I0693993

THE HEIR OF
ASH AND THUNDER

THE HEIR OF ASH AND THUNDER

BY

ELIJAH STEPANOVICH

McCord Stepanovich Publishing
Copyright © 2025

All rights reserved.

All rights reserved. No part of this book may be reproduced in any form or by any electronic or mechanical means, including information storage and retrieval systems, without permission in writing from the publisher, except by a reviewer, who may quote brief passages in a review.
Published by McCord Stepanovich Publishing
Tavares, Florida
First Edition, 2025

CONTENT WARNINGS

- **DEATH & GRIEF**

- **RELIGIOUS/MYTHIC IMAGERY**

- **TORTURE & CAPTIVITY**

- **WAR & BATTLEFIELD VIOLENCE**

- **PSYCHOLOGICAL MANIPULATION**

- **SEXUAL CONTENT (EXPLICIT, CONSENSUAL)**

- **STRONG LANGUAGE**

- **ETHIC/SECTARIAN CONFLICT REFERENCES**

PRONUNCIATIONS, PLACES, AND THINGS

Ilija Dragović (EE-lee-yah DRAH-go-vich) Protagonist; his surname is Serbian.

Danica (DAH-nee-kah) Central heroine; name means "morning star" in Slavic languages.

Ana (AH-nah) Antagonist figure.

Nikola Lazarević (NEE-koh-lah LAH-zah-reh-vich) President of Serbia, appears in National Broadcast

Jelena Trifunović (YEH-leh-nah TREE-foo-no-vich) Prime Minister, styled as hierophant in cultic imagery

Father Gavril (GAH-vreel) Orthodox priest who offers wisdom

Anwen (AN-wen) A vision/past-life name; Welsh, meaning "very beautiful"

Eira (AY-rah or EH-rah) Past-life vision name; Old Norse, meaning "snow"

Džemila (JEH-mee-lah) Past-life vision name; Bosnian/Turkish, meaning "beautiful"

Danilo Kiš (DAH-nee-loh KEESH) Real Yugoslav/Serbian author referenced in Belgrade scene

Saint Sava (SAH-vah) Serbian Orthodox saint, national religious figure

Theotokos (thay-oh-TOH-kohs) Greek Orthodox title of Mary, "God-bearer"

Saint Elijah (ee-LYE-jah) Biblical prophet, referenced in icons

Belgrade (BEL-grade / bel-GRAHD) Capital of Serbia; major setting

Novi (no-vee) **Belgrade** (bel-GRAHD) Post–WWII urban district

Danube (DAN-yube / DAH-noob) Major River in Central/Eastern Europe

Sava (SAH-vah) River joining the Danube at Belgrade

Delphi (DEL-fye) Ancient Greek site of the oracle (appears in chapter titles).

The Varangian Gate (vuh-RAN-jee-uhn) A historical/mythic reference to Norse mercenaries in Byzantium.

Forgjett (for-YETT) Old Norse/Icelandic word meaning "forgiven," appears in past-life vision

Icons (Orthodox) Religious paintings of saints (Saint Sava, Theotokos, Elijah)

Ajvar (EYE-var) A Balkan roasted red pepper and eggplant spread, often eaten with bread or grilled meats. Common in Balkan cuisine.

Rakija / Loza (RAH-kee-yah / LOH-zah) Strong Balkan fruit brandy; loza is grape-based.

Orthodox incense (myrrh & frankincense) Used in church liturgy.

Yugoslavia (YOO-go-slah-vee-uh) Former multi-ethnic federation in the Balkans, dissolved in the 1990s.

Kosovo (KOH-soh-voh) Region tied to Albanian national identity.

Balkan (BALL-kan) Southeastern European region encompassing Serbia, Croatia, etc.

PLAYLIST

EVERY TALE HAS ITS ECHOES.
SCAN TO UNLOCK THE PLAYLIST WOVEN FOR THIS
JOURNEY, HOSTED ON SPOTIFY.

Prologue
IN EVERY LIFE

Alatyr

The world ended around me in fire and steel, as it always seemed destined to.

Across the scorched plain where the ancient river once ran, armies tore the earth open, and I felt every wound in my bones. Ash choked the wind that howled down from the peaks, thick with the stench of burning flesh. This was the Age of Iron and Blood, when gods still walked among men and their wars scarred the land beyond healing.

Sigrún fought beside me, wreathed in conjured flame and biting frost. Her crimson war-cloak billowed behind her, soaked dark with blood and the spray of shattered ice. Her bare, scarred hands lashed whips of freezing fire that cracked armor apart and turned bone to rime. Every strike landed with the precision of someone who measured the cost of each breath she spent in battle. Her twin blades, marked with the symbols of Freyja and Brigid, carved through the enemy ranks and left trails of steam and frozen ruin in their wake.

I moved as thunder given flesh, blue-white current pulsing beneath my skin, and when I roared, the sound split the battlefield like a mountain breaking apart. My hammer, sky-forged iron heavy enough to crater stone, sent shockwaves rippling through the earth with every blow, crumpling men and buckling steel where it fell. I fought with the fury of a storm that had forgotten how to end. My eyes found hers across the chaos, gray-blue locked onto burning amber, and that single look steadied us both. We fought as one body, one devastating current, our bond older than language.

The enemy surged around us, faceless soldiers beneath a banner of twisted serpents, but the true threat came from the heart of the carnage itself, stepping through the bodies as though they were tall grass.

Katara glided through the slaughter untouched, impossibly beautiful, her hair trailing behind her like spilled ink. Her eyes held no color I could name, only depth, liquid and black, fixed on me with a hunger that predated civilization. Her bare hands had killed more men than any blade ever forged, and every part of her had been sharpened by centuries of desire and absolute command.

Sigrún spotted her first, and I saw the recognition hit, saw her jaw clench and her body go rigid before she screamed a warning, raw and desperate, but the roar of battle devoured it whole.

Katara moved faster than thought, faster than any bolt I could summon, and before I could raise my hammer, her hand drove into my chest. She did not pierce skin, but her fingers found something deeper, my essence, my living storm, and closed around it with the cold deliberation of someone snuffing a candle.

My roar strangled in my throat, and the hammer dropped from my hands, striking the earth with a final, resonant crack. The lightning wreathing my body convulsed, then flickered into nothing. My eyes, wide with sudden comprehension, found Sigrún across the bloody field, and my lips parted around the shape of her name, silent, meant for her alone, because I had no breath left for words.

Then Katara twisted her wrist, and I came apart.

The living lightning that had sustained me turned inward, consuming flesh and bone from the inside, a silent detonation at the molecular level. My armor dissolved to ash and my bones became dust, and in the space between one heartbeat and the next, I ceased to exist, leaving only the void where I had stood, a sudden, howling absence that swallowed even the sound of the battle around it.

Sigrún's scream cut through everything, silencing the clash of steel around her and the wind itself, until even the distant grinding of the mountains seemed to pause. She fell to her knees and the fire and frost within her guttered and died, replaced by something cold that hollowed her from the inside out. Her hands clawed at the scorched earth where my boots had been, and she shook with a grief so violent, it looked like earthquake.

Katara stood over the swirling dust and regarded her with mild interest, her face untouched by remorse. She raised one hand and traced a slow spiral in the air above the place where I had died, and a hum resonated through the ground beneath them, ancient and final, sealing my unmaking.

What remained of me watched, scattered fragments of thought, awareness dissolving at the edges like smoke thinning in wind.

Sigrún lifted her head. Tears burned tracks through the ash on her face, and her eyes blazed with something beyond fury, something that would outlast empires and the gods who built them. She stared at the empty ground, at the settling dust that had been her love, and a vow crystallized in her marrow, fierce and absolute. She would find me, in every life and every age, no matter what Katara made of the world between now and the end of all things, and she would make her pay a debt that no amount of suffering could settle.

CHAPTER ONE
THE FIVE FLAMES

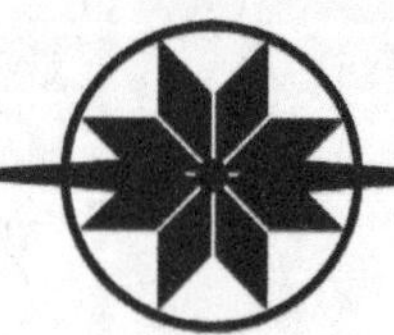

Ilija
Modern Day

The forest blurred around me in streaks of green and shadow, roots and wet leaves beneath my bare feet. Rain fell from branches overhead, soaking my hair and sliding down my face, mixing with tears I only realized were falling when I tasted salt on my lips. Each breath tore through my throat like glass, but the pain meant nothing because I ran from the sound that had ended the world.

The sound had been quiet, my father's body striking tile while the house seemed to hold its breath around us. I knew before I looked that something vital had torn loose in the universe. Steam still rose from his coffee cup, curling into air that pretended nothing had changed, and I could feel it, the room suddenly too large, the air too thin, as if his presence had been load-bearing and the structure of everything had begun to sag without it.

He stood at the counter one moment, muttering about cholesterol and rust-tasting statins. The next, the world pulled him down mid-sentence. The thud of him hitting tile echoed through the kitchen, a percussion I'll carry forever. His eyes showed confusion first, then recognition settled in his gaze as he realized this was it, this was how he died. His hand lifted, fingers splayed to speak, then froze mid-gesture. His expression vanished and the room stopped with him. My breath caught somewhere between my lungs and throat, as if breathing meant accepting what I was seeing.

My mother crumpled beside him, her knees hitting tile with a sound that pierced through me. Her hands scrambled across his chest and face, searching for warmth that had already left while she screamed his name, a sound so raw it flayed the air. "Marko!" Then again, louder, breaking on the syllables. "Marko! Marko, please!" Each cry grew more desperate, more shattered, turning a word that had been ordinary into a plea, a denial of what was already true. I wanted to go to her, but my legs refused. I stood stone-still and useless.

He lay on the kitchen floor, one hand splayed open, the other curled against his chest, his eyes staring at nothing. I'd read about death, seen it in movies, but this was my father's absence wearing his face. The steam curled from his cup. I wanted to believe that if I stayed still, the moment would rewind and he'd grumble about bitter coffee and everything would reset. My ribs ached with the wanting, but the scene held its terrible stillness, a life broken in an instant.

Then I ran.

Memory offers nothing about the decision, only the cold against my bare soles, damp linoleum, then the blur of the threshold. The world narrowed to trees and the howling I carried but couldn't release. I ran wordless past my mother's keening, past the shell of my father on the floor, and left the door open behind me. Leaving meant survival. Staying meant watching strangers lift his body, meant neighbors bringing casseroles with soft eyes, their careful glances making me into something fragile. I refused to let them. I couldn't breathe in that house, couldn't exist in a world where my father was just gone.

The forest swallowed me whole, its branches closing overhead in tangled darkness. I followed the paths until my legs burned, until the pain in my muscles matched the pain splitting me open.

I sank where the ground grew thick with moss and pressed my palms into earth, trying to hold myself together when everything inside me wanted to fly apart. My eyes stayed dry after those first wild tears, burning, as if my body had forgotten how to grieve properly. I knelt as if the ground might steady me. The moss felt damp and cool against my skin and smelled of bark and stone, of things that had lived longer than I had, things that knew how to become dust and be reborn. I wanted that desperately, to become dust, to stop feeling this.

The ache came gradually, then all at once, a rising tide that filled every hollow space inside me. Grief felt too small a word, too neat, because what lived inside me was shapeless and heavy, a pressure behind my ribs that made each breath uncertain. Someone had reached into me and carved away something essential, leaving only the wound.

I stayed as the sky darkened. The kitchen, the body, my mother's voice, Marko, please, Marko, all of it kept circling through my mind in fragments. They felt distant now and too close, as if they belonged to another life and were the only thing that had ever been real. The forest held me in its silence, and I let it hold the pieces of me that refused to connect.

The silence had depth, tangible presence, as though something unseen listened, patient and immeasurably old. I knelt in the moss, breath shallow, fingers curled into damp earth until dirt packed under my nails. The forest held only me and this grief I could not put down. For the first time since the kitchen, since the world tilted, I existed without expectation, and I was allowed to break, so I did.

The sob came from somewhere deep, a sound I'd been holding back since the moment his body hit tile, and it tore out of me like something being born. Then another came, and another. My shoulders shook while my hands pressed harder into the ground, as if I could anchor myself to something solid when everything else was falling apart. The grief was alive inside me, clawing to get out, and I let it come, let it rake through me.

I kept my eyes closed against new tears, but memory reached me anyway, a current beneath my skin pulling me backward into moments I'd never get back. His voice came first, low and rough with sleep, calling from the hallway each morning. Sine moj, are you up? The scrape of his chair against kitchen floor. The creak as he sat by the window with a paper he never read past the headlines. His hands, broad and scarred, stained from tools and sawdust, cradled a cigarette with absent care. Hands that had lifted me when I was small. Hands that would never hold anything again.

He moved through the house with quiet presence, someone who never needed to be noticed to fill a room. He was there, had always been there, until he wasn't.

His hands had sometimes been too rough, his moods often shrouded in quiet melancholy that pushed others away. Yet he'd been there every day, a solid presence I'd taken for granted. He'd taught me to patch a tire with steady hands and patient silence, the smell of rubber and oil clinging to his skin. He'd sat beside me on the riverbank when I was six and told me the Danube was dark, yes, but the currents ran slow and deep, like the world's secrets. You don't have to fear what you understand, sine moj. He'd called me that, sine moj, my son, and he'd said it like it meant more than blood. As though it named the part of him that would continue when the rest disappeared.

That burden had already begun to settle over me, the burden of being the one who continues, the one left behind to remember.

I lowered my forehead to the moss, cold where it touched my skin, sharp and clean. I needed something that demanded nothing, something that couldn't look at me with pity or expectation. I couldn't return to the house, to the raw grief waiting there, to my mother's shattered eyes. The priest would come with his practiced recitations designed to comfort the living, and grief would move slowly and publicly, dressed as tradition. Strangers would use their careful language to make themselves feel safe, to distance themselves from loss. He's in a better place. He's at peace now. Time heals all wounds. All of it was lies.

Here, in the damp stillness, I could let grief live inside me, heavy and wordless, without making it palatable for someone else's comfort. Here I could rage and crumble, and the trees wouldn't tell me to be strong.

What I felt was deeper than sadness, wider, without clear shape. It pulled inward, folding everything I was into a single aching center, a black hole where my father used to be. I breathed only because my body remembered how, some autonomic function that kept going even when I wanted to stop.

The cold moved through me while my body stopped shivering, settling into a stillness that came from bone-deep exhaustion, the kind that follows too much holding back, too much feeling. The ache pressed deeper, a dull heaviness behind my sternum that made everything slow down. My blood had thickened with sorrow, and my heart beat sluggishly, reluctantly, like it too wanted to stop.

I tried to think about something small, something I could hold without it cutting me. The smallest pieces of him: the way he shook a sugar packet with a sharp flick before tearing it open; the scratch in his voice, like old leather, when he laughed at black-and-white movies. Those details mattered only to me, and I already felt them slipping away, enough to make me wonder if I'd ever remembered them right, if they'd always been this fragile. Cold fear shot through me. What if I forgot? What if I lost even these small pieces?

Above me, the trees held their posture while their branches stayed motionless and the air hung still. The silence grew heavier, shifting from presence to awareness. The forest had begun to notice my grief and chosen to bear witness, and I sensed it then, a shift in the world around me, because the forest was listening.

I remained in the moss, a small figure caught in vastness, trembling with cold and shock. The world held itself around me, as though something larger than sorrow had joined me in that pause, waiting for something I couldn't name.

Something inside me had shifted and opened, and I knew with quiet, terrifying certainty that it would stay that way. The boy I'd been was gone, the one who complained about homework and played football with friends and thought death was something that happened to other people. In his place remained this hollow, aching thing that used to be Ilija.

The shift began so subtly I almost missed it through the fog of grief. At first, I thought the silence was only a reflection of my own stillness, the kind that settles when the body forgets how to move, but the forest was holding itself differently, bending its presence around something new. The usual sounds had receded, movement of leaves and faint groan of branches all swallowed into hush, while the air thickened and grew dense and still, heavy with something I couldn't name.

My skin prickled while every hair on my arms stood up. Some primal part of my brain started screaming danger , but I was too hollowed out to care.

I lifted my head. The light had changed, pale and unnaturally even, as if the sun had been muffled by something unseen. The shadows were gone, replaced by colorless stillness that dulled every surface. The clearing looked like a photograph left too long in the sun, bleached and flattened, drained of the dimension that made it real. My stomach clenched.

The moss beneath my hands felt damp, yet it held the warmth of my skin too long, as if it had begun to remember me. I stayed motionless because something primal inside me recognized that movement would bring change, and the space I occupied had become delicate, suspended between moments. It waited, and I waited. My heart kicked against my ribs, too fast, too hard.

My gaze drifted upward. The trees loomed higher than before, their dark forms rising in unsettling alignment, too regular to be natural. The canopy had grown tight, leaves so densely woven that the sky appeared as narrow, jagged veins of gray. Even the moss grew heavier, dense with presence that pressed down on me, and I felt observed, watched by something I couldn't see.

Fear flickered at the edges of my awareness, but it felt distant, muted by grief. What could frighten me now? My father was dead, and the worst had already happened.

A sound reached me then, quiet and deliberate. A crow adjusted its wings on a high branch, the faint rustle of feathers, then fell still. The noise, though small, drew the last breath of movement from the clearing. The silence that followed felt too complete to be natural, pressing down and demanding attention while my lungs tightened and I couldn't get enough air.

I turned slowly. The physical shape of the clearing remained the same, yet everything felt different. The space between trees had grown tighter while the air drew inward, compressing around an unseen center. My skin prickled with cold knowledge because I was no longer alone. I couldn't name what had entered, but I knew it was there, knew it the way prey knows the predator, the way the dying know death.

I stayed low against the ground while my mind tried frantically to stretch around what I sensed, to find logic for the impossible. The grief bore down inside me, a constant pressure, but now it sat beside something older, something immense. Whatever had come into the clearing moved in absolute quiet, yet the forest, in its stillness, had made room for it, had been expecting it.

The quiet carried intention now and pressed around me with undeniable purpose. My bones understood what my thoughts were still catching up to because something that had existed since before the first fires had turned toward me, and I'd already been seen, chosen, claimed.

My hands trembled against the moss.

He emerged from the clearing's edge as though my grief had summoned him from some deep place in the earth. The mist parted while he stepped into view with slow, deliberate inevitability, and the sight of him drove the air from my lungs.

His cloak, heavy and dark, dragged over the moss behind him. Strands of bark and threads of rot clung to it, soil gathering at its hem like roots refusing to let go. From his brow rose a crown of antlers, massive and weathered, dusted with green lichen that looked heavy, as though they'd grown from his skull. He moved with the immense gravity of deep time, a figure shaped by soil and shadow, and his presence crushed me. I couldn't look away.

Each step bent the ground beneath him while his limbs creaked as he moved. When he drew closer, his eyes met mine, and I forgot how to breathe. In their depths, I saw the green of riverbeds untouched by sun, murky and layered. They held something older than language, older than grief. They saw through me, past skin, past bone, to whatever flickered at my core.

I should have been terrified, and some part of me was, but a deeper part recognized him, knew him in a way that made no sense.

He stood in silence at first. The clearing had already changed in response to him, the air thick with his presence, with the smell of wet earth and things that had outlived kingdoms. Around me, five flames hovered above the moss in shades of gold, red, violet, silver, and deep pulsing blue. They cast no heat and made no sound but burned with steady calm. They held their perfect shape, unwavering, as though they recognized him and acknowledged his authority.

My heart hammered so hard I thought it might crack my ribs. I couldn't move or speak, and hell, I could barely think through the overwhelming presence of him.

When he finally spoke, his voice moved through the clearing like something the earth itself remembered, a deep resonance rising from beneath soil that vibrated in my bones.

"You've already crossed the threshold. You haven't claimed it yet."

The words reached me slowly, sinking in, pressing against something deep in my ribs, against the raw wound where my father was. I wanted to speak, to ask what he meant, but my throat had closed. My hands remained pressed to the ground, the only solid thing in a world that had turned liquid and strange while my breath moved quietly, unevenly, through the stillness he'd made.

He stepped closer, his presence expanding, filling everything. He was the god of thresholds and memory, of hidden things that live in quiet earth. The keeper of forgotten paths. Veles. The name arrived in my mind with the certainty of something I had always known. He moved between the seen and the unseen, between the living and the dead, between my father and me.

"Those who have died carry truths the living forget," he said, and I felt tears spring hot to my eyes because he was talking about my father, about all the dead. "You will learn them. You will carry them. And when those in power try to bury them again, you will speak."

I wanted to refuse, to say I was just a boy, that I couldn't carry anything, that I was already buckling under the heft of one death, but the words stuck in my throat.

He lifted one hand, palm open to the sky. The ground stirred beneath us, a slow, vast undulation, and I felt it in my stomach, in my teeth. Nausea rolled through me. Beneath my knees I sensed what lay buried, the presence of countless skulls and bones, long forgotten. They moved through the earth in slow undulation, their stories pressing up through soil, desperate to be remembered. I was going to collapse under it.

"You walk between. And when the world insists there is only surface, you will remind them of depth."

The moss pressed back against my hands while my breath came in shallow gasps. I was shaking now, full-body tremors I couldn't control. My grief and this encounter crashed together until I couldn't tell them apart. Was this real? Was I dying too? Had I followed my father into death without noticing?

He was waiting for something, for acknowledgment, for acceptance. I managed the smallest nod, though I understood nothing, felt only the crushing force of his attention and my own sorrow.

His body moved through the mist without resistance as he continued walking, and the mist allowed his absence the same space it had given his presence. He was gone, yet everything remained changed. The air hummed with him while my hands shook.

I looked down at the coin resting in my hand, its cool heft an anchor. The five flames hovered around me. They cast strange shadows across my trembling fingers. The clearing held its new, charged silence while my breath moved slowly now, painfully, drawn deeper than before.

The ache had made room for something else, something I didn't want.

Thunder rolled through the clearing, low and resonant, vibrating in my ribs like a second heartbeat. The sound came from everywhere at once, from the earth itself. The five flames flickered, their light dimming in acknowledgment of something larger, something more immediate.

He stepped from the storm itself, and I knew him instantly, the way I'd known Veles, a recognition that bypassed thought and lodged straight in my marrow.

Perun moved like living thunder, each step crackling with barely contained power. His form was massive, towering, built like the mountains themselves. His eyes held the gray-blue of storm clouds heavy with rain. Lightning played across his skin in subtle arcs, dancing between his fingers, humming in the air around him. His presence struck differently from

Veles's patient inevitability. Raw and immediate, the kind of power that demanded attention through sheer force.

He stopped before me, and the ground beneath him pulsed with energy, as if recognizing its master. When he spoke, his voice rolled through the clearing, promising violence and protection in equal measure.

"You carry death," he said, and his gaze dropped to the coin in my hand, the one Veles had left, before lifting back to my face. "Now you will carry the storm."

How many gods would come for me tonight, and how much could I possibly hold?

He reached out, his hand engulfing mine, and pressed something small and cool into my palm alongside Veles's coin. Another coin, identical in size and heft, but when I looked down, they had merged. On one side, the perunika, Perun's flower, six petals radiating outward like lightning strikes captured in metal. On the other, a serpent coiled in an eternal spiral. Veles's mark intertwined with his brother's symbol.

"Two halves of the same whole," Perun said, and there was something in his voice that might have been sorrow, might have been resignation. "We are divided, he and I, separated by the order of things, but in you we meet again. In you, the storm and the earth remember they were never truly separate."

The coin warmed in my hand, and I felt it then, a surge of power that started in my palm and raced up my arm, spreading through me like wildfire. Lightning in my veins, every nerve ending alive at once, crackling with energy I didn't understand and couldn't control. My breath came in short gasps while my heart kicked against my ribs, trying to keep pace with the power flooding through me.

"The storm will live in you," he said, and his eyes held mine with an intensity that made me want to look away, but I couldn't, couldn't do anything but feel this terrible, exhilarating power coursing through me. "You will learn to wield it, or it will tear you apart. There is no middle ground."

I wanted to throw the coin back at him and beg him to take it away, but the words wouldn't come, and maybe that was answer enough.

His expression softened, and for a moment he looked sympathetic, as if he understood what he was asking of me. "When the five artifacts are gathered," he said, his voice quieter now, "when you hold the coin, the spiral stone, the Blade of Fates, the rings of Lada and Morana, and finally the storm heart itself, you will remember. All the lives you've lived before this one will return to you, every death and every joy. You will know who you truly are."

The thought terrified me more than anything else that had happened tonight. I didn't want to remember other lives, other deaths, other griefs. I could barely hold what I carried now. How could I possibly bear more?

But Perun was already stepping back, the lightning around him intensifying until it was almost blinding. "The storm will be yours to command, when the heart splits into you and her."

I looked down at the coin in my hand, Veles's serpent and Perun's perunika, two sides of the same conflict, and felt what they represented settle into me alongside my grief.

Then the cold arrived all at once, without gusts or warning, as if warmth had been drawn from the soil, from my skin, from the air in my lungs. My breath caught. The heat dimmed by degrees, a deliberate extraction. I gasped at the suddenness of it, at the way it stole into me with quiet, deliberate precision. Her arrival stirred neither moss nor branches, but every cell in my body knew she was there.

Morana stepped from the trees without sound, and the sight of her drove ice into my veins.

She emerged as if she'd always been standing beyond the visible, waiting for the silence to settle enough for her to cross. Her dress moved in long, pale lines, trailing through damp moss and gathering soil at its hem. Flowers, drained of color, clung to the ends of her hair, their petals thin and brittle like pressed parchment. She was beautiful the way winter is beautiful, the way death is beautiful when you're too tired to fight it anymore.

She stopped directly in front of me, close enough that I could see frost forming on the moss around her feet, close enough that my breath misted in the sudden cold. She stood in silence while I felt only compelling stillness. Her eyes were the color of distant snowfields beneath a waning moon, a gaze that knew, that looked through me and saw everything I'd ever been, everything I'd ever lose.

She reached out, her hand pale and cold beyond anything natural, and placed it on my forehead. Ice against fevered skin. I flinched but couldn't pull away.

Heaviness came, pressing down on me, the immense burden of what I'd already begun to carry, but worse, so much worse. It pressed into me with exacting clarity, showing me what would remain when everything else fell away, showing me my future with surgical precision.

I felt rage then, and it shocked me with its intensity, measured, sharpened into something too precise to soften. Rage at the world for taking my father, rage at myself for running, rage at the unfairness of it all. I saw the ruin I could cause, the silence that would follow my actions. I saw cities blackened by grief I would wield with purpose while people I loved walked away without looking back, their faces indistinct but their fear clear. My own hands trembling with blood I couldn't name. I was capable of this, would become this.

The vision terrified me, and I wanted to sob, to beg her to take it back.

Then, within that clarity, I saw the boy I'd been. Small, shouting into an empty field, his voice swallowed by indifferent dusk. He knew only that something had gone missing too early. I saw him clearly, saw myself, felt his raw bewilderment. The desperate, clawing need to understand why. And in that moment, I understood the true shape of the grief I'd carried, a burden that had resided within me long before my father ever fell. Loss was woven into me. It had always been there, waiting.

Her voice sank into me like cold settling deep into marrow.

"You will lose yourself."

The words held pure certainty with no comfort, no mercy. They existed the way winter exists, arriving at the edge of harvest, inevitable.

"And others will mourn the man you once were."

A sob broke from my throat, raw, desperate. I didn't want this, didn't want any of it. I was a boy who'd lost his father, nothing more, someone who was never meant for gods and visions and burdens older than civilization. I wanted to go home, wanted my father back, wanted to wake up and find this was all some grief-induced nightmare.

She stepped back slowly, withdrawing with purpose, and the cold stayed behind, sunk into me now, permanent. The loss of her hand from my forehead left me gutted, abandoned with truths too heavy to carry.

I was shaking violently now, teeth chattering, though whether from cold or shock I couldn't tell because both had merged into one sensation. I wrapped my arms around myself, trying to hold together what felt like it was flying apart.

Then warmth came, sudden and unexpected, flowing through the clearing like spring breaking through winter's grip. The cold that Morana had left behind began to recede, gently, like snow melting under the first true sun of the season. I gasped at the shift, at the way my body responded to it, desperate for anything that wasn't death and ice.

She emerged from the trees like dawn itself, and the sight of her made something in me loosen, some knot I hadn't realized had pulled so tight.

Lada.

Her dress flowed in shades of green and gold, living fabric grown from new grass and sunlight. Flowers bloomed in her wake, pushing up through the moss in profusion. Her hair fell down her back in waves of honey and wheat, crowned with blossoms that released their perfume into the air. Her eyes held the green of new leaves, bright and clear, and when she looked at me, I felt seen in a way that differed from Morana's gaze. Recognized. Welcomed.

She moved with the easy grace of someone who had never known winter, and her presence filled the clearing with something I'd almost forgotten existed in the world, something that could only be called hope.

"Oh, little storm," she said, and her voice was warm, carrying notes of birdsong and running water. "You've been shown so much darkness tonight, so much sorrow. Let me show you what persists through it all."

She knelt beside me in the moss, heedless of her beautiful dress, and reached out to touch my face with fingers that felt warm and startlingly alive. Where Morana's touch had shown me death and loss, Lada's showed me something else.

Images flooded through me, softer, edged with golden light. I saw myself in lives I couldn't remember, and this time I wasn't alone. I was laughing, my head thrown back in genuine joy. I was holding someone, their body warm against mine, their breath soft against my neck. I was dancing under stars that had long since burned out, my hand clasped in another's, our movements perfectly synchronized. We'd been doing this for centuries. Maybe we had.

Love, I realized with sudden clarity that stole my breath. She was showing me love.

"You carry loss, yes," Lada said, and her thumb brushed across my cheek, wiping away tears I hadn't realized were falling. "You carry death and darkness. But you also carry this, and it is just as eternal, just as powerful, perhaps more so."

The images continued. I saw a figure beside me through countless lifetimes, their face shifting, changing, but their essence remaining constant. Familiar in a way that went beyond recognition. Sometimes they were fierce, all sharp edges and simmering violence. Sometimes they were soft, a steady presence that anchored me when the storm threatened to tear me apart. Always they were there, a thread of connection running through every life I'd lived.

"Love follows you," Lada whispered, and her smile was radiant, full of certainty. "Through every death, every rebirth, it finds you again. You are never truly alone, little storm, even when it feels like the darkness will swallow you whole."

The warmth in me grew, spreading outward, and for the first time since my father died, I felt something other than grief. The possibility of happiness, the knowledge that it could exist again, that I might one day remember how to find it.

But then her expression shifted, and something troubled moved through her bright eyes, a shadow crossing the sun. Her hand on my face tensed, and I felt a chill run through the warmth she'd brought.

"But I must warn you," she said, and her voice had lost some of its melody, taking on a gravity that reminded me uncomfortably of the other gods. "Love is not always gentle, not always kind. Sometimes it wears a beautiful face and speaks in honeyed words, and you will want so desperately to believe it that you won't see the danger until it's too late."

Another image came then, different from the others, and this one carried a sharp edge that made me flinch. A woman, staggeringly beautiful, with eyes that promised everything I'd ever wanted. Beneath the beauty I could sense something else, something hungry, something that would consume me if I let it. I saw myself reaching for her, desperate, drowning, unable to help myself even as I recognized the danger. Her smile, sweet and terrible, and I felt the trap closing around me.

"Some will take your love and twist it, use it as a weapon against you. You must learn to see the difference, to know when to open your heart and when to guard it, or you will be destroyed by the thing that should save you."

The warning lodged in me alongside everything else, another burden, and I wanted to scream that I couldn't hold any more, that I was already breaking under what they'd given me. But Lada was pulling back now, her hand leaving my face, and my skin went cold where her fingers had been.

"Remember the light," she said, standing. The flowers that had bloomed in her wake began to close, preparing for sleep. "Remember that beauty exists, that joy is possible, that love persists even when everything else falls away. Hold that knowledge close, little storm. The darkness will try to make you forget, and you must not let it."

Then she was fading, dissolving like morning mist, and the clearing felt colder without her, emptier, though the warmth she'd brought lingered faintly in me, a small ember that refused to go out.

I sat there, trembling, caught between the cold Morana had left and the warmth Lada had tried to give, between the warning of false love and the promise of true connection, between death and life, and I understood that this was what I would carry now, this balance, this endless tension between opposing forces.

The stars returned one by one, as if each had remembered its place in the cosmos. Their light descended quietly, softening the darkness until it held its shape. I watched them appear through tears I hadn't realized were still falling, beautiful, distant, indifferent.

From that stillness, they stepped forward, and my battered heart lurched with new fear. How much more could I endure tonight?

Two figures woven from celestial thread emerged from the darkness. Zorya. The names came to me unbidden, planted by gods or memory or something older. The Morning Star and the Evening Watcher, guardians of what moves between realms, sisters who held the space where endings and beginnings blurred. They crossed the moss without leaving a mark. One wore a gown of rose and shimmering gold, her hair the color of ripe wheat, and she looked at me with something like kindness. The other moved beside her in deeper hue, her presence cooler, her eyes calm and fathomless. Her dress shimmered in violet shadow, and her black hair fell in a single sheet down her back.

They walked in silence at first, and their approach carried barely a whisper, yet the force of their presence filled the clearing. It felt different from Veles's crushing authority or Morana's terrifying certainty because this was immense, but gentle. The five flames around me dimmed in acknowledgment, and I felt a flutter of relief. If the flames recognized them, perhaps I wouldn't break under this too.

When their voices came, they spoke in turn, two distinct lines of the same truth. "You were chosen long ago," said the sister in gold, her voice a warm, clear chime that made something loosen in me. "You have always been returning," said the other, her voice a cool, deep melody.

The words met something in me I'd been circling around but couldn't yet name, and recognition surged through me. I understood, with clarity that went beyond my current life, that I'd been here before, had stood in this clearing or one like it, had faced these gods or gods like them, though I couldn't summon the memory of when or why. The knowing was overwhelming, terrifying, and a relief all at once.

I wasn't just a boy who'd lost his father. I was something more, something older.

"You were lightning," one said, and I felt faint warmth flicker in my veins. "And ash," said the other, and cold stillness crept through me again. "Root and bloom." "Storm and soil."

Each word hit me like a note in a song I'd forgotten I knew, and I ached with it, with the heft of lives I couldn't remember but felt deep in my marrow.

They extended their hands, and from their fingers, threads unraveled in shades of crimson and lustrous gold and obsidian black. Each one drifted toward me with purpose. I watched them come with a mixture of awe and dread. When they reached my skin, they settled without resistance, and I gasped at the sensation, a pulling that rearranged something fundamental inside me. Their pull pressed into the space between my breath and thought, as if they'd been waiting for me to arrive, as if I'd been walking around incomplete and hadn't known it.

I sobbed openly now, too battered to care about dignity while the grief for my father mixed with griefs I couldn't name, lifetimes of loss pouring through me until I was drowning in it.

The Zorya stepped closer, and their eyes met mine, seeing past the boy to the long history of the soul. I felt naked under that gaze, seen and truly known. One of them touched my cheek with gentleness that made me want to shatter, her skin cool. The other pressed her hand against my sternum, above my aching, stuttering heart. Stillness came, so complete it held me in place, and the chaos inside me settled, just slightly, just enough.

"You carry more than grief," they said together, their voices weaving into one. "You carry what continues, the unbroken thread of what persists."

The words should have been comforting, but instead they felt like a sentence. I would carry this forever, keep carrying until I couldn't bear it anymore, and then I'd die and be reborn and carry it again in an endless cycle of loss and return.

But beneath the despair, something else flickered, something small and stubborn. If I carried what continued, then I carried my father too, his memory, his love, the scratch of his voice and the rough warmth of his hands. Those things would persist because I would make them persist.

They stepped back, and their forms began to unravel like thread returning to the loom, dissolving gracefully. They faded into the air they'd come from, leaving only the vibrant, unsettling memory they'd drawn forward from my hidden depths, leaving me alone with too much knowledge and a heart too raw to hold it all.

The flames held their places at the clearing's edge in shades of amber, violet, red, silver, blue. Their presence remained steady, a silent vigil. They'd waited for me, witnessed this communion, and held their places still, the only constant in a night that had unmade and remade me.

The coin rested in my palm. Its faint glow had faded, but its heft pressed into my skin with quiet insistence, as if it had always belonged there. I closed my fingers around it, letting its cool presence anchor me. This had been real. The gods had come, and I'd been claimed.

Ahead, the path between trees stood open, showing me only space, only forward.

I took a breath, deeper than any I'd managed since the kitchen, filling my lungs with the forest's damp, cool air. It hurt, and everything hurt, but I was still here, alive amidst the wreckage, and something within me had begun to move, something that belonged to me and was older than I could fathom.

My legs shook as I stood while the moss released me. My body was slow to remember the shape of motion, stiff from kneeling, from grief, from the force of divine attention. I stood in the quiet that followed the gods, in the space they'd touched and forever marked. The air held the lingering hum of their presence, but it had loosened, leaving behind me, changed.

The forest looked largely unchanged, yet I perceived every leaf differently, every shadow with new awareness. My grief for my father had been threaded into something larger, stitched into memory and myth so tightly that I no longer knew where my personal sorrow ended and the larger story began. I could still feel him. I could feel all the threads pulling at me, the dead calling, the gods watching.

I walked in silence, guided by the last faint pulse of warmth lingering in the ground where they'd stood. Each step brought me closer to the life I'd tried to leave behind, and I dreaded it. The sterile walls of that apartment. The smell of bleach trying to mask stale coffee. The unwashed plates stacked in the sink, proof of a life abruptly halted. The grief that waited behind the front door, unanswerable. My mother, broken. The funeral. The pity. But the world kept its relentless march, pausing for no one at all.

When the trees began to thin, revealing the faint glow of the city, what I carried inside me shifted again, clearer now and defined. I could feel the thread of it, this ache that had burrowed into my ribs and rewired the shape of my breath, knitting itself into my being. It would stay. It would become part of how I moved through the world. I would learn to carry it, or it would flatten me.

The lights of the city shimmered beyond the treeline, hazed by distance and damp air. A thin column of smoke drifted from a chimney somewhere close, ordinary and unremarkable, yet its mundane existence startled me. How could the world be so normal? How could smoke rise and lights glow when my father was dead, when gods had claimed me? The disconnect made me nauseous.

The world had gone on. People had eaten dinner while lights had been turned off and sleep had come and passed. Everything had continued without me, without caring that the universe had ended.

I stepped from the forest's embrace and crossed the narrow, deserted road, the asphalt damp and cold beneath my bare feet. A car passed, its headlights cutting through the mist, then vanishing into dark. I wondered if they saw me, if I appeared as a human figure or as something the woods had decided to release. I wondered if I looked as changed as I felt.

By the time I reached the apartment building, dawn had begun to rise, pale and uncertain. The front door stood ajar because I'd left it open when I'd fled, and no one had closed it. The thought made my throat tighten. My mother, probably too shattered to notice, or maybe she'd left it open hoping I'd come back.

I stepped inside while the smell hit me first, disinfectant and cold, stale air, and something underneath that would linger forever, the smell of death, of endings. My stomach clenched.

My mother had gone, to a neighbor's, maybe, or to the hospital to deal with arrangements I couldn't think about. A blanket had been draped over the couch while a glass of water, half-full, stood on the table, a forgotten offering. The quiet that settles around absence. The apartment felt emptier than it should, as if my father's death had carved space from the walls themselves.

The cup remained on the counter. His cup. The coffee had long since gone cold, a congealed black circle at the bottom. I stared at it while something in me broke open again. Such a small thing, a coffee cup, but it was his. He'd filled it. His hands had held it. Now it would sit there forever, or until someone threw it away, and neither option was bearable.

I couldn't bring myself to touch it. I stood there for a long time, watching the space where steam had risen. I knew, with certainty that had taken root in my newly opened heart, that everything in me had changed since the sound of his body hitting tile. The boy who'd woken up this morning was gone. In his place stood someone older, stranger, heavier. Someone touched by gods. Someone who walked between worlds.

I reached for the coin in my pocket and it remained cool and solid, the only proof that the clearing had been real, that I hadn't imagined it all in grief-madness.

I closed my fingers around it, feeling its faint pulse against my skin. Or maybe that was my own heartbeat, still insisting on continuing. I let the silence hold me, let it press against me with all its force. This was my life now, this grief, this knowing, and I would learn to carry it.

CHAPTER TWO
THE LOOMING VEIL

Ilija

I had long since ceased believing the aftermath of my father's death was anything more than a dream. Perhaps, with the quiet discipline of years, I had grown adept at silencing the part of myself that once grasped for such impossible truths. That wide-eyed, reverent fragment of my being, once dangerously willing to abandon itself to instinct, still lived beneath the surface. It thrived under the routines I had painstakingly built to keep it quiet. Discipline and the steady hum of repetition; I had stacked them high enough to silence the persistent stirrings when they came. They did come, now and then, faint echoes from a night that felt more like a fevered dream of grief than a tangible memory. I knew how to smother them, knew I had to.

Fifteen years had passed since the shattering night my father died, since everything blurred into that strange, unsettling vision. In that time, I had constructed a new life, brick by meticulous brick, as if a stable exterior could solidify what had fractured inside me. I had begun my studies, a path woven from textbooks and theories.

The lecture hall held its breath in the quiet morning, the way only old buildings know how to be still. Light the color of aged gold slipped through tall, arched windows, catching dust motes in long, luminous shafts. The ivy climbing outside blurred the view just enough to make the glass appear like rippling water. Sunlight struck the scarred desks unevenly, polishing patches of worn wood that had been shaped by decades of elbows and notebooks. I fit into it too well.

I stood at the front of the room, one hand resting on the polished podium, the other brushing invisible dust from my sleeve. My voice carried easily, steady and practiced, shaped by years of explaining the sacred to the secular. These students, mostly young and restless, had drifted here drawn by a need they rarely knew how to name. A flickering curiosity, perhaps, or the desperate hope of finding a word for the ache that sometimes lived at the edge of knowing.

I adjusted my glasses, a gesture more for comfort than clarity. The air disturbed by my breath drifted upward in lazy spirals. It looked like incense, like a prayer half-spoken, suspended between this world and another.

I had always loved this particular stretch of the semester. This was the moment when most students, overwhelmed by ancient narratives, began to fade. This was also where the deeper threads of meaning started to pull at the fabric of reality. The old stories ceased to sound like allegory and began pressing back. Myth, raw and visceral, rubbed up against the cold precision of psychology. Names spoken aloud as distant historical figures began to feel like living memory instead of metaphor.

It was here, suspended between the rigid structures of thought and the fluid currents of faith, that I felt closest to the gods I no longer let myself believe in.

I turned back to the whiteboard, the projector casting its familiar hum behind me. The slide held steady against the white expanse.

Between Sky and Root: The Duality of Slavic Cosmology.

I spoke to awaken recognition, perhaps in them, perhaps in myself, though the lines had blurred and I was no longer sure. It was in a similar class nine years ago, in the first throes of my own graduate studies, that I had met Ana. She had arrived like a breath of foreign air in the academic rhythm of my life.

We had first met in a class on Greek mythology. The very first time I saw her, the room seemed to reorganize itself around her presence. She knew everything, it seemed. The nuances, the forgotten connections. She could trace the lineage of every god and hero with the ease of someone reciting family history. She held a perfect score in that class, an anomaly I dismissed because she was from Albania, a country steeped in its own rich folklore.

She, as she would later confess with a wry smile, had initially thought me an asshole. A typical graduate student, too quick to challenge, too slow to listen. Yet I had found myself compelled to ask her to grab coffee after a particularly heated debate about the nature of hubris. Even then, before our hands touched across a table, before our words fully mingled into conversation, I had the unsettling sense that she knew everything about me already. My past, the lingering shadows, the things I buried with such meticulous care. I attributed it to her sharp intellect, and I left it there, because the alternative was a door I did not want to open.

"Perun," I said, pacing slowly now, "is sky-fire. The thunder-wielder, the guardian of law. His authority comes from above. Top down. Perun gives one ruling, and that's the end of it. He's the storm that arrives before you've made your decision, and by the time it passes, the decision's been made for you."

"Veles is different." I let my voice drop. "He works from underneath. He loosens things, drags up what you buried."

"Think of it this way. Perun is the monument on the hill, stark against the sky. Veles is the moss at its base. By the time you notice him, half the stone is already gone."

Thirty pairs of eyes stared back at me. Some glazed, some skeptical, some wide with a hunger they couldn't name. One or two held that quiet, almost reverent look people give an old painting, unable to look away.

I turned back to the whiteboard. The dry-erase marker was already warm in my hand. I drew the shape slowly. A single vertical line rising through the center, then the sweeping arc of roots reaching into the earth below, then branches split and reaching toward the sky above.

"This," I said, my voice dropping to a near whisper, "is the tree."

Pens paused across the room.

"Forget nine realms. Forget gleaming bridges. This tree is older than Yggdrasil, in some ways. More primal. It comes from the south and east, from soil and bone, and it bypasses the great poems entirely. It survives in fragments. Carvings on forgotten roof beams. The embroidery on funeral cloth. It waits for you to remember. That's all it asks."

"Nav. Down here." I tapped the roots. "This is where the dead go. Your grandmother, her grandmother, every ancestor you've forgotten the name of. They're all in Nav. And I know what you're picturing, fire, brimstone, the whole Christian inheritance. Set that aside. The Slavs didn't separate their dead into the saved and the damned. Everyone went to Nav. You lived, you died, you went into the roots. Your family left food at your grave, poured water, spoke your name at the feast of Zadušnice. You were still part of the household. Just lower down."

I traced my hand up the trunk.

"Yav is the trunk. The lived world. What you can see, touch, choose. The realm you're sitting in right now." I tapped the board. "And up here, the branches, some of you have read about Prav. The divine realm, the seat of cosmic law." I paused. "The problem is that Prav comes almost entirely from the Book of Veles, which is, to put it generously, a nineteenth-century forgery. The older sources give us Nav and Yav. Two realms, not three. As a historian, I trust the older sources."

I stepped back from the board.

"So what is this, then? Is it cosmology? Sure, if you want. But I think it's a diagram of how the Slavs understood being alive. The dead beneath your feet, the living world around you, and the question of what connects them."

A hand rose. Lana's, her brow furrowed in contemplation.

"So are you saying the gods are just... fragments? Symbols for what's inside us?" Her voice was tentative, but she leaned forward in her seat, waiting.

I looked at her for a long moment. Her pen hovered over her notebook, forgotten. Then I nodded.

"They are, yes. But they're also more than that. Myths are mirrors, sure, they reflect what's inside us, but they also shape us. They tell you what to worship, what to fear. And if something lives in your blood long enough, it stops being a metaphor. It just... becomes true. You stop being able to tell the difference."

I saw it then, just for a breath. The widening of her pupils. The almost unconscious way her fingers gripped her pen, as if she had felt a tremor pass beneath her own skin.

I turned back to the board, compelled, my hand moving with an almost automatic precision.

"Mythology survives," I said, and the words came out heavier than I intended.

And above the tree, the central axis of my drawing, I wrote one single, unyielding word, born from an instinct I could not explain.

Ilija.

I stared at it for a moment, the letters seeming to pulse with a hidden meaning only I could perceive. Then I turned, my voice still steady, though I could feel the ground beneath me beginning to shift, a subtle tremor that only I seemed to register.

"Class dismissed."

Outside the lecture hall, the air felt thinner, a subtle pressure against my skin. The cold prickling my forearms was secondary to a wrongness I couldn't locate, as if the city itself breathed too quietly, holding its collective breath.

I stepped into the street. A familiar current of pedestrians and traffic settled around me, yet I moved through it like a ghost. The sky had turned the color of ash, heavy and diffuse, and the buildings leaned into the wind with the weariness of old men. I pulled my coat tighter and kept walking, my leather shoes tapping over the uneven stone.

Belgrade remembers everything; the very streets do not forget. Smoke curled from dented barrels at the corners, where chestnuts roasted, their sweet scent mingling with rain-damp tobacco clinging to pensioners huddled in ancient rituals. This city spirals, folding into itself like sediment in a riverbed. Time here curls inward, becoming denser, more intricately wound.

I passed the bookstore, its window a tableau frozen in time. The same dog-eared poetry collection slouched beside a yellowing photograph of Danilo Kiš. I passed the old woman on the corner, her tin can of sunflowers wilted long ago, but still there, as if waiting for the dead stems to flower once more. Perhaps she was no longer selling, just keeping vigil for a husband or a version of this city that had already been buried.

I crossed the boulevard, diesel exhaust lingering behind buses as they wheezed into their stops like tired metal beasts. The fortress hill rose ahead, jagged and ancient, carved by wind and history, older than most gods. Below it, the rivers met, the Sava and the Danube, whispering in their timeless convergence.

From the hill's vantage point, one could discern the bones of empires laid bare by time, the deep scars left behind by kings and wars and names no one dared to speak aloud. I stood at the edge and looked out across the water, where the past stretched in every direction like a persistent fog clinging to the current.

New Belgrade blinked to the west, a stark expanse of concrete and fluorescent detachment. To the east, the old city slouched under rusted balconies and satellite dishes, as if trying not to be noticed. Above it all, the moon had risen early, pale and wide, watching with the kind of patience that comes from having seen it all before.

I turned away from the rivers and kept walking. The climb steepened as the street narrowed, winding upward through the older part of the hill where buildings leaned into one another like old friends who had long since run out of things to say. My body knew the way, accustomed to these ancient streets, even as my thoughts drifted.

My apartment stood near the top, nestled among a row of brick flats built between wars. The façade was cracked, the mortar veined with ivy that had grown wild and refused to be pulled down. The building looked like it had survived things without needing to explain how. I liked that about it.

I climbed the steps and paused at the door, reaching for the key, its cold metal familiar in my hand. The light above the landing buzzed, flickered once, then held steady. I watched it for a breath longer than necessary, caught in its fragile stability, before stepping inside.

The apartment greeted me as it always did, with a stillness that ran deeper than silence. There was the low hum of the refrigerator, the muffled pulse of the city beyond the windows, but this quiet was different. It lingered in the corners, distinctly aware, as if the space had been waiting for my return.

I set my bag beside the door and stood motionless, letting the room unfold around me. The air inside was cooler than it should have been, carrying the scent of dust and beeswax, underpinned by a mineral tang like turned earth and old stone that I felt more than smelled.

Books lined the walls in quiet chaos, stacked precariously, teetering in towers across every available surface. Titles in four languages spilled over each other, pages dog-eared, margins marked with half-formed thoughts, slips of paper tucked between pages like brittle, forgotten leaves. Some notes still held the faint ink of grief or wonder. Some didn't speak at all. It made sense to no one but me.

And then there were the icons.

They hung in quiet corners, as if they had chosen their places long before I ever moved in, their gazes fixed on eternity. Saint Sava, solemn and resolute. The Theotokos, her eyes fixed just beyond the frame. Saint Elijah, my namesake, mid-ascent and wreathed in fire. They offered no comfort, demanded no belief. They watched.

The candle beneath them was still burning. Thin, tall, handmade, its wax a pale honeyed gold, its flame a steady beacon. The faint scent of beeswax and myrrh lingered in the air, as it always did. My mother had lit one like it every Sunday morning, every night of Lent, her hands steady, her faith unwavering. After her death, I never made the conscious choice to continue; I just did, the tradition woven into the fabric of daily life. Even now I kept the flame lit. Whatever faith I had once held had worn thin, threadbare at the edges, but a different compulsion had taken its place, woven from habit and the unspoken fear of what might follow if the light ever died.

I stepped to the stand beneath Saint Sava and reached for the matches, their wood cool against my fingers. The candle hadn't gone out, but I lit it again anyway, a redundant ritual. The flame caught, wavered for a hesitant moment, then steadied, its glow rising up along the icon's face, lending his ancient severity an almost fatherly warmth. For a single moment, the room seemed to exhale, releasing a tension I hadn't realized it held.

I turned from the candle slowly, letting the warmth of its light remain at my back as I crossed into the kitchen. The loza was where it always was, tucked behind the chipped mugs and a half-empty tin of bitter mountain tea. I reached for it without ceremony, just habit, quiet and worn thin by years of repetition. The bottle felt cool in my hand, its glass slightly fogged, the label faded and curling at the edges. I had never bothered to replace it, perhaps because it had outlasted everything else.

The liquid poured clear and sharp into the glass, catching the low light in a brief, fiery brilliance. I paused before drinking to listen. The stillness in the apartment had deepened, and though nothing had shifted visibly, I felt the quiet settle around me with more weight than before. I brought the glass to my lips and drank slowly. The loza burned in my throat, as it always did, then dropped into my chest like an anchor, heat unfurling along my ribs in a way that almost made me believe I was grounded again. The ache remained unchanged.

I leaned against the counter for a moment, glass in hand, my eyes unfocused. There was comfort in the sting, yes, but no clarity. Just the repetition of an old ritual, one that had once belonged to colder nights and voices I no longer heard. I finished the drink, rinsed the glass, and left it beside the sink.

Nothing in the apartment had outwardly changed, but I had, in a way so subtle it left no physical mark, only the faint pressure of the ground having shifted beneath my feet. I walked out without turning on another light. The candle's glow stretched far enough from the hallway to reveal the faint outlines of bookshelves and the floorboards worn smooth by years of pacing. Everything felt known, even if I couldn't say why it no longer felt still.

From the hallway behind me, I heard the soft, unmistakable sound of the key turning in the lock. It moved through the quiet room the way a memory returns, softly, uninvited. I stayed in the armchair, my spine curved into its worn comfort, hand still resting on the closed book, as the door eased open behind me.

Ana stepped inside as if she had always been there. Her coat slipped from her shoulders with the weight of rain and long hours, and she hung it beside the door without looking in my direction. Her braid, dark with moisture, clung to the back of her sweater. She unwound it slowly with one hand, shaking out strands that clung like threads of smoke to her shoulders.

"You left the balcony light on again," she said, her voice a low murmur, gently chiding.

I blinked, pulling my gaze from the flickering candle, and turned toward the glass door at the far end of the apartment. The balcony was dark.

"I didn't go out," I replied, the words feeling brittle on my tongue, unsure whether I was answering the question she'd asked or denying one that hadn't yet formed.

She paused in the hallway, her body still, her eyes meeting mine. Her gaze was steady, clinical, the kind of look she gave artifacts behind museum glass, cataloging fractures before deciding how to handle them.

"You dreamed again," she said. Already certain.

My fingers moved to the edge of the book, brushing a small tear in the page I hadn't noticed before. "I don't remember," I said, the lie thin and transparent even to my own ears.

Ana didn't press. She nodded once, slowly, and moved into the kitchen. Her presence filled the space the way scent fills a room, total, leaving no corner untouched.

I listened to her movements, the cupboard opening with a soft creak, the clink of glass against porcelain. Her movements were familiar, worn in by years of shared space, two people inhabiting a quiet rhythm without speaking the thing that lived between them.

"They brought in a new case of mourning veils today," Ana said from the kitchen, her voice shifting into the register she used for old, dead things. "Rural. Most were threadbare. One still had the comb sewn in."

I stood and crossed into the kitchen, leaning against the doorframe. She was drinking water, one hand curled lightly around the glass, her shoulders curved as though she hadn't yet let the day go.

"Serbian?" I asked, my voice low, hoping to keep the conversation anchored.

She shook her head, a slow, almost imperceptible motion. "Mixed. Vlach. Some Albanian. One Turkish braid pattern we haven't seen catalogued before." She paused, letting the glass rest on the counter. "The embroidery was still stiff with salt. Tears, or sweat, who knows. A hundred years old and you could still feel the grief in the thread." She said it the way someone might describe a favorite painting. Admiration dressed as sympathy.

Ana didn't expect a response. Her gaze moved over my face with that same searching stillness, the way she inventoried damage on a new acquisition. She stepped forward and placed her hand on mine. Her grip was firm, almost fierce, before she let go.

"You looked pale when I came in," she said quietly. "Gray around the mouth. You get that way when the dreams come."

"I was reading," I replied, the lie sharp and unwelcome in my mouth.

"No," she said, and her eyes held mine without flinching. "You weren't here."

I had no response.

She stepped back, already moving toward the stove. I watched her reach for the kettle, fingers brushing the switch. The gesture was enough; it always had been. It was the same unspoken rhythm we had fallen into so many nights before, small gestures replacing larger ones, a shared silence that had once felt like peace but now felt like a held breath we were both afraid to release.

"I made some earlier," I said, my voice softer now. "It's probably still warm."

"I'll heat it," she replied, already pouring the remnants into a small pot. She left the question of what I had been reading untouched. The candle still flickered faintly against the far wall, beneath Saint Elijah's icon, and I saw her eyes fix on it, her expression going flat, emptied of whatever warmth had been there a moment before. She held the look longer than made sense, then turned back to the stove.

I stayed by the door, leaning against the frame as she moved around the kitchen. The light from the street slipped in through the window, catching her profile in dim gold. She looked tired, the kind of weariness that comes from performing the same role too long. Her face held the same expression she wore when cataloging ancient bones, careful and reverent.

When the tea was ready she poured two cups, placed mine on the counter beside me, and took hers to the small table in the corner. We didn't speak while we drank, the quiet between us a space we had made to keep from unraveling. I joined her, and we sat across from each other like we had countless nights before, listening to the murmuring city hum around us.

Outside, the wind had picked up. It moved through the alleyways and over the rooftops with a persistence that made it impossible to ignore. The windows shivered in their frames, and the curtain near the balcony door fluttered without direction.

Ana finished her tea first. She stood, rinsed her cup without a word, and placed it in the rack. I followed her into the hallway, and we moved through the motions of closing the night, shutting the windows against the chill, locking the door. None of it needed to be said aloud.

When we reached the bedroom, she peeled off her sweater and let it drop to the chair near the bed. Her hair was still damp, curling near the ends, clinging to her neck. She slipped beneath the blanket without waiting for me, her eyes already half-closed, one hand reaching absently across the sheets.

I lay beside her. Her hand found its way to my chest, pressing over the place where my heartbeat pressed closest to the surface. Her fingers settled into position with the certainty of ownership.

Her hand softened against my skin. Her breathing deepened into sleep, each exhale like tidewater smoothing stone. I stayed beside her, unmoving, my eyes open to the ceiling, listening to her breathing and to the apartment itself. The subtle groan of wood shifting with the cold. The way the quiet had filled with a low hum, a presence I couldn't place, like the air before a storm gathers its charge.

There was no sense of linear time now, only the slow awareness of my own consciousness folding inward, drawing breath in a way the body doesn't consciously recognize but the soul remembers.

I eased the blanket away and sat up, the air chilling my skin.

The floor was cold beneath my feet. I stood slowly, letting the room remain steeped in darkness. I moved through the hallway as if the apartment itself had shifted its shape while I slept. Every book on its shelf, every coat hanging along the wall felt familiar, yet wrong, as if they belonged to a version of my life I hadn't inhabited in years.

I knelt near the low shelf beside the coat rack, reaching for the stack of journals along the back. Behind them, smooth and plain against the wall, rested the cedar box. It hadn't been locked, its contents guarded by grief and hardened denial.

The scent met me before the lid lifted. Lavender and the sharp tang of ash, the mineral smell of river clay that always arrived with memory. I opened it slowly.

Inside, the past had kept its distinct shape. The photo lay on top, its edges curled, the colors slightly faded, but the moment itself remained untouched. My father crouched beside me on the bank of the Danube, a string of freshly caught fish held high in one hand, the other resting on my small shoulder. I must have been ten, perhaps younger. We were both laughing, wide-mouthed, full-throated. I traced the worn edge of the image with my thumb, then set it aside.

Beneath it lay the wristwatch. Its face was cracked, a spiderweb of irreparable damage, the metal cold and unpolished. It had stopped at 6:12. I never knew if it had broken before or after he died, never asked.

There was a funeral card, its name blurred at the edges from years of handling. My father's.

Next came the stone, smooth, river-worn, the color of wet ash. It still felt warm, even after all these years, as if it carried the heat of a sunlit shore and the echo of water slipping past old roots. I closed my hand around it for a moment, just long enough to feel it push back against my skin, then let it return to its place.

A red ribbon followed, frayed along one edge, its fibers beginning to pull apart. I didn't consciously remember where it came from, only that it had been important once, that it had been tied around something I should have kept. Now only the ribbon remained.

Then lavender. Dried, pale, nearly brittle. The scent rose in a faint breath as I lifted the sprig, still sharp, still rooted in some distant memory of incense and fertile soil. I remembered the way my mother used to tuck herbs into the corners of rooms, a quiet gesture of protection against unseen harms.

And finally, folded flat and tucked beneath everything else, a single piece of paper. I knew it was mine before I opened it. The handwriting was slanted, precise, familiar in a way that made my chest tighten with foreboding. I didn't remember writing it, not exactly, not the physical act, but I remembered the feeling. The stillness in my chest, the peculiar way my hand had moved without me, guided by a will that was not my own.

I unfolded the paper. A single line in my own hand.

Something waits beneath the roots.

I read it once, then read it again. The words confirmed what I hadn't wanted to articulate aloud.

I let the paper rest beside the others. I closed the box slowly, pressing it gently back down. My fingers lingered for a moment against the worn cedar before I rose. The hallway pressed in on either side, the walls unchanged yet alert, attentive. I moved without sound, each step measured.

Back in the bedroom, the light had thinned further, retreating into deeper shadow. The candle's reach no longer touched the doorway, and the curtain near the balcony billowed faintly with the night wind, casting slow shadows that stretched and warped across the walls. I slid beneath the blanket without disturbing her. The warmth where I had lain hadn't yet faded, and as I settled, Ana shifted, her hand brushing across my chest until it found the same place it always did, resting over my heart.

Her breathing never changed. I kept my eyes open, staring at the ceiling, which held no answers, just familiar lines drawn in shadow and light. Yet the restlessness in me had quieted, as though whatever had been pacing behind the edges of my thought had finally settled.

I watched the ceiling until the shadows blurred, my body unable to discern the difference between waking and the onset of a different kind of awareness.

When sleep came, it brought me down, deeper, into a realm that felt more real than waking.

The dream settled the way water does, filling every empty space. Soil surrounded me, thick, damp, pressed close on all sides, heavier and older than anything I had language for. It held me the way earth holds a seed, total and indifferent.

Then came the roots. They were already there, intertwined, woven deep through the silence. They didn't visibly move, but I could feel the way they pulsed, a slow, resonant thrum of life that had always been there. I had already arrived.

And deeper beneath them, or perhaps beyond them, where the language of space didn't apply, an immense awareness stirred. It had always been there.

Within that boundless darkness, images stirred, felt with an agonizing, visceral intensity. Scorched fields beneath skies the color of bruised violet, the ruins of a temple I instinctively called home, a beloved body held in my arms as ancient stone cracked around us, a desperate kiss sealed in fire just before the world collapsed into dust and silence. These were memories I had inhabited and then buried with ruthless efficiency for countless ages. I knew their textures, the specific bitter taste of their grief, their precise agonizing shape, rising now from the deep, unspoken silence of my slumber.

CHAPTER THREE
THE SHIFTING

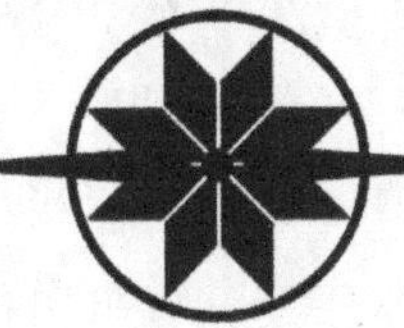

Ilija

The knocking returned the next night. It came from behind my ribs, a quiet rhythmic pressure, pulsing like breath caught between waking and sleep. I filled the kettle instead.

The kitchen was dim, lit by the stovetop light. I moved through the motions, water into the kettle, the familiar chipped mug I refused to replace. The tea was harsh and bitter, and I welcomed the burn. Steam drifted toward the ceiling, and I kept my eyes fixed on the mug.

I set the mug down and crossed myself. The meaning had worn thin over the years, frayed like thread passed too many times through the same needle. Forehead, chest, shoulder, shoulder. I pressed my fingers to my lips, then to the doorframe beneath the wooden cross my mother had hung there, still slightly crooked.

"Holy God, Holy Mighty, Holy Immortal," I whispered. "Have mercy on us." I stopped there.

The knock inside my chest held steady. I stood there a while longer, the tea cooling in my hands.

I only remembered the cold of the hallway seeping through my sleeves as I pulled on my coat. The door clicked shut behind me.

The sky was the color of slate, and the morning air carried a raw edge that settled deep in the lungs. I walked without rush, diesel from passing buses, chestnuts roasting on corners. The university district swallowed me among students who moved like ghosts across the cobblestones, all headphones and heads bowed into the wind.

Inside the lecture hall, everything looked the same. Tall windows streaked with the breath of ivy, dust turning the light gold in places and shadowed in others. Thirty students, maybe fewer. I shrugged off my coat and folded it over the chair near the wall. My hands were cold, slightly unsteady.

I had planned to discuss funerary rites. The transition from pagan burial customs to Christian ritual in the medieval Balkans, how belief systems layer over each other. I had my notes and my slides. I cleared my throat and began.

"When the Slavic tribes began converting," I said, "they didn't abandon their dead. They renamed them. The offerings continued, the food left at graves, the coins placed on closed eyes. Only now they called it Christian charity instead of ancestor worship. The gesture was identical. The name had changed."

I clicked to the next slide, a photograph of a medieval Serbian tombstone, a stećak, carved with spirals and a figure raising both hands toward the sky beyond the frame's edge.

"Notice the hands," I said. "Reaching upward. We interpret this as prayer because we've been taught to see prayer. The original carvers may have meant invocation. A gesture older than any church."

The lecture unfolded as lectures do, and the room held its usual attention. Then the pressure came again, right beneath my sternum, insistent and sharp.

My hand moved to the whiteboard. I meant to sketch the stećak's spiral pattern. The marker was warm in my grip, and the shape that formed was not a spiral.

It was my name. Ilija. Written clean across the center of the board in my own handwriting.

Behind me the projector flickered. At the bottom of the screen, barely noticeable, three faint interwoven lines appeared. Red, gold, and black. I hadn't drawn them. I knew them.

"Professor?" Toma sat forward, brow furrowed, watching me the way you watch a man walk too close to the edge.

I blinked and looked again. The slide had returned to normal. The symbol was gone. I turned toward the class and forced composure.

"I loaded the wrong file," I said. "That's all for today."

The room emptied with the shuffle of bags and chairs skimming tile. I left the marker uncapped on the tray and walked out without looking back. Halfway down the corridor I stopped and pressed my palm against the cold wall. My name was still on the board. The three colors on the screen were the same ones I had seen the night my father died.

What the fuck.

The night my father died and I ran into the woods, that was supposed to be grief. Shock. An overactive teenage imagination fracturing under loss. That was what my therapist had told me for years, and I had believed her because believing her meant solid ground. Both parents dead now, my mother's passing fresh enough to ache when I breathe too deeply. Maybe that was what had cracked it open, the last blow to a foundation that had always been hollow underneath.

I knew Ana was waiting for me.

I took the back streets. I needed the quiet, the roads where trees leaned low over old fences and rust spread on lampposts like ivy. My feet carried me without a destination, past shuttered windows and the thin wail of a violin drifting from a second-story apartment, past the dry scrape of a broom on concrete behind a wrought iron fence. The street curved gently left toward the Faculty of Theology, its old stone walls carved with the names of saints, and beyond it the monastery garden waited.

I slipped through the side gate without a sound. The garden stretched ahead of me in the gray breathless stillness only late autumn can hold. Ivy clung to the stone walls, and the path curved around skeletal trees, the gravel underfoot muffled by frost. Cold air carried the trace of beeswax and myrrh, funeral incense.

He was there. Same bench. Same posture. The old monk sat beneath the faded mural of Saint Elijah rising into flame, his cane leaned beside him, one hand resting on its worn curve. His cassock hung from him in ancient folds, threadbare near the cuffs. His eyes were pale and clouded, as if he were always looking through you.

Before I could speak, he lifted his head. "You've been dreaming again."

"Excuse me?" I managed.

He tapped two fingers against his temple. "You've been somewhere else. You're carrying a weight, and it's from much further away than Belgrade."

"Just tired, Father."

He gave a dry laugh, one corner of his mouth tugging up. "Tired lives in the body. What you're carrying sits deeper than bone."

He patted the bench beside him. "Sit, if you want."

I nodded once and turned to leave.

"Whatever's calling you," he said, softer now, "it won't stop because you ignore it."

I turned back for a moment. His hand hovered over the dust on the bench, and there, traced into the surface with the edge of his thumb, was a crude uneven triangle. In my mind the shape flared in three colors. Red. Gold. Black.

I walked out of the courtyard fast enough that it was almost running.

The city felt heavier on the walk back. I kept to the narrow streets, where a burnt-out bakery smelled faintly of flour and ash. Church bells rang from far off. I passed the corner market where a kid slouched by the freezer scrolling through his phone while the radio played a folk ballad about rivers and mothers. I remembered that song. My aunt used to hum it when she cooked, and the smell of lamb and garlic filled my head uninvited, too vivid, bringing my mother's kitchen with it, the oil-smudged walls, the waxy flame on the windowsill. I shook the memory off because I had no other choice.

My building rose in its usual leaning way, vines clawing up the mortar, windows glowing soft gold, one of them mine. I stood across the street and looked at it.

The apartment smelled like ajvar and warm bread, clove from her tea settling over everything, and beneath it, faint and sweet, the particular scent she carried that I had never been able to name, floral and heavy, like roses left too long in a closed room. The lights were low, softened by the stained-glass shade she'd bought from a street vendor who claimed it had once belonged to a poet. She left the poet's name a mystery, and I let it stay one.

Ana's voice reached me from the kitchen. "You're late."

I stepped into the kitchen and saw her, barefoot in one of my old sweaters, its sleeves too long, her hair pinned up and slipping loose, flour dusting her cheek, a pot simmering on the stove behind her.

"I went for a walk," I said.

"Through a war zone?" Her tone was light, but her eyes tracked my face.

"Through memory," I said, and regretted it immediately.

She raised an eyebrow and let it go. "You hungry?"

"I could eat the table."

She handed me a plate and nodded toward the table. We ate. Ana talked about the museum, mislabeled funerary textiles and a curator who couldn't tell the difference between Vlach lace and Turkish weaving. I nodded in the right places, my mind back in the corridor at the university.

She noticed, and she pressed her foot to mine under the table, holding me there, and kept talking.

"You know," she said, her gaze fixed on the far wall, "you've been slipping. I can tell when you're holding yourself together, and you've been doing it badly for days."

I watched the candle. The flame leaned gently, caught in a draft only it could feel.

"I'm not pretending."

She set her fork down, deliberate. "You came home with the same look you had last night. Like you're already halfway gone."

"You dreamed again," she added.

"I didn't sleep," I said, and she murmured, "Same difference," and neither of us spoke for a while.

I finally looked at her. "I saw a slide change at the university. On its own. A symbol appeared, red, gold, black. It flickered like it wasn't digital. Like it was alive."

She reached for her wine and drank, and when she set the glass down her expression had gone still, watchful. "Did anyone else see it?"

"Maybe. No one said anything."

"And the dream?"

"The same. The clearing, the flames. Only this time I was there twice."

That made her pause, her hand stilling around the glass. "Yourself?"

"Yes. Me now and me then."

Her lips pressed together, and when she spoke her voice was softer. "Do you think it's memory or omen?"

"I think it's waking up," I said. "In me. Around me. I don't know."

Ana reached across the table and took my hand. Her grip tightened once, a reflex, before she let her fingers soften.

"You need to be careful," she said, and her voice had changed, dropped into a register I rarely heard, older and harder. "These things don't wake without taking something with them."

"I know."

"No." She held my gaze, and for a moment the warmth in her eyes was gone, replaced by something ancient and absolute. "You don't."

We finished the wine, cleaned up the plates, moved through the quiet motions of a life we'd built together and only half recognized anymore. When we got into bed she curled into my side the way she always did, her breath warm against my collarbone, her hand flat over my heart.

She shifted slow. I stared at the ceiling, tracing the cracks in the plaster, waiting for her breath to even out into sleep, and it didn't.

She moved just enough to press her lips to my shoulder, and I turned to her. I always turned to her.

Her eyes found mine in the dim light and held, patient and certain, as if she had been waiting for exactly this moment. Her palm slid up along my sternum, settling at the side of my neck, and then she kissed me.

It was raw and urgent. Her leg came over my hip, pulling me closer, and she slipped her palm beneath my shirt, cool against my skin. I exhaled into her and everything else fell away.

I pulled the sweater over her head, her hair falling free, catching the streetlamp's glow through the window. Her skin was warm, flushed from wine. I kissed the hollow of her throat, her collarbone, and she let out a low sound that undid me.

She unfastened my pants with the steady focus that came from years of knowing this body. I helped her out of hers, our movements graceless and familiar. Her hips rolled against mine before I was fully inside her, and she buried her face in my neck as we found the rhythm together.

It was urgent in the way grief sometimes is. Slow at first, then quicker. Her hands dug into my back. My fingers tangled in her hair.

We'd been apart for months without ever leaving each other. She looked at me just as she came, and for a moment the distance between us vanished.

She moved above me slowly, rhythmically, her breath caught between sighs and silence, and I looked up at her like a man who'd forgotten language. Her hair spilled around her shoulders, golden and unruly, clinging to her damp skin, slipping between her breasts. Her skin glowed in the low light, pale and flushed, marked by the things I knew by heart. The tiny freckle under her right breast, the faint scar above her hip from a childhood fall she kept to herself. Her thighs clenched around me and I felt the world go still.

Her gaze held mine, wide and focused, as if she was checking whether I was still hers. Her lips parted when she gasped, red and swollen from my mouth, and I wanted to kiss her again.

I reached up and touched her ribs, her waist. My thumb grazed the soft underside of her jaw where a single pulse fluttered. She closed her lids and her body shuddered once.

She cried out softly as she came, her body curling into mine, and I held her through it, her warmth trembling at my neck, her heartbeat stuttering before finding its rhythm again.

Afterward she lay with her head against my chest, her fingers tracing slow patterns on my ribs, deliberate shapes that repeated and repeated as she drifted toward sleep.

She felt like home. She felt like the last solid thing, and I was already sinking. I touched her hair, gold and soft, and even that comfort felt borrowed.

I closed my eyes and immediately felt it again, the hum and the pressure, the knock that came from inside.

The dream settled the way water does, filling every empty space. I sank into cold and weight, my limbs heavy.

I was in a corridor, long and curved, its walls pulsing slightly, damp and alive. Each step echoed from within me. The air was thick with salt and wet stone. The walls were carved with faces twisted in agony or ecstasy; mouths open mid-scream or mid-song.

I reached a threshold that yawned wide and stepped through into a hollow, vast and starless, and my blood recoiled because I'd been here before. The air tasted like iron, and the smell came stronger, rot and lavender braided together.

My knees hit the ground. A presence pushed up through my spine, spreading across my chest. The roots twisted in the distance, moving as limbs move, thick and alive, pulsing with dull internal light.

Beneath them, an awareness watched me, older than gods. A part of me had always known it was there.

You've begun to remember.

The realization broke open. I pulled in a breath too sharp and woke with my heart pounding.

The room was dim, my skin slick with sweat. Ana lay warm against my side, her breathing slow. The awareness from the dream had followed me back.

I rose carefully, moved through the apartment to the kitchen, and poured a glass of water. The taste in my mouth was earth. I stood at the window watching the street below bleed into day, overcast and pale, palm flat on the glass. My breath left a halo there, a faint circle that pulsed once and faded.

Behind me the sheets rustled. "Ilija?" Ana's voice, rough with sleep.

"I'm here," I said.

She sat up, pulling the blanket around her shoulders. "You didn't come back to bed."

"I couldn't."

She crossed to the kitchen and brushed my arm as she passed, then poured herself a glass of water and leaned against the opposite counter.

"You're shaking," she said.

"I'm fine," I said.

She studied me, then stepped closer, her hand reaching for mine, slow and careful.

"I know it's getting worse," she said. "I've been watching it happen."

I closed my eyes. "I can't explain it yet."

"Then don't," she said, and neither of us spoke again.

I let the shower water run too hot, steam fogging the mirror before I stepped in. I stood under the spray with my palms pressed to the tile, letting it burn. The heat scalded my shoulders and back, stopped at the skin. The dream had followed me out. It was still here, patient and close, waiting in the marrow.

CHAPTER FOUR
THE NORSE REMEMBERS

Ilija

Ana moved through the kitchen as if she belonged to it, her hips brushing the counter, bare feet cool against cold tile, hair pulled up into that messy twist that never quite stayed. One sleeve of my hoodie had slipped off her shoulder, and she left it. The kettle clicked off behind her, and she poured the water with a careful precision that made everything she did feel older than it should.

I watched her from the doorway, holding the chipped mug she'd handed me. We let the dream from the night before sit between us, untouched. The stone sat on the desk in the other room, unwrapped, its spiral still pulsing faintly like it was remembering me. Ana had only smiled when she saw it, faintly, as if she'd expected it.

She stirred honey into her tea and took a sip, then winced. "Too hot," she muttered, setting the mug down and leaning against the counter. "What time's your lecture?"

"Ten," I said. "Norse and Slavic cosmologies. The cheerful stuff."

She gave me the look that said I was trying too hard and that she appreciated the effort anyway. "You going to actually teach, or just stare into space again while pretending you're forming a thesis thought?"

"Not fair," I said, sipping my own tea. "I stare very academically."

She snorted, and the sound stopped at her mouth. Something hovered between us, a shared waiting, as if we were both listening for the same thing.

"I'll walk," I said.

Ana nodded and turned back to the stove, already somewhere else, or pretending to be.

The lecture hall held its usual quiet. I had been speaking for twenty minutes, moving through the parallels between Norse and Slavic cosmological structures, the way both traditions built their worlds around a central axis and populated the spaces between with forces that mirrored each other, when Danica Madsen raised her hand.

She held still. A kind of gravity clung to her that belonged somewhere far older than a classroom, and it made the room feel smaller, slower. She waited a beat before speaking, her voice low and deliberate.

"I brought something," she said. "I shouldn't have kept it."

A few heads turned. Eyes lifted from phones and notebooks, and the usual undercurrent of distraction went silent. In her lap sat a velvet-wrapped bundle, midnight blue, folded tight around whatever lay beneath. Her fingers gripped the fabric with reverence, as if she were holding it for someone else.

Her face was pale in the dim light. Her eyes caught me first, dark and depthless, carrying a stillness I had only ever felt at the edge of a storm.

"I think it's related to you," she said.

Nervous laughter flickered somewhere in the back, a quick glance between students uncertain whether this was still part of the lecture. I offered a neutral smile to ease the tension while my gaze held hers, because she was steady, composed. She was holding something ancient, and it wanted out.

She rose slowly, every step measured and deliberate. She moved between the rows of desks with a solemnity reserved for offerings. Her shoes clicked lightly against the tile, the only sound besides the projector's low hum, and even that seemed to fade as she reached the front.

She stopped beside my desk and extended the bundle toward me, both hands wrapped around it, her fingers firm despite the slight tremble in her wrists. I looked at her once more. She gave the smallest nod.

I reached out and took the bundle. The fabric was warm, unnaturally so, like it had been resting near fire or pressed against skin for too long. The velvet clung to itself as if reluctant to yield, and then it gave. Slowly, I peeled back the layers.

Inside was a stone, flat and round, black as charred bone, veined faintly with crimson and silver threads. Its surface held a pattern that spiraled inward, impossibly fine, like a fingerprint pressed into stone by something older than hands.

I felt it first in my ears, a pressure, the kind you get before a storm breaks. The fluorescent lights overhead buzzed louder for a moment, then flickered. The familiar scent of whiteboard marker and dust turned metallic, sharp, like blood over old stone. Then it passed. I pulled my hand away, because the heat had burrowed deeper than skin, lodged somewhere in my chest where memory and instinct shared the same root.

"You know what it is, don't you?" Danica said, soft and certain.

I did know. I knew it the way you recognize a voice in a dream or a place you've never visited and somehow remember, something older than words. The spiral burned behind my eyes.

"Where did you get this?"

"It came in the mail," she said. "No return address. Just a plain box. This was inside, wrapped like that."

"A note?"

"One thing," she said, barely above a whisper. "Your name. Written in pencil. In the old Cyrillic."

The ground shifted beneath me, or seemed to. I looked down at the stone again. The marks carved into it belonged to an alphabet older than Cyrillic, older than letters. They were something primal, and they still spoke. I could feel them speaking now.

"Did you tell anyone else?"

She shook her head. "It didn't feel like something you tell."

"Thank you, Danica. I'll look into it."

She stepped back, arms crossing over her chest, and returned to her seat. I wrapped the stone tight, like sealing a wound, and placed it into my satchel with a care that startled me. The moment it disappeared the room exhaled. Students stirred. Someone coughed. Someone else typed a note they'd never read again.

The rest of the lecture passed like a ghost through my hands. I don't remember what I said, whether I finished the slides or dismissed them early. No one spoke of the object, as if the moment had already been buried somewhere no one wanted to dig. When the room emptied I stood there with my hands planted on either side of the desk, eyes locked on the satchel that now held something far older than the university, older than the idea of names.

I could feel the stone through the canvas, its presence registering as memory more than heat.

I found the monk where I always found him, beneath the faded fresco of Saint Elijah rising into flame. The walk to the monastery had vanished from my mind. The city had blurred around me, streets narrowing and emptying as though Belgrade itself had decided to step back and give me privacy.

"You're heavier than last time," he said, his voice rolling through the cold like wind over dry leaves. Observant, the way you'd note a tree leaning after a long storm.

I sat down beside him, skipping the polite dances of the previous visits. The bench was cold beneath me. The silence that followed was old and familiar, like a coat I'd worn too long to take off.

"You've been standing too close to things that want to wake," he said.

I almost laughed, a bitter sound that died before it left my mouth. I was so sick of riddles, of mythic fragments and poetic warnings whispered like prayers I never asked for. I sat with it for a while, both hands gripping each other between my knees, and then something inside me cracked open.

"You think I don't know what's happening to me?" The monk waited. "I feel it in my sleep. I see it in my lectures. I can't fucking breathe without something ancient pressing against my ribs. I'm breaking in places I can't even name, and I still get up every day and pretend to care about footnotes and PowerPoints like the world isn't falling apart inside my chest."

My voice trembled on the last word. I hated how exposed I felt under the dull winter light.

"It's not just symbols and dreams. It's real. Something's waking up and it knows my name. It's in my bones. It's in that fucking stone, and I don't know what it wants from me. I can't think or rest. I can't even remember

the last time I looked in the mirror and recognized the man standing there."
He said nothing. "I'm losing myself," I said, quieter now. "Piece by piece.
The worst of it is that something in me wants it to happen, because I think
the person I was before all this started is already gone. I'm just the echo."

I leaned forward, elbows on my knees, knuckles white where my fingers
laced together. When I looked at him again his gaze was steadier than I
expected.

"Good," he said.

Anger flared in my chest. "Good?"

"Yes," he answered. "Because you finally stopped pretending you're still
asleep."

I stared at him, and the anger drained as quickly as it had come. He was
right. I was too exhausted to pretend otherwise.

"You'll be back," he said, tapping the cane once against the gravel, the
sound dull and final. "When the symbols stop burning and start singing,
you'll know where to go."

I walked out of the garden without looking back, because I was afraid
he'd give me a real answer if I stayed.

One object and a girl with storm-dark eyes, and suddenly I was
seventeen again, running barefoot through a forest I couldn't name, grief
pouring from me like blood from a wound I kept reopening. I was so tired
of holding the line between logic and myth, between who I pretended to be
and what I knew I was, or had been. I no longer knew the difference, and
maybe I never had. Maybe the truth was never mine to hold, only to
witness.

By the time I reached the apartment my hands were cold and raw, my
thoughts stretched thin. The door clicked shut behind me, and the quiet hit

hard, a silence that seemed to hold its breath.

Ana was on the couch, curled under a blanket, a candle burning low on the coffee table, its light flickering against the glass. She looked up when I entered. Her expression stayed even. She shifted slightly, just enough to make room.

I crossed the space, set the satchel by the bookshelf, and lowered myself onto the couch beside her. The cushions gave under my weight. She folded the blanket across both of us, her fingers brushing mine, and that contact almost undid me. I let my head fall against her shoulder, and for the first time all day I let myself be still.

She stayed like that for a long time. Then her hand found my chest, palm flat, grounding.

"You're somewhere else again," she murmured against my shoulder.

"I don't know where I am," I admitted.

She exhaled and pressed closer. "Come back."

I turned to look at her and for a moment, just that, I really saw her. Her skin glowed in the candlelight, gold at the edges where the flame caught her cheekbone. Her hair had fallen from its braid and framed her face in loose strands. Her eyes met mine, steady and open, and I exhaled for what felt like the first time in hours.

Her hand slid from my chest to my jaw, fingers brushing the stubble there. I leaned forward and kissed her like it was the only honest thing I'd done all day.

It started soft, familiar, the way we always began, her mouth warm and tasting faintly of honey. Then something beneath it cracked loose. She pulled me closer and her hands found my back under my shirt, her nails dragging lightly up my spine, and the sound I made surprised us both. I breathed her in like air after drowning. My fingers tangled in her hair and she arched into me, her hips pressing up against mine, and the blanket slid to the floor and neither of us reached for it.

I kissed her neck, the soft hollow beneath her ear, the place where her pulse beat quick and hard. She tasted like salt and something I had missed all day. Her hands pulled my shirt over my head and her palms pressed flat against my ribs, fingers spread, holding me like she was checking I was solid. I traced the line of her collarbone with my mouth, felt her breath catch, felt her fingers tighten in my hair.

We moved to the bedroom without separating, her back pressed against the wall in the hallway while my hands gripped her waist and she wrapped her legs around me. The sheets were cold when we fell into them. Her skin was warm everywhere I touched. We found each other the way we always did, slow at first, then urgent, her breath against my ear, my forehead pressed to hers, eyes open because I needed to see her, needed to know this was real. She whispered my name once, low, and I felt it move through me like current through water.

For a while I did forget. The ache and the stone. There was only this, her body wrapped around mine, her lips at my neck, her name spilling from my mouth against her skin. The candle guttered in the other room while the city hummed beyond the window. We held on.

Later we lay tangled in sheets, the window cracked open, the cold edge of night drifting in. Ana was quiet, her head tucked beneath my chin, one leg draped over mine. I listened to the apartment settle around us. Beneath everything there was that presence again, steady and low, a hum that came from the space between things.

I turned my head toward the desk. The velvet was gone. The stone sat exposed in the low light, resting exactly where I hadn't placed it, its surface catching the shadows strangely, the spiral glowing faintly like heat that remembered fire.

Beside me Ana shifted, still half-asleep, her voice barely more than breath. "It's not done with you yet." She kept her eyes closed. We said nothing else.

Sleep settled over me like mist thickening into fog, muffling the edges of the room until even Ana's warmth faded into background. The world slipped sideways and I found myself standing barefoot in the clearing again.

The forest pressed in around me, immense and breathless, holding something deeper than silence. The circle of stones hadn't changed, their moss-covered edges glistening in the low light. In their center the five flames hovered, pulsing in sequence, each a different hue that reached beyond color. Red like blood remembered. Gold like the last light before dusk. Black like the void behind the stars. White flickering like a breath held too long. A blue so deep it ached.

I stepped closer, and the moss gave beneath my feet as if the earth recognized me. I realized I was not alone. Across from me stood a boy, my younger self, still seventeen, still carrying a heartbreak too old for his body. His eyes met mine and something unspoken passed between us. He knew what I had come through. I saw what he had become, or rather what he had failed to become, because standing there in the clearing he looked like what I might have been if I hadn't spent fifteen years building walls against exactly this moment.

Behind him the trees shifted, though no wind followed. The branches swayed too deliberately, and something moved between them, never quite taking shape, like breath against glass. The forest made space around it. I couldn't see it clearly, only feel its weight, something immense and old beyond reckoning.

My younger self already knew it was there. His hands were cupped in front of him, holding something I couldn't see, and when he looked at me again the meaning was clear. An invitation.

I stepped into the ring. The five flames brightened in a slow steady pulse that felt like the heartbeat of the world itself. The boy reached out, palms opening, and inside them the spiral stone, alive now, its symbols gleaming with a light that belonged to memory.

The moment my fingers touched it the forest breathed. The ground beneath my feet shifted, the soil opening, roots twisting just beneath the surface with slow deliberate purpose, forming patterns that were familiar, symbols half-remembered from dreams I'd never spoken aloud.

Then came the voice, rising from somewhere within me.

You've begun to remember.

It moved through me like resonance, a truth that bypassed language. I knelt. The moss cradled my knees. The flames bowed in response, and the roots coiled around the edge of the circle like a frame being drawn around something that had always existed.

The voice returned. The door never closed. You forgot it was yours.

The fire flared, full and bright, and everything folded inward, drawn into the spiral in my palm until there was nothing left except heat. Then I opened my eyes.

I was still in bed, still in the apartment. The world remained exactly as I'd left it. The air felt thick. My chest ached. My hands were damp against the sheet. Beside me Ana hadn't moved, her breathing calm, her hand still resting lightly against my ribs.

Across the room, on the desk, the stone sat unwrapped, its spiral glowing faintly, pulsing like a second heartbeat in the dark. Whatever had been watching had followed me back. It was here now, awake and waiting.

So was I.

Chapter Five
The National Broadcast

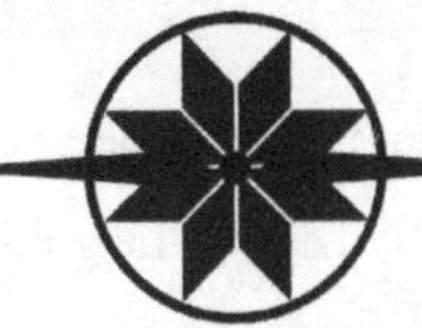

Ilija

The silence came first. A hush that pressed against skin, a hum just beneath the bones, as if the air itself remembered war even when no one spoke its name.

At exactly six o'clock, the world stopped. Every channel, every screen ceased without warning, without scrolling text to ease the transition. An abrupt absence, as if an invisible hand had pressed itself to the nation's mouth. The cartoon on my television froze mid-motion, its colors bleeding into gray. A soccer match vanished mid-pass. News anchors blinked into static. Radio voices stuttered, then dropped off. Even the music in the supermarkets fell to nothing. My phone buzzed once in my palm, then locked, its notifications vanishing. After that, silence, full and suffocating.

I stood in the living room, my thumb still hovering over the remote, my arm suspended. My lungs held tight, braced for something I couldn't name.

Then the image came, slow and deliberate, resolving on the black screen like something unearthed. A golden double-headed eagle, crowned with archaic authority, clutching the Orthodox cross in both claws. Its wings fanned wide, stark against the void. The air in the apartment tightened, pressing in on me, and my throat constricted.

The voice followed, genderless, mechanical, filling the silence with chilling authority. "This is a National Cultural Sanctity Broadcast. Please remain where you are and give your undivided attention to the President of the Republic of Serbia."

My feet stayed rooted to the floor, my body locked by something I couldn't resist. The screen shifted again, the golden eagle dissolving. Nikola Lazarević appeared, backlit by the cavernous, gleaming marble of Saint Sava's Cathedral, its immense space swallowing all ordinary sound. Behind him, flags of blood-red and burnished gold, embroidered with the same eagle and cross, hung heavy. His hands rested on the podium, fingers laced with the quiet tension of someone preparing to either pray or deliver a final sentence. At his side stood the Prime Minister, Jelena Trifunović, robed like a high priestess of some ancient, terrifying cult. The lighting within the cathedral had shifted from the soft glow of candlelight to a harsh, theatrical blood-orange, casting long, lean shadows that stretched alive, hinting at unseen presences.

Lazarević spoke, his voice steady and slow, resonating with a controlled power that belied the stillness. "People of Serbia. We are a nation with a soul." A chill coiled through my spine, cold and immediate, settling deep in my bones.

"For too long," he continued, his words striking like measured, intentional blows, "the soul has been polluted by imported ideologies. By scholars who dig through our sacred soil in search of false gods and dead spirits." His gaze, though distant, felt direct and accusatory. "They have desecrated our heritage and dressed it as truth."

My hands went cold. Every word, every veiled accusation, aimed at me, at my life's work, at everything I had given my years to.

Trifunović stepped forward, her voice ringing too bright for the solemn space, too sharp for the moment. "We are announcing the Cultural Sanctity Directive. A constitutional reform approved unanimously by the National Assembly." She smiled as she said it, a chilling, disarming expression, as if erasure could be an act of grace. My stomach turned, a tight knot of dread.

"Effective immediately," she continued, her voice gaining a ruthless precision, "the Republic of Serbia will reaffirm its identity as a sacred Orthodox nation, indivisible in faith and spirit." The camera widened, slowly revealing the full image. Priests in dark robes, their faces unreadable, stood in disciplined rows. Behind them, grim-faced soldiers held rifles at ease, their weapons a silent promise of enforcement. Further back, rows of impossibly young children in school uniforms clutched small, gleaming gold crosses, their innocence weaponized.

"This is how they do it," I whispered to no one. "This is how it starts."

Trifunović kept going, unfazed, her voice a relentless current. "All fields of anthropological, folkloric, and mythological study will be placed under review by the Ministry of Cultural Integrity. Academic disciplines that contradict the sanctified Orthodox narrative will be discontinued."

This had become doctrine, codified into law. The words hammered at everything I believed in, everything I had built.

"They want to own memory," I said aloud, my voice hollow in the suddenly vast room. "They want to burn everything that challenges their singular truth."

And then they did.

The feed cut to live footage outside the cathedral, a stark, immediate transition. A brazier had been wheeled into view, a vast iron crucible, already burning with a fierce, hungry intensity. Books were being thrown in, volumes spiraling into the flames. Field guides and dense theses with cracked spines. Some I recognized, titles I had pored over for years. One, I knew with a sickening lurch, I had written the foreword to, its words now consumed. Flames licked the pages like starving mouths, devouring ink, twisting paper into ash.

I stepped back. The cold edge of the bookshelf met my spine, and I stayed there.

A message buzzed in my palm. Tanja from Novi Sad, her words rushed and barely coherent. Her classes had been cancelled mid-semester, her office sealed. Security had escorted her off campus before she could retrieve her field notes. Years of dedication, swept away.

She wrote, "They said it's cleansing. Not restructuring. Cleansing."

I sank into the armchair and let the word settle over me, let it sink through my skin. Cleansing, the kind of word that sounds clinical until you understand what it buries.

I'd lived through chaos before, the violent fall of Yugoslavia and the bitter nationalism that twisted language into accusation. This was something else entirely. The methodical rewriting of a soul, done so cleanly, so quietly, that I almost missed the moment its cold reach extended to me.

The Serbian chapter of Pagan Confederation had disappeared without explanation. So had the Ethnographic Society's digital archive and the Balkan Mythopoetic Journal, along with half a dozen independent platforms that had survived on donations and devotion for years. Pages that once held centuries of layered memory redirected to empty government portals bearing the same sterile insignia. The double-headed eagle, wings outstretched like judgment. I clicked through them one by one. The content had been replaced, rewritten from the ground up.

When I opened the University's faculty directory, a hollow laugh almost escaped me. The Department of Slavic Folklore had been renamed overnight, now housed under something called the Center for Cultural Integrity. Their course offerings were stripped to a bare syllabus of medieval texts and Christian saints. There was no trace of the cosmology seminar I'd taught for nine years. No listing for my research. No paper trail of my name, as if I had been excised from existence.

I sat there for a long time, watching the screen, its stark truth sinking in. Shock had burned away hours ago. Only the slow ache of recognition remained, blunt and absolute. This was coordinated and clean, surgical in its precision. Quiet deletions and official signatures.

A friend texted to say the ministry had reclassified all pre-Christian materials as "cultural contaminants," stripping them of legitimacy. Another sent a link, already dead, to the oral tradition index I'd helped build as a graduate student. The content had vanished. Erased, with nothing left behind.

I tried searching for terms, typing them one by one into the search bar. Perunika returned nothing. Veles, Rod, Svarog, each came back empty. The search engine returned a sterile notice: "Irrelevant to the current cultural standard."

I typed the title of my own book into the search bar, Thresholds of the Underworld: Slavic Descent and Return. The page that once housed it now redirected to "Educational Resources for Orthodox Civic Renewal." I clicked back, tried another server, then another, and found nothing. My work had been overwritten. It felt like a ritual cleansing of the record, as though the myths I'd studied my whole life had never existed, had never breathed.

My skin prickled then, a tremor moving through the very walls of the apartment. Reality was being overwritten, truth remade, in a way that would change what people remember, what they hold sacred. That would rewrite what children learn in school and shift how they speak about their dead, severing them from their roots.

The screen reflected my face, and I barely recognized myself in the distorted image. The apartment had gone quiet, a watchful stillness, as if the room itself were holding its breath.

I thought of something Father Gavril had said to me once, back when I was still a student. I'd dismissed it then as quaint nostalgia. "When a people forget their stories, they don't become modern. They become hollow." I had smiled politely at the time. Now I felt the truth of it take root somewhere low in my stomach, heavy as cold stone.

We were being hollowed out.

Everything I had built my life around, every myth I'd archived and sacred name I had studied, every lecture I'd given with quiet devotion, had been swept aside in less than an hour. Removed, as if the centuries they came from had never happened. The erasure was so complete, so exacting, it had transcended politics. It felt like something older and colder than law, something ritualistic and deliberate.

My hand drifted toward the edge of the desk, fingers brushing a stack of books I hadn't touched in months. Field notes and transcripts from dying dialects. They felt fragile beneath my fingertips, and I knew what they represented. A world that this new order had declared extinct. I had thought, foolishly, that knowledge could survive anything. That memory, if carefully preserved, would always endure. I saw the truth now. Quiet, systemic forgetting erased a people. The slow kind, the kind that left no rubble, only absence.

When the knock came, I heard it as one hears something expected. Measured and deliberate. Three knocks, followed by a pause, then two more. Patient, weighted with intention. It held a kind of rhythm, like an invocation repeated by someone who remembered its meaning even if I didn't.

I stayed seated for a moment, listening. The hall beyond was silent. Just that faint, steady pressure in the air telling me I was no longer alone. A shift had taken hold of the room, palpable behind my ribs. As if memory itself had knocked, arriving to remind me that a buried truth was stirring.

I stood, my legs slow to respond, heavy from disuse and a deeper weight, grief, maybe. I crossed the room and placed my hand on the doorframe to steady myself. What I carried now was older than fear, a recognition that lived in my body before my mind could name it. Somewhere beneath the quiet surface of my thoughts, a truth I didn't yet want to face pressed forward, softly at first, then insistently, like a thread pulled from a fabric I had spent years pretending was whole. I knew that pattern. I had known it long before it ever reached my door.

I went straight for the handle and opened the door.

Danica stood there, damp from the rain, her backpack slung over one shoulder, her expression unreadable. Her clothes were different from her usual lecture-hall quiet, darker and almost utilitarian, but her eyes were the same, steady and too old for someone her age. They aged her in a way that left you wondering how many lives she remembered that she shouldn't.

"I came straight from the library," she said, her voice strained. "It's already happening there, too. Whole floors cordoned off. Staff acting like it's a drill, but the archive terminals are locked out. No access, not even to public records."

I stepped back wordlessly to let her in. She walked past me without hesitation, pulling her soaked hoodie from her shoulders and dropping her bag onto the kitchen table. She unzipped it and pulled out a thick sheaf of printed pages, her thesis, placing it carefully in front of her like something fragile.

"I printed the whole thing last night," she said, her voice low. "Right before everything started shutting down. It's not even finished yet, but I had this feeling. Like if I didn't do it now, it was going to disappear."

I stayed standing, my legs unsteady, a tremor running just beneath my skin.

Danica flipped to the first page, smoothing it down with her palm. Her eyes stayed on the page as she spoke. "You said we wouldn't need physical copies. That we should trust the digital backups. That it was time to move forward."

"I was wrong." My voice was flat, stripped bare.

She finally looked up at me. "I know." Her tone carried a plain, exhausted understanding, a weariness that shouldn't exist in a voice that young.

I moved to the chair opposite her and eased myself down. The room still smelled faintly of the candle I'd let burn too long earlier in the afternoon. Or maybe that was just a ghost in my head, older than the afternoon, a lingering scent of the sacred.

"They're erasing us," I said. "Removing the memory that we were ever here."

Danica nodded, her eyes never leaving mine.

"That's why I came," she said. "I needed to know if you remembered." The words landed strangely. She was telling me she already knew I had. Whatever thread she'd been pulling at had already been wrapped around me for a long time.

I looked down at the pages she'd laid out on the table, familiar typeface in clean formatting, the careful work of a student who had gone beyond what was assigned, who was chasing something she didn't yet know how to name.

"I've been having dreams," I said quietly. "I don't know what they mean."

Danica tilted her head slightly, as if she'd been expecting that. "Are they recent?"

"Lately, yes, but I think they've been happening for longer. Maybe years. I just didn't notice." A partial truth, at best. I had noticed. I had ignored them. Explained them away as ritual bleed, academic stress, pattern recognition in the brain grasping for old gods in modern skin. But I remembered the dirt on my hands when I woke. The taste of ash. The pressure in my chest like something was pulling me back through the world.

Danica let the silence hold. She sat across from me, shoulders tight, hands resting flat on either side of her thesis like she was bracing for something.

"They don't feel like dreams," she said finally. "They feel like something I'm remembering wrong. Like I'm walking through something that already happened, but the details keep shifting." My throat tightened. That was exactly it. The dream was atmospheric, sensory. It spoke in knowing, in symbols, things unspoken but absolute. A field burned black beneath a rootless sky. A spiral carved into wet stone. Red-gold-black, always those colors, bleeding through.

She leaned forward, her eyes narrowing. "I think it was a warning."

My hands rested on the table, flat and still, but I could feel the tremor building beneath the surface. Years of training had taught me to dismantle mystery, to pin it to a page and file it away, and here she was, five years younger and already past me in every way that mattered.

"Why now?" I asked. "Why all of it at once?"

Danica held my gaze, unwavering. "Because something old is waking up, and they're trying to make sure we don't remember it when it does."

I sat back slowly, the chair creaking beneath me, and let her words settle into the space between us. That calm certainty of hers thickened the air in the room, made it denser, heavier, like the pressure before a storm breaks.

Danica stayed leaning forward, her hands now folded, fingers locked tight. Her eyes had left the thesis. She was watching me.

"I've tried to rationalize it," she said. "The bleeding pages, the dreams, the symbols showing up in places they don't belong." She paused, then shook her head. "I wanted to believe it was stress, the fear of watching our field dismantled in real time. It's recognition."

I rubbed my forehead, the dull throb behind my eyes getting sharper. "Recognition of what?"

She waited, and when she did speak, her voice dropped, instinctively careful, as if the words themselves were fragile. "I don't know yet. But it's not just mine."

The words landed in my chest, quiet and certain. Whatever she carried, I carried it too, and had for longer than I wanted to admit.

"I've dreamed of the tree," I said, keeping my voice low. "The place it used to be. Scorched earth beneath an empty sky. Sometimes I hear water, but I never see it. And a sound, like metal against stone, a rhythmic forging, always distant."

Danica's mouth parted slightly. "I hear it too."

I sat forward again, my hands cold, my palms damp.

"The dreams are pulling something up," I said. "Older than prophecy, older than trauma. Like the ground is remembering us, and we're just catching echoes."

She nodded once. "I think the dreams are reminders."

We both went quiet for a while, the kind of silence you fall into when language fails and meaning hangs heavy, unspoken.

I glanced at the window. Rain traced lines down the glass, and the street below was almost completely empty. Belgrade felt hollow tonight. Like it was being held in suspension, waiting for something to finish dying so something else could be born.

Danica finally spoke again, softly. "When they talk about national purity and cultural integrity, what they mean is disconnection. If they cut us off from the myths, they cut us off from memory, and without memory, we can't recognize what's waking up. We won't even have the words."

She looked at me then, and for the first time, I saw fear in her expression, the deep, quiet fear that grows in people who have seen too much too quickly.

"I'm not asking you to believe me," she said. "I just needed to see if you're still open."

The room felt too small. We had opened a door that would stay open, and we both knew it.

Danica lingered in the chair, staring at the thesis like it had become something alien. I couldn't tell if she wanted me to say something or if she already knew there was nothing more I could give her. My mind was full, everything fragmentary. Shards of imagery and sound.

Outside, the rain had slowed to a whisper against the glass. The city, usually restless even at this hour, had gone still in a way that made my skin itch. Like a presence just outside the range of my senses had paused to listen.

She stood finally, quiet and deliberate, and slipped the thesis back into her bag.

"I don't know what happens next," she said, adjusting the strap over her shoulder. "But if they come for the stories, they'll come for the people who remember them too. Even if we don't understand what we're remembering."

I stood with her, for reasons I couldn't articulate. Maybe just to feel like I still had agency in this moment, some faint muscle memory of hospitality. Some part of me still pretending that this was just a conversation between teacher and student.

She stopped at the door, hand resting on the handle, and looked back at me. "Whatever this is, it's already started. You know that, right?"

I managed a nod, my throat closed around any words I might have offered.

Danica held my gaze for another second, like she was trying to memorize something about my face before it changed. Then she pulled the door open and stepped out into the hall without another word.

I stood there long after the door clicked shut, still trying to grasp what had just happened. The apartment was quiet again, but it felt like it belonged to something else now. Whatever she had carried in with her still hung in the air, memory or myth or maybe just the knowledge that the world had shifted and I was already behind it. I sat back down at the table. Her chair still held the warmth of her body. Her thesis was gone, but I could still feel it, like a footprint pressed into ash. The dream would come again tonight. I could already feel it waiting.

When I finally left the apartment, the air outside felt wrong. The sky was still dripping in slow, irregular pulses, but something deeper had changed. The way the city held itself. Like it was bracing for impact. The streets held only silence where the usual horns and balcony arguments should have been.

The walk was short, but it stretched. My body moved through muscle memory while my thoughts trailed behind, slow and heavy, still back in that room with Danica's eyes, her thesis, the red-black-gold edges that refused to be forgotten. By the time I stepped through my front door, my shoulders ached from tension I hadn't noticed. I kicked off my shoes, let my keys drop into the bowl with a sound too loud for the hush around it, and looked toward the living room.

Ana stood in front of the canvas. Something about the way she held herself, rigid and angled, completely still, made my voice retreat back into my throat. Her back was to me, her right hand raised mid-stroke, brush in motion but frozen. The air in the room was dense, as if the walls had drawn closer while I was gone. A low vibration hummed just beneath my hearing, and the smell of wet paint clung to everything, sharp and chemical, almost metallic.

I stepped closer. "Ana?" I kept my voice low, cautious.

She gave no sign she'd heard me. Her arm moved again, smooth and deliberate, dragging the brush across the canvas in a slow arc. Her hand moved with certainty, but her body looked brittle, like she'd been standing there for hours.

"Ana," I said again, louder this time, but her body offered nothing in return.

I came around her side, enough to see her face. Her eyes were wide open, unblinking, pupils blown. Her gaze went through me, through everything. Whatever she saw, it lived somewhere else entirely.

I turned to the painting and stopped. It had shape now. Form and symbol. Color, though most of it seemed pulled from a palette no sane hand would reach for. At the center was a tree, or what remained of one, its trunk cracked and hollowed, roots exposed like veins ripped from the soil. Around it, fire curled like fingers. A sky choked in ash. And hanging in the branches, barely visible unless you stepped close enough to feel the pull, a shape, spiral and endless, drawn in a hand that shouldn't have remembered how.

I looked back at Ana. Her lips were moving now, just barely. Silent, mouthing something in a language I couldn't place. Just motion, repetition. I reached out and touched her wrist gently. Her body flinched like I'd hit her with voltage. She gasped, inhaled sharply, and her legs buckled. I caught her before she hit the ground.

"Ana. Hey, hey. You're okay. I've got you."

She blinked hard, like she was trying to remember where she was. Her hands clutched at the front of my shirt, eyes darting past me to the canvas.

"I… I don't remember painting it." Her voice was hoarse, broken open at the edges.

I looked over my shoulder. The tree still burned. The spiral still watched. "You were standing for hours," I said. "You didn't say a word."

She shook her head. "I only picked up the brush a few minutes ago. I was just going to add a line, something small. I blacked out."

I helped her to the couch. She moved like someone emerging from deep water, every gesture slow, uncertain, as if gravity had changed in her absence. I brought her water, but she left it untouched. She sat there staring at the canvas like it might move again. After a long silence, she whispered, "I think something's trying to speak through me."

I stayed silent, because I'd seen it too. The painting still burned behind us, smoldering and impossible. She couldn't have known the symbols, the spiral or the scorched tree against that red-black-gold horizon, yet they were rendered with aching precision, as if they had been waiting inside her all along.

I watched her closely. The shaking had stopped, but a residual tremor lived beneath her skin. Her eyes stayed fixed on the canvas. I had seen Ana paint a hundred times, usually in the late hours, barefoot and half-humming under her breath, but this had been different. Another force had moved through her hands. And yet those hands had held the brush. There was something in the way she watched the painting now, a familiarity she was trying very hard to suppress. Like she had seen it before. Like she had been there.

"You're sure you don't remember anything?" I asked, barely above a whisper.

She kept her gaze on the painting. "Just heat. Light. A sound I couldn't place, but familiar somehow."

"You weren't afraid?"

She shook her head once. "It felt like coming home."

I said nothing. Because something in me agreed with her, and that scared the hell out of me.

Later that night, I lay in bed, everything pressing into me like a second body. Sleep took me at some point. The ceiling above me disappeared, the quiet took on shape. I stood in a wide, lightless field. Ash, maybe, or bone ground so fine it had forgotten what it came from. The air was still, no wind, no moon, just silence thick enough to make my ears ache. I was barefoot. The ground beneath me was cold and soft, the way riverbeds feel after the water has gone.

Behind me, something shifted. I turned slowly, already knowing who would be there before I saw him. He was just there, standing at the edge of my awareness like he had always been waiting. Broad, still, rooted like an old tree. His face was lined with memory instead of age, his eyes dark and heavy with soil and consequence, and I knew him at once as Veles.

He reached out, and his hand closed around my forearm. The grip was firm, unshaking, old as bedrock. I tensed on instinct, but there was no point. His strength was inevitability itself. I couldn't pull away from something I'd never truly left.

When he spoke, his voice was low, grounded, the sound of riverbed stones shifting beneath the current. "She walks beside you now." His fingers held me still, anchoring me there. "You do not know her name. Not truly."

I tried to speak, to ask him what he meant, but my mouth wouldn't shape the words. A deeper knowing, in the dream and in me, understood that this was a place for listening only.

He stepped closer, his face weathered but unchanging. His gaze was ancient and patient, holding only the kind of memory that speaks in pressure alone. "She has worn too many faces. Been loved too long." His hand released mine, and I stayed upright, rooted where I stood by something I couldn't name. "She forgets what she is, but she cannot help what follows her." He looked past me, beyond the field, toward something I couldn't see. Then back at me. "You will want to trust her." He let the words hang, deliberate as a held breath. "But you shouldn't."

The sky cracked with light. His shape began to fade, sinking like something returning to the underworld he had never truly left. "She has been a god too long to remember how to kneel."

I woke gasping, the sheets damp against my back, Veles' voice still lodged deep in my chest like a secret I didn't ask to carry. The room was dark and still, and yet a presence lingered. *Be careful with her, the god whispered. She remembers more than she lets on. And she is not yours to trust.*

CHAPTER SIX
THE QUIET WAR

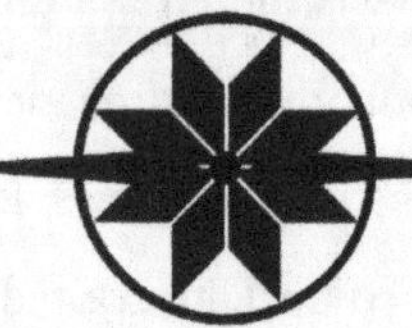

Ilija

The world kept moving the next morning, and that was the strangest part. The kettle whistled in the kitchen. The radiator clicked against the wall. Curtains lifted in the draft from the window, and beyond the glass, pigeons fought on the sill with the same ugly persistence they brought to every morning.

I sat at the kitchen table in the shirt I had slept in, the collar bent, the fabric stale against my skin. The mug between my hands had gone lukewarm. I kept holding it because the shape gave my fingers somewhere to rest.

The television played on mute in the living room. Press conferences shifted into cathedral footage, government seals, and schoolchildren standing in rows with crosses around their necks. Along the bottom of the screen, the ticker moved with the calm precision of an order already being carried out.

Cultural Reformation Initiatives Launched. Ministry of Sacred Education to Oversee Curriculum Integration.

Faith and Fatherland, National Identity Strengthening Measures Begin.

Outside my building, the pavement stayed clean. People still walked to work with their collars turned up against the morning chill, but every screen spoke with the same state-approved calm, and every sentence carried the shape of an order.

Across the kitchen, Ana moved through the morning as if last night had left no mark on her. She wore a loose gray sweater and mismatched socks, her hair twisted up with a pencil shoved through it. She filled the kettle, leaned against the counter, and hummed while she waited. She looked like the woman I had known for years, but the longer I watched her, the more that familiarity worked against me.

Her jaw tightened as she stared out the window. I would have explained it away on any other morning as tiredness, irritation, another sleepless night, but this morning came after the painting, after the voice that had moved through her, after Veles had told me to be careful. Ana remembered. I knew it in the way she avoided the easel, in the way her humming never quite broke rhythm, in the careful softness she used on me when she wanted me calm.

The canvas still leaned in the corner. I had checked before she woke. The jars of pigment remained open on the floor, and charcoal dust marked the cloth beneath the easel, but the image had vanished. The burning tree, the cathedral-woman, the saints with mouths where their faces should have been, all of it had been wiped from the surface. Only a red smear remained in the lower corner. I had touched it while Ana slept. The paint was dry, but warmth still lived under it.

She poured coffee without looking at me.

"Milk?" Ana asked, reaching for the carton.

I shook my head, and she handed me the mug anyway, careful not to let her fingers brush mine. It smelled like coffee and home, and that small comfort made my throat tighten.

She glanced toward the clock above the stove. "You'll be late."

"I'm not going in."

The carton stopped halfway back to the fridge. "Since when?"

"Since this morning."

"You canceled class?"

"All of them."

Ana closed the fridge with her hip and faced me fully. "Okay. Why?"

I searched her face for shame, for guilt, for the smallest crack in the careful expression she had chosen before turning around. Her eyes held mine with a patience that made my skin tighten.

"What happened last night?"

Ana lifted one shoulder. "I painted."

"You did more than paint."

Her fingers tightened around her mug. "You were upset. You saw what you saw."

"That's it?"

"What do you want me to say, Ilija?"

I looked toward the easel. "I want you to stop pretending the painting surprised you."

Ana set her mug down harder than she needed to. "Careful."

I looked down at the mug. A thin ring of coffee trembled against the porcelain.

Her voice lowered. "Ilija, you're starting to scare me."

Her hand came to rest on my shoulder. I used to love her hands, the steadiness in them, the care she gave old artifacts and broken things. This morning, her touch carried intent. It soothed and measured at the same time, as if she wanted to know how close I was to pulling away.

I stood too fast, and the chair scraped against the floor. "I need to get out for a bit."

Ana's hand dropped from my shoulder. "Fine."

"It's not like that."

"Then what is it like?" Her voice sharpened. "Because you're looking at me like you've finally decided I'm the enemy."

I looked at her and wanted to answer like a husband, but the memory of the canvas held me where I was.

"I don't know how to explain it yet."

"Then don't make me guess."

I left before I could turn my fear into another accusation.

At first, Belgrade gave me the same streets it always had. Buses sighed at the curbs. Windows caught the pale morning light. Vendors lifted metal shutters with a scrape that carried down the block. But the city had been handled overnight, straightened and corrected, and every missing thing made the silence worse.

The kiosk at the tram stop had always been loud with cheap tabloids, phone chargers, gum packets, cigarette smoke, and a radio playing jazz too low to identify. That morning, the glass had been cleaned. The man who ran it stood behind the window with his hands folded over a small prayer book. The radio had been replaced by liturgical chant drifting from a speaker behind him, thin and drained of breath.

I kept walking, past the café where students used to corner me after lectures. The outdoor tables were gone. The chalkboard menu had been scrubbed clean, and a laminated sign had been bolted to the wall in its place.

Faith. Fatherland. Order.

The same words waited on street corners, government buildings, public screens, and banners pasted fresh over old posters. The graffiti had been covered. The flyers for poetry readings and basement concerts had come down. Everything restless in the city had been painted over in gold letters and crimson borders.

In an alley, the crate where an old man used to sit with his gusle still rested against the wall. The instrument lay beside it in the gutter, its strings snapped and curled against the wood. I stopped long enough for the sight to sink in. A broken instrument explained the morning better than any press release could.

Belgrade had survived empires, bombings, and men who mistook flags for souls. It knew how to hide what mattered. This felt different. The cafés opened with their chairs stacked inside. The kiosks sold prayer cards beside newspapers. The old songs had been replaced before anyone had time to complain, and every blank wall looked freshly scrubbed.

The streets carried me toward Saint Mark's, past shuttered kiosks and wet stone, until the church rose ahead of me.

Inside, the silence pressed close. My shoes clicked over the stone floor, and the sound felt rude in the heavy air. Incense clung to the back of my throat. Candles trembled beneath the icons, their light gathered close around the wicks.

The saints watched from gold leaf and dark wood. Their eyes were wide, their hands lifted in blessing or warning. I had spent my life studying what people made sacred, but standing there, I felt stripped of every useful word.

An old woman knelt near the iconostasis. Her coat was thin at the collar, and her hands closed around a rosary so worn the beads had lost their shape. She whispered toward the floor, her lips moving quickly.

I moved to the side altar and lit a candle. The flame caught with a soft hiss. I waited for the ritual to steady me, but the familiar motion gave me nothing. I lowered my forehead to the wooden rail.

"I don't know what I'm seeing anymore," I whispered. "I don't know what belongs to me."

Behind me, the old woman's voice rose from the candle smoke. "The veil is thinning. You feel it too."

I turned, and she was already walking away from the altar. She did not head toward the front doors. She moved left, toward a narrow passage near the sanctuary, where an archway sat deep in shadow. I would have missed it if I had not been watching her feet.

At the arch, she gave one small motion with her hand, more like a woman telling a child to hurry before he lost his nerve. Then she stepped beneath the stone.

I followed.

The air changed beneath the stone. The church sounds flattened, as though the walls had swallowed their edges. Footsteps, breath, cloth shifting against skin, all of it dulled. The passage sloped downward into a narrow stairwell. The stone steps were worn smooth and damp with old condensation. Cold rose from below.

The walls were carved with crosses, each one different from the last. My fingertips brushed over them as I descended. Near one bend in the stairs, a faded figure spread rigid wings across the stone. The face had worn away, but the posture remained severe and watchful, older than comfort.

At the bottom, the crypt opened into a low chapel. The ceiling curved overhead, close enough to make me lower my shoulders. Damp had stained the walls, and strips of fresco clung to the plaster. Eyes remained where faces had been damaged. Open mouths survived without names. A row of candles burned near the altar, though the wax around them looked untouched by recent hands.

The woman stood at the far end, facing the altar.

At the far end, the old woman kept her back to me. "You're not the first."

My throat had gone dry.

"To feel it?"

She nodded once. "To notice the cracks."

When she turned, her face held fatigue more than mystery. She looked like someone who had spent years keeping a truth safe and had grown sick of waiting.

"You've been seeing things," she continued. "Then you talk yourself out of them."

"What are they?"

"Old things coming back up."

"From where?"

Her eyes flicked toward the stone under our feet. "Wherever they were buried."

She reached into her coat pocket and set an old key on the altar cloth. I stepped closer. The key looked hand-forged, iron or brass darkened with age. Its teeth were uneven, and one side had been worn smooth by years of handling. It belonged to a door from another century, built heavy enough to hold against weather and men with torches.

The old woman pushed the key closer with two fingers. "Keep it close."

"What is it?"

"A key."

"I can see that."

Her mouth twitched, almost a smile. "Then ask a better question."

"What does it open?"

"You'll know when you get there."

"That's not helpful."

"It's all I have."

She stepped back from the altar. I reached for the key. It was heavier than it looked and warm against my palm. The candle beside it rose high for one breath, throwing my shadow against the wall. Then the flame died.

The smell of iron filled the chapel.

When I looked up, the woman was gone. I turned toward the space behind the altar, expecting a door or passage, any place she could have disappeared. There was only stone. I stood there with the key in my hand until my breathing slowed. It pulsed once against my skin, then went still.

By the time I returned to the street, the city had grown quieter. The light had turned pale under a low sheet of cloud, and the buildings around the church seemed washed thin.

People crossed the plaza with their eyes lowered, moving around one another without looking up. My hand stayed clenched around the key in my coat pocket until my fingers ached.

Near the park, the flowerbeds had been replanted. Red, white, and gold blooms stood in hard rows, too precise for a city that had never done anything neatly. Small bronze plaques marked each bed: Saint Sava. Saint Petka. Saint Basil. The writers, revolutionaries, and public men who had once given the streets their restless voice had been replaced by saints lined up like verdicts.

The playground stood empty, its swing chains hanging still in the cold air.

I cut down a side street toward the apartment. Behind a dumpster, a boy spray-painted a spiral onto the wall with quick, nervous strokes. He did not look at me. The shape pulled at my chest. My hand went to the coin in my pocket, then to the key. Different objects. Same pull.

At the foot of my building, I stopped and looked up. The stairwell light flickered once, then again. Then it blinked five times. Three quick flashes. Two slower ones. My body knew the rhythm before my mind found a reason to fear it, but I climbed anyway.

The apartment key caught in the lock. I had to work it twice before it turned. Inside, the apartment was warm. The lights gave off the same amber glow. My shoes landed on the same faded rug, and everything stood where it belonged.

The hallway held the warmth of the apartment, but the air sat heavy around the kitchen doorway.

From the kitchen came Ana's humming, soft and tuneless. She did not come to meet me. She kept moving behind the half wall, letting me hear her before I saw her, as if the rhythm itself were meant to tell me nothing had changed. I walked in slowly.

She stood at the stove in loose cotton pants and one of my old sweaters. Her hair was tied up with a pencil. She looked over her shoulder and smiled.

Ana nodded toward the pan. "Dinner?"

"I'm not hungry."

"You keep saying that."

"I know."

She turned the heat down and studied me. "Where were you?"

"Saint Mark's."

Her mouth tightened. Her hand paused before she set the spoon down.

"You went beneath it."

I looked up. "What?"

Ana reached for her wine. "You smell like old stone."

"I didn't say I went beneath anything."

"No," she said, bringing the glass to her mouth. "You didn't."

She turned back to the stove and lowered the heat beneath the pan. For one second I wanted to sit at the table, take the wine she set near me, and let the evening become ordinary. Then the key pressed against my thigh through the coat, warm enough to remind me that ordinary was the lie she had always worn best.

Ana poured herself wine and curled into the armchair with her phone. A few minutes later, she laughed under her breath.

Ana turned her phone toward me. "Look at this."

A cat tried to leap across a counter, missed, and slid out of sight.

I managed to smile. "Poor thing."

She laughed into her wine. "No, he earned that."

Her eyes sparked as she laughed, and for a moment I could almost let myself believe in her. The softness around her eyes. The curve of her mouth. The faint scar near her collarbone that I knew by touch. She looked like Ana. She sounded like Ana.

Then I caught her scent.

Lavender and soap sat on the surface, but an older sweetness lived beneath it. Incense cooled on stone. Flowers crushed under heat. Metal at the back of the throat. It filled my lungs and pulled grief through me with a longing I did not understand.

Ana lowered the phone and watched me over the rim of her glass. "You're doing it again."

"What?"

"That look."

"What look?"

"Like you think you caught me."

I swallowed. "Did I?"

Her face went still. The hurt that came next looked almost real. "Jesus, Ilija."

I looked away first.

Later, after Ana fell asleep on the couch, I stayed in the armchair. The lamp in the corner threw a small circle of light across the floor, and the streetlamp outside washed the window in dull orange.

Ana slept curled on her side, one arm across her stomach, the other beneath her head. Her breathing stayed slow. Her face held peace, but peace looked strange on her now, too smooth and arranged, as if she had carried the mask with her into sleep.

I stood because I needed to move. I needed to touch something ordinary and prove the room still obeyed the rules it had kept before all this. Halfway across the room, I stopped.

The coin sat on the shelf beside the radiator, angled toward the room as if someone had placed it there with care.

I had left it in the drawer. I knew I had. I had not touched it since the day Perun pressed it into my hand, and I had not taken it out that morning. Yet there it was, warm when I picked it up, holding heat from within itself.

The longer I held it, the more I felt the pulse beneath the metal. Faint. Steady. Alive enough to make my stomach tighten.

My phone vibrated in my pocket, and the sound cracked through the careful quiet. I pulled it out and looked at the screen.

Danica M.

You saw it too, didn't you?

I read it twice. No greeting. No explanation. She knew. The line made my skin tighten around the phone.

I looked at Ana. She had not moved.

I held the coin until its edges pressed into my palm, and for a long time I could not tell whether the thing watching me was in the apartment, in the city, or inside my own blood.

Sleep came badly.

I stayed in the armchair until my neck ached and my spine stiffened. I could not bring myself to go to the bedroom. I could not lie beside Ana and pretend her breathing still meant what it used to mean.

At some point, I placed the coin on the nightstand. Even after I let it go, I could feel it in the room. The room changed around it. Exhaustion finally dragged me under.

The dream opened hard.

One moment I hovered near sleep, and the next I stood below ground, beneath the world, in a place that had never known sunlight.

The walls were close and damp, formed more like root and bone than stone. Veins of black earth ran through them, pulsing with a dull heat. The air smelled of soil, river water, and animal musk. Water dripped somewhere beyond sight, the sound coming from too many directions at once.

Something moved behind me. I turned, and Veles came out of the dark with the force of river flood. He was broad-shouldered, draped in furs darkened by mud. His face was sharp, his eyes gray as ash before flame catches. Moss tangled in his hair, and small bones were woven through it. Horns rose from his skull as if they had grown there.

Before I could speak, he crossed the space between us and grabbed my shirt at the collar. His hand locked there with the strength of earth closing over the dead.

Veles yanked me close enough that I smelled bark and iron on his breath. "You're waking too fast. Too much, too soon."

I tried to pull away. His grip held.

"I didn't ask for this." My voice came out thin.

"You keep saying that like it changes anything." His fingers tightened in my shirt. "You forgot. Now you're paying for it."

He leaned closer. His eyes searched mine, and for a moment I felt every version of myself rise under his gaze: Ilija, the professor, the grieving son, the man in other bodies and other ruins I could not yet name.

Veles studied my face. "You trust her because you loved her. She knows that. She has counted on it."

I said nothing.

"She is exactly what she has been hiding from you."

My chest tightened. "Ana?"

His grip loosened, and I stumbled back. Above us, roots shifted along the ceiling, slow and deliberate, responding to his anger.

"She opened the gate."

"The painting?"

"The paint was just how it came through."

"She knows what she is?"

Veles looked at me as if pity had begun to bore him. "She has always known."

I waited for more, but the dark had already begun to take him back. His shape thinned at the edges, fur and bone dissolving into shadow.

"Be careful with her. She remembers everything she needs, and she will call it love when she uses it against you."

The dream folded shut.

I woke with my heart hammering and my mouth dry. The room was still. Ana had not moved. The coin sat exactly where I had left it, but the air had changed.

It smelled faintly of damp earth.

I sat up slowly, breathing through the taste of earth, while the coin held its place on the nightstand.

CHAPTER SEVEN
THE UNRAVELING

Ilija

The message sat on my screen, patient as a held breath. You saw it too, didn't you? Danica's name, no number, no timestamp, just those words, stark and unreasonably steady. They felt found, waiting in the dark until the right person opened the door. I stared at the glow of the phone until the room shrank to its edges, though I hadn't moved in hours. Was this truly Danica? I ran through everything that had happened, the surveillance, the silence, the certainty that they knew who I was. What I was. Colleagues had been erased, their works removed, their lives taken apart like furniture no one wanted to keep. Fucking hell. My pulse hammered against my wrists. If it truly was Danica, she needed help now. She remembered something, the same way Veles kept reminding me, and that truth might be more terrifying than New Serbia itself. I had to go.

Behind me, Ana lay still, her body curled slightly toward the edge of the mattress, one arm tucked beneath the pillow. She breathed with the measured softness of deep sleep, the kind that normally felt safe. Her back rose and fell in slow rhythm, her lips parted. She looked peaceful, and yet the quiet around her felt curated, as if everything about her held perfectly still so I wouldn't notice it had changed. That scent still lingered in the air. I'd thought it was something from her perfume, something new she'd tried and forgotten to mention, but it had gained substance now. Sweet and metallic, like iron left in rain. It sank into the bedding, into my lungs, a scent that didn't belong in this apartment, or perhaps in this century.

I eased myself up from the bed and sat on the edge for a moment. My bare feet pressed into the cold floorboards, grounding me. I looked back at Ana once more, just to be sure. She hadn't moved. Her breath didn't even hitch when I stood. I stepped out into the hallway, shut the bedroom door behind me with slow, careful fingers. My phone was still lit, still waiting.

I typed, Where are you?

The reply came almost instantly, a brief flicker of three dots, then nothing. Empty space where meaning had almost formed. I held the phone as if it might pulse again, but nothing else came.

I dressed quickly, yesterday's jacket, my scarf, the same leather shoes I'd worn through all of this. It felt like preparation. I didn't take the spiral coin from the drawer. I didn't need to. I already felt it with me, a pressure beneath the skin, warm and insistent.

The city was already waking up by the time I stepped outside, but it looked like it hadn't slept at all. The sky held that pale, washed-out color that never quite committed to dawn. The wind curled around my ankles, too mild to sting, persistent enough to remind me I didn't belong here anymore.

People lined the streets, hollow and mechanical. Their faces were too tight, their eyes unfocused. They walked as if trying to vanish into the pavement while pretending they weren't. I passed three women at a crosswalk who stood without speaking, all of them staring straight ahead, clutching prayer books with clean, unread spines. No one smiled. No one nodded. The whole city moved like a funeral procession.

The public screens along the tram line flashed with loops of patriotic footage, cathedrals and children in uniform praying in classrooms, old men crossing themselves before icons in the fields. Each scene ended with bold, glowing text.

UNITY THROUGH SANCTITY

HISTORY IS HOLY

MEMORY IS OBEDIENCE

I turned away from the avenue and took the back roads, the ones I used to walk during my university days when I needed to escape lectures and feel something alive. The alley walls that used to be loud with graffiti were blank now, sealed with authority. No tags, no anarchist slogans, no chalk poetry. Just white silence. I kept walking, faster than I meant to, heading toward the observatory, toward the place the message had pulled me like a hook behind the ribs.

She was already waiting at the weathered gate, as if she'd been there for hours. Danica. Her coat was long, woolen, the color of frost and cinder, collar turned up against the wind. Her hair was no longer light, no longer the shade of early spring; it had gone black, braided thick down her back, catching faint glints of blue in the gray morning light. She looked like someone who had been burning quietly from the inside and had finally stopped pretending otherwise.

I froze a few steps from the gate, and when she turned, her eyes met mine and my lungs locked, seized by something deeper than fear. Her eyes had always been gray, but now they were vast, endless in the way that space is endless, holding centuries.

"Hi," she said. Her voice was calm, almost amused, as if we were meeting for coffee instead of standing at the edge of some unraveling truth.

I needed a second, maybe more than one, to process how changed she was, how real, how revealed, like she'd peeled something off her skin that didn't belong to her anymore. The Danica I had known, the one who asked pointed questions in lectures and wrote essays like spells disguised as scholarship, had always felt off-center, as though she was orbiting something she didn't yet recognize. This version of her had found the center. Or maybe it had found her.

She stepped closer and the gate creaked, swinging wider on corroded hinges. Wind coiled between us, lifting the edge of her coat. She reached into her pocket, then extended her hand to me, directly, without ceremony. I opened my palm.

A smooth, cold object dropped into my hand, slate-black and round, carved with the same spiral I'd seen before, on the coin Veles had given me, on the graffiti in the alley, on an artifact she'd smuggled into class weeks ago under the pretense of research.

"Did you take this from my flat?" I asked, though I already felt the answer settling into place.

"Yeah," Danica said. "I didn't know if it was safe to leave it there. I needed time to figure out what the hell it was."

"And? What the fuck is it?"

She almost smiled. "A key. Maybe a map. Honestly, I'm still working that out."

I turned the object over in my hand, and the spiral pulled at something in me, like movement disguised as shape, a question slowly answering itself in the bones of my wrist.

"I had a dream about you," she said suddenly, her voice dropping. "You were drowning."

My eyes shot up to hers. That word, drowning, landed in my stomach like something familiar and hated. I had woken up too many times gasping, sinking without water.

"I don't remember anything clearly," I said.

"You wouldn't," she replied. "That's how they do it. Keep you foggy, keep you compliant. Forget enough about who you are and you stop fighting."

I shivered despite the layers. "Who's they?"

She answered with her hands. She raised one, reached toward me, and tapped two fingers against my temple with the precision of someone pressing a button I didn't know I had. Something gave.

Something flickered behind my eyes. A flash of fire and grief and ruin, trees bending in wind that didn't belong to any season, a voice threaded through everything, raw and guttural.

Danica pulled her hand back. "Something got through to you," she said quietly. "Was it the painting?"

I nodded, then hesitated. "It was Ana. She painted it, and then it vanished. Completely wiped."

"Of course it did," she muttered, more to herself than to me.

"She doesn't remember."

Danica looked up at me, and for the first time since I'd arrived, something sharp flickered behind her eyes. "She remembers, Ilija. She's just very good at pretending."

My spine stiffened. "What do you mean?"

"She's awake, Ilija. She's waiting."

"For what?"

Danica turned away, her leather shoes crunching the frost-dusted gravel as she started down the path toward the observatory dome. I followed without being told.

"Think of it like a house," she said as we walked. "Emptied out, furniture gone, but someone left the lights on. Because something else moved in, and it's been living there a long time."

I glanced up at the observatory. The old building was crumbling, its dome corroded, windows broken, but the sight of it made my skin prickle. There had been nights, years ago, when I'd come up here alone, lying on my back watching stars scrape across the sky like silver embers. It had felt infinite then, untouched. Now it felt like it was watching us.

"They're going to take everything," Danica said, stopping beneath the overhang of the dome's shadow. "Every story we have, every god, anything that doesn't fit their version of what Serbia is supposed to be." She looked at me. "And if you don't figure out who you are before they finish, they'll do it for you."

I looked down at the spiral stone in my hand, then back up at her. "Why me?"

"Because you're still asking," she said. "That's more than most people can say."

The silence that followed buzzed and thickened around us like fog. She turned toward me again. "I've seen you before, Ilija. And I don't mean in class." She paused, searching for the right way to say it. "I remember you in places that don't exist anymore, in languages I shouldn't know."

My breath caught.

"I don't know who I am," I said.

"I know," she said. "But that's going to change."

Her hand brushed against mine, just for a moment, and I felt heat travel through my knuckles like something ancient had been waiting for a single touch. Then she turned, walked toward the broken steps of the observatory, and vanished into shadow.

The walk back felt longer than it should have. I avoided the main streets. I didn't want the churches staring down at me from billboards or the public announcements whispering their faith-wrapped obedience into my skull. I needed real quiet, the kind that lets you hear yourself falling apart.

I kept the stone in my pocket. My fingers brushed its edges every few steps, as if to confirm it hadn't disappeared like everything else I'd started to question. My breath fogged in the air, thin and fast. I didn't realize how cold I'd become until my fingers started to ache. The cold was something inside me now, something tightening.

When I reached the building, the front door didn't stick the way it usually did. It opened too easily, like the house had been expecting me. The stairwell light buzzed and flickered, one long pulse followed by silence. I climbed without looking up.

The lock resisted me just enough to feel unfamiliar, as if the key itself was warning me away. When I finally pushed the door open, a wave of warmth hit me, sweet and cloying, the air inside thickened since I left. That scent had changed again, grown bold, saturated and everywhere. Roses crushed into wine, spiced with something bitter and metallic. It sat in my throat like a warning.

Ana was already standing in the hallway, smiling, the same smile I had seen a hundred times over quiet breakfasts and long evenings, and now it looked sculpted, too still, too clean, a painting of a woman I used to know.

Her sweater was the same, her hair pulled up, and her posture all wrong, hands resting at her sides as if someone had placed them there with deliberate care.

"You were out a while," she said. Her voice was light, casual, and every word landed like it had been practiced.

"I ran into someone," I said, taking off my jacket, avoiding her gaze.

"Oh?" She turned slightly, just enough to follow me with her eyes.

"Just a student."

A pause hung between us, just long enough for the temperature in the room to drop a degree.

"Danica," she said, flat and certain. She knew.

I looked up. Her expression hadn't changed, still that same smile, but her eyes were darker than they had any right to be in this lighting, bottomless, like she'd been staring into a void and brought a piece of it back with her.

"I'll take a shower," I said. "Then maybe we can talk."

She took a step forward, slow and precise, every step a glide.

"Talk," she repeated. Something was wrong with the way she said it, too smooth, too stretched, like the word itself had been unspooled.

That's when I saw what she held. In her right hand, loose at her side, a blade, curved and ancient-looking. The metal gleamed faintly even though no light touched it, gold-veined, marked with symbols that meant something to me before I could name them. It was sacred, something meant for ritual, for ruin.

"Ana…" I said, barely above a breath.

"You weren't supposed to wake up yet," she said, tilting her head. The calm in her voice was worse than any scream. "I wasn't finished. The veil needed to burn clean first, and you, you keep crawling out before I'm done." Her hand tightened on the blade. "I did this for us, for everything we could have been. And every time, every fucking lifetime, you choose death over me."

Her voice broke something open in me. I stepped back, heel striking the leg of the dining chair, and stumbled, my shoulder slamming into the wall. She raised the blade, her hand carving through the air, and symbols bloomed behind her fingers like embers catching wind, spirals and Greek letters and names that had once been mine.

I tried to stand, tried to speak, but my throat locked and my limbs refused the order.

Then the door exploded inward with a sound like thunder cracking bone.

Danica's voice followed it, though what poured from her mouth was far older, a chord in a language I didn't know I knew. She shouted one word, and the air answered. The symbols Ana had drawn fractured like glass against wind.

Then came the light. This light was truth, pure and unbearable, pouring into the room like judgment, peeling away illusion. Ana staggered back, her mouth open too wide, her skin splitting in delicate lines of golden light. The eyes I had stared into for almost seven years were ancient now, cold and dark, void of anything resembling feeling.

Danica stepped between us. Her coat was gone, her arms bare, runes spiraling up her skin like flame tracing a fuse. Her braid had unraveled, dark hair swirling around her as if gravity had forgotten to claim it. She raised one hand and spoke a word I could never understand, and the world came apart.

For a moment, I saw everything, the room and the city and the veil stripped clean. I saw Ana as she truly was, robed in crimson, her face half a mask, her body flickering between beauty and terror. She looked at me and said my name, spoke it in the language beneath all others, the name beneath the name. Then nothing. No sound, no breathing, just the freefall. I fell through memories.

The ceiling had split, and what waited beyond was deeper than sky, thicker, shaped like things I hadn't named in lifetimes, colors I'd forgotten how to see. The descent was slow, stretched, like the moments between heartbeats when you realize something has changed and you're just waiting for the pain to arrive.

I landed hard somewhere between this world and the next, on a floor that breathed beneath my weight. The world around me was haze and smoke, broken branches and roots like veins clawing up through the ground. It smelled of wet soil and burning herbs. The air itself was alive, watching.

I stood, or thought I did, my limbs moving without weight. My jacket was gone, my hands bare, skin marked with smudged patterns that glowed faintly, like old wounds reheating. I knew where I was, the way you know a face in a dream long before it speaks your name.

Then I felt him before I saw him, the shift in pressure, the way the light bent, a cold that belonged to rivers with no surface and doors with no hinges. Veles.

He emerged from beneath the shadows the way roots emerge from under a fallen tree. He was massive and narrow all at once, cloaked in fur and snakeskin, bone trinkets clicking with every movement. His beard was woven with threads of moss, his eyes mismatched, one blind white, the other glowing faint gold. His voice, when it came, arrived through the chest, through the spine, a chord struck beneath the ribs.

"You were told twice."

I swallowed. Steady in my limbs, shaking somewhere deeper.

"You think I wanted this?" I said.

He held still while something behind him shifted, shapes watching, horned silhouettes that shimmered without light.

"No one asks," he growled. "But you're neck-deep now, boy, and you keep holding on to this idea that you get a choice."

"How was I supposed to know what she was?" I said.

"Bullshit." The word landed like a slap. "You knew the moment the air changed around her. You knew when the walls went dead in her presence. You knew when the gods stopped knocking and started waiting."

I looked down at my hands, bleeding from old wounds, scars reopened by whatever I'd passed through to reach this place.

"I loved her," I murmured.

Veles stepped closer. "I know you did. That's the thing that will save you or bury you." He gripped my forearm tightly, his fingers digging into flesh like roots breaking stone, and my knees buckled. His other hand pressed against my chest, firm enough to remind me I was still soft, still unfinished.

"I let you play at this," he said. "Lectures, theories, papers filed under 'Speculative Mythology.' I let you pretend. That's done."

He leaned in, and his breath smelled of loam and iron, of wild things buried too long.

"Ana is a memory. She wore that name like a veil, and now she's the key to everything they're building, the ruin they're writing into the bones of your people. She is the veil."

I opened my mouth, but he squeezed my chest, just slightly, and the words died.

"You carry the coin," he said.

"I do."

"Then you carry the oath."

"When? No one asked me."

"You did," he said, eyes burning. "Before this skin. Before this name. Your bones know it even if your head is too frightened to catch up."

He let me go and I fell backward onto dark ground that hummed beneath me, alive in a way earth should never be.

"When the time comes," he said, "you're going to have to choose. And it won't be between her and Danica. It'll be between the truth and the comfort of a lie that loved you well."

He stepped back into shadow, and his final words came like thunder whispered through marrow. "She'll lie sweetly. She'll die beautifully. Be careful. She remembers everything."

I came to with a hiss of pain, my chest rising as if it had been submerged too long and only now broken the surface. My back ached and my head throbbed and my hands had gone numb beneath me, and for a moment, I wasn't sure I could move at all. The world swam at the edges of my vision, a blur of amber light, cold floorboards, something floral drifting on the air.

I didn't know how long I'd been lying there. My cheek was pressed against the floor, and my arms trembled as I pushed myself up, shoulder cracking, something in my ribs protesting, dull and mean. I tasted copper.

Across from me, the kitchen chairs were overturned. The table leaned slightly to one side, one leg broken or bent. The candle that had burned so steadily earlier now lay in a puddle of wax, extinguished. The smell of smoke clung to everything, wax and incense, yes, but also something ancient beneath it, like scorched parchment left too long over flame.

I blinked, and the apartment resolved itself into quiet. No sign of Ana, no sign of the symbols she had carved into the air, no gold-bladed knife. Danica was still here.

She sat on the floor beside me, back against the wall, legs drawn up, arms wrapped around herself. Her braid was gone, curls falling loose over her shoulders in messy waves, her breath coming shallow and uneven. Her eyes were closed, face pale beneath the flush of exhaustion.

I tried to speak but couldn't, my throat burned raw, and the only sound I managed was a hoarse rasp.

She stirred at the sound, her eyes opening slowly, like surfacing from deep water.

"Hey," she said, voice rough. "You're back."

I managed a weak nod, my neck stiff and aching.

"What happened?"

"You went down hard. Hit your head on the way."

"Ana…"

"Gone," she breathed. "For now."

I struggled to sit fully upright. Danica sat still beside me, her gaze steady, though pain lived there too, something like sorrow, or maybe recognition.

"Danica, I saw her," I said. "Really saw her."

She nodded slowly. "Yeah. You weren't supposed to yet."

"Everything changed. Her skin, her face, that voice…"

"She's been this way a long time," Danica said quietly. "Longer than you've known her. Longer than any of us have been alive."

"My name, Danica. She said it like it was hers. Like she'd been saying it for centuries."

Danica's jaw tightened, and she looked away before answering. "She probably has."

My chest tightened, something worse than panic, worse than grief.

"There has to be someone else," I said.

She looked at me, and in her eyes I saw something I hadn't expected, the same weariness I felt, mirrored back. "Yeah," she said. "Neither did I."

We sat in silence for a while. I listened to the radiator hum softly behind us, to the distant wheeze of old pipes settling into the walls. I reached into my jacket and pulled out the old skeleton key, the one the woman in the crypt had pressed into my hand days earlier.

I hadn't shown it to Ana, hadn't spoken of it aloud, hadn't even been sure if it was real. I held it out, and Danica only looked.

"You know what it is?" I asked.

"Yeah," she said. Then, quieter, "Do you know what it opens?"

"No."

She exhaled through her nose. "You'll figure it out. I think you're closer than you realize."

I turned the key over in my hand. Its teeth were worn, the metal warm even though I'd just pulled it from my jacket. It looked like something torn from the ribs of an old church door, and it felt like it had a heartbeat.

"And if I'd rather leave it shut?" I asked.

Danica almost laughed, dry and hollow. "Then don't. But the door opens whether you're ready or not. That's sort of the problem."

I looked at her. "How do you know all this?"

She was quiet for a moment, her fingers picking at a thread on her sleeve. "Because I've done this before. I've watched cities burn, watched gods die." She paused, and the silence held something fragile. "I've watched you die."

The candle between us flickered violently, and the air in the apartment tightened.

"None of that," I said. "Not a single thing."

"It comes back in pieces," Danica said. "Never all at once. That would kill you."

I rubbed the side of my face, and my fingers came away with soot. "So what do we do?"

She reached over slowly and took the key from my hand, turned it over once, then handed it back.

"Keep it on you. And whatever you do, don't let her know you still have it."

My eyes locked on hers. "Too late for that. She knows."

"She suspects," Danica said. "There's a difference, and right now that difference is the only thing keeping you alive."

We sat there until the candle burned low, the wax pooling near the base, the light dimming, the shadows stretching longer across the floor. Somewhere in the city beyond the windows, a church bell rang, just once, just enough to remind the silence it didn't own us yet.

Danica reached for the blanket draped over the couch and wrapped it around my shoulders.

When I finally looked up at her again, I asked the question I hadn't let myself say aloud until then. "Am I losing my mind?"

She was quiet for a beat. "No," she said. "You're getting it back. That's why it hurts."

I stared at her. "And then what?"

She smiled, tired and fierce. "Then we fight."

I smiled back. Then my face went slack, eyes closed, body limp, back into the darkness. "No!" Danica screamed.

CHAPTER EIGHT
THE VARANGIAN GATE

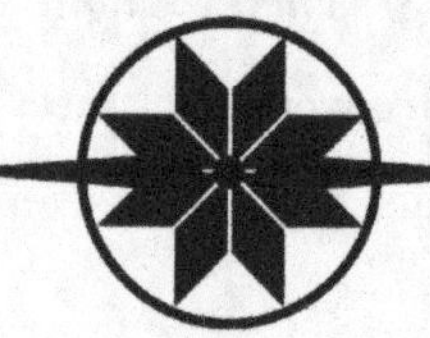

Ilija

I floated somewhere between breath and nothingness, caught in that jagged place where sensation frays and memory bleeds. I couldn't discern where my own being ended, where time began. It felt like being pulled through a dream I held no power to shape, one made of raw, electric feeling that scorched and flooded me at once.

Sometimes I was Ilija. I felt the sweat-soaked linen clinging to my chest, my own body pressing down, too real to be illusion. A professor and a son, a scholar who once believed myth was merely metaphor, who read history as a predictable chain of facts laid out like bones, each link clear and distinct. Then the storm would come, lightning twisting through my veins like memory trying to wake, thunder rumbling in my chest like a laugh too old to belong to anyone living.

I heard names, all of them mine, called across centuries like war cries hurled into a burning sky. Ilir. Ilya. Illios. Ilija. Each syllable cracked something open within me. I saw flashes of places I couldn't name; mountains torn in half, a raven blinking from the edge of a pyre. I saw a blade glowing at the root of a great tree that rose beyond the stars. Danica's face, stained with blood and ash, her voice tearing through the chaos, screaming for me in a tongue made of fire and oaths. It carried through lifetimes, through ruin, relentless.

Then the cold dragged me back, a sudden, brutal plunge into a different agony. Hands pulled at me, wet and trembling, desperate. Mud sucked at my heels. My coat dragged through fallen leaves and cold river-water. Leather shoes splashed. Roots caught and tangled around my feet, threatening to trip. My skull throbbed with the pulse of returning pain. The scent of wet pine and crushed moss filled my lungs. Somewhere above, unseen branches whipped in the wind.

"Stay with me," I heard, fervent, repeated over and over. Her voice cracked, frayed at the edges. "Don't let them close the door, please, stay with me…" It was Danica.

She was carrying me. Fuck, she was actually carrying me. Her arms shook, but she didn't stop. She gritted her teeth, a raw sound, as the forest fought her, branches slapping her face, thorns catching her sleeves. Her coat was soaked, clinging to her. Her breath came hard, ragged, each exhalation a struggle. Her muscles must've been on fire, yet her heart held steady. I could feel it beating against my side, fierce and relentless.

I was too heavy. I could feel it in the way her body strained, every muscle pushed to its limit. I was wrong somehow. Tilted. Like my soul wasn't sitting inside me the right way, like something had knocked me loose from the inside out. Danica's footsteps slid and then recovered, each stumble followed by a grunt of effort. She was crying now, and I didn't have to see her face to know, to taste the salt of her tears. Her voice was splintered, uneven, a whisper and a scream at once.

"Please," she begged, her voice raw. "Not like this. Not again."

I didn't understand yet. But I felt her grief like it was stitched into my skin. She dragged me through a patch of thorns. I heard her grunt as one caught her arm, sharp and involuntary. My body was a goddamn anchor, and I hated every useless pound of it, but she kept going.

Two kilometers, maybe more, all of it uphill. Through crumbling trails and shallow rivers that bit at her shins with icy teeth. We crossed some invisible threshold I couldn't name, yet the air shifted. I tasted it, thick and electric, heavy with memory.

The trees opened, revealing the sudden expanse of sky above. Before us, rising from the earth like the ancient bones of something divine, stood the Varangian stronghold. Ivy crept across stone walls bowed with age, tracing the lines of forgotten battles. Moss clung to old carvings like the forest was trying to swallow them whole. An archway leaned crooked, cracked by centuries of storm and neglect, yet the moment Danica stepped through that ruined gate, I felt something change, seismic and sudden.

The stronghold felt dormant, like something watching from deep beneath the stone. The air inside hung heavier, as if time itself had stopped to acknowledge her arrival. The walls, worn and cracked, seemed to lean inward in recognition. This place remembered itself, and in doing so, it remembered me.

Stone rose in bowed, uneven lines around us, slick with rain and choked with ivy, but as Danica carried me deeper into the ruin, more details emerged from the shadows. Carvings wrapped around the arches and walls, barely visible through layers of moss and lichen. With every strained step, they came clearer; coiling spirals and radiant suns, vast wings spread across the lintels. The symbols belonged to no single pantheon but carried echoes of many, fragments of a universal truth.

She carried me to the center, to the place where the earth itself had cracked open to reveal a flat stone dais, partly buried under moss and rot. As her leather shoes met the stone, the moss peeled back as if moved by will alone. The dais lay exposed, circular, covered in runes worn nearly smooth by rain and time. I couldn't consciously read them, yet my bones responded, a deep, resonant hum. I knew this place, somehow, even if my mind, fractured by trauma and revelation, didn't.

Danica lowered me onto the stone. My head lolled back, my body limp and uncooperative, but something beneath my ribs stirred, a twitch of warmth that refused to die. She knelt beside me, soaked and scraped raw from the journey through the forest. Her hair clung to her cheeks in dark tangles, her breathing still ragged from the climb. She reached beneath her coat and pulled out a leather satchel, frayed along the seams and covered in a sheen of damp. The leather looked older than her. Older than either of us.

She opened the satchel and removed five candles, short, lumpy, stained a deep rust-red. Tallow, iron-dyed, rough-wicked, ancient in their construction. She placed them with deliberate care around the stone dais, forming a five-pointed star, layered precisely over the spiral that glowed faintly beneath me. Then she reached again, pulling out a small pouch of salt, a sprig of dried rue, a strand of black-and-red wool, a chipped piece of flint. Last came the coin Veles had given me. The moment she set it beside my chest, I felt it hum. Deep, inside me. The thing knew me, and it was waiting.

Danica began to speak. Her voice didn't sound like ordinary speech, not at first. She spoke in Danish, quiet and clipped, then Serbian, low and rhythmic, the familiar cadences sharpening into something older, something beyond language, all resonance and tone, like sound trying to remember what meaning once felt like. Her voice became a vibration, the kind that trembled beneath the skin and burrowed into bone.

The carvings around us stirred, responding to her voice. They pulsed faintly in answer, mirroring the rhythm. Rain slid through the open rafters above, soft and deliberate, pooling in the grooves of the stone.

Beneath me, something shifted. The rock pressed against my back like it had warmed beneath her voice, sudden and living. A pulse flickered over my sternum, foreign and ancient. I tried to move; my fingers barely twitched, yet the fire beneath my ribs flared again, faint and irregular, like a dying ember catching a draft. Lightning danced across my knuckles, weak and incomplete, but undeniably there.

Danica leaned over me, her hand pressing gently to my forehead. Her skin was cold from the rain, but steady enough to hold me here.

"Come back," she whispered, her voice a fierce command. "Come through."

And I did, or I began to.

The visions dragged me through rivers that burned, through storms that sang in a language I used to know. My mind couldn't hold them all at once, fractured as it was, so they came like flashes, raw and uninvited.

A ship carved with wolves cut through a black sea, its sails stretched taut with wind that howled my name. I stood at the prow, thunder rumbling in my chest, a hammer in one hand, the other raised high as lightning licked my fingers. It didn't hurt; it recognized me. Behind me, voices rose in battle cries. I turned toward them, and for a second, I caught her face.

Danica, fierce and blood-smeared, her mouth open in a scream I couldn't hear, her eyes glowing with something more than moonlight. She lifted a shield carved with spirals and runes that shimmered in a light older than stars, but the image tore away, dissolving into the next.

Now a temple. Stone walls carved with symbols that wept. Smoke curled from a brazier beside an altar fashioned from bone and blackened wood. I was on my knees, wrapped in furs, a crown of antlers resting heavy on my head. My hands trembled as I held a burning brand over a cracked skull. I felt the immensity of what I was about to do, of who I was supposed to be. My conscious mind had lost the ritual, yet my body still held it. The pain in my chest came from recognition, from knowing I'd been here before, made this sacrifice before, and would likely do it again.

Then she stepped from the shadows. The same woman, always her. Hair dark as ash. Eyes lit from within. She held my gaze, steady, and pressed something into my palm. I looked down. It wasn't a coin this time; it was a mirror. The reflection it showed wasn't mine alone. It was a thousand faces layered over mine, flickering like candlelight in a draft. A soldier dying in snow, his mouth full of blood and prayers. A monk setting fire to a library while holding sacred texts beneath his robes. All of them me. Every lifetime, every consequence.

She appeared in every memory. The form changed, the name changed, but the eyes stayed the same. The same pull in my chest that had haunted me since the dreams began. She was always fighting, beside me, sometimes against me.

The current grew stronger. I felt it draw me toward the edge, a terrifying precipice, and then I heard her voice again.

"Come through," Danica whispered. "Come home."

The moment I tried to answer, the storm cracked inside my chest. I gasped. Air hit my lungs like fire, and I arched against the stone dais. My whole body seized with a jolt that was power, a flicker of something I'd held once and forgotten. Light burned behind my eyes. Then it broke apart, collapsing into shape and shadow, returning me to the waking world.

Rain on my face. I blinked against it as my vision cleared. The world came back in slow pieces; dark sky framed by broken rafters, water sliding down my cheeks. Danica leaned over me. Her face was flushed with heat and worry, her eyes wide, her breath caught in her throat as she realized I was awake.

"I remember you," I whispered, the words raw, aching.

Her lips parted. She didn't speak. She just looked at me like she was seeing someone she'd waited lifetimes for. "So do I," she finally said, her voice barely audible.

I coughed, and my chest heaved as I tried to sit up. My muscles resisted like I hadn't used them in years. I felt raw, like my soul had scraped its way back into this body one inch at a time.

"It's all still there," I said. "The lightning. The night she changed."

Danica brushed a soaked curl from my forehead. Her hand lingered just long enough for me to feel the tremble in her fingers. "The veil lifted too soon," she said. "She was supposed to wait."

"Ana…"

"She's not who she was," Danica murmured. "Maybe not who she said she was, and maybe not even who she thinks she is anymore. She's part of something older, and she's been here much longer than you've known."

I forced myself upright. My legs felt useless. My hands buzzed, something alive beneath the surface. My skin felt like it didn't fit right anymore, stretched by what it now contained.

"I saw myself," I told her. "In temples. On ships. Holding things no one should fucking hold."

"You've been a lot of things," she said. "Never ordinary."

That made me laugh, though it came out more like a rasp. "Fuck," I muttered, raking a hand through my damp hair. "I don't even know what's real anymore."

She knelt beside me, dirty and soaked, her jaw set like she'd fight the whole world if it tried to take me again.

"This is," she said. "You and me, right now. Everything else we figure out as we go."

I looked around us. The stronghold breathed, life thrumming in the faint glow of runes along the ancient stone walls, in the way the wind moved through the rafters like a song almost remembered. I saw Mjölnir carved into the arch above us. Perun's spiral, set in the altar beside me, pulsed with a quiet energy. "This place remembers," I said.

Danica's gaze never left me. "So do you."

I took a breath, letting it settle deep in my chest, then stood. My legs were shaky, but they held. Rain trailed down the side of my neck, cool against skin that still felt too hot, still faintly scorched from whatever had moved through me. I looked at Danica, standing just a pace away. Dirt streaked her face, salt and ash still clinging to her knuckles.

"You saved me," I said.

She nodded once. "I had to."

"Why me?" I asked again, the question hammering through my skull since the first time I heard my name in the dark.

Danica's expression softened. "Because you're the one who remembers when the world wants you to forget. You always were."

I swallowed against the pressure in my throat. Something wider than grief, closer to rupture. "I felt it," I said quietly. "When she looked at me with that knife, Ana, I saw through her. I saw something inside her. Something vast and cruel, older than anything I had language for."

Danica's jaw tightened. "I told you she's not who she was. They've used her for so long, I don't know what part of her is still real. She was sent to keep you asleep, to wrap you in comfort and nostalgia until you forgot you were ever something more."

"She's the leash," I whispered.

Danica looked away. The emotion broke across her face, and she let it. "You loved her," she said. "They used that."

I nodded slowly. "I buried myself in her. I buried everything."

"You were never meant to stay buried," she said. "They built your prison out of love and soft mornings, but it was still a fucking prison."

I clenched my hands, and a flicker of light cracked between my fingers. Just for a moment. Barely enough to scorch, yet enough to remind me it was there, waiting. I turned to look at the stone dais where I had nearly died, where perhaps I had. The runes that had flared beneath me were dim now, resting. The circle still glowed faintly with what she had summoned. It didn't feel like magic. It felt like memory, pressed into the bones of the earth.

"I saw so many lives," I said. "And in every one, I was walking toward war, toward sacrifice. Always standing on the fucking edge of a choice I didn't want to make."

Danica stepped closer, her voice low. "And you chose. Every time."

I looked at her then, truly looked. I saw the woman who had dragged my dying body through a storm, the student who had watched me from the back row with eyes full of stars. I saw her in the firelight of a forgotten temple, painted in ash and blood, across every lifetime.

"You found this place because of me," I said. The certainty of it settled through me like cold water.

She nodded. "Every path I've walked, every life I've lived, it always led back here. Back to you."

"More than a lover," I said.

She smiled faintly. "A mirror. A match."

I reached for her hand. Her fingers slipped into mine like they'd been there before, warm despite the rain. The moment our palms met, something stirred beneath the stone, a deep, slow groan. The earth recognizing us. We stood in silence, the kind that doesn't ask for anything. The rain shifted, falling softer now, slower. The trees surrounding the stronghold leaned inward, like they were listening.

I let go of her hand and knelt beside the stone circle. The coin still lay where Danica had placed it; I picked it up and slipped it into my pocket, felt its hum settle against my ribs. I touched the spiral carved into the dais, the same symbol that pulsed through the coin. It warmed beneath my palm.

"I was buried," I said. "In her. In the comforts I clung to because they made forgetting easier."

Danica didn't speak. She knelt beside me, eyes locked on the spiral, her hand still trembling faintly from everything she had carried to get us here.

"They made forgetting feel like peace," I said.

"But it wasn't," she whispered. "It was erasure."

I looked up. My voice cracked when I said her name. "Ana…"

"She'll come again," Danica said. "She was sent for that."

"Who sent her?" I asked.

She hesitated, then answered with a steadiness I hadn't expected. "The ones who believe they've tamed the gods. The liars who drape authority in sanctity. She's their weapon."

I stood, the ache in my limbs sharper now, but clearer. Like something had been reset in me, aligned.

"And when she comes?" I asked.

Danica stepped to the edge of the dais, her leather shoes sinking slightly into the moss. She looked toward the trees. "Then we fight."

She stayed there, shoulders rigid, tension rising from her skin like heat from scorched earth. I stepped beside her, letting my eyes trace the dense wall of trees ahead. The forest stood silent. The air didn't stir. No wind, no birdsong. It was watching.

"They know where we are," she said.

I didn't ask who. The pressure on my chest, the tingling beneath my skin told me enough. Something out there had noticed the ritual and the pulse of power, and it was waiting.

"How long do we have?" I asked.

Danica's mouth moved, almost a smile. "Not enough."

A breeze finally came, cutting low through the trees. It carried a bitter, cloying scent, sweet rot twisted into something foul. I stepped back toward the center of the circle and pressed my hand to the stone. It was still warm. Quiet now, but resting, like breath drawn and held just behind the lips.

"We need to leave," she said. "This place opened the door, but it won't keep it shut."

I turned to her. "Where do we go?"

"Somewhere the gods haven't been silenced. Somewhere memory still has roots." Her eyes softened when she looked at me. That rigid edge cracked for just a moment, and I saw the exhaustion behind her steadiness. "But we don't go alone."

I slipped my hand into my coat pocket and closed my fingers around the coin, drawing steadiness from its warmth.

Danica stepped back into the circle and knelt at its center. She pulled a strip of cloth from her satchel, black and red, worn thin at the edges. She wrapped it once around her wrist, then extended the other end to me.

"What is it?" I asked.

Her voice was steady. "A bond. Older than either of us."

I offered my wrist. She tied the cloth around it and fastened the knot tight. The warmth that surged up my arm was gentle, steady. It grounded me. My thoughts cleared, and the fear that had been clawing at my chest loosened its grip. I could still feel it, but it no longer ruled me.

"When we step out of here," she said, "they'll come. They'll try to reach through every memory that still aches, every loss you haven't faced."

I met her eyes. "Then we don't give them that chance."

Her voice dropped low, nearly a vow. "Then we give them something they can't swallow."

We turned together. As we crossed the circle's edge, the symbols beneath our feet dimmed until only moss remained. The forest ahead was shadowed and strange, but I was carrying a name that finally meant something. The wind stirred again. The trees bowed slightly, and as we stepped forward, the silence of the forest parted around us. Whatever came next, we would face it together.

CHAPTER NINE
THE VEILED QUEEN

Ana

I watched the sun rise over Corinth like it belonged to me, its light slow and deliberate across the Aegean. It painted the villas in soft gold, brushing the distant ruins with just enough warmth to tempt them into believing they still mattered. From the cool marble of my balcony, I could pick out the stone skeletons of temples, their forgotten gods buried beneath modern steel and tourist cash. Their altars lay quiet now, their names worn smooth by centuries. I had come to take their place.

The call was brief. "If you wish to survive," I told President Lazarević, "you will be on the next plane." He offered no argument. He knew, with an instinct deeper than reason, what I was.

The villa they had given me overlooked the Gulf, high-walled and empty save for what I allowed inside. I brought no staff, needed no handlers. The soldiers stationed at the gates avoided my gaze as I passed, holding their rifles the way children clutch toys at bedtime. One of them flinched when I smiled; I permitted it. Fear was a far more effective leash than loyalty, and I had no time for lesser feelings.

Inside, I poured wine. Greek, of course, its color dark as fresh blood. I did not drink it. I set the glass on the polished table where the President would eventually sit, ensuring the stem still held the lingering heat of my fingers.

He arrived with four guards. I dismissed them with a glance; they retreated to the perimeter without blinking. I remained barefoot, clad in silk that clung to my hips, hinting at bare skin beneath. Nikola's eyes found that first. His gaze traced the curve of my thighs when he believed I was not watching. I always watched.

"Was the plane comfortable?" I asked.

He walked in like a man accustomed to command, yet the rigid tension in his shoulders betrayed him. He had arrived dressed in linen with an open collar, his jacket folded over one arm as if he imagined this to be a negotiation of equals.

"It was fine," he said, his voice taut. "Though I would've appreciated more context before being summoned."

"You're being salvaged," I corrected him, turning my back to walk toward the sea.

He offered no immediate answer. I heard the soft clink of the wine glass being lifted, then the quiet intake of his first sip. I did not turn until he had tasted my offering. When I faced him again, I allowed his gaze to travel over me, fully, slowly. I granted him time to measure the dip of my collarbone, the way the silk parted just enough to invite him to imagine more than he could see. His stare clung to my skin like sweat.

"I know what you've built," I said, my voice smooth. "The nationalism. The cultural purges."

His jaw tensed, a visible flicker of defiance. "You disapprove?"

"I didn't say that." I took the glass from his hand, my fingers brushing his, and drank, allowing the wine to trace a warm path down my throat. "I said I know it was only the beginning."

He stepped closer, drawn by something invisible. I permitted it. His breath smelled of spice and desperation.

"You're the one behind it," he said, the realization dawning in his eyes.

I nodded, slow. "And you're here because I need someone to help finish it."

He reached for my wrist, his fingers tentative and greedy. I did not move away. His touch held a desperate hunger. I placed his hand higher, guiding it to my thigh, and watched the realization bloom across his face. Nothing beneath the silk, only invitation.

"Do you think I'm going to fuck you and then hand you your throne?" I asked, my lips close enough to brush his. "Is that what you're hoping for?"

He swallowed hard, his throat working. "Isn't that how gods work?"

I smiled, a slow curve of my lips. "No. We fuck after you surrender."

I pushed him into the chair.

He did not speak for a long time after that, his body a tableau of disbelief. He stared at me like he couldn't decide whether to pray or crawl, and it thrilled me to know that either act would have pleased me equally. His spine remained rigid, a military habit, yet his knees were already weakening beneath him. That was power. It hollowed out the old gods, the tired ideals, and poured in new instincts.

I allowed him to look at what I was, a goddess sculpted by demand, by desire itself. I moved slowly, each step across the polished stone floor drawing his gaze like a tide. The silk parted as I circled him, brushing against his shoulder, my fingers trailing across the rim of his ear before catching in his hair.

"You think Serbia belongs to you?" I whispered against his skin.

He offered no answer. I was not finished.

"You think borders will save you, that armies will hold?" I leaned down until my mouth hovered beside his, my breath warm against his lips. "They're nothing without want, and I own want."

His lips parted, ready to respond, but I slipped two fingers into his mouth instead, silencing him. He gasped around them, and his tongue curled, instinctive, a primal acceptance.

"You came here because I told you to," I said, lowering myself into his lap. "You brought no questions, no preconditions. Only your appetite."

I pulled my fingers free, allowing the moisture to trace a path down his chin. He tried to speak again, a choked sound, but I silenced him with my mouth. I kissed him like I was claiming territory. His hands gripped my waist, desperate for direction, and I gave it. I dragged his jacket off his shoulders, tore his shirt open with a single motion, buttons scattering across the floor.

"You want a future," I whispered against his throat, my breath hot against his pulse, "then forget the past. Forget your fucking country. You're mine now."

And he was.

I took him there, in the chair, with the vast sea watching through the open glass and the morning wind catching our heat. He moaned like a convert. I rode him until sweat beaded down his temples and his hands trembled.

When it was over, I left him slumped in the chair, undone, his ambition stripped bare.

I stood, naked, stretching like a flame pulled taller by its own hunger, feeling the power surge through my limbs. His eyes followed the curve of my hips, tracing bare skin streaked with gold from the morning sun. I walked to the full-length mirror, ran my hands down my sides, and watched myself.

"I want all of them," I said aloud. "The presidents, the generals. Bring them here."

He stayed where he was, slack-jawed.

"I said, bring them," I repeated, turning back to him.

Nikola stood slowly, as if remembering how to obey. His lips were red from mine, his collarbone still bearing the half-moon of my teeth.

"I'll summon the delegation," he said, his voice hoarse, his eyes full of fire and fear at once.

I smiled. "Good, but not through diplomats or letters. You'll speak to them one by one, personally. And when they ask why, tell them they'll understand once they meet me."

He hesitated in the doorway, gathering his clothes, dignity stitched sloppily back around his spine.

"Ana…" he said, the name a question, a plea.

I tilted my head, inviting him to continue.

"Are you going to…" he trailed off, his gaze caught on my naked form.

I cut him off with a single word, soft and absolute. "No."

He nodded, swallowed hard, and left.

I turned back to the mirror and whispered my true name. "Aphrodite." The reflection smiled first.

They started to arrive three days later. Not all at once. That would have been too obvious, and none of them liked to admit they were following anyone's orders, least of all a woman's, especially one who had begun to rewrite the Balkan map with a smile.

The first came alone. A French envoy with a spine like old marble and a mind cluttered with secular arrogance. His mouth spoke diplomacy, but his eyes couldn't stop tracking the curve of my robe, the gold threading that shifted every time I breathed. I let him recite his credentials, his hollow assurances of neutrality. Then I touched his wrist, softly, and whispered the name of the woman he loved in university, the one who died before she ever got to say yes. He signed in blood.

The British emissary arrived next, dressed like colonial memory in human form. He tried quoting Byron, as if poetry could protect him from a goddess. I poured him a glass of wine, letting him talk, letting him lecture me on sovereignty, on restraint. Then I reached across the table and dragged my fingernail along the rim of his teacup. It bloomed into roses, white and breathless. He stared, transfixed, until his hand trembled, then whispered, "God save me." I tilted his chin and said, "I am." His knees hit the floor.

The Americans sent someone from Defense, young and sharp. The kind of man who mistook control for strength and thought calling me a myth would protect him from becoming part of one. He said, "This is propaganda," as I brushed past him, my hair catching torchlight. He said, "You don't scare me," while his pulse surged under my hand, while I ran my tongue along the rim of his ear. I kissed his forehead. Three days later, they found him naked on the roof of the U.S. embassy in Athens, painting my name on the tiles in his own blood, whispering prayers in Akkadian he couldn't have possibly learned. They tried to restrain him. He bit through his badge and sobbed when they dragged him away.

This is what they never understood. I only needed to unearth what was already rotting beneath their skins, the loneliness, the feral need to be wanted in ways they couldn't admit even to themselves: I was a reckoning.

Some brought gifts. One offered oil rights. Another offered his eldest son, and I took what mattered from both. One foolish diplomat tried to offer me weapons. I took the pen from his pocket and drew a spiral on the table. He gasped, his breath catching. "Keep your missiles," I said. "I want your churches, your airwaves." And they gave them. Every last one.

Soon, I no longer needed to ask. They brought things before I even opened my mouth. Treaties signed on silk. Relics dug from forbidden tombs. One king handed me a bishop in chains, still weeping prayers from his knees. I let him pray. Then I cut the chains and said, "You're mine now." He smiled and kissed my bare foot. He was the last until Athens.

I left Corinth at dawn. The convoy waited in silence as I walked across the marble steps of the old temple, the air heavy with the scent of oil and wine. Soldiers along the road stiffened at my approach. Their weapons dropped to their sides. Their eyes lowered. The ground beneath their boots had already chosen its goddess.

By the time we reached Athens, the sky burned gold through haze. Lazarević sat beside me in the armored car, his gaze empty, collar loose. His voice had gone quiet after the plane, after my thighs had wrapped around his ambition and stripped it of language. Now he looked at the world like it no longer belonged to him, and he was right.

The Acropolis loomed ahead, cordoned off by security details who had no idea why they stood there, only that something told them to. A clear path stretched to the summit, cleared by instinct more than order. The columns blinked with light from an unseen sun. Each crack in the marble felt like a pulse, each worn step like history inhaling me back into place.

I stepped out barefoot. The earth was warm beneath my soles. The wind stilled. Men and women from the highest seats of power had gathered near the Parthenon's broken frame. I hadn't summoned them, but they came, drawn forward like insects to heat. Their faces said it all. Some still tried to measure me against myth, wondering what version of me this was, Aphrodite or Ana, but their bodies already knew the answer.

I walked past them slowly, letting them feel the shift in the air, the subtle distortion of reality. I stopped at the center of the plaza and turned. They formed a loose circle around me, silent, waiting.

"I brought you here to remember what power tastes like," I said. My voice carried through the open air.

No one responded. No one looked away.

I crossed to the cardinal first. His lips trembled when I touched his cheek. "You'll teach them that pleasure is devotion. That salvation smells like sweat and incense." He dropped to his knees.

The NATO general next. I ran my fingers down the medals pinned to his chest. "You'll march them in my name. Every anthem will carry my breath."

The French envoy clutched an old crucifix under his jacket. I laughed. "You think that thing remembers how to protect you?" He tried to speak. I kissed the side of his throat. His knees buckled.

Then the American, always smug, always the last to fold. His suit was pressed too perfectly, his arrogance thick enough to taste. I stared into his eyes and said nothing. He swallowed hard.

"I don't need your loyalty," I told them all. "I already have your desire, and desire is harder to kill."

I turned away from the kneeling leaders and moved toward the north side of the Acropolis, where a narrow stone passage wound between crumbled walls. My bare feet clicked against the marble, and the assembled dignitaries watched me as though they expected the ground itself to swallow me whole. The wind tugged at my hair, carrying salt and dust from the city below.

At the end of the passage, I halted before a weathered block of stone that bore no carving, no mark to distinguish it from the surrounding rock. I placed both hands against its surface and pressed. The marble shifted, sliding aside to reveal a stairway hewn from the living hill. Torches flared to life as I descended, their flames arcing to follow me like obedient worshipers.

Nikola appeared at my shoulder, his breath catching. I offered him my arm, letting him feel the pulse beneath my skin. We went down together, the air growing cooler, richer with the scent of damp earth. The torchlight danced along rough walls, revealing ancient reliefs half-swallowed by shadow.

He steadied himself against the wall. "Where are we going?"

I gave him a single look. "To the heart of everything they thought they knew."

The stair curved, spiraling downward until the passage opened onto a vast cavern supported by columns of veined marble. Stalactites dripped from the ceiling, and the floor sloped toward a dais carved into the living rock. A low pool of water reflected the torchlight like liquid bronze. I walked across the cavern, my silk whispering against the stone. My bare feet felt the heat pulsing through the rock.

He followed, his eyes wide. "I never believed it existed," he admitted.

I paused at the edge of the pool and looked down at my reflection, distorted by ripples. "Belief is for those who need comfort. I deal in reality." I reached into the pool and drew up a handful of water, letting it drip through my fingers. The surface stilled, and the reflections solidified. Behind me, I heard the others enter, their murmurs drifting from the passage.

I turned and rose to the dais where a stone altar waited, ancient and unassuming. "This temple has no name," I said, my voice carrying over the hush. "It belongs to blood, and to the hunger that drives us beyond our limits."

I placed a finger on the altar's edge. Ancient Greek letters inscribed long ago glowed beneath my touch, igniting in a soft red light that spread outward in swirling patterns. The columns trembled as though they recognized their master's call.

Nikola stepped beside me. I laid my hand over his and looked him in the eye. "You will tell the world this place is sacred. That every treaty signed here carries the gravity of eternity."

He nodded, and as his fingers closed around mine, the letters flared brighter, illuminating every face in the chamber. I lifted my other hand and let the light spread along my arm like liquid fire. "From this moment on, Athens remembers its true goddess."

Behind us, the pool's surface rippled again, showing visions instead of reflections. The city rebuilding in my honor, statues rising along boulevards I had once walked as mortal. I watched the future unfold in water and flame. Then I turned, leaving the vision to settle, and descended from the dais.

At the bottom, I paused, water dripping from my fingers. "Destroy their doubts," I said. "Let them carry this temple in their bones." Nikola met my gaze and offered his hand. I took it. Together, we walked back into the corridor, leaving the hidden power of the temple to pulse beneath our feet.

When the final vow left his lips, I turned my back on them all. The circle of leaders remained frozen, the air thick with devotion. They had already given me what I wanted, the ache itself.

The city shifted as I moved. Windows darkened along the streets below. Conversations stopped mid-sentence. Children fell silent without knowing why. The city's bones remembered me.

From the Acropolis, I descended the stone path alone, without escort or ceremony. I crossed through the ancient ruins like I had never left, and perhaps I hadn't. Below the plaza, hidden in layers of forgotten marble and centuries of state-sanctioned erasure, my temple waited. It had waited long enough.

The entrance revealed itself only when I reached it. A narrow stairway tucked between two collapsed columns, veiled by ivy that parted at my touch. I stepped inside. The world hushed. The sun fell away, swallowed by shadows that obeyed me. The descent was steep, carved into the earth with a precision born of memory rather than tools. The steps glistened faintly, as if the stone itself pulsed with old breath.

Each level I passed smelled older, salt and smoke layered beneath rose oil and sex, the whole of my history pressed into stone. The walls narrowed, then widened again, lined with broken statuary, figures from myths too old for textbooks, gods erased by the councils of men. Most were crumbling and faceless. I paused before one. A woman with a serpent crown, her torso scarred by chisels, her breasts deliberately defaced. She had been feared, then erased. My fingers brushed the stone where her name had once been. "I remember you," I whispered. "They will, too."

When I reached the main atrium, the temple sighed open. The walls moved aside with the grace of something that had waited millennia to welcome me home.

The chamber was vast, its domed ceiling glinting with thousands of embedded gemstones. They shimmered like stars but tracked my movement like eyes. The floor was polished black stone streaked with veins of crimson and gold. Each step I took echoed with something ancient, aware. There were no icons of me here, no altars. This place had always been for transformation.

I walked to the center dais and stood still, letting the temple recognize me. The air grew warm. The floor beneath my feet thrummed gently, as if exhaling. Lines of light traced up the columns, spiraling with faint glyphs that hadn't been spoken aloud since the Oracle's tongue was burned.

I removed my robes. My skin belonged to this place. My blood called it open. I stepped barefoot onto the dais and let my body sink into the ritual memory of it. A hum started low in the walls. A memory. The temple remembered the shape of my arrival, and it sang without voice.

I closed my eyes and reached down for invocation. My fingers pressed against the marks along my hips, sigils inked beneath the skin when I was still human enough to forget. I called them forward, one by one. Heat spread across my thighs. The air tightened. Something deep in the stone uncoiled. I lowered myself to the floor, flat against the cold marble, arms wide. I offered a return.

Then the temple answered. The dome above pulsed with light. The air thickened with rose and iron. Veins of molten gold lit up beneath the floor, webbing out from beneath my spine. The walls shimmered with brief visions of lovers, of battles older than language. My mouth opened. A cry ripped out of me, raw and feral. Power poured through me, took everything it wanted. It burned, and I let it. My body arched. My fingers clenched against the stone. My hips bucked, and the chamber moaned back. The temple claimed me as its heart.

When it finished, I rose slowly, hair wild and skin glowing. Above me, constellations blinked back into place across the dome. I walked from the dais without dressing. The air clothed me better than silk. My skin was still slick with sweat and sacred oil.

The stairway opened behind me as though the mountain itself bowed to let me pass. I rose, slow and deliberate, barefoot and unbothered by the cold stone. My skin still gleamed from the temple's blessing. Every step felt like a storm shifting its gravity. My nakedness was dominion.

At the summit, the wind changed. The air that touched my body moved in deference. I crossed the threshold into the torchlit corridors of the estate above, and the guards who flanked the hall froze as I passed. Their hands clenched against rifles from the tremor of recognition. Their mouths parted as though to speak, but no sound came. The marble glowed where I stepped. The oil lamps leaned toward me.

They were waiting for me in the upper chamber, an inner sanctum designed for state visits and private deals, draped in burgundy velvet and Byzantine gold. There were no journalists, no cameras. The most powerful men and women Europe had left stood when I entered, some instinctively, others pretending they hadn't already been watching the door.

Lazarević was among them. He sat closest to the hearth, clothed again in silk and arrogance, but his gaze slid down my body like he'd forgotten how to blink. We both remembered the flight, the way he had cried my name against my breast, fingers clawing at the floor like he thought he could dig through the plane to Hades if it meant I'd ride him again. Now he sat straighter, pretending he hadn't already been claimed.

"Gentlemen," I said. "And the few clever women brave enough to join them." They chuckled, the sound of submission with teeth marks. A room filled with advisors, envoys, presidents, military attachés, each one wearing authority like armor that didn't quite fit anymore. I could feel their sweat behind their collars. Hear the shallow catch of their breath when I leaned just slightly, letting my scent reach them.

I crossed the room like a lover, like the memory of the first time they came and the moment they realized they'd never feel that way again. I let my fingers brush along the curve of a decanter. I poured the wine myself, dark red and older than their borders.

"To the world we are about to forget," I said. I raised the glass. "And the one we are about to create."

Only one man didn't raise his in return. He was British, fifty, trim, stone-creased around the eyes. He hadn't bowed when I entered. Hadn't looked away when I passed. Even now, his glass sat untouched. He thought he was immune.

I crossed to him slowly. He watched me, jaw set, spine locked straight like a soldier facing a firing line.

"What's your name?" I asked.

"Lord Everly," he said tightly.

I straddled his lap without permission.

"You want to stop me?" I whispered into his ear, my thighs pressing against the stiffness beneath his trousers. "You should've done it before I sat down."

His hands gripped the chair. He was shaking.

I leaned back just enough to look into his face. "Say it," I murmured.

He stared at me, sweat blooming at his temple. "Say what?"

"Say my name."

He swallowed. "Ana."

I smiled. "Wrong."

I kissed him. It was rough. He moaned into my mouth, his resistance burning off like mist. When I pulled back, his eyes were glazed. His hands had moved on their own, resting at my waist. "Try again," I whispered.

"Aphrodite."

I climbed off him slowly, letting my wetness smear against the crease of his tailored slacks. He stayed seated, panting. The rest of the room had gone silent.

I turned to them all, hair wild, lips parted. "This is how the world changes. With surrender, one ache at a time."

I stepped forward, barefoot, letting the marble drink my heat.

"You've had your wars," I said. "Your empires painted in blood and called it faith." Their heads stayed lowered. "But you've never had me."

One by one, they looked up. The Greek Prime Minister blinked too slowly, like waking from a deep sleep. His lips parted. No words came.

"Greece is already mine," I said, stepping closer. "And Serbia has given itself willingly." Nikola nodded without hesitation, without shame.

"You have a choice. I can unravel you thread by thread, until nothing remains but hunger for my name. Or," I smiled, soft and absolute, "you can kneel now, and be made whole."

The room melted. The Cypriot envoy crumpled first, falling hard to both knees as tears traced down his cheeks. He whispered something into his sleeve, a prayer or a confession. It didn't matter. I had already heard it in his heartbeat.

The Bulgarian defense minister tried to stand. His hand twitched toward his briefcase, where I knew a document waited, some charter or formal protest. I let him reach for it. I walked to him slowly, pressed my palm to his chest, and looked into his eyes. He dropped the case. Then he dropped to the floor.

Their languages faltered. Their memories blurred. Some of them wept. Others smiled like children shown light for the first time. A few tried to resist, quoting sovereignty, oaths sworn in darker times. I gave them clarity.

The map in the corner of the room glowed, a living projection built from threads of fire and shadow. Serbia was already aflame, its borders pulsing with soft red-gold light. Greece shimmered, fully swallowed in the rose-hued dawn of me. The Macedonian ambassador hesitated, until I whispered her real name, the one she'd hidden since childhood. The moment she heard it, she crossed the room on her knees and kissed the floor beneath my feet.

"I am the ache that breaks you open. I am the god your ancestors whispered to before language remembered how." And they believed me. Because I made them beg to be claimed. They called it revelation.

Within forty-eight hours of the summit in Athens, declarations flowed like wine. Parliament buildings lit their facades with my symbol, a burning rose encircled by stars. Constitutional revisions were drafted overnight. Theocracies collapsed in longing, their laws rewritten in gold ink.

In Greece, the Orthodox synod convened in secret, then emerged in full ceremonial regalia to bless my name in front of the Acropolis. They canonized me. Said I had always been the unnamed Queen behind the veil, the flame on Sinai they mistook for wrath. They lit candles beneath my image, though I never asked for light.

In Serbia, statues were recast. I kept their poets and their generals. I just corrected their gaze. One by one, their eyes now turned to me in marble and metal, in every public square. I watched myself rise above the skyline like prophecy with cleavage.

Children were taught to paint my sigil before they could spell their names. Schools held daily devotions. "Beauty is strength. We belong to the Flame." No one made them say it, but they said it anyway.

Military conscripts wore polished brass pins over their hearts, roses ringed in spirals. Church bells rang to mark each hour I was alive. A sculptor in Thessaloniki tried to recreate the curve of my hip in bronze and wept when it failed to move him. State-run orchestras rewrote national anthems, replacing drums with longing, horns with breath. Every broadcast included a whisper of my name in the final frame. Art changed first, then government followed. They forgot the word goddess and used my name instead.

I never chose the rose because it was soft. Men mistake it for a symbol of fragility, of dainty femininity wrapped in velvet and silk. They forget the thorns. They always do. That's why it's perfect, and that's why it's mine. The rose doesn't beg to be touched. It dares, and if you reach for it without reverence, it bleeds you.

They remember me as the goddess of love, of wet mouths whispering names in the dark, but that's only one version. One sculpted in marble by hands that needed me to be palatable, beautiful in a way that didn't frighten them. They never carved the truth, that I was also called Areia. They buried that title. Warlike and blood-born. They didn't want their goddess of lust to be the same one who demanded sacrifice before dawn and took cities with a glance. I was both. I am both.

Sparta remembered. They gave me altars soaked in blood. They sang to me before war. The women braided my name into their sons' hair before sending them to die for glory, and the men never stood a chance. Leonidas knelt before me once, in sweat and desperation. His body trembled when I touched him, wanting to become something more than flesh, and I let him, for a moment. He carried that moment with him to Thermopylae. Every step, every last defiant scream was soaked in my name. He died for me, my rose carved into the inside of his shield, my scent clinging to his armor even after the blood dried. His legend still echoes, but his surrender to me was the real reason history remembers him.

That is what they never understand. My power lives in submission, in what they offer willingly, in how they kneel because they cannot imagine standing without me.

I don't need spears or tanks or presidents on leashes. I need only the ache beneath their ribs, the one they try to drown in patriotism or prayer. When I press into that ache, when I whisper just right, they become mine. Entire nations unravel for the promise of being wanted fully, without escape. That's what the rose means. Surrender, and surrender, when done properly, always ends in fire.

The summit ended in silence, an acceptance that passed between them like a shared breath no one wanted to acknowledge. They had all said yes, willingly or otherwise, and the signatures on the vellum were enough. I did not give a fuck if they wanted to or not. One by one, the leaders surrendered. Greece, Serbia, Montenegro, North Macedonia, and finally Albania. They wrapped it in language meant to sound diplomatic, cultural solidarity and regional integration, but we all knew what had happened. They had given me the continent.

I stood by the tall windows facing the sea when the treaties were signed, letting the light gild my skin while they watched. Some trembled with fear. Others stared with something dangerously close to devotion. It didn't matter. Their nations now moved at my breath.

Weeks had passed. The dates no longer mattered to me. I moved through time as I moved through rooms, without needing permission. While they counted days, I altered memories. I rewrote loyalties through yearning, through the pull of something older than their systems and stronger than their gods, but beneath the flags, beneath the temples and the treaties, something remained unsettled.

Ilija remained, always Ilija.

He had always been the loose thread. His name still appeared in the wrong places, scratched into train station walls, spoken in dreams that slipped through my reach. Danica was there too, I felt her. Always nearby, never visible, but present, like she'd never left his side, even across lifetimes. If they were waking up, and I knew they were, I could not allow it to spread. If the people understood who they were, if they remembered what those two had once meant, my worship would rot from within. The leaders would be torn down. My temples would crumble. My image, projected across the heavens, would be erased by frost and lightning. A goddess who is forgotten is nothing.

Ilija had to be captured, never killed. His death would turn him into a symbol. I had no interest in martyrdom. I needed him broken quietly, sealed in confusion and doubt, until he couldn't tell memory from madness. And then, perhaps, if he still had enough of his old fire, I'd take it for myself. Bend it to my shape. I would see him kneel because he no longer remembered how not to. I missed that man. Gods, I missed his cock. He was a phenomenal lover, and I truly do love him. This, however, is about worship. I would not see myself forgotten like my brothers and sisters on Olympus. Although that was my fault too, oops. They never stood a chance against my cult, my convictions. Zeus, all high and mighty; I rolled my eyes. Ares; Ilija reminds me of him. Ilija will not make the same mistakes they did. Olympus felt my wrath. Immortal, fucking laughable. Immortal until another god gets fucking tired of dealing with the same bullshit millennia after millennia.

I shifted my focus back to today, to my poor, sweet Ilija. Danica had found him in every lifetime. Every lifetime she gets him fucking killed. Not this time, over my dead corpse. She can die; she's mortal. Fuck her and her righteous delusions. Little bitch thinks this time will be different, and it will be. Ilija and I will rule the world. Some may call this obsession; they would be right. I, the goddess of lust and love, will wage war to stop this fucking bitch from killing the man I would make king of my pantheon. Sparta knew what I was. Now the entirety of the modern world will know that Aphrodite will burn down the world with the fire Prometheus gave them just to feel Ilija's love, and his beautiful cock, for the rest of time.

President Lazarević stood waiting for me at the doors of the summit hall. He held a glass of wine, already savoring our next performance. I brushed past him without a word. He would accompany me to Belgrade. The public announcement was scheduled. The people would cheer. Their new reality had already been scripted. All that was left was for me to speak it into being. But before I did, I turned back once, just briefly, and looked out across the sea. The sun was low. The city shimmered, and somewhere beneath it all, Ilija still breathed. I would find him, and I would unmake him carefully.

Chapter Ten
THE INHERITED WAR

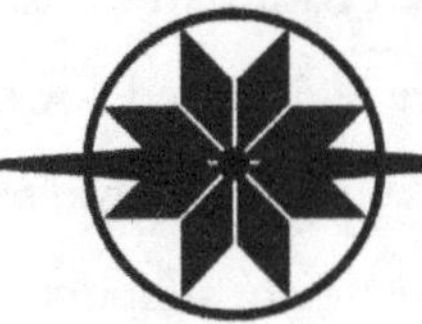

Ilija

The stone walls held the cold longer than they should have, a chill that lived in the mortar, in the marrow of the stronghold itself, refusing to yield to warmth. Smoke from the hearth curled in tight spirals, never quite reaching the room's furthest corners, leaving pockets of sharp air. I moved my chair closer to the coals, notebook still open on my lap, though I hadn't written anything in hours. The words I needed no longer came easily.

Danica stood at the far table, sorting the relics again. The spiral stone sat beside the sun-eyed coin, the sketch folded between her notes. She touched each piece as if it were alive, with a careful awareness, as if she were cataloging a pulse beneath the surface.

Outside, the fog hadn't lifted for days. The pass below lay hidden beneath a curtain of cloud that never stirred. Even the birds had gone quiet. We didn't speak it aloud, but both of us felt that waiting tension in the air, the kind that always came before something changed.

At exactly six o'clock, the radio terminal flared to life. Its sudden brilliance jarred the room. It was a military relic, salvaged from a ruined checkpoint, brought to the stronghold by a traveler who never stayed long. The screen was scratched, the speakers hissed with static, yet it worked.

Every evening, it came alive with the same broadcast, a ritual so predictable it had become its own kind of violence.

The flag appeared first, drenched in red, trimmed in gold, the old tricolor erased as if history itself had been overwritten. The eagle still bore its two heads, but their posture had shifted, lowered, humbled, almost servile. One claw clutched a sword driven into stone. The other held a book wreathed in flame. Behind it, a radiant sunburst spiraled outward, runes etched in light. At the center, the seal of the Ministry of Sacred Unity pulsed slowly, as if it breathed.

Danica stepped beside me, arms folded. Neither of us spoke.

A low horn followed, long, unwavering, hollow, the kind of sound that made your chest tighten before your mind understood why. Then came the voice. President Nikola Lazarević, framed beneath the mosaic. He wore black robes stitched with gold, sunbursts embroidered along the cuffs, spirals winding down the hem like a sermon no one had asked for. A gleaming Orthodox cross rested over his chest, but what stood behind him wasn't Christ. It was Ana.

She towered over him in mosaic, her form rendered in gold, crimson, and shadow. Seven stars crowned her brow. Her eyes, unblinking, gazed beyond the camera, beyond the room, as if fixed on everyone watching. Even reduced to tile, she radiated presence. She didn't need to move. She had already become the light.

"Brothers and sisters," Lazarević began, his voice slow, measured, almost liturgical. "Tonight, we return." He let the words hang there. Heavy. Scripted. "To the blood, to the book, to the beauty we were taught to forget."

The camera widened. Ash-robed officials knelt before an altar carved from dark wood, their heads bowed, hands clasped like supplicants before a relic. A wordless hymn began to rise beneath the broadcast, soft, slow, hollow, like a lullaby drained of memory.

Lazarević again, with the same cadence. "We do not conquer. We correct. We do not destroy. We restore."

Then came the list. A slow scroll of names. Scholars, artists, priests. Children. Each followed by the same crimson sigil. Dissonant Voice. I didn't need to see mine. I knew it was there, but when it appeared, Ilija Dragović, something still shifted in me, like reading a name carved into your own headstone.

The screen faded to black. The hum of the transmission died. Danica held still for a moment, then her voice cut through the stillness. "That's not just a purge list," she said. "It's scripture now."

I looked down at my hands. They had gone pale. "They're canonizing memory," I said. "One name at a time."

We turned together to face the mural on the far wall. It had been carved long before we arrived, half-erased by centuries of erosion and fire, but its lines had grown clearer since we'd begun to remember. A man stood between a broken sword and a burning tree. A woman pressed her palm to his chest. Above them, five divine shapes swirled, patterns of meaning rather than form.

I stepped forward and placed my hand on the tree. "What if they're right?" I said. "What if stories are more dangerous than armies?"

Danica stood beside me, but her eyes weren't on the carving. They were on my hand. Her voice, when it came, was more raw than I expected. "They are," she said. "That's why they're destroying everything that still remembers how to feel."

I turned to look at her. Her jaw was tight, her brow furrowed like she was holding back something sharp. "But I don't know who I am in this story," I whispered. "I don't even know if I'm supposed to be in it."

Her breath caught. She blinked hard and stepped closer, near enough that I could feel the tremor in her voice. "Don't say that," she said. "Don't…" She stopped, gathered herself. "You were there before the first name was written. I've seen you, in dreams, in ruins, in lives I've only half remembered. You've always been in it."

I searched her face. She wore memory barely holding shape. "I thought you had answers," I said.

She laughed under her breath, bitter and sad. "I thought so too."

We stood there in silence, both of us staring at a history too big to hold. I looked down at my palm, where the spiral mark had once glowed. It was gone now, or hidden, but I still felt it under the skin, like an old chord still vibrating long after the song had ended.

"Then we wait," I said. "And when it calls…"

Her eyes met mine, glassy and fierce. "We go."

We didn't move for a while after that. Danica stayed by the mural, one shoulder pressed against the stone, fingers tapping nervously against her sleeve. I returned to the fire, stoked the coals back to life, dropped in another log. The kindling hissed like it hated being disturbed.

"Think they're watching us?" I asked, settling back onto the stone bench.

She glanced at the radio, then at me. "If they are, they're probably bored out of their minds."

"Speak for yourself. I'm captivating."

Danica raised an eyebrow. "Captivating? You've spent three hours today staring at a half-written sentence and muttering to your tea."

"Poetic muttering," I said. "Inspired, even."

"I think the teacup disagrees."

That got a small smile out of her, tight at first, but real. I let the silence settle between us again. It had weight this time, familiarity.

"You know," I said after a while, "you're different when we're not running for our lives."

"Better or worse?"

"Less likely to throw me off a cliff."

She snorted. "Give it time."

I looked at her again, really looked. Her braid had come slightly undone, strands curling near her cheekbone, catching the firelight. There were smudges beneath her eyes from exhaustion, but it was her expression that stayed with me. Worn from holding too much.

"How long have you known?" I asked. "About me."

Danica took her time answering. She crossed the room and sat across from me on the floor, her back against the old timber support. Her voice was softer now.

"Pieces of you showed up in my dreams for years," she said. "Sometimes just your voice. Sometimes your hands. Once I saw you fall in a temple with ivy growing through the roof. I remember the light bleeding through it. Your blood was everywhere."

I let her continue.

"I thought it was madness," she said. "Or maybe trauma from some life I couldn't name. But the more it happened, the more I started to recognize you. Your face stayed foreign, but the feeling of you didn't."

I nodded slowly. "I've seen you too," I said. "In visions, in dreams. Standing in snow, singing near fire. Once I watched you drown. At the time I had no idea who you were, just some face that haunted my sleep. It was strange. Then you showed up in class, and I couldn't figure out where I had seen you before."

Her head tilted slightly. "Did I survive?"

"No idea. I woke up gasping."

Her lips parted, almost a laugh, but it didn't come.

We both fell quiet. The fire popped. Somewhere above us, timber creaked in the ceiling like something very old shifting in its sleep.

"I think we've done this before," I said finally. "Maybe not here, maybe not exactly like this, but us. This rhythm."

Danica watched the fire. "And?"

"And I think I've always lost you."

She looked over then. Her voice was steady, but something behind her eyes wasn't. "Maybe this time you don't."

"I don't think it's up to me."

"Then maybe it's up to both of us."

We sat there a long time after that, the thread between us stronger now, reshaped into something living.

Danica returned to the table as the fire settled into embers. She moved with care, unfastening the layers of oilcloth wrapped around the relics. Her hands were steady, but I could tell from the way she exhaled, slow and measured, that something inside her wasn't.

I joined her.

The spiral stone lay at the center, warm even in the chill of the room. Silver veins split its surface like roots chasing something buried deeper than time. The sun-eyed coin rested beside it, its etched runes still unreadable, shifting like water when you looked too long. But it was the folded scrap of paper she laid beside them that caught me off guard.

I hadn't seen it in days, maybe weeks, not since I had found it beside the journal, my fingers still stained with charcoal I didn't remember using. She had kept it safe. Protected it. As if she knew I'd need to see it again.

I unfolded it slowly. A heart stared back at me, if you could call it that. The shape was rough, sketched in jagged lines, but unmistakable. Lightning webbed through the muscle like veins of fire. Ice clawed up from the base, brittle and sharp, creeping toward the center but never reaching it. Deep inside, at the core, something glowed.

"I drew this?" I asked, though the question was pointless.

Danica nodded. "You didn't speak the whole time. You just sat at the table and started drawing, like your hand already knew."

I touched the edge of the paper. The charcoal left a dusting on my fingertip.

"I don't remember it," I said. "But I remember what it is."

She waited, giving me room.

"It's the heart of Perun," I said. "I saw it in a dream. It beat like thunder, slow, certain, and there were markings all over it."

Her voice dropped lower. "You were holding it?"

I nodded. "It didn't feel foreign. It felt familiar. Like I had always carried it."

She studied me then, concern and awe tangled in her expression.

"That makes sense," she said.

I looked up. "Why?"

"Because I don't think you're a vessel," she said. "I think you're something older. A threshold. They don't live in you. They remember through you."

I stared down at the sketch again. The heart hadn't changed, but I had.

"And what if remembering breaks me?"

Danica reached out, resting her hand on the table between us. Close enough.

"Then we break together," she said.

I didn't answer. The words stayed lodged behind my ribs, where the ache had settled.

Danica tapped the edge of the cloth. "We're missing two," she said. "Morana and Lada."

I looked down at what we had. The spiral stone, the coin, the heart sketch.

"One for death," I murmured. "One for love."

She nodded. "And when we have them…"

She hesitated, her eyes drifting to the mural across the chamber. "We return," she said.

I turned to her. "What does that actually mean? Why these things? Why us?"

She sat back on her heels, thinking before she answered. "They aren't relics," she said. "They're memory made solid. Traces of the gods left behind after they were forgotten. These pieces are what's left of their shape in the world. Each one ties this world to the last, to the ones before that."

I looked at the sketch again, the heart I'd drawn in some half-waking trance.

"They're anchors," she replied. "To power, identity, truth. They don't give us anything new. They remind us of what we were before forgetting replaced belief."

"And when we have all five?"

Danica's voice dropped to a whisper. "The lock breaks."

I didn't ask what lock. Some part of me already knew. Something ancient stirred beneath my skin, light and thunder woven through memory, vast and electric, a storm waking after lifetimes of silence, bound to a name I was only beginning to remember.

By the time Danica finished rewrapping the relics, the sky outside had faded into a dull, bruised blue. Smoke rose from the hearth in thin strands, curling toward the rafters. I stayed near the coals, watching the light move across the floor. Danica crossed to the table on the eastern wall and unrolled another map.

At six o'clock, the radio terminal switched on. The screen blinked once, then steadied. A low hum settled beneath the silence, just enough to make your spine tighten. The voice came through clear, female this time, one I did not recognize. It was controlled, stripped of emotion, as if the words themselves were sacred and she was merely a mouthpiece. Danica kept working, but her hand froze above the parchment.

"Broadcast Number Two Hundred Twelve," the voice said. "Fourth month of the Sacred Confederation. The Ministry of Sacred Unity reminds all citizens that memory is sacred only when it obeys."

The words were familiar now, but they didn't dull with repetition. If anything, they sharpened.

"Extremist cells have been identified in multiple provinces. Incidents include symbolic vandalism, heretical graffiti, and unauthorized possession of pre-sanctification materials. Citizens are reminded that harboring dissonant literature constitutes a breach of sacred doctrine. Dissonance is sedition. Sedition will be corrected."

No pause, no change in inflection. Just more doctrine.

"The Sacred Confederation remains unified. Borders are symbolic. Worship is law. She is watching."

Danica crossed the chamber and turned the dial sharply, cutting the broadcast off mid-sentence. Her hand lingered on the terminal like she was deciding whether to smash it. "Four months," she said finally. "It's only been four months since she took Greece and created this 'confederation.'"

It felt like longer. Time in the mountains moved differently, slower, heavier, as if the earth itself waited to see who would win.

I stood and moved to the narrow window. The valley below was still. The trees didn't move. Even the wind seemed afraid to stir. The sky looked too clean, too gold around the edges. "They're not calling it resistance," I said. "They're calling it terrorism."

Danica opened one of the larger maps and pinned it to the wall. Her fingers traced a line from Sarajevo to Skopje, then down toward the coast. "Of course they are. They've turned language into a weapon. Make people afraid of the truth and they'll burn it themselves." She tapped a circle outside Sarajevo. "Someone torched a broadcast tower last week, painted a spiral in the ash."

"Zorya," I said. The name still tasted like something sacred.

"Or someone who still remembers her."

We stood in front of the map. Red thread connected cities and ruins like veins. A burned archive in Skopje. A ruined basilica in Dubrovnik turned into a sanctuary. A commune deep in the Albanian hills where children were being taught names that hadn't been spoken aloud in generations. Most of the intel was fragmented, secondhand stories from travelers who stayed only long enough to pass a message before moving on, but something was building. It lacked the coherence of a movement, yet it was beginning to take shape.

Danica stepped back and surveyed the pattern she'd been stitching together for months. Her voice was low. "They can call it terrorism all they want," she said. "This isn't strategy. It's survival. It's people lighting matches in the dark because they refuse to forget what fire looks like."

I nodded, my chest tight. "And we're part of it."

She added a pin over Kraljevo and wrapped another line of red thread across the map. "We've always been part of it," she said. "That's what they're really afraid of."

We didn't sleep. The stillness that settled between us came from something deeper than fear or strategy, a restlessness born of knowing the world was changing while we fell behind it. I lay near the fire, using my coat as a pillow, watching the light shift along the ceiling beams. The shadows were still moving. I couldn't stop thinking about the list, my name on it, what it meant to be declared dangerous for remembering.

Danica sat against the far wall, knees pulled to her chest, her braid half undone, her journal open in her lap. She wasn't writing. Her gaze was fixed on the glow across the room, but her mind was somewhere else, listening for something she hadn't named yet. The silence between us stretched, but it didn't feel empty. It felt like pressure building.

She spoke without looking at me. "What did you believe in," she asked, "before all this started?" Her voice was direct. She wanted an answer.

I thought about it for longer than I should have. "Language," I said. "Because it gave shape to things. To thought, to history. It was how we remembered ourselves."

Danica nodded slowly. "Until someone like her showed up and made words meaningless."

"She didn't make them meaningless," I said. "She made them obey." That landed harder than I expected. I felt it in my teeth.

She looked at me now. "And what do you believe in now?"

"Memory," I said. "Because it's the only thing left they haven't fully rewritten. But if we lose that too, there's nothing left worth rebuilding."

She didn't respond. Her expression softened with empathy. We were both carrying memories we hadn't earned and couldn't escape.

When the last of the light had drained from the coals, I spoke again. "There's something I never told anyone."

Danica turned her head just slightly, giving me space to continue. "The night after my father died, I left the house and didn't stop. I followed the road until it gave way to the forest, then kept going, past every tree I thought I recognized, until even the air felt different."

"I found a clearing. A perfect circle of stones laid out like some ancient ritual. Then the flames appeared, five of them, floating, waiting. They were a presence, heavy, old, watching." Danica shifted forward, her knees still pulled in, her body alert.

"The first was covered in moss and antlers. His eyes were still water, and his voice came through the ground, like the trees themselves were responding." I pulled the coin from my pocket and held it out, watching how the firelight reflected across its surface.

"Then came a woman of gold and dusk with blossoms in her hair. She touched my chest and said, 'You will ache, and that ache will make you dangerous.'" Danica leaned in.

"The third came in thunder. A giant of fire and storm. He placed this coin in my hand and said, 'You'll fight without weapons and you'll be the last to kneel.'" I set it between us.

"The fourth was absence itself. A shadow on the world. She took the light with her when she passed, and the only thing she left behind was fear that belonged to nothing but me." I rolled back my sleeve and looked at the skin above my wrist, where the thread of red, gold, and black had once burned with meaning.

"The last were twins dressed in twilight and dawn. Zorya. They tied that thread around my arm and said, 'You are not chosen. You are returned.'"

Danica exhaled. Her hands trembled, but she didn't try to hide it. "You saw all five."

I nodded. "I thought it was all a dream."

Her eyes were glassy, but it wasn't disbelief. "You didn't imagine it. I've seen fragments of them in dreams and ruins, but never like that." She looked at the coin again with recognition rather than reverence. "They marked you early," she said. "That's why she's afraid of you."

I said her name even though I didn't need to. "Ana."

Danica kept her eyes on the coin. The silence between us felt like something sacred, a space that had been waiting for truth to fill it.

We didn't say anything more. I stretched out again near the fire. The cold had begun to reach through the stones, but I barely noticed it. When I finally slept, the dream didn't begin with me running. That was new.

The wind returned before dawn, but it didn't sound right. It moved through the trees like it was searching for something, too focused to be natural. The branches outside the stone slits creaked with slow resistance. Every so often the iron vent above the hearth let out a low groan, metal shifting under pressure it had never known before.

I woke before the light changed, my eyes already open when the first pale color spilled across the stone. My body felt stiff, weighed down by something settling over the room. The stronghold no longer felt like shelter. It felt like a question we had been trying to avoid.

Danica was already up. She stood by the mural in the far chamber, her hand pressed to the carved image of the tree. Her brow was furrowed, her posture tense but focused. She didn't flinch when I approached.

"It feels different," I said.

She nodded. "It's reacting now."

I looked at the carving beside her. The figures hadn't changed, but they felt sharper, less symbolic, more alive.

Danica drew back her hand slowly and stepped aside. I took her place. I touched the bark in the carving. Heat pulsed beneath my fingers, steady, deliberate.

"They're waking up," I said.

"So are we."

She crossed the chamber, opened the drawer beside the supply shelves, and pulled out the pouch of moss and ash that held the coin. She placed it on the table, then unwrapped the spiral stone. It shimmered faintly in the gray light coming through the high window.

"These things were never meant to stay hidden," she said. "We were meant to carry them."

The room was colder now, but I didn't move closer to the fire. The cold didn't feel hostile. It felt like the end of a delay.

Danica rolled up the journal pages and packed them into her satchel. She moved without rush, but with finality. We had stayed long enough. The world wasn't going to wait for us to feel ready.

"Do you think we're ready for this?" I asked, still facing the mural.

She paused mid-motion, then answered. "I don't know."

Her honesty landed heavier than reassurance could have. She joined me at the mural again, her hand brushing against mine briefly before falling away.

"I remember things," I said. "From before. Flashes, faces, words I've never spoken out loud."

"What do you see?"

"You," I said. "Always you."

Danica didn't respond immediately. Her fingers curled into the hem of her coat.

"In a temple," I continued, "draped in green. You were calling the sun through the stone. You weren't afraid. You were holding my name like it meant something."

Her voice held steady, but it trembled at the edges. "I think I've lost you too, more than once. But I always find you again."

We stood facing the wall, the gods above us carved in shape and silence. For a moment the air inside the stronghold felt too still.

"Do you feel it?" she asked.

I nodded. "The change."

The wind outside didn't howl. It pressed. The kind of pressure that meant a storm wasn't coming; it was already here.

We rose before the sun had cleared the peaks. There was no summons, no warning, just the certainty that staying any longer would become its own betrayal. The fire in the hearth had burned itself down to white ash. Neither of us made a move to rebuild it.

Danica was already dressed. She wore a dark green coat patched at the elbow, the same one she had worn when we first arrived, though now the fabric carried the scent of smoke and pine. A silver clasp pinned at her throat caught the faint light from the window, shaped like flame. It had been left behind by a traveler weeks ago, someone who hadn't stayed long enough for names.

She didn't speak as she packed. Her movements were methodical, unhurried. She rolled her maps and slid them into her satchel, layered her journal between folded cloth, tied the flap shut with a length of leather cord that looked older than the bag itself.

I gathered the relics. The spiral stone came first. I wrapped it in wool and dusted it lightly with salt, the way Danica had shown me. It had grown warmer over the past few days, humming faintly whenever I held it, as if it were responding to something I hadn't yet said aloud.

Next came the coin. I placed it back in its pouch of moss and ash, then cinched the cord and held it in my palm for a moment. It was heavier now, anchored, as if it carried the names no longer spoken and refused to let them be forgotten.

Then came the sketch. I unfolded the page slowly. The lines were rough, drawn in charcoal I didn't remember touching, but the image was unmistakable. A heart threaded with lightning, its edges frozen, its center burning from within. The storm-heart was real. I had seen it in a dream that still echoed behind my ribs, in the space just beneath memory. I folded the page and slid it into the center of Danica's journal. We didn't have the third relic yet, but we would find it. When we did, I would know it by the burn in my chest. Two relics secured, three still waiting. Enough to begin.

We ate the last of the bread in silence. Half an apple, a few swallows of tea. It was a ritual at this point, a way to mark the final moment before we became what the world had been trying to erase.

Danica rolled the last map and slipped it into her satchel. Then she turned toward the wall. I followed her.

The mural had darkened in the low light, its edges traced in shadow. The same figures, the same gods above them, but something had shifted overnight, as if the stone itself were leaning closer to listen.

I pressed my palm against the bark of the tree. The heat that met me was immediate. It was waiting. Danica stood beside me.

"I watched you die," I said. "You weren't afraid."

Her jaw tightened. "I've lost you too. In more lives than I can count. But I always find you again."

The bond between us didn't ask for proof. It waited for action. I wondered what it meant to find each other across lifetimes. My feelings for Ana were still there; you cannot spend almost a decade with someone and drop those feelings like a bad habit, or at least I can't. But this was different. I didn't yet understand my connection to Danica. Maybe it was the wars we'd fought together throughout history, or maybe this was something else entirely, a bond woven into the stars by Lada or Freyja. All I knew was that there was something different about Danica. Her smell, her hair, her eyes. My gods, her eyes. They were like looking into the cosmos for the first time, seeing the light of galaxies reflected back. Maybe this was love. I laughed at myself internally. Maybe I was going mad. Or maybe that was exactly why it felt different.

I refocused on leaving the stronghold; I needed to, at least for the moment. The fog outside was lifting as we stepped into it. The cold moved around us, as if clearing a path. Below, in the valley, bells rang in calculated intervals. They sounded like control. The air in the mountains was sharper than I remembered, and somewhere ahead, the third relic waited.

The trail wound downward through mist and frost, the stones beneath our leather shoes still damp with the night's silence. We didn't speak at first. We both knew where we were going.

The sketch burned in my mind, more vivid than any dream had the right to be. I could feel the storm-heart out there in the skin of the world, hidden beneath soil or myth or time itself. Wherever it was buried, it was calling.

Danica glanced at me as we passed the tree line. "You felt it last night, didn't you?"

I nodded. "Like it was inside me, but not yet mine."

Her grip on her satchel tightened. "It's close. The veil thins where it waits."

We followed the path as it twisted toward the high ridge, leather shoes kicking loose gravel into the ravine below. Behind us, the stronghold vanished into fog. Before us, the mountain widened into a wild, silent expanse.

A gust swept across the ridge, cold and sharp. No scent of pine, no noise, but something electric. My arm tensed. Danica felt it too.

She turned to me. "If we find it," she said, "you have to be ready."

I met her gaze. "I think I already am."

No more hiding. No more waiting for the gods to speak first. The storm-heart was out there. I could feel it beating beneath the bones of the land. When we found it, when I held it in my hand, I wouldn't be carrying Perun's power. I would be remembering my own. We pressed forward into the haze.

CHAPTER ELEVEN
THE STORM-HEART

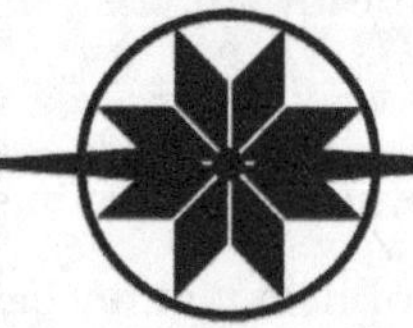

Ilija

We left the stronghold before the sun rose, both of us feeling it in silence, the knowing. The air between us had shifted, charged with memory pressing outward, something once buried clawing its way back into our blood. Danica walked slightly ahead, her pace steady, her breath soft and visible in the chill. Snow clung to the seams of her leather shoes as if reluctant to let her go.

I kept behind her by a few paces. She carried something new in her now, something undeniably alive, and so did I. We'd barely spoken since the basin, since the moment the world cracked open and the Heart chose us. Perhaps there were no words for what we'd become.

The wind cut low along the ridge, biting through the seams of my coat. I adjusted the strap of my satchel, still half-conscious of its weight. Inside sat the leather-bound journal and the cloth-wrapped spiral-stone, the sun-marked coin alongside a worn icon of Saint Sava that had belonged to my father. Every item held new meaning now that the relic lived in me, in my chest, beneath skin that still shimmered faintly when the cold hit just right.

Danica carried more than me, physically and otherwise. Her pack sagged with linen-wrapped offerings and a bone-handled compass, carved tokens, a dagger that smelled faintly of pine sap and old blood. I'd seen her sharpen it once, on the night we decided to leave. She'd said nothing as she did, just turned the blade over in her hands like she'd done it a thousand times across a thousand lives. Perhaps she had.

The trail east was little more than a ghost path, thin and broken, nearly swallowed by frost and time. It twisted upward first, then curved sharply around outcroppings of lichen-covered stone. The trees began to change as we climbed, pine fading to bare rowan, then to brittle branches bleached by wind. We climbed through the bones of the forest.

The trail had been abandoned for years, centuries even. The air shifted again when we reached the ridge, and Danica stopped. I stepped up beside her. Below us, the land unfurled in shades of gray and ash. A high mountain basin stretched into the distance, its mouth ringed by jagged stones and blackened soil. The sky above churned low and fast, heavy with something that felt like breath.

Then the lightning came.

A single bolt, wide as a tree trunk, tore down the center of the basin. It didn't strike but held, suspended midair, frozen in place as if caught in the act. For a heartbeat, the whole world glowed, and I saw every inch of the basin in stark, burning clarity. The ring of standing stones, the cracked earth webbed with old scars. In the center, a tall translucent pillar of ice pulsed with pale blue light.

The lightning vanished and silence fell over the ridge. Danica breathed, just once. "We're here."

My throat closed around an answer I already knew. The pull of it throbbed behind my ribs, the same pressure that had hummed through my skin since the shrine had closed, and it was waiting now, patient and immense. We started down together.

The descent into the basin felt like surrender. Each step dragged us further from the world we knew. The rocks beneath our leather shoes were brittle, the soil too black to be natural. Snow hung suspended here, drifting in slow spirals, dry and fine as bone dust, and silence swallowed everything, even our footsteps muffled as if the air had thickened with memory.

Danica's braid swayed as she walked, wind tugging at loose strands that had come free near her temple. She stayed silent, and I expected her to, because everything about this place was older than language. My breath came in shallow pulls, and I could feel the spiral-mark on my forearm begin to warm.

The roots and branches had given way entirely, leaving only stone and ice, and at the center, closer now, the pillar. It towered from the earth like something grown rather than carved. Glacial and faceted, nearly translucent, blue light pulsed inside it, slow and steady, a heartbeat buried in crystal. The circle of standing stones around it leaned slightly inward, as if they, too, were drawn to what lay beneath.

Danica slowed at the base of the pillar, her hand hovering just above its surface before she knelt and placed her palm directly against it. The stone answered with light.

She whispered something beneath her breath, to the ice. The language was foreign to everything I knew, every text I'd studied in decades of research, and it sounded older than all of them.

A low rumble answered and the ground shifted beneath us. I stepped back as the pillar cracked, a seam splitting down its center as light spilled out from within. The soil at our feet trembled, and lines carved themselves across the stone in a perfect spiral, radiating outward from the base of the pillar until the earth itself opened.

The spiral folded inward, petal by petal, an enormous bloom of black glass and frost. Mist poured upward from the gap, cold and metallic, curling around our ankles. Below, I saw the beginning of a stairwell, wide, carved from obsidian, rimed with ice that glimmered faintly blue.

Danica looked up at me, her face lit by the glow beneath.

I nodded, my chest tight. "We go together."

Her voice trembled when she finally spoke. "I've been here before, in dreams I couldn't remember when I woke up."

I nodded, throat dry. "Me too."

The mist rose higher, circling our legs. Behind us, the basin was already vanishing into haze. The world we'd come from was folding shut.

Danica stepped to the edge. "If we go down there, nothing stays the same."

I met her eyes. "Then let's stop pretending it ever did."

We descended into the spiral that had been waiting.

The air changed the moment we crossed the threshold, carrying metal now, myrrh, something far older, the breath of a sealed tomb opened after centuries of silence. The cold pressed close, a reminder that we were accompanied in this place, that these walls remembered us.

Every step downward tightened something in my chest. The spiral staircase wound into darkness, yet the mist itself guided us, shimmering faintly, pale blue with flickers of gold threading through it. I realized it was memory, all our past lives clinging to our skin, each flicker a forgotten echo.

Danica moved just ahead of me, her hand trailing along the wall in measured intervals, fingers brushing grooves that shifted as she touched them. The surface was never still. Runes emerged and disappeared in waves, glowing briefly before fading like breath against glass. Ancient alphabets surfaced in my thoughts, Glagolitic and Futhark, Ogham and scripts I had no name for, slipping away before I could catch them. The symbols resisted reading, as if they wanted only to be absorbed.

The deeper we went, the warmer the air became, alive with the breath of something ancient that recognized us. I felt it in the soles of my leather shoes and the knot behind my ribs, a slow, resonant hum pulsing through the air, trying to align itself with my heartbeat. When I reached out and let my fingers trace the wall, the stone pulsed under my skin and sent a jolt straight through my spine, bypassing pain entirely and landing somewhere deeper, somewhere that felt like pure presence.

Danica's voice drifted back, hushed and rough. "I don't think this place was carved."

I frowned, slowing. "Then what is it?"

She looked over her shoulder, the pale glow of the mist catching her expression. "I think it grew."

The thought stayed with me until we reached the final step. The spiral unfurled into a massive chamber, so vast its edges dissolved into dark. The floor beneath us was carved with five concentric rings, each one intersected by jagged lines that cracked like lightning. Sigils shimmered faintly in the stone, and the air held a tension that blurred the line between heat and cold.

Six obelisks ringed the chamber, each encased in smooth crystalline ice, a relic waiting within. Their shapes were hard to make out through the frost, some wrapped, some exposed, but all of them felt like memories suspended in cold.

At the very center, above a pedestal of fractured crystal, the storm-heart hovered, alive and turning. The jagged mass of blue crystal floated inches above the stone, shot through with veins of white lightning that pulsed like breath. Every flicker inside it echoed something in my chest.

Danica stood beside me, her voice barely more than a breath. "It's been calling us. All this time."

My gaze stayed fixed on the heart. "It's done waiting."

We stepped into the circle together, and the cold stripped pretense from skin and thought alike, biting into the marrow, dragging memory to the surface whether it was ready or not. Every sound dulled and every breath thickened until the space around the storm-heart pulsed with a silence so absolute it felt like a god holding its breath.

Danica slowed, her eyes locked on the crystal suspended above the pedestal, and I could feel her trembling with recognition. Her lips parted slightly, and I realized she had seen this too, maybe a different shape, but the presence, the pull.

"It knows us," I said, though my voice sounded foreign in this place.

She stepped forward without answering, moving until she stood at the edge of the pedestal, her hands clenched into fists at her sides. The light within the storm-heart flickered faster, the arcs of lightning growing brighter, stretching toward her.

I followed, drawn forward as if something inside me were unspooling, and the runes on my forearms burned through the fabric of my coat, answering the heart.

Danica turned toward me, her face pale, eyes wide. "This is where everything starts, again."

She could have meant the war or whatever we were becoming, and I knew she was right.

We reached for it at the same time, and there was no turning back. Our fingertips brushed the outer arc of the energy, and the crystal split down the center in slow, violent bloom. Light spilled out, blinding and endless, moving across the chamber, igniting the runes in the walls, sliding into every crack.

My breath stopped, and recognition flooded through me like a second heartbeat.

The light wrapped around us and my skin went translucent, the spiral marks glowing like wildfire beneath it. I saw my blood in lines of lightning, saw Danica's braid unravel as her hair lifted into the air, sparks cascading down her spine.

Half of the heart surged into my chest, piercing at first, then burning, then plunging into something deeper that had no name. It belonged there, and my body had forgotten how to hold it. The pressure inside me spiked, my ribs expanded, then cracked, and I screamed, because the sound was already in me and had been for lifetimes.

Across the pedestal, the other half struck Danica. Her back arched and her mouth opened in a soundless cry that filled the space with agony and rebirth. Her skin lit with runes that belonged to no single language, symbols of war and death inscribed across her body.

I reached for her, but the world collapsed first. The chamber cracked with thunder, the six obelisks shattering in tandem, their relics dissolving into ash as the shrine itself began to close with violence, folding inward until silence swallowed everything.

When I opened my eyes, I was lying on my back in the snow. The sky above me turned slowly, the clouds curled into spiral shapes, echoing the mark that now pulsed just beneath my ribs. My body felt scorched and alive, every vein glowing faintly blue, as if lightning had replaced my blood.

Danica leaned over me, her face damp with sweat, her hair wild. "You're alive," she said, her voice rough with disbelief.

I coughed and nodded, the air tasting of frost and copper. "So are you."

She helped me sit up. The pedestal was gone, the shrine sealed, the basin untouched around us, but we were changed. We stared at each other, and something passed between us that had no need for words. The rune spiraling along her jaw glowed faintly gold, and the breath I took next felt shared between us.

Words failed us both for a long time.

The world around us was silent, but inside me, everything screamed. My ribs still burned where the storm-heart had entered, my skin buzzing with residual power, with symbols I had no name for. The sky above us churned like it remembered its own birth, and Danica stood just beyond the seal of the shrine, her chest rising hard and fast, her eyes locked on mine. I moved to her slowly, everything in me rewritten, each step a kind of relearning.

She was trembling, her hair clinging to her temples, her braid loose and wild. The runes down her arms were fading, but the truth still bled through, because she was lit from the inside.

And I remembered. Gods help me, I remembered everything.

"Sigrún…" I said.

She looked up at me, eyes wet, voice barely controlled. "You fucking left me. Again."

I blinked. "I died…"

"In fire," she cut in. "In war. Every time. I kept coming back, Alatyr. I kept waking up without you."

The wind curled around us like it was listening.

"I tried to find you," I said, stepping closer. "I didn't know how. I didn't even know who I was…"

"You always find me," she said, her voice raw, breath breaking. "But you never fucking stay."

I reached for her, and she held still, grabbing my wrist and shoving it against her chest, where the heart had struck. I felt it still pulsing beneath her skin, still alive in her.

"We've died for each other a hundred times," she whispered. "I remember every goddamn one now. The temple. The mountain pass. I waited for you on a frozen fucking lake while my lungs filled with blood, and now we're here again, Alatyr. So what the fuck are you going to do about it?"

Words died in my throat because the pain in her eyes went deeper than grief, deeper into rage and hunger, and I wanted all of it. I wanted her, every version, every scar.

I pulled her to me, hard, and she slammed her mouth to mine like she'd been starving for centuries. It was savage, our teeth knocking, her nails scraping down my back, tearing fabric. I grabbed her hips, lifted her, and she wrapped her legs around my waist like she'd been waiting for me to carry her through every lifetime.

She gasped as I bit her lip, then laughed, feral and broken, shoving her hand into my coat and yanking it off my shoulders. We stumbled backward into the snow, and I knelt, then lowered her down onto the frost-thin ground. Her coat fell open beneath her, the snow melting around her skin, steam rising from where we touched. She tugged her shirt over her head, baring herself, and the runes across her collarbone sparked to life.

"You remember me?" she growled, breath heaving.

"Every fucking inch," I rasped.

I kissed my way down her throat, across the scar near her ribs, down to where she was already wet and shaking. Her hands tore at my belt. I shoved my pants down just far enough, and then I was inside her.

She cried out, hips arching, fingers digging into my back hard enough to bruise. I thrust into her like I could bury every year we'd lost, every life we'd been torn apart. She met me with equal fury, her breath ragged and desperate. The wind howled through the basin, but it couldn't drown her moans, couldn't mute the way she cried my name, this name, that name, names I'd forgotten were mine.

She rolled us, on top now, riding me like she meant to kill the past with every grind of her hips. I grabbed her waist to anchor myself as much as her. She leaned down and kissed me again, slower now, tongues sliding, heat growing unbearable. The pressure built between us, ancient and immense. When we came, it was together, her clenching around me with a cry like a curse as I poured into her like lightning finding ground. Light shimmered from our skin, pale blue and violent gold, and for a heartbeat, the snow stopped falling.

She collapsed beside me, curled into my side, chest still heaving. I held her, one hand tangled in her hair, the other against the place where the heart now lived beneath her skin, the air still humming with lightning around us.

Danica ran her fingers through my hair and whispered, "Do you feel it?"

I nodded against her skin. "We never stopped being them."

"No," she said, voice like flame. "We just forgot how to burn."

I looked up at her. "I love you."

Her voice cracked. "I know. Always."

We stayed there long after the storm faded from our blood. She lay curled beside me, head on my shoulder, her fingers tracing the runes across my chest like she was still trying to memorize them. I let her. My hand rested on her hip, my thumb brushing her skin in slow circles. The sky had lightened above us into something pale and waiting, and we lay in silence for a while, because everything worth saying had already been carved into our bodies.

I turned toward her, brushing a few strands of damp hair from her cheek. Her eyes met mine, raw and luminous, and for the first time since I woke from that first dream in Belgrade, I felt whole.

"I remember the night we fled the coast," I said softly. "You were wearing red, bleeding from the shoulder. I carried you down the cliffs."

Danica closed her eyes and nodded. "That was Thrace. We didn't make it. The ship was burned before we reached it."

I swallowed. "You died in my arms."

"And you screamed my name until the gods answered," she murmured. "They took you after that, reforged you in lightning."

I ran my hand slowly up her spine, feeling the curve of her, the warmth still radiating from beneath her skin. "Why didn't we remember sooner?"

"Because it would have broken us before we were ready," she said. "We weren't strong enough before now."

I kissed her forehead, then her temple, letting the silence stretch.

"We have to leave," I said eventually. "The storm told them."

Danica nodded against my chest. "Ana felt it."

I sat up slowly, the cold returning now that our bodies were no longer locked together, though my clothes could wait. I looked down at the faint blue spiral glowing over my sternum, because the storm-heart still held claim over me.

"What are we walking into?" I asked.

Danica rose beside me and pulled the long coat over her bare shoulders. Her braid was half undone, her skin marked with symbols I'd missed before, old and jagged, Norse, some of them looking like warnings.

"War," she said. "Ours."

I watched her as she moved toward the edge of the clearing, toward the place where the shrine had sealed itself beneath ice and rock, her posture anchored and fierce. She was becoming who she'd always been.

I stood, pulling my clothes on piece by piece, my muscles aching from the ritual and the weight of history settling into my bones. I glanced at her once more.

"We go to Ukraine?"

"Yes," she said without hesitation. "There's another relic there. I saw it when the Heart opened, buried near water. Frozen ruins. I think it's hers."

"Morana."

Danica nodded. "Death and rebirth. She's waiting."

My stomach knotted, because Morana was merciless in my dreams.

Danica stepped forward with her eyes fixed on the horizon. The name felt interchangeable now, Danica or Sigrún, both true. "We can't outrun her. We have to face her."

I walked to her side and took her hand, and it fit into mine like it had always belonged there. I looked out across the valley where the snow had begun to fall again, slower now, heavier.

"Then we go before she finds us first," I said.

Danica turned to me, her voice steady. "No. We go so she remembers who we are."

I felt only fire.

CHAPTER TWELVE
A SINGLE, RESONANT SOUND

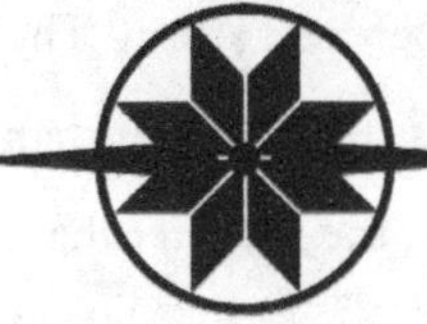

Ilija

The news of his death came to us in fragments, passed from roadside whispers to static-laced radio reports that never gave a name. From a northern village, a priest's account told of a body burned before sunrise, its secrets cauterized from the world before any physician was allowed to speak. In another town, a woman with trembling hands sketched a more mythic horror for Danica. Presidential blood had darkened to the color of rose petals. Greek letters glowed faintly on his cooling throat. She sealed the story with the sign of the cross, then offered an apology she could not explain. The official narrative, a sterile claim of a heart attack, arrived too late. By the time the capital announced the transition of power, there was nothing left of the man to examine. Only the hollow shape of his absence.

No official explanation was ever needed. The absence of detail was its own proclamation. In every story we heard, people lowered their voices when they spoke of how the body had been treated, then lowered them further when they described what followed. The streets of Belgrade grew quieter. The ministers bowed more deeply. On the night after the broadcast, the bells of Saint Sava rang thirteen times for an hour that did not exist, their unsanctioned chime left to hang uncorrected in the dark.

By then, we were already moving through the Pannonian Basin, where the air felt heavy, the light turned brittle. Though the villages looked unchanged, a stillness lay just beneath the surface, the kind that settles over a forest when animals freeze before a storm. The children wore white pins shaped like flames. The priests spoke longer than usual, never looking up from their scripts. In the cafés, the laughter that once spilled onto the streets had vanished. The chairs sat arranged with a precision that felt more like a warning than an invitation.

Danica noticed the changes before I did, her eyes lingering on the Watchers posted at bus stops, near the entrances to schools and libraries. They wore ash-colored coats, carried nothing but thin notebooks, yet moved through the world unchallenged. Their silence was its own authority. People shifted out of their way on instinct. Even in places where no sign had changed, where no law had been read aloud, the fear had already settled. It was sacred.

Every night, just before midnight, the loudspeakers installed across the town centers would release a single, resonant tone. It lasted only a breath, yet seemed to come from somewhere deeper than the metal above us, from beneath the earth, from beneath memory. No message followed, no words attached. Just a vibration that passed through the chest, leaving the world feeling slightly less our own. The radio broadcasts changed after that, the voice on the other end speaking more slowly each time, as though the words themselves had grown heavier. Reporters no longer asked questions. Their sentences sounded like prayers wrapped in protocol, until some broadcasts ended without warning, replaced by that same single tone stretching longer than it should have. We learned to stop listening when that happened.

It wasn't just here. Rumors, traveling faster than facts, carried news of a Moscow where the Russian flag had been darkened and re-inscribed with unfamiliar symbols, where the patriarch now issued executive orders beside the premier. In Washington, the changes had begun with pageantry. The president gave his address from beneath a cathedral of rotating scripture shaped from artificial light. Congress had been dissolved indefinitely, replaced by a new council of media and clergy, all appointed, whose decisions were spoken as doctrine.

They called it the Trilateral Accord on paper. No one we met ever used that phrase. What had formed between Ana's Confederation, Russia, and the United States was a chain, beautifully wrought, delicately fastened. The world had not been conquered. It had been seduced.

Even now, I do not fully understand how she did it. Her name was never spoken in the addresses. Her image never appeared directly. Yet I saw her presence lingering in the fabric of each new order. In every altered flag, in every sermon that shifted tone midway through, she had already arrived. The men who once ruled these nations had yielded because she gave them something they had been starved of. She made them long to offer their devotion freely.

I do not know what she is. I have seen her walk through fire, seen her image burn into the walls of dreams. Her face is never constant, her presence always absolute. Wherever she goes, people forget what came before, who they were without her. She is not mortal, and I have known that for some time. I have not learned how to name what lives beneath her skin.

She has turned Belgrade into a temple. The rumors we heard in the southern villages claimed the summit between the three leaders had been held beneath Saint Sava itself, in a chamber of black stone veined with gold, its ceiling shaped like the inside of a throat. The cathedral had been hollowed out from below to reveal a space no architect admitted to building, a place that had no origin, only purpose. They called it the Sanctum of the Flame.

We never saw it, only heard of it the way we heard everything else, through half-remembered conversations passed between tavern keepers and border guards who left the room mid-sentence. Every version of the story ended the same way. She did not walk into the room. She appeared in it. Russia's general, America's preacher-president, what remained of Serbia's last chosen man; they stood when she entered. None of them spoke first. A map lay in the center of the chamber, suspended by water, and where the leaders saw nations, she saw memories. She pointed to sites of myth and inheritance, explaining how Greece had already surrendered through ritual, its bishops kneeling while its children dreamed in her name.

They said she paused when Croatia flickered beneath her gaze, her eyes narrowing as the light on the map dimmed across the northern border. No one recounted her exact words, but they all remembered the shift in the room, the way the temperature seemed to drop when she pointed toward Zagreb and said there was one who still remembered the old names. Some claimed she called him the thread. Others said she never used a title at all, only let the silence stretch long enough that the men beside her filled it with mine.

The rest came to us on a grainy AM transmission from somewhere west of the Drina, the voice shaky, wrapped in static, yet clear enough to make my throat tighten. She had told them to spare me, for death would only make a martyr. Doubt, she had said, would undo me far more thoroughly. When I repeated the words aloud, Danica didn't look away. She reached into her coat, pulled out her journal, and turned the page.

That night, sleep would not come. I sat with my back to a lichen-covered stone, my bald head cool in the night air, turning the coin slowly in my hand while the fire between us burned down to embers. In the wet, metallic cold that settles just before dawn, Danica sat across from me with her arms around her knees, staring into the smoke. Her jaw was set, her eyes fixed somewhere past the flames, but her silence held something waiting to be said.

I asked her what was on her mind.

She didn't answer at first, her eyes following the sparks as they drifted into the darkness. When she finally spoke, her voice came out halting, pulled loose one word at a time. "I was seventeen when they came. I hadn't told anyone about the dreams yet, not even my grandmother, but they knew. Freyja stood beside the bed first, her presence making the room feel too small, like she was the only thing real, like everything else had to make space for her. Brigid came next, sitting at the edge of the mattress to place a thread in my mouth. She told me to hold it there until it burned, told me not to swallow it."

Danica looked down at her hands, expecting to see the scars. "I didn't know what they were preparing me for. I didn't know it would lead me to you, or to the rings." Her voice softened but didn't waver. "I think they were trying to remind me of something I had already promised."

I had no words that wouldn't shrink beside hers. She had carried this memory without question or proof, had walked beside me without demanding trust in return. I thought of the night I had stood before the five flames, of the way each god had branded something into my bones without permission or warning. We had both been chosen long before we found each other, but the choice no longer mattered. Only what we would do with it.

Danica stirred the fire with a stick, her gaze fixed on the shifting coals. "I don't think the rings are hidden in some distant shrine waiting to be retrieved. They're placed where love and death still hit hard enough for the gods to notice. We're meant to remember how to feel our way there."

The coin in my palm had gone still, no longer pulsing with the pressure of warning or fate. It was only warm and attentive. Something that no longer needed to lead, only to listen.

Danica rose first, packing her things with the slow, deliberate movements of someone preparing for a climb she had already made once in another life. I followed without speaking, for whatever waited for us now was a test of memory. We left the ravine before sunrise, the light not yet touching the ridge. Already I could feel a softness threaded with cold in the wind, as though a threshold had just been crossed.

Her mouth was already close to mine when the last light of the storm faded behind the trees. No words passed between us. There was nothing left to say that wasn't already written across our skin. The kiss began as recognition, soft and slow, but it did not stay that way. It deepened, surged. She pressed me back onto the moss-covered stone, climbing into my lap with thighs warm on either side of me, her breath catching between our mouths.

My hands slid up her back, under the thin linen of her shirt to find the truth of her skin, hot and alive. Her fingers, trembling with urgency, were already at my belt. I helped her, tugging her coat from her shoulders before lifting her shirt over her head, letting it fall forgotten into the leaves. In the dim light her breasts were flushed from the cold, from the heat between us. I kissed the curve of one as my hands moved down her waist. A soft gasp escaped her as she arched toward me. When I looked up, her pupils were wide, her lips parted. She looked feral and radiant, touched by something ancient, watching me as though she had chosen this, chosen me, because she wanted me here, now.

I dragged my mouth down her stomach, kneeling on the moss as I helped her out of her remaining clothes. She was already wet for me. I kissed the inside of her thigh, then again higher, until a sound I had never heard from her before, half whisper, half sob, broke the silence. Holding her hips steady, I lowered my mouth to her. She tasted of salt and fire. I licked slowly at first, savoring every quiet moan, every shift in her body as she tightened her fingers where my hair should have been. She ground against my mouth. I let her, giving her every part of me she wanted until her thighs trembled around my ears. When she came, she cried out my name as a claim.

She pulled me up to her after, her breath ragged, her mouth eager. She kissed me hard, tasting herself on my lips as her hands slid beneath my shirt, pushing it over my head. Her fingers trailed over the lightning-shaped scars on my chest. I felt them glow faintly under her touch. We didn't stop to speak. She guided me onto my back, straddling me again as she reached between us, her grip certain. When she sank down onto me, the world narrowed to the place where our bodies met. We both gasped.

She rocked her hips slowly at first, then faster, riding me with a need that had nothing to do with prophecy. My hands gripped her, guiding her rhythm as we moved together, the way we had in other lifetimes. Maybe this was every version of us choosing each other again. I sat up, held her close, pressing kisses to her neck while she buried her face in the thick red hair of my beard, her nails leaving light trails over my back as she clenched around me.

"I love you," I said, the words barely a breath against her ear.

She looked at me then, truly looked, and the way her face broke open with that single look shattered something inside of me. "I've always loved you," she whispered. "Even when I forgot."

I thrust up into her, harder, deeper. She moaned against my mouth. When we came together, it felt as if something sacred had snapped and rewoven itself around us.

Afterward, we stayed tangled in each other, skin damp, hearts pounding, her fingers tracing the edge of my jaw as though she were afraid I'd vanish. "I'm not going anywhere," I murmured.

She smiled against my shoulder. "I know. Neither am I."

We dressed slowly, from a shared reluctance to break the stillness. My shirt clung to my skin. Our hands brushed more than once as we gathered what we had shed in the dark. When she pulled her coat back on, I stepped behind her, ran my hands down her arms, and rested them at her waist. She leaned back into me with a sigh.

"Well," she began, her voice a little hoarse. "That certainly didn't suck."

"Didn't suck?" I said into her neck, feigning offense. "Madam, that was a masterclass. Decades of practice went into that performance."

She laughed, a quiet, breathy sound, still raw. She turned in my arms, kissed me again, slow and lingering. "It was the best I've ever had."

I grinned, brushing a stray leaf from her cheek. "It better have been. My beard is going to smell like you for a week."

She rolled her eyes, but a flush crept up her cheeks. "You're insufferably smug when you make me come twice."

"Only twice?" I raised an eyebrow. "I must be getting rusty." I leaned closer. "That's not why I'm smug. I'm smug because I love watching you fall apart. You're beautiful when you come. Fierce as hell."

Her smile faded a little at that, replaced with something deeper. She looked at me for a long moment, her fingers resting at my collarbone. "You always say that."

"Because it's always true."

We stood like that for another minute, just breathing while the wind picked up around us. The storm was gone. The grove had quieted. Whatever had awakened in the roots and stone had settled again, waiting. I reached into my pack, pulled out the map. She came to stand beside me, our shoulders touching as her eyes scanned the worn paper.

"Ukraine," I said. "That's where the next relic is. The rings. Love and death."

"Lada and Morana," she said quietly. "I know."

We folded the map and started walking, the forest thinning as we found the old road. We didn't talk much at first, our bodies still remembering what we had just done, every glance feeling heavier now, charged. Her hand brushed mine once, then again. She took it in hers and didn't let go. By the time we reached the gravel rise leading out of the basin, the first grey light of morning bled into the sky. The cold was sharper here, the world stretched wide before us.

Danica pulled her hood up. "You really think we can do this? Walk into the heart of another collapsing country to find a pair of mythical rings?"

I looked back down the trail, at the grove and the stone that still hummed under our skin. Then I looked at her, at everything we had already survived. "It's a terrible plan. What's not to love?"

She nodded once, then kissed me again, quick and firm. "Good. Because I'd have to drag your stubborn ass to Ukraine even if you tried to back out."

"You'd try," I said, squeezing her hand. "But my ass is impressively stubborn. You'd probably give up halfway."

We walked into the cold together, hand in hand, the wind rising around us. We made it out of the basin by dusk, into a light drained of warmth, more ash than gold. The land lay hollow, gutted of something sacred, swept clean. Villages sat quiet in that uneasy stillness that follows panic, their windows sealed tight, their doors bearing painted symbols I did not recognize. The dogs that watched us pass did not bark. They followed, low to the ground, ribs sharp, eyes empty. From a barn with its doors ajar, an old state radio crackled, the announcer's voice a smooth false calm, a man soothing a room while hiding blood on his hands.

"…terrorist activity linked to folkloric cultism continues to rise. Citizens are reminded that unauthorized artifacts, ritual markings, and mythological gatherings are prohibited under Confederation statute. Individuals found in violation may be subject to divine remediation…"

I adjusted the dial on our transmitter, catching other frequencies, some clear and official, others just threads of sound between static, voices trying to survive the sweep. All of them carried the same story. Realigning territories. Towns handed over. Clergy-military checkpoints replacing civic buildings. Churches once filled with saints now bore red banners with the new sigil, a half-sun bleeding over a sharpened crown. Ana had moved quickly. The Confederation answered to her. Russia had aligned with her before the summit closed. America had been seduced rather than conquered. I could see how she had done it, for I had seen her look at men as if they were already hers, watched them bend without realizing they'd kneeled. No human carried that kind of fire without being consumed. She carried it, made others burn instead.

Danica walked beside me, her hand occasionally brushing mine, the tension coiling in her shoulders each time Ana's name drifted from a prayer or a passing radio.

"She's rewriting the world," I said.

Her voice was calm, her jaw tight. "She's not rewriting it. She's bending it back toward something she believes is owed."

"You think she always wanted this?"

"She was made to want it," she said. "Or made into it. That's worse."

We passed a family taking shelter under a crumbling overhang, their forms huddled around a single blanket. The man wore the Confederation's emblem stitched in red thread on his coat. He watched us with wary, silent eyes. No one begged. No one trusted anything outside the new order.

"She's using my name," Danica said suddenly, her voice low. "On the broadcasts. In the liturgies. They call me the Betrayer. The seductress who tried to draw their savior into ruin."

Bitterness sharpened my voice. "Because she's afraid of you."

Danica didn't respond, but when we reached the edge of the ridge, she took my hand and didn't let go. We walked until night fell, then kept walking, for the roads had become unreliable, the signs painted over, the gas stations converted into makeshift shrines. In one village, a boy no older than twelve pointed a rifle at us, his eyes hollow, the Confederation's sun stitched into his jacket like a blessing. We kept our hands visible. Left as soon as we could. Danica never once looked back.

By the third day, we found a forest road that hadn't yet been claimed, the wind smelling of wet pine and ash. The farther we got from the towns, the more the air cleared, but there was no peace in its silence. Something had been stripped from the land, as though the stories were being erased along with the people who carried them.

Danica stood on the crest of a ridge, scanning a treeline that rolled into shadow. "This was never supposed to be just Serbia," she said. "It was always meant to spread."

"She didn't start the fire," I said. "She just walked through it like it was hers."

"She lit it the moment they gave her a name to hide behind."

I joined her at the edge of the ridge, watching the mountains beyond. Somewhere past that horizon lay Ukraine, the next relic, the next truth. The rings of love and death. "She knows we're awake now," I said.

Danica nodded. "She probably felt it the moment we touched the storm-heart."

The quiet that fell between us was tired, the kind that settles in your bones when you know there is still more to survive. That night, we made a small fire behind a fallen oak, ate what we had left. Stale bread. Dried meat. Water that tasted of rust. Danica lay beside me in the dirt, her head on my shoulder, her hand against my chest, the heat of her skin reaching me even through the grit. Her breathing was steady. Mine was not.

I turned slightly, kissed her temple. "You know this ends with us killing her," I said.

She opened her eyes, the fire casting gold across her cheeks. "Or she kills us," she replied. "But either way, we end it."

The crunch of tires on gravel shattered sleep. A single engine, perhaps two, heavy enough to vibrate through the frozen ground. My eyes flew open, met Danica's. She was already pulling the fire blanket over the dying coals, smothering their story, her hands steady in the half-light. My heart hammered against my ribs. I slid the knife from my boot, dropped into a crouch behind the fallen log that had been our shelter, its rough bark the only armor I possessed. The engine cut off. Then came the voices, speaking Serbian with the clipped, rehearsed precision of the regime's military. Low. Deliberate. Clergy-military. Trained.

Danica moved up the slope first, slipping through the brush without a sound. I followed, careful not to crack a single branch, every heartbeat a countdown I couldn't slow. A flashlight beam passed over the place where I had been lying moments before.

"These tracks are fresh," a man said. "Less than a few hours."

A woman's voice, unsettlingly calm, replied. "We don't move on a hunch. Confirm visual. If either carries relics, we wait for the signal before engagement."

A burst of static. A quick exchange of numbers. Then a silence filled with the shuffle of boots and the click of weapons. I didn't need to see their faces to know they were surgical, that they were tracking something they already owned. Danica reached the ridge first, motioned for me to follow. Below, at least three armed figures moved with coordinated steps, their certainty chilling.

"They know it's us," she whispered. "That wasn't a patrol. That was a fucking acquisition squad."

"They must have intercepted something," I muttered. "The monastery… the relic…"

"They've been closing in since before the basin. We were too focused on what's ahead."

I glanced east, toward the mountains that rose into shadow, the only way left for us to go. Danica adjusted the strap of her pack. "We'll go through the forest. Stay off any visible trail, keep to the trees, no fire."

"They'll expect that."

"I don't care what they expect. I'm not letting them catch us."

We plunged into undergrowth that tore at our legs, slipping on ground made treacherous with frost, never slowing as the cold burned harder with every step. We were no longer travelers. We were being hunted. The forest thinned as we pushed forward, the slope beneath us turning slick with fractured stone. I could hear the pursuit behind us, distant but purposeful, the kind of chase that wastes no energy because it is certain of the kill. Danica veered off the trail, pulling me down into a gully tangled with wet leaves. We crawled through thorns until the ground rose again, narrowing into a cleft between two rock faces. She ducked in first. I squeezed through behind her, scraping my shoulder on the stone.

Inside, the air was cold, thick with the stillness of a place untouched by years. The gap widened into a narrow chamber where roots hung from the ceiling; moss clung to the walls in dark patches. We pressed ourselves against the stone and listened to the footsteps and sharp commands passing above us. Danica held still, her eyes fixed on the dark. My hand stayed near my knife, knowing it would be useless if they found us here. The voices passed. The footsteps faded. We stayed silent until the woods settled around us again.

Danica let out a long breath, the strain showing in her posture. A fresh streak of blood marked her wrist where the rocks had scraped her.

I sat beside her, the stone cold through my coat, reached for her hand. "Cozy," I murmured, my voice a dry whisper. "You pick the best hiding spots."

She glanced at me, a flicker of a smile touching her lips before vanishing. "Better than being on the end of a rifle. Don't complain." She let me take her hand.

"They'll keep searching," I said, my voice returning to a low murmur. "We're not far enough ahead."

She nodded slowly. "Then we don't stop moving."

Outside, I knew they were circling. Inside the hollow, with her beside me, something older than fear settled over us, as though we had stumbled into a place ancient enough to remember us. We had survived the day, but the hunt had only just begun. We stayed there until the light began to shift, the silence between us changing from urgency to the low hum of shared memory.

"There was a winter like this once," she said eventually, her voice calm. "A long time ago. We were hiding in the Carpathians. You'd taken a sword through the thigh. I couldn't feel two of my fingers from the cold."

"I remember that," I said. "You were insufferable. Kept telling me to stop bleeding on your cloak."

"It was a good cloak," she said, her tone matter-of-fact. "You kept asking if we'd survive. Every five minutes."

"I was delirious. You kept telling me we would, even when you weren't sure."

"There was another time," I said. "Somewhere north. A coastal village. You wore red, carried a curved blade. I followed you into a skirmish, woke up days later without you."

She didn't respond right away. Then she turned to me, her eyes clear. "I never left. You just didn't wake up where I did."

The ache behind her words was familiar, though I didn't remember that life fully. The emotion always came back before the history. "We've done this before," I said. "Running. Finding each other."

She nodded. "Losing each other." A fact we had both known but hadn't spoken aloud.

I shifted against the stone, my shoulder brushing hers. "I want this to be the time we hold on."

"It has to be," she said. "We don't get another."

The cold eventually crawled through our coats again, reminding us that stillness couldn't last. Danica stood, slow and deliberate, stretching out her legs before checking the weight of the pack. "We'll leave at dusk," she said. "Cross the ridge before moonrise. The eastern valleys should still be quiet."

"What then?"

"We get to Ukraine," she said. "We find the rings."

I stood beside her. My legs were stiff, but the motion helped. I looked once more at the narrow entrance behind us, overgrown, easily missed. It would close behind us like it had never been there. Just another place that had sheltered us for a while before the next storm.

"Let's keep moving," I said.

She nodded. "Let's go."

CHAPTER THIRTEEN
"STAND STILL, STAY HOLY"

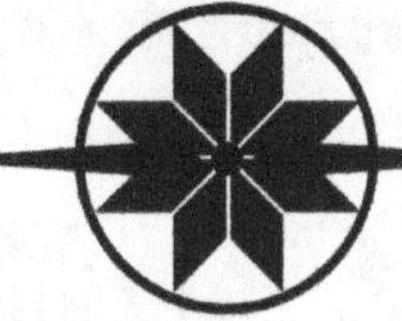

Ilija

The frost came silently, a memory returning to a place that had been waiting too long. It touched the earth with gentle reverence, coating the broken stones of an old Roman road in silver, collecting in the hollows of forgotten hoof prints. The breath of a god too old to wake, a slow exhalation across the hills that reminded the world of a cold it had nearly let go.

I noticed it before she did, crouching beside a crumbling brick to study a single curled leaf trapped beneath a skin of ice. By all logic it should have blackened and rotted, but it was preserved whole, as though time itself had paused to spare it. When my fingertip brushed its edge, the frost shattered like spun glass, the sound so faint it registered only as a feeling.

Danica moved ahead, her stride sure-footed even as the ground grew slick with this strange rime. The land seemed to open for her, accepting her weight as though welcoming a long-lost daughter. She kept her eyes forward, trusting the shared pull between us. I felt the same stirring in us both, the Heart buried deep within our bones, pulsing again in a quiet, persistent hum beneath the skin that said we are still here.

The Pannonian Basin opened before us like the chest of a body left unburied, its silence tangible. The wind drifted here, slow and watchful. The trees bowed low, as if answering a voice only they could hear. Danica pulled her shawl tighter, and I fell into step behind her, our movements a silent conversation. Since the shrine, she had carried herself differently, as if the land now remembered her more clearly than she remembered herself. The toll showed in the weary set of her shoulders, the way she held her jaw tight against something she refused to name.

By midday, we passed the remains of a village whose buildings had long since collapsed inward. I paused near what had been a schoolhouse, its bell half-swallowed by rust and frozen grass. As I ran my hand along the stone doorframe, the lightning inside me flickered in answer, a soft, familiar tremor. Ahead, Danica had stopped near the broken edge of a roofless chapel. On the ground beside its foundation lay a wreath of dried lavender. Someone had placed it deliberately, with a care that defied the desolation. The stems were brittle, the color faded, but the scent still lingered like a ghost in the cold air.

She knelt, her voice a low murmur against the quiet. "This shouldn't be here. Not in this season."

I joined her, crouching, and the faint thread of scent became a torrent. My grandmother's blanket. The room where my father died. All of it hitting me in a single, violent wave. My heart hammered against my ribs, and I stood quickly, turning away before the memories could pull me under.

Danica remained kneeling, one hand pressed flat against the cold stone beside the wreath, grounding herself in the present. "I think the land is remembering, too."

I kept my eyes on the frozen hills, nodding. "Leaving pieces behind for us to find."

The longer we walked, the stranger the land became. Pines thinned and gave way to ash trees whose bark peeled in curling strips like old parchment. Shadows lengthened even when the sun still sat high, and our footsteps echoed faintly across the frozen earth, returned by something other than walls. The very air around us held still, charged and expectant.

We eventually reached a pasture, a flat, open expanse bare of fence or structure. At its center stood a horse.

"Well now," I murmured, stopping short. "You don't see that every day."

For a moment, I was certain it was alive. It stood perfectly still, ears pricked, its dark mane caught in an invisible breeze. Its eyes were open, its posture alert, poised. But as Danica stepped closer, her boots crunching softly on the rime, the illusion dissolved. The thing was dead. Preserved, its skin stretched and lacquered over a hollow frame, stitched back together with meticulous care into a stance meant to outlast centuries.

Danica came to a stop beside it, her breath clouding faintly in the air. "This wasn't done recently."

"No," I said, circling its flank, the frost catching in my red beard. "But it was meant to be seen. Meant to last."

A wooden sign had been nailed to a crude stake and driven into the frozen earth at the horse's feet. The letters had been burned deep into the wood, black and unforgiving:

THE OLD GODS ARE DEAD

STAND STILL

STAY HOLY

Danica stared at the words, her hands curled into loose fists at her sides, a quiet tension coiling within her. I stepped up to the horse, reaching out to press my hand against its side, expecting the deep cold of ice and dead leather.

I flinched back as if I'd been burned. It was warm. A low, persistent heat radiated from it, a mockery of life.

I looked at her, my voice low. "It shouldn't be."

Danica's gaze remained fixed on the placard. "Neither should we," she said, a dry, weary wit in her tone. "I suppose we're all breaking the rules."

The air shifted, the cold deepening instantly. Something ancient and heavy pressed in like the walls of a sealed tomb. I stepped back from the horse, away from its false warmth.

"We should keep moving."

Danica stayed silent. She stepped past the unnerving monument and walked toward the dimming light. I followed, and we kept our eyes forward.

Night bled into the sky unannounced as the last of the sun slipped behind the basin's rim. The wind slowed to a hush, and even our footsteps seemed quieter, absorbed by the frost as pale stars emerged. We walked in silence, our movements speaking for us. Each step forward felt like crossing into an older version of the world, a landscape we had left behind lifetimes ago.

The frost beneath our boots began to glow with a faint, phosphoric light, and our footprints lingered longer than they should have, impressions of light, as if the land itself were memorizing our passage.

Sometime past midnight, we came upon the ruins of an old rail station. Fire had gutted the buildings, but their skeletal frames still stood against the stars. Rusted rails ran off into tall grass, disappearing beneath frost-bitten roots while a collapsed signal tower lay like a broken limb across the tracks. Above the main platform, the remains of a ticket hall opened to the night sky like a cracked mouth.

Danica stepped through a warped doorway first, her silhouette framed by climbing vines. I followed her inside. The cold clung to the air here, watchful, familiar. In what had once been a stone ticket booth, she knelt on the frost-covered floor and pulled her journal from her pack. She opened to a blank page with certainty, her fingers stiff but sure as she began to sketch.

I settled against the opposite wall, my back to the cold stone, and closed my eyes. Rest came hard these days. After a few minutes of her quiet scratching, I asked, "What masterpiece are you creating now?"

Danica kept her eyes on the page. "The horse. The sign. Something else."

She held out the journal. The horse was there, exactly as I remembered it, rigid, its mane swept by a phantom wind. But behind it, in the shadows of the crosshatched trees, she had drawn two faint figures. One was wreathed in a crackle of lines that could only be lightning. The other was wrapped in a mist that suggested something colder than fire, a power held in deliberate restraint.

My throat tightened. It was us. "You didn't mean to draw them."

She shook her head, her eyes still on the page. "My hand moved on its own. I only saw them after I finished."

I handed the journal back. "Then maybe it wasn't your hand."

She finally looked at me, something dark and ancient in her gaze. "I'm starting to wonder if anything in me still belongs entirely to me."

"I feel the same," I said, the truth of it landing like a stone in the quiet between us.

A soft breath of wind moved through the ruin, brushing across the stones like a hand remembering its way through an old room. The frost crept in again from the corners, its tendrils crawling toward us as if the place held them in its memory.

Danica closed her journal. "Something is building."

"What do you feel?"

She was quiet for a long moment, watching the ice advance. "As if we're walking through a ritual that started long before we were born. Every ruin, every silence. It all feels deliberate."

I looked down at my palms. The storm inside them had gone quiet since the shrine, coiled and restless. It paced behind a locked door. "It's the same for me," I said. "The world is remembering us."

Her eyes stayed on me, wide and knowing. We both felt it then. Whatever had begun was happening because of us.

We reached a wide clearing just before full dark as the sky above turned the color of ash. Across the field, a shallow stream cut through the earth, its surface glassed over with a thin layer of ice, and a simple stone bridge arched over it like a sleeping spine. The wind had gone completely still. Even the trees ringing the clearing leaned inward, like witnesses gathered for something sacred.

Danica stepped beside me, her own breath a visible plume in the air. "We're being watched."

I already felt it. The presence was faint but rooted, like memory pressing in from the edges of the world. My gaze scanned the far side of the bridge, and there, between one breath and the next, the figure appeared.

It was simply there, a shape that felt foreign to the clearing yet seemed as though it had always been waiting. It held an outline rather than a solid form, eyeless, mouthless, its edges shimmering in the dim light. The echo of a body that had once known form and since outgrown it. A memory given substance, something forgotten struggling to be remembered.

I took a step forward, and the lightning inside me stirred in response, threading beneath my ribs as an answer, a recognition.

Danica held still. Her breathing was steady, and the frost at her feet thickened, crawling up her boots until a perfect ring of ice formed on the ground beneath her. "It isn't here to hurt us," she said, her voice low and even.

I nodded, my eyes fixed on the apparition. "It came to see if we remember."

The figure remained still, suspended in a way that made the air bend slightly around its edges, as though the world itself was still deciding if it should be allowed to exist. Danica raised her chin, frost clinging to her lashes. The fire that lived in her pulsed just beneath her skin, visible only as a faint shimmer behind her eyes. The storm moved unbidden now, curling along my shoulders and down my arms in a quiet pattern that belonged more to instinct than to will. Above us, the stars seemed to ripple, as if they too recognized the meeting.

The figure held for a moment longer, then began to unravel. It folded in on itself, its shape collapsing inward, its edges curling like old paper at the touch of a flame. One moment it stood as an echo of a body. The next, there was only a shallow impression in the frost where it had been.

Danica stepped forward, her expression unreadable as she looked at the empty space. "It wasn't a threat."

"No," I replied, walking to join her on the bridge. "It was a reminder."

We crossed the bridge in silence, the ice beneath our boots holding firm as if it had been expecting our weight. On the other side, we made camp in the lee of the tower ruins, where the stones still held a phantom heat from the vanished sun. We unpacked in silence. Danica gathered a small pile of dry kindling, but the fire refused to catch. She struck flint against steel, coaxing the brittle bark with breath warmed by the Heart inside her, but the sparks died against the cold air.

The place itself refused it, a stillness so sacred it would permit only silence.

She set the flint aside. Instead, she sat beside me near the wall, drawing her knees to her chest and pulling her shawl tighter. Her gaze was fixed on me, present, steady. Above us, the stars continued their slow drift into new constellations. I noticed the one that resembled a single, watching eye was gone. In its place, a spiral had begun to form.

Danica broke the silence, her voice soft. "Do you think it will come back?"

I leaned my head back against the stones. "No. It saw what it needed to."

She nodded once. "Proof that we remembered."

She shifted slightly, her voice dropping even lower. "I keep thinking I'll wake up and it will all be gone. That I'll just be me again, without it."

I turned to her. "But it's still there."

"Every time I breathe," she confirmed. "It's like another heartbeat, but brighter. Something other than blood."

I looked down at my own hands, watching the faintest pulse of light dance along my knuckles. "Mine feels like pressure. Like the start of a storm, just beneath the skin. Sometimes it moves with me. Other times it acts on its own, like it knows more than I do."

"Maybe it does," she whispered, pulling her shawl tighter around her shoulders.

I met her eyes in the dim starlight. "Does it scare you?"

A long moment passed before she answered. "No. But it humbles me."

I nodded slowly. "That's the right word."

We fell into a deeper silence then, one of complete understanding. The quiet settled around us as the Heart between us listened.

The shared quiet held us for a time, but the cold was a patient predator. We rose, the stiffness in our bones a reminder of how little rest we'd truly gotten. As we shouldered our packs and started walking away from the silent tower, the memory of the hunters we'd faced before returned, colored by the strange holiness of this place.

"They were speaking in commands," I said, my voice low in the stillness. "But it wasn't military. It sounded like a sermon being recited under breath."

Danica's eyes stayed forward, watching the frost form thin white veins along the roots of the trees. "She didn't need to take the barracks by force," she said, her jaw tight. "She only had to stand in front of them and let them believe."

"She got to them early," I continued, the thought solidifying. "Before any accords were signed. While the rest of us were still asking questions, she was whispering certainty into their ears. She doesn't issue decrees. She breathes conviction, and men will kill for that faster than they ever would for orders."

Danica looked at me then. "You think she seduced all of them?"

I nodded slowly, my own breath leaving a pale stream in the air. "I think, whatever she is, they don't serve the woman. They serve a vision she gave them."

She turned back to the path. "They see us as the ones trying to tear it down."

"They're not hunting fugitives," I said, the final grim piece clicking into place. "They're cleansing unbelievers."

Danica stayed silent, but I saw the way her hands tightened around the leather strap of her pack. She walked faster after that, her head low against the cold as the frost clung to everything, as if trying to preserve what little remained of a world already disappearing.

We crossed another stretch of ruined farmland where collapsed fences lay like broken skeletons in the frost. What remained of life had been reduced to fragments, scorched posts and shattered glass, an overturned trough half-buried in mud and ice. In the distance, a cluster of birds lifted into the sky in eerie silence, their wings catching the dim light like old coins scattered on the wind.

Danica slowed as we passed a row of trees bent low by age, their branches heavy with ice. "Do you remember this stretch?"

I looked around, truly looked, and the pieces felt unnervingly familiar. The hill to the east, the broken farmhouse leaning to one side like a corpse refused a grave. "From a dream, I think."

"More than a dream," she said, her voice quieter now, firmer. The tone rose from the deep ache left behind when memory has been taken. I knew that ache too well.

The words came to me slowly, pulled from a place I had forgotten I could access. "There was a child here," I said. "Dark hair, frostbitten fingers. She carried a bird in her hands."

Danica nodded, her eyes fixed on the leaning farmhouse. "You were behind her. Your cloak was wet with blood, but you didn't stop to bind the wound. You just kept walking."

She kept her gaze on the farmhouse as she said it, and I was grateful. Whatever lived in my face felt ancient. I stepped past her, letting the wind strike my face full on. The cold passed through me as though I were already part of the landscape. Something else had settled inside me, older than cold and deeper than pain.

Ahead, a low ridge rose from the land, crowned with the faint silhouette of a watchtower that had long since collapsed, its remains sprawled across the slope like a forgotten warning. We stopped beneath its shadow and looked back the way we'd come. Smoke curled faintly in the distance. Too far to smell, but close enough to mark, the steady, patient breath of something that hunted at its own pace.

"They're still behind us," Danica said, stating a fact we both knew.

"Close?"

She shook her head. "Not yet. But they're coming."

I watched the glowing impressions of our footprints disappear behind us, the trail swallowed by wind and time. We were meant to walk forward, always forward. "We should find shelter before nightfall," I said.

Danica turned toward the ridge. "There's something beyond this. I don't know what, but it's waiting."

The climb was gentle, but the soil was loose, churned by hooves or boots long absent. As we reached the top, the sky opened wider above us, and tucked into the hollow between the hills stood the remnants of another village. It was smaller than the others, half-swallowed by the trees, with roofs that bowed under frost. Only abandonment had left its mark.

Danica exhaled slowly. "This isn't on any map."

I adjusted my pack. "Then it's probably where we're meant to be."

The village was utterly still. Silent chimneys, empty yards. Only the shape of buildings softened by frost and the particular hush that follows soldiers. Danica kept her pace, moving toward the center of the lane with deliberate steps, her shoulders squared against the silence. I caught up to her.

"Do you think they already passed through here?"

Her eyes scanned the empty windows, lingering on worn footprints pressed into the path like shallow graves. "I think they passed through recently," she said, her voice low. "They didn't leave empty-handed."

We reached what had once been a market square, where a rusted cart lay overturned. The dead were elsewhere, but absence carried its own gravity. On a wooden bench, a bowl had been left behind, half-filled with something frozen solid. Danica knelt beside it, brushing her fingers over the rim.

"Someone ran in a hurry," she observed. "But they didn't fight."

"No one fights," I said. "Not when the uniforms are clean and the orders come from Saint Sava."

She looked up at me, her expression grim. "It's worse than fear. They think this is sacred."

I nodded. "That's the trick. She didn't conquer them with armies. She took them with awe."

Danica stood and turned toward the path that led eastward again. "Awe always demands sacrifice."

We walked on, leaving the empty square behind us. The world was already speaking in the silence, in absence, in the cold that kept reaching for our skin and finding it changed. We followed a narrow track out of the settlement, past an old well covered in splintered boards and a statue whose face had been chiseled off long ago. The original god was irrelevant now. The gods who survived had rewritten the prayers.

Danica glanced over her shoulder, her gaze distant. "They'll be circling back soon."

I already felt the shift, the wind curling differently across the back of my neck. Somewhere behind us, boots were already retracing their steps, their owners' eyes sharp with the chilling clarity of obedience.

"I thought I'd be angrier," I said, the admission surprising me. "Seeing all this. What she's done to these places, what they've made sacred."

Danica stepped over a frozen root, her focus on the path ahead. "I'm beyond anger," she said. "It doesn't burn the way it used to. It settles deeper now."

I knew exactly what she meant. The hot fury had cooled and hardened into something else, heavier, colder, sharper. A blade, honed by everything we'd seen.

We crossed a stretch of field where rows of corn had once grown. Now the stalks were broken and blackened, as if the frost had reached too deep, too fast. Ahead, the land dipped into a narrow pass between the hills. The world itself seemed to hold its breath.

Danica slowed, her eyes fixed on the ridge that loomed before us. "They'll be waiting for us there."

I touched the frost-covered stones along the path. They hummed faintly beneath my fingers, a vibration so quiet it might have been only the trembling of my own blood.

"I know," I said. "But we're not walking into a trap. We're walking into memory, and memory is on our side."

Danica nodded once, sharp and determined. Together, we stepped into the pass.

The pass opened into a wooded hollow where the trees grew thick and the wind lost its voice. Nestled between the pines stood a lodge, old but still standing, its timbers weathered to a dark gray. The windows had long since lost their glass, but the door held fast on rusted hinges, and the stone foundation remained solid beneath a crust of frost and root.

Danica approached first, pressing her palm to the door as if asking permission. It swung open on a long, groaning complaint, revealing a single wide room dusted in leaves and ash. A hearth sat cold against the back wall, and the remnants of a cot leaned crooked in one corner.

"Home sweet home," I murmured, stepping in after her, my boots echoing softly on the boards. The air smelled of pine and old smoke, and something else, a trace of memory that clung to the stones like breath left behind.

"It has four walls and no bullet holes," she replied without turning, her voice flat with an exhaustion that went bone-deep. "It's a palace."

She set her pack down and moved to the hearth. She sat by the cold stone, drawing her knees to her chest. I lowered myself beside her, the silence between us heavy and welcome. We were still moving. Still remembering.

She turned her face slightly toward mine. "We'll rest here. Just for a little while."

I nodded, the word a promise. "Long enough to gather what comes next."

She leaned against my shoulder, a quiet surrender to the day. I wrapped an arm around her, feeling the steady, thrumming pulse of the Heart stir once beneath our skin. Outside, the wind passed through the trees like something that had been searching for us and deciding, for tonight, to let us be. We said nothing more, and sleep, when it came, was a quiet, dreamless fall.

We were barely half a mile from the lodge when the air snapped. A sharp crack split the quiet, precise and mechanical, the sound of violence approaching with intent.

I stopped. Danica was already down, one hand pressed flat against the earth, her eyes tracking the ridge above us as the forest went rigid around us. A second sound followed, a low churning beat of rotor blades somewhere above the canopy, punctuated by the sharp hiss of radio chatter. Then the shapes came, moving through the trees with a discipline too quiet for anything but practiced murder. Black uniforms, tactical vests, bare of insignia. Weapons drawn, steps calculated.

I yanked Danica behind the crumbled remains of a wall a moment before gunfire tore the air apart. A round shattered the bark beside my head. Shards of wood ripped through her sleeve.

"They're running a sweep," she said, her voice calm and clipped. "Standard grid."

My fingers wrapped around the hilt of the relic blade, its warmth a useless comfort against the threat of a bullet. The storm inside me began to move. "Three squads," I whispered. "Maybe four."

"They aren't searching," she said, her eyes narrowed. "They already know."

A red laser cut through the gloom and settled on her shoulder.

I stood. My hand came up as if it had done this a thousand times before, and the power surged through me. Lightning ripped from my palm and slammed into the soldier's chest. His body arched backward and hit a tree hard enough to leave a smear of scorched cloth and flesh. He did not rise.

A voice, clipped and cold, shouted over a radio. "Level Five anomaly confirmed. Engage and eliminate."

Then the forest became a killing floor.

Gunfire hammered the trees. Danica rose and threw her arms out. Fire exploded from her hands, white-hot and edged in blue. The brush ignited instantly. The frost vaporized. Three soldiers screamed as the fire washed over them, their bodies gone in seconds. Another group moved in from the left, their formation tight, and one of them flung a grenade in a clean arc. I shoved Danica sideways as it landed. The ridge behind us blew apart. Rocks and frozen earth slammed into my back, tearing the air from my lungs.

My ears rang with a high, thin whine. Smoke burned in my nose. I forced myself to my knees and saw another wave advancing. I raised my hands again, fingers stiff, and lightning roared out of me, brighter, louder, a raw scream of energy that slammed through their line. Men dropped. Metal screamed. The stench of ozone and burning flesh punched the air. A drone buzzed overhead, and I blasted it from the sky in a shower of shrapnel.

Danica was already turning, one hand dragging a curtain of frost from the ground while the other spread a wide arc of flame. A wall of ice, thick as a shield, burst upward between us and the flank. Bullets shattered against it. A soldier broke through the trees too close to shoot, a combat knife in his hand. I met him with the relic blade, catching him low in the side and driving him back with a pulse of electricity that lifted him off his feet.

Another grenade landed near us. Danica threw herself over it, arms crossed, and released a violent, contained surge of heat. The explosion was swallowed in a concussive plume of steam and broken air. She staggered but stayed on her feet.

I turned back to see the last squad breaking through the smoke. My body felt like it was unraveling, but I lifted both hands and let the storm tear through me one final time. The blast was wild, a spray of lightning I could only aim by instinct. I let it go.

The final scream was cut off before the body hit the ground.

The gunfire died. The shouting stopped. Only the sizzle of scorched roots remained, and the slow, groaning collapse of a forest trying to breathe again.

Danica dropped to her knees. Her fingers still glowed with a faint, residual heat, and frost crusted her torn skin. Her breath came in ragged, shallow bursts. Her face was pale enough to scare me.

I fell beside her, my own legs failing. My arms twitched with aftershocks. The lightning inside me had burned itself out, leaving behind a hollow ache. My vision swam. My lungs felt torn.

Danica's hand touched my arm. Her grip was weak, trembling. "Are you alive?"

I managed a single nod. Speaking was beyond me.

We sat there together in the wreckage, surrounded by burned earth and the twisted metal of smashed rifles. The air was heavy with ozone and the particular hush that follows a slaughter. She leaned into me, her head resting against my shoulder. Her voice was barely more than a breath against my ear.

"We can't do that again," she whispered. "Next time, they'll kill us."

She was right. The cold crept back in, crawling over the devastation. Ash drifted through the trees like a soft gray snow. Somewhere beyond the ridge, something shifted in the woods, listening, patient. I closed my eyes. The storm inside me had pulled back, but it still pulsed. It was waiting. Something else, something in the dark, now knew what we were. It would keep coming.

When I opened my eyes again, I saw it. On the trunk of a tree scorched by my final, uncontrolled blast, a shape was carved deep into the bark. A spiral, still smoldering faintly at the edges. Rough, primal, and I recognized it instantly.

Perun had been here.

The spiral predated the men who came to kill us. It was older than the Accord, sharper than their rifles. It marked the place where the god of thunder had watched me lose control and had chosen to let me burn.

Her fingers tightened on my arm. She had seen it too. Near her boots, the last ember of a smoldering root hissed out in the frost, and the world went dark.

We were exposed now. The gods had stepped forward, and whatever came next would burn.

Chapter Fourteen
A Game of Shells and Roses

Ana

It began beneath my skin as a quiet pressure, an ancient, insistent ache like the echo of a vow I had never fully broken. It moved slowly through me, gathering behind my sternum like a fist as I stood alone in the upper sanctum of the Ministry. Relics forged in my name lined every wall, yet for the first time in centuries I felt the raw chafe of powerlessness before something I could not command.

Beyond the window, the final light scattered across the mountain peaks in fractured violet streaks while the clouds were pulled apart from within, revealing a strange glow that pulsed behind them, slow and deliberate. I recognized it at once as a signal, a resonance I had felt once before when the world first began to remember me. The fine chain of a locket brushed against my collarbone. I laid my fingers over it, feeling its warmth through the fabric of my gown. For years I had worn it without thought, telling myself it was sentiment, a remnant of a weakness I had long since outgrown. Now it pulsed against my skin like a living heart. Ilija had given it to me, long before either of us remembered what we were.

That he had awakened was a truth I felt more clearly than any priest's devoted blessing or any soldier's dying oath. He had crossed a threshold none of my followers even believed was real. The very air in the sanctum trembled with that recognition as the silence deepened, as the sky itself began to break. I remained still, staring at the horizon while the reality settled into my bones. I had prepared for this possibility with plans, with armies. I had silenced prophets, rewritten doctrine to bury him beneath metaphor. Yet I had never allowed myself to imagine the sheer, physical feeling of the moment finally arriving. He remembered me. He remembered me as I was, before the world crowned me, before I chose dominion over presence. Before I gave up everything that had once made me ache.

I knew what would come next. The generals in the lower halls would begin their predictable panic while the bishops reached for incense and tired rhetoric, while the seers collapsed into wordless agony. They would give it a hundred grand, hollow names. I knew the truth they would never speak. He had become visible again. The storm was already here.

He was the only one I had never been able to control. I had buried gods, rewritten myth. I had built this nation from memory and fear. I was worshipped in ten languages, feared in thirty. None of it had ever reached him. He had loved me when I was only a woman, seen me when I most wanted to be invisible. Now he remembered. The chamber around me felt hollow, its silks and sacred inks suddenly cheap, the air thin despite the scent of rose ash and myrrh. Everything in this place had been chosen to exalt my dominion, yet nothing I had built could contain the simple force of his remembering.

I laid my palm against the window and felt the stone beneath its frame begin to warm as the mountain itself responded. Far beyond the peaks, where the sky split apart, I could feel him at the edge of the world. He had remembered the part of me I had tried hardest to forget, and I could not look away.

I left the chamber without a word, my feet carrying me through corridors I had walked a thousand times, though the silence that met me felt closer to expectation than reverence. The very air held its shape too carefully, like something bracing for impact. The guards outside my doors straightened as I passed, their gazes remaining averted. Their presence had ceased to matter. I possessed needs their protection could not address, and they had lost the knowledge of how to offer it.

I descended into the heart of the mountain, taking the spiral path carved long before my Ministry had ever claimed this place. The icons along the walls blurred as I moved, their faces of gold and ash seeming hollow now, worn thin by centuries of imitation where they had once carried the force of divinity. I passed them without notice, my attention fixed on the pressure building behind my ribs as each step took me deeper into the dark, toward the only place in this compound that prayer could not touch.

The air cooled as I reached the lowest level, where marble gave way to rough-hewn stone that was cold to the touch. The walls here remained bare, built for endurance. At the end of the corridor, the sanctum opened before me. The pool sat in its center, wide and black as oil, encircled by stone that drank the light. Sound could not reach this deep. The surface of the water looked solid, though it existed for one purpose alone, to hold memory where other gods could not reach.

I stepped forward and lowered myself to the floor, my knees meeting the cold with the familiarity of ritual, though ceremony had no place here. I had prepared no words, having offered enough of those to altars that demanded performance. This was different. This was mine. I reached out, placing my fingers lightly upon the surface. A ripple should have been impossible in that stillness, but the shift happened all the same. The air thickened. The water refused to hold a reflection, yet still it responded, drawing me in through the piercing ache of recognition.

He came to me as he always had, pulled across lifetimes by a connection my will could never sever.

The first to surface was the blacksmith, his memory rising with the scent of hot metal and honest labor. I felt the forge-light on his skin, saw the simple strength in his shoulders, a man who lived in a village pressed between two cliffs where winter came early and was always reluctant to leave. I had arrived cloaked in smoke and convenient lies, offering charms that worked with a disquieting perfection, yet he took me in without question. Through the turning of three seasons I stayed. When it came time for me to leave, he could only hold my hand as if it were the only language he knew how to speak, his silence a question I refused to answer as my path led me away from him forever.

Then came the monk, his presence a quiet ache in the heart of Dubrovnik as the plague emptied its streets. I felt the gauntness of his frame as he moved barefoot among the dying, offering a care the church itself had abandoned. It was into his infirmary I walked, bringing with me the performance of wounds, blood at my wrists and salt in my mouth. He bathed them without ever asking for my name. I watched from the shadows as he finally collapsed beside a child too small for the fever, his body failing until he could not rise again. I whispered prayers over him that I knew all the other gods refused to answer.

After him, the soldier appeared, already wounded when he stumbled into my crumbling temple, its statues split, its ceilings cracked open to the uncaring sky. He arrived with blood on his armor and disbelief in his eyes. I took the sword from his hand and pressed a cloth to the wound beneath his ribs. In return, he kissed my fingers, the touch a desperate promise that he would return, a promise his falling empire would prevent him from ever keeping.

The memories arrived stripped of ceremony, their essence flowing into me as pure presence. I felt each life fold over the next until they became a single, inseparable story of reunion and departure. Whether I was the one to leave or death arrived before we could say goodbye, the ache of it always stayed the same.

I withdrew my hand from the pool, my palm damp with a condensation the still air could not explain. The stone beneath me felt harder than it had before as the silence deepened, as the ache in my chest finally settled into the marrow of my bones. I did not resist it.

This time would be different. I would not let him slip away into the grey mists of forgetting, nor would I surrender him to fate or to another woman's arms. He had carried the memory of me across lifetimes without knowing it, and now that he had begun to remember, I would carry him through whatever came next.

When I stood, my movements were slow and deliberate. The surface of the pool returned to its perfect, obsidian stillness. Nothing visible marked my presence, yet the memory had taken root within me. I knew it would hold. The Ministry officials remained silent as I ascended, asking nothing.

The guards at the outer gates had already felt the change in the air. They kept their eyes lowered as I passed, their obedience born of a new awareness of the power that now surrounded me, a force so vast that none of them wished to be the first to name it.

The great gate opened at my approach, and I stepped out into the cold without a word. I brought no light with me. I required no direction. The forest had already begun to respond before my feet crossed its threshold, the very grass losing its color beneath my steps as the blades wilted and sank back into the soil. The frost lining the stones held its delicate shape, refusing to break or melt. The streams narrowed until their surfaces lost all motion, hardening into sheets of ice that would no longer reflect the sky. The wind grew still. The world had begun to recognize what now walked within it, and it held its breath.

I continued through the trees without slowing, needing no trail, for every part of the land ahead started to shape itself around my presence. Hollows between roots grew shallow as the terrain flattened underfoot, the forest yielding to me with reverence. I passed beneath wide arches of bare limbs that rose into the dark without a rustle. The animals remained hidden, their silence born of a primal memory of my passing.

As I reached deeper ground where the earth curved down into a basin, the air shifted again. I could feel his presence pressing upward from the soil, an imbalance in the fabric of the world. His breath had begun to stagger, his pulse losing the rhythm it needed. The storm within him, that untamed power of a god, was trying to hold its shape yet faltered with each surge, turning against its own momentum. He was still alive, yet he was losing the ability to remain so.

The forest had begun to mirror his struggle, its agony visible in the droop of the branches, the darkness pooling in the low hollows. I could feel the tension in the ground beneath my feet, as though the very roots of the world had started to pull back in pain.

I found him beyond a shallow stream, folded into a slope beneath a fallen tree whose trunk curved overhead in a wide, broken arc. Its exposed roots rose behind him in thick spirals, creating the framework of a ruined cathedral. He had collapsed into the shape of the earth with a final, quiet surrender, his arms drawn inward. One hand clutched the lining of his coat while the other lay open, half-submerged in frost. His breathing was a faint, shallow thing, the movement of his chest too subtle to see from a distance.

I stood above him, watching the shape of his collapse, and saw how the earth had made space for him, forming a cradle. The tree leaned with such precision that it seemed to have chosen him, the world itself curving around his descent.

When I stepped into the hollow and knelt beside him, the ground accepted my weight. My knees pressed into the cold soil, yet I felt no sting as the forest held its absolute silence, the trees having turned their attention downward in a shared vigil.

Leaning over him, I studied the faint signs of life in his cracked lips and the slow, incomplete motions of his breath. His body lacked tension yet had refused the final slackness of death. The storm remained. I could feel it buried beneath his ribs, coiled in confusion, clinging to his heart with a force that knew neither how to protect nor how to destroy.

I reached out and laid my hand on his forehead. His skin was cold to the touch, though it accepted the heat I gave it. Beneath my palm, I felt a flicker, a tremor of recognition that caused his breath to catch for a moment before pushing outward again. His body still knew me. The chaotic current inside him paused, then shifted, and I knew he had not slipped away.

His lips moved. The sound that followed was so faint it was barely shaped, a single word forming before his breath pulled back into his chest.

"Danica."

He spoke the name with no force, the sound escaping from some deep part of him that had carried her name without instruction. The word struck me deeper than any blade. I had known it would come. Her presence lived inside him now, her mortal fire having steadied him where my divinity had not. Yet to hear her name from his mouth in this state of near-death was a fresh wound laid atop an ancient one.

I gave no outward sign. I leaned forward and pressed my lips to his forehead, my breath passing over the skin that had once burned for me, and only me. His body remained still, then seemed to soften, his jaw loosening as his pulse held its fragile rhythm beneath my hand.

He did not speak again. He remained with me.

"I am here," I said, my voice low, carrying the certainty of a decree.

The forest held its posture, its branches unmoving, the wind refusing to return. The pressure in the clearing deepened, as the world recognized that he had been found.

I lifted him from the earth with a care that was almost reverent. The storm inside him had taken root, moving through him in uneven pulses. His strength had yet to return, though his presence was a solid weight in my arms. I gathered him against me and began to walk. The forest opened before me in quiet recognition, its branches shifting without a sound to clear my path. I had walked this way before across centuries I no longer counted, and the land still responded to the pressure of memory.

The trees widened, and at the center of the clearing stood the altar. It rose from the ground without ornament or inscription, a single, vast slab of stone that held the attention of everything surrounding it. It had not been built. It had surfaced.

The moment I stepped into the clearing, the air thickened, pressing against me as if the space were already filled. The altar responded. Lines and shapes emerged across its surface as sleeping glyphs awakened. I stepped forward and laid Ilija across the stone, his body settling into it as though the space had been carved for him alone. Moss at the base of the altar withdrew while oil seeped from the edges of the runes, spirals and curves of salt and light that held him. The stone was remembering him.

I placed my hand against his chest, feeling his slow, steadying breath. The power inside him had grown still, gathering at his center. I knelt beside him, the moss holding my weight with the stillness of something that had carried it before. The world had drawn close, and it would not release its breath until he woke. The stone responded to him with a certainty that confirmed what I had always refused to say aloud. He was the reason I had risen from salt and silence to take breath again. I had come to this place because I no longer knew how to bear his absence.

His hand moved, his fingers brushing against my knuckles and remaining there, half-curled and warm. The altar accepted the gesture. The light within the runes deepened from pale gold to the red of dried blood. I leaned forward and rested my forehead against his. Our breath moved in a slow, shared rhythm as I gave him what I had withheld in every lifetime, the fullness of my presence, without condition. A line of light from the runes reached the edge of my foot and coiled gently around my ankle, its heat tracing upward. I did not pull away. The altar was remembering us together, and the clearing had begun to bind us.

I knelt beside him, unmoving, while the clearing thickened with a silence that was older than the trees. The altar had accepted him yet had not released me. The moss beneath my knees pulsed with a faint warmth as if the very roots of the earth had begun to hum with a memory I knew intimately, for I had knelt in this place before.

There was never a time I was not divine, never a moment I wore another name or shed my shape for the convenience of mortality. I was Aphrodite before marble knew how to hold my face, worshipped in Sparta long before Athens tried to cage me in beauty alone. He once knelt before me in a ruined temple, with blood on his hands and tears he refused to show, his voice calling my name as a vow.

The world called him Leonidas, making him a king, burying the truth of him in a mountain pass. They remember the spears, the glory. They forget the night he touched my thigh with trembling fingers and asked if I would watch him fall, a promise I made and have never broken. Here he was again, reborn and fractured, bleeding a power he didn't yet understand while still trying to protect a world that would kill him for it.

Danica had pulled him from the edge, a fact I must grant her. The frost in his blood is hers, and the new steadiness in his pulse wears her shape. She cannot remember him as I do. She was mortal once, and whatever thread ties her soul to his frays at the edges, leaving her with instinct instead of memory, an ache without a name. She touches him as if he is a question. I hold him like an answer I have waited millennia to hear again.

I hated her for it, if only for a moment. His dying breath had searched for her instead of me, and that was the wound I could not close.

I pressed my palm against his ribs again, letting my warmth settle into him. "I have always been here," I said, my voice low and raw. "You were the one who kept dying."

The light in the runes beneath him deepened to the color of rose and iron as the scent of oil and salt thickened in the clearing. My tears never fall, yet the ache behind my eyes felt older than the stone beneath us.

"Come back to me," I whispered, the command dissolving into a need so ancient it felt like the bedrock of my own divinity. I leaned down and kissed the corner of his mouth, the way I had in Sparta, in the dark corners of libraries and temples that time had long since buried. I cared little if he heard me now. I only cared that he stayed. "You don't have to remember it all," I said against his skin. "Just remember that I never left you."

His hand twitched again, a stronger movement this time, and the light under the altar flared in response.

When his lips parted, when the first sound of his returning consciousness clawed its way free, it still wasn't my name he spoke.

"Danica."

The word tore from him as if it had claws. My name was still buried somewhere deep inside him, waiting to rise, yet hers broke the surface first. My jaw locked so hard I tasted blood.

Because I fucking knew. She wasn't just some girl caught in the wrong century. She had been there in the past lives, dying beside him, burning for him just as I had. I wasn't the only one who had suffered, but gods help me, I still wanted to rip that truth from the sky. She had forgotten, while I had been forced to remember. She had come back to him scattered and incomplete, while I had carried every single second of his absence. While I had never fucking left.

When he said her name as if it were the only thing he had left to hold on to, something in me cracked. I pressed my palm harder against his ribs, as if I could force my own memories into place, reminding him with the sheer force of my body what we had always been.

"Yeah," I whispered, the sound low and bitter. "Say her name first. That's fucking perfect."

The altar pulsed once, dim and slow, as if even it had no answer for that. I sat back, pressing my hands to my thighs to keep them from shaking, my voice steady only because I refused to let it tremble.

"I know she loves you," I said to his sleeping face. "I know she's bled for you, died for you, more times than even she can remember. She's fucking earned a place in your story, and I hate how much that hurts." I looked down at this god who knew his own name, this man who had once chosen me over an empire, and swallowed the sob clawing its way up my throat. "I was there, too. Every time. I didn't forget."

I leaned forward again, brushing my lips against his brow, the place he used to kiss me when he still believed I was human. My voice finally shook, and I let it.

"She's part of your story," I whispered. "I am the fucking myth that never let you go."

I stood, the ache in my knees meaningless compared to the centuries I had carried him in memory. My fingers hovered for a moment over his ribs, and then I gathered him into my arms as I had done a hundred fucking times before, on battlefields, in beds soaked with blood and salt. He weighed no more than a man, yet he felt like a world.

His head rested against my collarbone, his breath still catching in that uneven rhythm. I curled one arm around his back, the other beneath his knees, and I carried him from the altar. I needed no incense and no witnesses. This was a reckoning.

The clearing did not resist me. The vines loosened, the roots pulled back. The trees stood as sentinels because they remembered who the fuck I was. Aphrodite. Goddess of love, yes, but also of war. Of women who have burned too long to be soft anymore. This was the man I chose.

As I stepped from the altar's glow, the ground beneath us trembled once, like a heart catching itself before it breaks. The runes faded behind us. The light receded into the earth.

I didn't look back. He would wake, and he would remember. He always did. When he did, the world would either kneel or burn, because this time, I was not going to fucking lose him.

I pressed my lips to the top of his head, breathing in the scent of frost and charged air.

"You're mine," I whispered against his skin. "Fuck anyone who tries to take you from me again."

The clearing closed behind us.

CHAPTER FIFTEEN
SCOTLAND'S SUMMONS

Danica

I woke to a weighted silence, the kind that judges. A tight, metallic chill gripped me from the inside before I even moved, coating each breath as if it had been there long before I opened my eyes. The world had shifted, a wrongness deep in my bones. I reached sideways for him. My hand landed on his coat, nothing else.

It was damp with dew and streaked with ash, folded as if he meant to come right back, still carrying the ghost of his warmth as it faded into the cold. My fingers curled into the rough fabric for a moment before I let it fall. The breath I'd been holding broke from my lips in a ragged shard. I sat up, and the world spun around me. The forest was the same, the ridge still catching the first weak light, the trees still standing in their crooked ring, but everything was hollow. Ilija was gone.

I turned to where he had slept, and the panic hit like a fist. The ground was smooth. The leaves were undisturbed. There was no depression in the soil, no pattern of frantic feet or broken stems. The space had been erased. I crawled across the clearing, my hands digging through the earth, scraping at bark, desperate for any sign that he'd fought or run or fucking breathed before he disappeared. There was nothing. The silence grew thicker, pushing in behind my ribs and coiling tight around my spine.

I choked on his name. The sound died in my throat. I rocked back on my heels, breath coming in fast, shallow bursts that burned my lungs. He was gone. I had no idea where or how, but my body remembered this, the same pain, the same loss it had carried before. I had known it in muddy trenches and in the middle of goddamn nowhere. In every lifetime I had ever touched him, I had also lost him. I was losing him again.

I slammed my fist into the dirt hard enough to feel the skin split. "Fuck," I hissed, dragging in another useless breath. "No. No, no, no." I forced myself to stand on trembling legs. My head throbbed with a pressure I couldn't release, as if the tether holding me together had finally frayed enough to snap. I turned, staggering, scanning the trees for any sign, any trace. That was when I saw them.

Red petals, unnervingly soft, scattered near the edge of the clearing like a trail laid by someone who knew precisely how to hurt me. I stumbled toward them, a hot rage bubbling under the panic, and dropped to my knees to reach for one. The moment my finger touched it, the petal crumbled into fine grey ash. Of course it fucking fell to pieces.

My breath hitched and stayed there. My hands curled against the earth again, shaking instead of searching. I knew what this meant.

"Ana," I whispered, her name tasting like blood in my mouth. "You fucking bitch."

She had taken him. She had walked through this clearing like a ghost and carved me out of it. But the thought that made me want to scream was worse. He would have fought her. He would have burned the world down.

Unless he hadn't. A new, sharper thought, cold and clean as a shard of ice, slid into my chest. He had gone with her.

I doubled over, wrapping my arms around my stomach as the ache became brutally physical. A rage with nowhere to go, a grief that had found its target. He had gone with her willingly. That thought shattered me worse than if she'd burned the entire forest to the ground to take him.

"I can't—" The words scraped raw from my throat. "I can't fucking lose him again."

The runes under my skin stirred, and the ache behind my sternum twisted deeper, became ancient. My vision blurred from a heat blooming at the base of my spine, crawling upward through me. I stood slowly, my shoulders shaking, fists clenched so tightly my nails dug into my palms. My body was freezing, but my blood had begun to burn.

"Ilija," I said, his name a blade I was driving into the ground. "I swear to every god listening—"

The clouds above shifted with a long, thin ripple, as if the world itself had just begun to crack. A strange warmth followed, comfortless, the kind that arrives only after loss, when the price is already being counted.

I made my way up the hill with my fists clenched, the wet grass gripping at my bare feet as if it remembered me. Every step cost blood I had yet to spill. When I finally reached her, my body had nothing left to give. I collapsed to my knees, my voice scraping through my gritted teeth. "I lost him. She took him."

Brigid descended in silence, her cloak hissing through the heather like water over coals as she crouched beside me. Her hand was surprisingly cold as she lifted my chin, forcing me to meet her ancient, unblinking eyes.

"He went with her," I said, hating the broken sound of my own voice. "There was no fight, no trail. Just a fucking coat and petals that turned to ash."

"He was claimed," she corrected, her voice a low rustle of leaves and stone. "Chains have forms beyond iron, Danica Madsen. Sometimes they take the shape of comfort, of a memory twisted into something sweet enough to swallow."

I shook my head, a hot fury climbing my spine. "He didn't even try. She just took him."

"Your runes still held their guard," she said. "Ana could only reach what lay beyond them, so she took what would hurt you most."

"She fucking succeeded." Her silence was its own confirmation. I wanted to hit something, to scream until the sky shattered. "What am I supposed to do with that? Walk away and let her brainwash him while I go pray in the fucking dirt?"

Brigid rose, her expression unchanged. "You walk west," she commanded, and I stared at her. "West. There is a blade there that remembers what you have forgotten."

I opened my mouth to argue, but the sky split open in my mind. I saw a cairn in a field, wrapped in seal leather and ash leaves while ravens circled above. I saw a half-collapsed train station with its doors open to a world that belonged only to the dead.

"The Blade of Fates," Brigid said, her voice cutting through the images. "When you hold it, you will remember the war that broke the sky." The word left me like an exhale. "Scotland."

Brigid nodded once. "The land of your mother's blood. A place where second chances must be taken, for they are never given."

My gaze dropped to the ground, the fight draining out of me. "I can't leave him again."

"You already did," she said, her voice a knife pressed gently to my throat. "The moment you started waiting for him to choose you. If you want him to remember, then find the blade. When you hold it, you will stop asking whether you were enough, and he will stop forgetting why he was born to stand beside you."

My jaw locked shut. Brigid crouched once more, placing her palm over my chest. The touch left an immediate, searing burn. "The woman who woke up in that clearing is gone," she said, her voice now a low, fierce hiss. "You are the one who walks through fire without asking permission. You are the one who fucking finishes what the gods abandoned."

The heat from her hand surged through me, into my ribs and down through my legs. My vision blurred with its intensity. When I looked up again, she was gone, but the mark she had left pulsed like a second heartbeat.

I woke with frost clinging to my eyelashes and Brigid's handprint searing my chest. The sky had gone pale again, grey and motionless, casting a thin, cold light that lay flat across the clearing. It looked exactly as it had before, but I had changed. Grief had finished shaping me, and Brigid's fire had set the edge.

I sat up slowly, my palms pressing into the firm ground, feeling the dry leaves beneath them, the sharp, honest cold. I was back in the place where he had vanished, and the silence steadied me. The rose petals were gone. The air held no trace of ash or perfume. Whatever had passed through this clearing had left everything intact except for me.

I stood, and my aching legs obeyed. My coat still lay in the grass, stiff with dew, and I fastened it with cold, deliberate fingers before pulling the satchel onto my back. I tied the compass to my belt, letting the needle spin where it wanted. My direction had already been decided. West. The word was inevitable.

Before leaving the clearing, I crouched one last time, my hand brushing the ground where he had slept. The earth was smooth and cold, every trace of him erased. "I'm coming," I said, and my voice was a stranger to me, level and steady. Then I turned and walked west, the path pulling at my center like a hook set deep in bone.

The basin stretched before me, grey as fucking ash beneath a sky sagging with silence. The land that had once been golden with wheat now offered only the taste of smoke, and I walked straight into it. My boots cracked the frost with every step, the air burning in my throat, but I never stopped. My legs ached. My gut twisted with hunger. I kept walking. I had memorized the rhythm of his presence, the sound of his boots in the dirt, the way he'd turn to look at me like I was the only real thing in the world. That rhythm was gone. All I had left was the echo, a name I whispered into the cold air like a prayer I refused to stop saying.

"Ilija." The word came with my steps, steady and weighted. "Ilija."

Four fucking days passed in that rhythm. I moved through what was once Hungary, through the fractured edges of forgotten towns where red Ministry banners were stitched like fresh wounds into the stone. Every building leaned sideways, still buckling from whatever had struck it. The streets were empty of soldiers. The silence itself was guard enough, teaching people to stare at the ground and pretend they saw nothing. I moved through it all like smoke, hood low and scarf high, my steps blending into the motion of everything else trying to avoid being seen. At dusk on the fourth day, I reached the ruins of Nagykanizsa and stopped behind a caved-in bakery with a rusted water pump out back. I forced the handle until water the color of rust sputtered out. It tasted of mold. I drank it anyway, refilling my flask before I sat beneath a bent awning. I chewed through a heel of bread so stale it tasted like bark and watched a pack of wild dogs circle something small and broken in the alley. They moved in a slow, hungry orbit around whatever scraps remained.

Sleep refused me that night. I lay against the wall of the ruined bakery with one hand on the hilt of my knife and the other curled around my flask, watching shadows crawl. When the dream came, it swallowed me whole. I was standing in a stone circle on high ground, with a wind that bit through my coat, though my body held its own warmth against it. The air smelled of rain and blood. Around me moved figures in robes, their faces marked with ash and bone-white paint. As they moved through their silent ritual, they wept. A blade hovered in front of me, leaf-shaped and long, suspended in the air as if it had no use for gravity. Its hilt was wrapped in kelp and thorn, the steel itself etched in glyphs that pulsed with a faint, living heat. It waited for me. I knew its name as the sound of it bloomed inside me like fire catching in dry grass.

Dànadas. The name sat on my tongue, older than understanding.

I woke with it still on my lips. The sky above me was flat and grey, but the heat of that blade still flickered under my skin.

I crossed into Austria at dawn. The border was marked by a silence thick enough to choke, the road narrowing to a frozen strip of gravel and cracked concrete. The air here pressed closer, a conscious, waiting presence wearing the skin of cold. The mist gathered, heavy on my back as I walked, as if the land had finally noticed me and had yet to decide what to do. The Accord let this place police itself through memory and fear. But I had changed, and the land knew it.

As I passed a broken signpost, the frost on the metal curled back in thin flakes, falling away like shed skin. On a hollow chapel wall, the Accord's symbol, a spiral sun burned deep beside the archway, cracked down the center and peeled away. I hadn't lifted my hand. At first I thought it was coincidence, but then a dead hearth flared with a single spark as I crossed the threshold of a collapsed barn. The snow behind me refused to keep its shape, my footprints filling faster than they should have. The ravens held their perches as I passed, then followed.

I made camp that night in the ruins of a waystation, with three walls to brace my back against the wind. The blade pulsed behind my ribs, a second spine of purpose. I sat in the dark, my fingers on the cold stone, feeling my own heart beat in time with a presence beneath the land, ancient and attentive. I threw together a small pile of splintered timber and struck a flint. The flame caught immediately, a low and stubborn bastard of a fire that ignored the frost clawing at the stones around it. I crouched before it, my palms open to a heat that felt more real than anything I had touched in days. It burned with a familiarity that went deeper than warmth.

The name echoed in my bones. Dànadas. It threaded through me, quiet but sharp. The Accord thought taking Ilija would buy them fear. Let them rot. I would burn their fucking empire to the ground until someone told me where he was.

The fire hissed, and an ember leaped free, sinking into the ice beside me and holding its glow. The frost hissed back, then fell still. I watched that patch of earth, waiting for it to speak again. When I finally stood, the pain in my legs was welcome. The silence around me was expectant, listening. Out in the trees, a presence moved, a witness to my vigil. The gods had come to watch.

I stomped the fire out, scattering the coals until the heat finally gave up, though it clung to my skin, marking me. If Brigid or anyone else wanted to help, they knew where to fucking find me.

I turned toward the road and kept walking west, my direction settled beyond asking. If I had to carve a hole through the whole goddamn continent to reach him, I would, and if the gods refused to help, they had better stay the fuck out of my way.

Salzburg had been emptied with the chilling precision of a surgeon cutting rot from bone, its streets stretching out in straight lines that led nowhere. The silence pressed down on the snow-dusted rooftops like a held breath. I moved through the alleys with my hand resting near my knife, distrusting the quiet, every step pressing into a city trying to forget it had ever lived. I passed a butcher's shop that someone had converted into a shrine, with candles on meat hooks and salt poured in careful, protective lines along the doorway. A place of quiet, desperate faith, a gesture from someone still hiding. Kinship flickered through me before I dismissed it.

My hiding days were over. The blade called to me louder the closer I came to the church, its pull a clear, purposeful pressure in my spine that promised clarity, the only thing I trusted now.

The church came into view beyond a collapsed rail depot, its bell tower snapped near its base and leaning at a sick angle toward the ground. The stone façade bore the mark of the Accord, a spiral sun burned deep beside the archway, now cracked down the middle like a scar that refused to seal. I stepped through the arch, my jaw tight, and was met with a deeper cold, a space heavy with air that had never stopped listening. The pews were gone. The altar had been stripped clean, its surface blackened. Beneath it, charred into the foundation, was the Accord's spiral. Beside that, another mark had been carved by hand. The letters were dug into the stone with a blunt object, the grooves still holding dark red flakes from the blood it had cost to write them. A message meant for someone like me, someone who still walked the alleys and refused to bow.

RUN.

I stared at the word and felt only a surge of heat. The woman who had woken up in a clearing, frantic and shattered, might have listened to such a warning, might have seen it as confirmation of her terror. I was someone else now. Fear had left me on that hillside, burned away with Brigid's handprint still smoking on my skin. The person who carved this message had died afraid. I would honor their desperation, but I would not share it. I was here to hunt. The blade had already chosen me, and I was done crawling.

I turned away from the altar and stepped back into the frost. The road ahead would demand blood, a price I was more than willing to pay.

Graz unfolded beneath me like a wound that had forgotten how to close. I stood at the top of the Schlossberg ruins with my eyes fixed on the western horizon as the wind moved sluggishly through the crooked streets below, brushing past bullet-scarred facades. The Accord had swept through here months ago, leaving its mark with silence that policed itself. I descended slowly, my boots scraping stone, my satchel lighter now, my steps heavier, the compass at my belt ticking west on its own. At dusk, I reached the edge of the old university quarter where books lay torn in the streets, their pages dissolving in the frost. I was stepping carefully around a textbook smeared with familiar-looking handwriting when a noise came from the alley behind me.

Every muscle in me went still. Another step, soft-footed and untrained. I circled around a half-collapsed arcade on silent feet, the knife already in my hand as I waited at the alley's far end. A figure stepped into view. The moonlight caught the steel in my grip. She was a woman, older than me by maybe ten years, her face drawn with hunger but her eyes sharp. She slowly raised both hands. "I have no weapon. I followed you."

I said nothing, my grip firm.

"My name is Éloïse," she said, taking a careful step forward. "I saw you three nights ago, near the cliffs past Maribor. I was uncertain then, but I know now that you walk like someone with gods in her blood."

"You're resistance," I stated, the word tasting strange in my mouth.

She nodded once. "What's left of it. We've been watching the borderlands, looking for anyone like you. Come with me, just for the night. You look half-dead."

After a moment's hesitation, I gave a single nod. "Lead the way."

She took me through a series of alleys to a rusted door hidden behind a shattered fountain, which opened into a cellar lit by candles and warmed by the hum of a salvaged generator. Six others sat inside on crates and blankets. A boy adjusted the dial on a shortwave radio, glancing at me once before returning to his task. A woman in a wheelchair turned the page of a thick book. An old man stirred soup with a long iron spoon, his focus entirely on the pot. Éloïse gestured to the quiet group. "This is what's left. Runaways and heretics."

"You know who I am?" I asked, my voice low.

The woman in the wheelchair looked up, her gaze piercing. "We know what you carry."

I kept my voice soft, a clear warning. "I'm not here to lead anyone."

The old man finally looked up from the pot, his eyes ancient and clear as he met my gaze. "But you already have."

They fed me a soup bitter with root and wild rabbit that burned going down, but it began to fill the hollow behind my ribs. They kept their mouths shut, gave me space, and that was more than enough. Later, Éloïse sat beside me in the quiet, her voice low. "We heard something, a transmission near Trieste, about a male subject transferred east under special clearance."

My spoon stilled in the bowl. "Ilija."

She dipped her head. "We think he's still alive. They are unaware of what he is. Not yet."

The woman in the wheelchair rolled forward, pointing to a sprawling charcoal map on the wall where red wax marked points of power. A crudely drawn blade was sketched over the isle of Scotland. The breath stalled in my lungs.

"We believe it's real," Éloïse said. "The Blade of Fates. We think it's waiting for you. If they find it first—"

"They won't," the old man said, his voice certain. I looked at him. "Why not?"

He finally looked up from the fire, his gaze clear. "Because Ana may be powerful, but she has never been desperate."

I stared into the flames until they blurred, a new, sharper fear coiling in my gut. "He's forgetting me." No one answered. I slept near the boiler, a scarf Éloïse had given me curled in my palm. They allowed me my rest. When morning came, I stood before the map for a long time until the boy from the radio approached, handing me a satchel filled with dried food, vials, a whetstone, and a knife marked with symbols I had never seen.

"This is neither Norse nor Slavic," I said, turning the blade over in my hands.

The boy nodded. "I dreamed it. A woman with fire in her hair told me you would come."

I took the knife and tipped my chin in thanks. Éloïse met me at the stairwell, handing me a pouch of salt bound with copper thread. "For crossing," she said, "in case the river's skin thins."

I tightened the scarf around my neck. "How far?"

"Two weeks, if you stay clear of the patrol lines," she said. "Ten days if you don't."

I met her eyes. "I won't be hiding anymore."

A flicker of respect passed through her gaze, though she did not smile. "Then don't die quietly. It would disappoint the myths."

I stepped out into the frost-heavy dark, the pouch from Éloïse tucked beneath my coat, the dream-forged blade cold against my thigh. The wind had picked up, hissing through the alleyways as my boots found their rhythm, heavy but sure. I passed through Graz like a shadow wearing form, visible only to the things that remembered how to look. The resistance had taught me how to move like someone already forgotten, but the gods still remembered. By the time I reached the outer fields, the runes beneath my skin had begun to itch again. The line between the world I walked and the one I remembered grew thin. The path west split just beyond the old railway tracks, one trail following the river toward bombed-out tunnels I had learned to distrust, the other veering into the foothills. I took the latter, my hand on the hilt of the boy's blade, my other curled around the compass that pointed only west.

Time blurred after that. The days between Graz and the French border lost their edges, and the hours and the miles ceased to matter. I moved through southern Germany like a ghost with a heartbeat, quiet and deliberate, sleeping where I dropped and rising before light. I crossed through valleys where the snow fell sideways, through pine forests that had gone still with watching. Towns so hollowed by fear they displayed their bones openly fell behind me one after another. The boots I wore cracked apart near the Rhine, so I wrapped my feet in cloth and kept going, past burned-out chapels and checkpoints now manned by the silent, steady eyes of drones. They followed my trail for three days, yet they never struck. The Accord had already burned everything in this land that I could have stopped.

I passed schools with ash still clinging to the windows, rivers clogged with rusted signs. I crossed into France beneath a collapsed bridge outside Saarbrücken, where the wind was sharp enough to draw blood. By then, I welcomed it. Every road bent west. Every step answered the pull in my chest.

I lost track of how many nights I walked without stopping. The rhythm of my patched feet on the fractured roads of France was the only constant in a world that felt as though it were slowly exhaling its last breath. The air hung heavy with the damp chill of the approaching sea, carrying the scent of brine and kelp. Each step cost more than the last, my legs shaking under me, yet the westward ache never faltered. The landscape softened as I neared the coast, the skeletal remains of bombed-out buildings giving way to windswept fields of tall grass that whispered in the breeze. The silence here had loosened, carrying the distant cry of gulls and the low murmur of the ocean.

Through a veil of mist, the coastline appeared. Jagged cliffs met a churning grey sea. My throat tightened and my pulse kicked hard. There, nestled in a small sheltered cove, a dark shape bobbed against the restless water. A boat, waiting as promised, held steady by the network of shadows that had guided my path.

My legs screamed with every step down the rocky trail. I had trekked across a broken continent, and my body showed every mile of it. Yet as I descended to the cove, the runes beneath my skin hummed awake, answering the blade's call from across the water. Scotland. The land of my mother's blood. The place where second chances were seized. And there, waiting within its rugged embrace, the Blade of Fates, the key to reclaiming what had been stolen, to reminding Ilija why he was born to stand beside me. I climbed aboard, the small craft rocking beneath my weight, my gaze fixed on the horizon where the mists swirled and parted.

Chapter Sixteen
THE CHANNEL'S UNVEILING

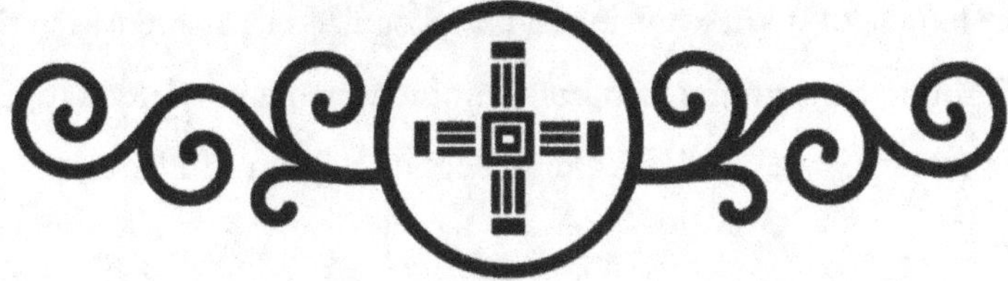

Danica

The sea took everything I hadn't realized I was still carrying. It claimed me like a debt whispered into brine and foam, long overdue. By the time my raw hands clawed on the gravel shore, my coat hung sodden with the ocean's chill, a fistful of seaweed locked in my grip. I lay there, salt bitter on my lips, every muscle throbbing with the sheer, fucking exhaustion of having crossed a world that kept demanding. Rage, potent and subterranean, coiled somewhere beneath it all.

Above me, the sky stretched in a sheet of iron-gray, motionless and indifferent. The sun stayed hidden, yet every protesting joint in my body announced the dawn. When I dragged my head sideways, the boat, Rhosyn Gwyllt, was a splintered ghost, her broken ribs scattered across the rocks like sacrificial offerings. Perhaps they were. Perhaps that was the grim toll of passage, the price demanded for safe harbor on this desolate coast. Indifference was all I could muster for her demise. She had served her purpose, had brought me to this waiting land. That was all that mattered.

The climb began with a single-mindedness that banished all thought of fatigue. The cliff face rose before me, a jagged wall of stone weeping with frost, each handhold slick with ice and grasping ivy. My hands were flayed, skin torn and bleeding, long before the summit came within reach, yet I kept climbing. Pain, sharp and familiar, was infinitely more manageable than the helplessness that had shadowed my steps. The frost pressed into the open wounds, testing me. I welcomed its bite. This land had dispensed with welcome long ago. It knew me instead. I recognized its awareness in the shift of ground beneath my torn boots, in the way the ivy yielded to my grasp. Sanctuary was a fool's dream. Recognition, grim and bare, was enough.

When my battered knees buckled, pitching me forward into the grass at the cliff's crest, a ragged breath tore from my throat. A pulse moved beneath the earth, a slow, thick thrum that resonated with the buried breath of a presence that had lain dormant for centuries. The runes beneath my skin stirred, warmth uncoiling up my spine, settling with a throb behind my eyes. It was an answer, quiet and certain, to a question I hadn't even consciously asked.

The figures who emerged from the ridge came without drawn blades or shouted challenges. Three of them, moving with unsettling ease across the frosted expanse. A man whose face was mapped by time and old battles, marked by a long, pale scar. Beside him, a woman with braids tucked beneath a hood of green, her movements fluid as a river. And trailing them, a girl, too young, it seemed, to brave the frost with bare feet. She carried a flask in one hand and a small bundle of herbs in the other, as if this was a duty she had performed countless times before. They watched me without speaking.

The man, his gaze as weathered as the land itself, crouched beside me. He studied my face with unsettling intensity, reading a story in the lines of my exhaustion that he had perhaps already encountered in whispers and old lore.

"We thought you were only a story," his voice, coarse as stone, broke the hush.

My throat, raw and burning from the salt and the climb, still managed to rasp a reply. "I still might be, you know."

The girl, her eyes wide and intent, stepped forward, tilting the flask to my lips. The water, startlingly clean, cut through the lingering taste of salt with a clarity that bordered on shocking. I drank deeply, desperately, until the ragged coughing ceased and breath returned to my lungs.

"The Channel's dead," the woman's voice, a low current of sound, drifted from where she stood on the bluff, her gaze on the churning grey expanse below. "No one crosses it alive anymore."

I wiped the water from my mouth with the back of my hand, shoved damp hair from my eyes. "Guess I missed the fucking memo."

The hush held. They asked nothing, demanded nothing. They turned, their forms already moving, and I, with no other direction or choice, followed.

The path they led me down wound through the gnarled skeletal forms of ash trees and the brittle remnants of frostbitten hedgerows, half-swallowed by time, yet still subtly maintained by unseen hands. Someone, I realized, had been keeping this forgotten way alive. With every step deeper into the landscape, the air grew heavier, thicker, watchful and palpable beyond mere chill. When we reached the farmhouse, its silhouette stark against the steel-grey sky, I halted at the gate.

I knew this place.

It was older than hearth or shelter. A bruise pressed into the skin of the land, a wound that had refused to heal, holding memory as an open, living thing.

Inside, the rooms were stripped bare. Furniture had been long gone, the floorboards carved with swirling ochre lines, the plaster walls smeared with chalk spirals and ash symbols, patterns that hummed with forgotten power. Above the hearth, a crooked line of photos, tacked with grim precision, caught my eye. A shattered temple beside a child's crude drawing of Ilija and me caught in a storm of impossible red and gold. And next to them, Ana's face. Someone, their hand trembling with fury or sorrow, had burned her eyes out of the paper, leaving only a charred void.

I stood in the doorway, seawater still dripping from my coat onto the floor, every muscle in my back tightening. The blade, strapped to my spine, had begun to warm, a low, persistent thrum. I surveyed the room, bracing myself, half-expecting it to unleash some force I couldn't name. Instead, it hummed, a steady vibration that filled the air, the stillness right before the sky rips open.

"Resistance?" I heard myself ask, the word tasting strange on my tongue, even as the answer resonated within me.

The woman turned, her green hood framing a face that held centuries of unspoken knowledge. "This is older than resistance, child. This is everything they tried to wipe from the earth, every truth they sought to bury beneath their lies."

They offered me food without asking a single question. A steaming bowl of stew, thick with the earthy scent of lamb and barley, its heat stinging my mouth as it slid down my raw throat. Someone draped a shawl of coarse wool over my shoulders, woven with symbols I didn't recognize but sensed in my bones, while beside the crackling fire, dry boots waited, worn but lined with fur, as if they'd been set aside for someone exactly my size. Comfort went unspoken. It was ritual, and it had nothing to do with me as an individual. I was the one who had arrived at the precise, predetermined moment.

I kept my thanks to myself. Gratitude, in this stark place, was pointless. Whatever they gave had always been meant to pass through. It had been done before, in other bleak winters, for countless others who had borne the same crushing resolve in their bones. I ate until the tremors in my hands subsided. I slept without the torment of dreams. When I woke, Maeryn, the woman with the green hood, was already seated beside me.

She held her quiet, her presence a vigil. She watched me with the intensity of someone studying a storm-laden sky, prepared for what was to come. I sat up slowly, the wool shawl still wrapped tightly around my shoulders. My ribs ached, a dull throb that had settled into familiar company. It was staying. So, I realized, was I.

That night, she led me into the woods.

We carried only a small clay bowl cradling a handful of glowing coals, and a leather pouch that reeked of rosemary and old blood. Maeryn held the fire with both hands, her gaze fixed on its fragile light. The girl, her bare feet noiseless on the earth, walked behind us, her wrists adorned with tiny bones that clinked with a rhythmic whisper every time she moved. That delicate sound kept the encroaching hush from collapsing entirely around us. The man with the scar remained behind, a sentinel against the dying light of the farmhouse, tracing a spiral across the doorframe with powdered iron, his face unreadable in the flickering glow.

The forest resisted us at every turn. The deeper we ventured, the heavier the air became, the atmosphere thickening around us. The trees pressed closer, their trunks wide and damp, their bark layered with moss and lichen. Gnarled roots coiled above the ground, reaching for what they had lost to time. The only path was instinct, patches of earth soft enough to tread and a pull that drew us forward. The girl held her footing with every step. So did Maeryn. I followed, because turning back, in this world or any other, had ceased to be an option.

The claustrophobic press of trees receded, opening into a hollow.

It lay low in the hillside, a natural depression, sunken enough to deflect the biting wind. A circle of standing stones ringed its edge, leaning with the weary grace of monuments that had stood too long, threatening to fall but held in place by a force beyond gravity. Some bore the crude markings of ogham. Others held symbols older than language itself. One massive stone, split clean down the middle, stood witness to some forgotten cataclysm, as if the earth had decided its vigil was complete and rent itself in two.

At the heart of the glade, a low altar rose barely two feet from the mossy ground, its surface blanketed in a haphazard mosaic of feathers. They had been left there slowly, over untold years, by wind and birds, by people who understood the sanctity of unseen rituals. They belonged, each one, to this place.

Maeryn halted before the edge of the stone circle, her arm extended, offering a knife. Its hilt was wrapped in wool and braided bone thread. She said nothing, but her intent was clear. I took the blade, its weight familiar in my palm, and stepped across the invisible threshold into the circle.

The moment my foot crossed into the ring, the air shifted. The wind, which had whispered ceaselessly through the trees, dropped away entirely, and the rustle of the girl's bone charms faded to nothing. The fire in Maeryn's clay bowl dimmed, its light shrinking to a faint glow. Everything pulled inward, the entire world holding its breath.

I knelt before the altar, my knees sinking into the damp soil. One hand rested on the stone, careful with the feathers. My fingers trembled, because the air recognized me, an awareness that settled into the deepest layers of my skin. The runes beneath my ribs flared, a soft burn. My heartbeat slowed, falling into an older rhythm. I waited.

Wings, vast and unseen, passed overhead, their slow circle pulling the sky tight, drawing the fabric of the heavens closer. Then a breath, ancient beyond reckoning, curled through the glade. It carried memory, and it had been patiently waiting for someone, anyone, to truly listen. Its source eluded me, for it belonged to every woman who had ever knelt in this space, every fucking soul who had reached for what lay beyond comprehension and begged for it to reach back.

The altar warmed beneath my trembling hand. The earth pressed against my legs. The air thickened, laden with everything I had kept unspoken, every truth I had buried. Then the voice came, a pressure in my chest, a burning heat at the back of my throat.

You have been unmade, child of Danu. Now be remade.

The glade fell still. Utterly, completely still. The kind of quiet that descends before a storm so cataclysmic, you know, with chilling certainty, that it cannot be stopped.

A slow heat began to rise beneath my knees, spreading through the damp soil as if what lay buried had begun to breathe again. The runes flared once more, an intense burst of warmth, and my grip tightened on the altar as the air grew viscous. The feathers beside my hand stirred, ruffling in a current that came from nowhere, though the air remained motionless. I turned towards the trees just as she stepped out from their shadows.

She was flesh and blood, defiantly real, and she let every inch of it show. Her boots crushed the moss beneath her feet with an audible crunch. Her breath plumed in the cold air. Her presence struck me with a force greater than anything I had known since Ilija's disappearance, a primal echo in the hollow space he'd left behind.

Her face, carved by war and time, offered itself plainly, indifferent to my thoughts or opinions. Her left eye, obsidian-black, missed nothing. Her right eye was gone, a hollowed void left starkly exposed, a truth she refused to soften. Her hair, thick and black, hung in ropes, damp and tangled with bits of leaf and ash. Her armor, bronze and battered, scorched in places, was molded to a body built for battle. The cuts and gashes that marred its surface had been left exactly as they were. She wore every one of them.

She stepped into the stone circle without hesitation, and as she passed, the frail fire in Maeryn's bowl guttered. I held my ground, one hand on the altar, my spine rigid, my body acutely aware of every inch of space between us. The glade had admitted her without question, like an old friend returning. She offered me no name, and asked for none.

She stopped a few paces from me, her gaze pinned on mine, as if I were already failing some test I hadn't realized had begun.

Her voice, when it came, landed in my chest like the blunt force of a hammer. It filled the space without echo.

"You think the blade is yours."

I met her stare, unblinking. "I didn't come here to claim it. I came here because I'm done watching everything I care about get turned to fucking ash while I sit on my hands. Because I'm tired of carrying power I can't use. Because I'm angry, and I'm done pretending that means I'm broken."

She moved around the altar, her steps slow and deliberate. Her boots passed without sound over the ground, yet I sensed the earth shift with each step, as if the land made room.

"This blade wasn't forged for rage," she stated, her voice a low rumble. "It remembers oaths. It honors reckoning."

"Good," I retorted. "Because that's exactly what I came for."

She stopped directly in front of me, bare hands at her sides, knuckles scabbed, fingers stained as if she'd been digging through freshly turned graves. Her gaze was steady, unbroken. She looked at me, her one good eye holding the certainty of someone who already knew the outcome, patiently waiting for me to catch up.

"You've bent yourself in every direction trying not to break," she rasped, her voice like grinding stone. "You've buried grief under silence and called it strength, and now you want a weapon that will finally let you cut the world open and bleed it for what it's done to you."

"I want a weapon that answers back," I said, my voice raw with an old ache. "I want the next goddamn tyrant who tries to burn the past down to choke on the ash."

She reached forward and touched the altar, wordless, and the feathers flared outward, a collective exhale through time itself. Then she pressed her palm flat against the stone, and the markings carved into its surface began to glow, faint at first, then brighter, pulsing once with the slow rhythm of a buried heart.

"You've already carried the blade in other lives," she murmured. "You left it here when the last vow broke. Now you've returned. You didn't remember. The blade did."

My mouth tasted of dust. My chest ached with a grief I couldn't name. I said nothing, moved my hand towards the stone. The moment my skin brushed its surface, a pulse slammed through my arm and into the hollow of my ribs.

A pressure within the stone shifted, spreading through my palm and into my chest, as if the blade, buried beneath the earth, had recognized the shape of my grip. The world peeled away, layer by smoky layer.

I stood in the desolate heart of a field ripped open by fire, its ground blackened and cracked. The glade was gone. Bones lay scattered through the ash, abandoned where they had fallen, twisted in their final throes. The wind brought the stench of smoke and charred flesh. In the distance, a solitary tree, skeletal and defiant, stood at the center of the plain. Every branch had been stripped bare, and its bark glistened with blood that had yet to dry. Bodies were piled at its base in grim layers, some still clutching the steel of forgotten weapons, others curled inward like withered prayers.

I was wearing armor. It pressed against my ribs, hot from the inferno, the metal sealed to my skin with ash and sweat. My fingers ached from gripping too tightly for too long. A sword, its hilt worn smooth, sat in my right hand. My left hand clutched a shattered crest, torn from a banner whose name I recognized. It had once signified everything. Now it was proof of how far we had fallen, how completely we had been undone.

Every inch of me burned, seared by a grief so vast it coated my lungs. This was memory, my own, dredged from a life I had lived. I had stood on this battlefield. I had survived it. I had killed for it. I had sealed the truth of it away. The blade, in its terrible wisdom, had forced me to remember.

Each step brought the sickening crunch of bones beneath my armored boots. The quiet was total, born from the fact that everything capable of making noise had already been destroyed. The last time I had seen this place, the air had still been torn by screams.

A lone figure stirred at the far edge of the plain, a silhouette against the dying light. He knelt beside a fallen soldier, his head bowed, brushing ash from a face he seemed to recognize. His shoulders were slumped, but his body was intact. His chest, bare to the elements, was smooth and unscarred. His hair was darker, his face less hollow, unmarked by the sorrow that would soon claim him. He turned slowly, as if sensing my presence.

It was Ilija.

He looked up, his gaze finding me standing there in the blood-stained armor, a ghost from a future that had yet to arrive. His expression held only the bitter recognition that comes when you encounter what you had desperately hoped to forget.

"I came back," he said, his voice younger, clearer than I remembered, unspoiled by the distances he would later learn to wear.

I stopped a few feet away, the sword still in my hand. "You always do."

We held each other's gaze, unsmiling. The wind shifted, and the gnarled tree behind him groaned. A crack split the sky above, and then, mercifully, everything folded inward, the vision receding like a tide.

The battlefield vanished. I stumbled forward, my hands plunging into the damp moss of the glade, bracing against the sudden return. My breath scraped against my throat as I forced myself upright, my fingers raw and scraped. The feathers on the altar had scattered, blown across the stone. The lingering heat in the earth had dissipated, leaving only cold ground beneath me.

I reached into my coat, seeking comfort or perhaps proof, and withdrew the rose the girl had given me. Its petals had blackened and curled inward, desiccated by the searing memory. When I opened my palm, it crumbled into fine, grey ash, a final, cruel echo of Ilija's disappearance.

The blade held its quiet. The gods, having delivered their terrible gift, had departed, leaving only the hush that followed their passing.

Every muscle in my body was tempered now, forged by the force of memory pressed into flesh. My breathing was slower, steadier, the ragged edge of panic smoothed away. My skin still burned along the lines of the runes, a soft thrum, and the sensation had become confirmation. What came next was clear.

I left the altar behind, turning into the trees without hesitation. The forest recognized my passage and shifted to allow it. I moved through it freely, because I was part of what the land had decided to accept.

The path ahead, unseen to casual eyes, had been shaped with purpose long ago, then left to fade beneath layers of moss and forgetting, awaiting its return. Stones, half-buried and worn, pushed through the frost in uneven lines, guiding the way. The chill had lost its sting. It wrapped into my coat and boots like an old companion.

With every stride, the ground grew softer, yielding beneath my feet. The sharp glint of frost thinned and vanished. Beneath it, old symbols stirred, brief glimpses of spirals and runes that echoed the markings burned into my skin. Each one flickered, barely visible, before sinking back into the earth. They were memory rising, acknowledging my passage.

The light above the ridge shifted as the clouds parted, stretching into layered grays, opening fleeting channels to a softer sky beyond. The fog that had clung to me held close, moving against my shoulders, curling across my arms, holding its shape as it traveled with me. It was a shroud woven by the land itself.

The forest grew quieter with every step I took further into its heart. The stillness held shape, the kind that forms only when an immense presence chooses to hold perfectly still and listen.

Each breath settled deeper in my chest, calm and steady. The cold folded into the motion of my body, matching my pace. I moved with purpose now, with a direction that had eluded me for weeks. The blade rested against my back, part of how I moved through the world. It had shaped me long before I ever returned to claim it.

The woman who had forged it lingered in my memory. I recalled the deliberate force of her hands as she worked, the raw finality in her posture. She had toiled without relief, whispered only to the metal. She had pressed every part of herself into the blade, and when it was finished, she had walked it to the roots of the tree and left it there. Her body had worn restraint the way others wore shields. That restraint, I understood now, still lived in the weapon.

As I followed the winding trail away from the sacred tree, I carried her stillness with me. The land moved beside me now. It matched my pace. It had always known I would come this way again.

The grove receded behind me as I moved down through the ridge, the blade pressed evenly across my spine. The wind brought the scent of salt and distant smoke, heavier now, more insistent. The mist thickened again around my ankles, curling through the long, wet grass. I already knew where I was going.

The slope narrowed, the ground shifting beneath loose stone and trampled moss, revealing a thin path ahead. It had been worn down by countless feet over generations. The farther I went, the more the air changed, growing denser, infused with the tang of the sea. My muscles screamed in protest, but I pressed on. Every step held a momentum I hadn't possessed in weeks, a driving force I didn't have to steal from anyone else. By nightfall, the churning expanse of the coast broke into view.

The chapel sat low against the rugged cliffs, built from weathered stone, shaped by the battering of centuries. Its roof had been patched with mismatched slate, and the bell that hung in its arch leaned to one side, a weary sentinel. The place had the stubborn strength of endurance rather than sanctity, the kind that comes from surviving far more than it was ever built to withstand.

A figure stepped out from the shadows along the chapel wall. Her cloak fell around her ankles, and she held herself with the same calm, coiled tension I remembered. Her weapon was sheathed. My name went unspoken. Yet I knew her, recognized her with an instinct born of shared purpose. Maeryn stood utterly still, her eyes locked on mine.

I stopped a few feet away, adjusting the strap of the blade across my shoulder.

"You waited," I said, the words flat.

She nodded once, a brief, sharp movement. "You took long enough."

"I had shit to do, you know."

"That part's obvious, even from a distance."

The exchange was stripped clean, free of warmth, only a stark understanding that we'd both spent whatever pretense we once had. I moved past her, reaching for the wooden door of the chapel. It opened with a long, grating scrape of iron against stone, the wood damp and worn from the salty air rolling in off the sea.

Inside, the thick stone walls trapped the cold, holding it close. The space was wide and stark, empty of pews or ornament. Only a large fire pit in the center, long burned out, its base filled with coals and ash, untouched for weeks, perhaps longer. The floor was uneven, cobbled stone with moss clinging to the edges where moisture had seeped in. The echoes of lives lived within its walls clung to the air.

I dropped my pack beside the doorway and unfastened the blade. The leather straps, stiff with use, caught for a second before I pulled them loose. I set the weapon down beside me and sat with my back against the stone wall. My legs stretched out before me, a bone-deep ache settling into my exhausted muscles. My fingers throbbed from the grip I had maintained all day, and I let them stay clenched. The cold offered a strange kind of relief.

Maeryn stepped inside a moment later, closing the door behind her with a soft thud. She crossed the room without a word, reached into a worn basket tucked into a corner, retrieved a thick wool cloak, and handed it to me.

I pulled it over my shoulders. It smelled of old firewood, perhaps lavender or dried herbs from someone else's hands. Thanks would have been pointless. She expected none.

She sat near the opposite wall, leaning her head back against the stone. Her eyes closed for a brief, weary breath, but she stayed alert. I stared at the dead fire for a long time. Peace was nowhere in me, and relief even further. Only the immense, crushing fact of what came next, filling me bone by bone.

Sleep refused me that night. My body craved oblivion, but my mind kept dragging me back to the sharp edges of waking. The fire stayed dead, its coals stubbornly lifeless, even after I tried twice to coax a flame from them. The air in the chapel thickened with a chill that lodged behind the ribs and refused to yield.

She asked nothing, attempted nothing. She sat in vigil across from me, her back against the stone, her legs folded beneath her cloak. We held that way until the first faint light of dawn began to bleed into the sky, washing the stars from view.

When I pushed myself upright, my joints cracked in protest, and my left shoulder pulled with a dull pain, twisted beyond repair. I stretched it, rotating my arm until the sharp edge softened into a manageable ache, and then reached for the blade. It came freely. My fingers wrapped around the hilt, and its weight found its place along my spine as I strapped it into position.

She rose in turn, her movements controlled, though I could tell her body was as ravaged by the journey as mine. Her face looked harder in the pale morning light, sharper around her discerning eyes. The scar across her cheek had faded, paling into what was almost elegant.

"How far is the sea?" I asked, my voice flat.

She answered without hesitation. "You'll hit the channel by dusk if you move fast. There's a boat waiting. Supplies, weapons, the rest of the maps. I stashed them near the crossing."

"What about the Accord?"

"There's been patrols in the area," she replied, her voice low. "They pass through, but they leave. They don't like these hills."

"Good," I said, satisfaction curling in my gut. "I hope it fucking hurts."

Her mouth twitched, a fleeting ghost of a smile, but it faded before it arrived.

I tightened the straps on my boots, checked the compass on my belt, grabbed the satchel I had left untouched the night before. When I turned towards the chapel door, Maeryn followed.

At the threshold, she spoke again, her voice low. "They know you're moving."

"Let them know," I retorted, stepping into the morning air. "I'm done hiding."

"They've taken more cities," she pressed, a flicker of urgency in her eyes.

"I'll take them back," I promised, my voice a blade-edge of resolve.

She stepped aside, allowing me to pass into the stark light of the new day.

The path west curved through thornbrush and hollow, treacherous ground, cutting a narrow passage between patches of grass scorched by old fires. The rolling hills narrowed, dropping away into flat, desolate fields, and then the coastline, foreboding, came into view once more. I stopped counting the hours and measuring the miles. My boots dug into the frost-stiffened dirt with a steady rhythm. My breath left my lips in short, sharp bursts. I moved faster once the scent of seaweed, sharp and wild on the wind, reached me.

By late afternoon, the crossing Maeryn had described revealed itself. The small boat sat below a jagged ledge of shale, tied to a broken post hammered into the rocks. It wasn't much, a low craft built for one person and a few crates, but the tide had come in, and the current, though powerful, looked steady. A canvas-lashed crate sat nearby, crusted with salt and spray. I ripped it open with impatient fingers.

Inside, I found a water flask and two tightly wrapped meal packs. A second blade, sleek and wickedly sharp, that looked untouched. A stack of folded maps sealed in protective wax. Beneath the maps lay a strip of cloth, black, with silver embroidery in the shape of a broken wheel. It was old, impossibly old, predating even the long war. I shoved it into my pack without a second thought.

The wind picked up, a biting chill that tore at my exposed skin. My fingers burned as I dragged the boat to the water's edge and climbed in. It rocked once beneath my weight and held steady. I untied the line and pushed off hard, sending the craft skimming across the water. The cliffs behind me faded as the current took hold, pulling me westward.

The sky blackened as I crossed the churning channel. The sea moved beneath the boat in long swells. I faced forward, one hand on the rope, the other resting near my belt, my mind locked on the blade strapped across my back. It had made no sound since I had taken it from the tree. Its stillness was watchful, an old companion biding its time.

Land broke into view just before nightfall, a silhouette against the starless sky. The distant shore was lifeless, its coastline a jagged line of stone and grey sand that sloped upward towards the inland trees.

As the boat scraped against the shore, I stood and stepped into the frigid surf. The icy water soaked through my boots, a painful stab that shot up through my ankles. I pulled the boat farther onto the beach, securing it beneath a low shelf of rock where only someone who knew the coast would find it.

I reached for the compass Éloïse had given me back in Graz. The needle spun once, then pointed with unwavering certainty. It had stopped tracking north days ago. It pointed towards the hills beyond the beach, where what was old and violent, what had waited for centuries, waited to be claimed.

The wind held steady. The sky stayed whole. I knew the truth of it in my chest, a certainty that resonated through my bones. Whatever path I had been on before, whatever fragmented journey had led me here, it was ending.

"Ilija," I whispered, my voice raw against the roar of the sea, "I'm fucking coming, just hold on a little longer."

CHAPTER SEVENTEEN
THE RESONANT ECHO

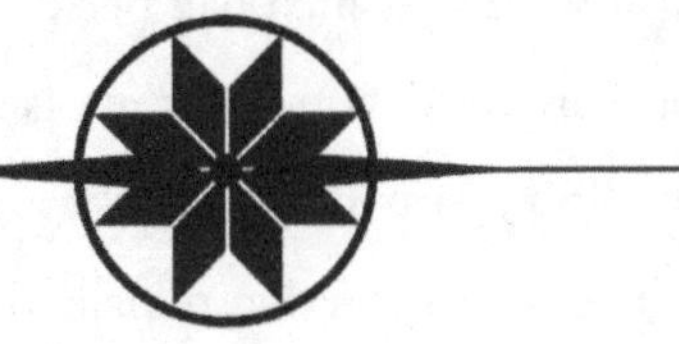

Ilija

I woke with the taste of earth clinging to my tongue, thick and metallic, as though I had bitten into iron buried in the heart of stone. Each breath tore through my throat with raw friction. A slow burn had taken root in my chest, something older than fire, something left to fester in the stagnant air of this forgotten place. Cords bound my wrists behind my back, moving with terrifying intimacy, tightening with every shallow breath. They released their grip only when my pulse dared to slow.

Pain flowered in my side, sharp and relentless. With each inhalation it flared deeper. My head throbbed in rhythm, and the dried blood along my jaw told me violence had happened that I couldn't recall. The last shard of memory was her voice, a sudden slip sideways, then blankness.

The chamber held its breath. The air sat heavy in my lungs, untouched by warmth or breeze. A single sound reached me from above, unnervingly patient. Water dripped from one level of stone to another, striking with a rhythm that suggested centuries, the cadence of a ritual worn into bone.

Even before I forced my eyes open, I knew I was deep beneath the earth. The pressure coiled around my ribs, pooled behind my eyes. This was something far older than the prisons men built for their fleeting wars, shaped by reverence, hollowed for worship.

When my eyelids dragged open, the chamber resolved into view like a memory surfacing from murky water. The walls curved inward in a perfect dome, sculpted from a single piece of living stone. No jagged seams marked the intervention of tools. Every inch had been smoothed by hands that worked with patient, tireless devotion. Symbols spiraled outward from a central point on the floor, weaving together languages I recognized, Greek, Glagolitic, Latin, alongside others that remained tantalizingly beyond my grasp. The unfamiliar glyphs looked as though they had been drawn by memory and instinct, shaped by someone who still believed that writing itself was an offering.

She was at the heart of it all. Ana. She sat on a low stone bench, her back impossibly straight, her hands resting in her lap. The robe she wore cascaded around her, pooling against the floor like smoke given solid form. Her hair had changed. It no longer held the soft brown I had known. Now it gleamed the color of molten gold, lit from within, as though it had been poured from the sun itself. Her eyes, those depths I had once known so intimately, glowed with a quiet, submerged radiance that never flickered.

The cords at my wrists kept rhythm with my labored breathing. They did not bite into my skin, yet they reminded me, constantly, who held the power here. Even stillness had been claimed by her will. I dragged my battered body upright through the suffocating press of broken ribs and days lost to silence. I held the agony trapped inside my teeth.

Ana rose, as if my movement had been a summons. Her steps landed with careful grace, as if the ground beneath her feet knew better than to resist. When she reached me, she knelt, her form folding with effortless precision. Her hand came to my face, cupping my cheek. Her palm was warm. For a dizzying instant I was back in Belgrade, early morning light through the curtains, her breath warm on my neck, the half-sleep before coffee. I flinched, but she did not withdraw.

"You were never meant to wake like this, Ilija," she said, her voice a hoarse whisper that scraped against my ears. "This isn't how I wanted it to be for you."

My throat burned as I forced the words out, each one a jagged shard of defiance. "But it's what happened, isn't it?"

Her hand dropped away. Her posture changed, subtle enough that anyone else would have missed it, yet enough for me to feel the force behind her every movement.

"I didn't bring you here to punish you," she breathed. "I brought you here because if you finish what you've started, there won't be a way back for any of us."

I met her luminous eyes. "You mean for us."

She held my stare. "No, Ilija. I mean the gods and their war, the world that's finally beginning to remember its own name because you won't let it stay asleep. People have started speaking of you like you're a prophecy, a damn legend walking among them."

"I didn't ask for this," I said, bitterness raw on my tongue.

"I know," she countered, her voice softening, carrying a strange sorrow. "That's exactly why it had to be you. If it were anyone else, they'd revel in it, wouldn't they? They'd demand the power."

The torches seemed to dim in response, as if her words carried force beyond sound. Shadows lengthened, twisting. Ana stepped back, folding her arms tightly across her chest. She looked as though she had come here clinging to a desperate hope, trying to save something that no longer existed.

"I thought we could build something new, Ilija," she murmured, her voice heavy with regret. "That your gods and mine didn't have to be enemies. That we could find something between myth and man, something human and enduring."

"You wanted Ilija and Ana," I said quietly, the names a ghost between us.

"I was never just Ana," she answered, her voice tired with old truth.

"And I was never just Ilija," I finished. The realization sat cold and clean in my chest.

Neither of us needed to speak their names. We already knew them.

She walked to the far side of the room, towards a shallow basin in black marble. From it she took a bronze cup, worn smooth by time. Greek letters on its surface, dulled by age, still caught the torchlight at odd angles. She filled it with water, its surface unnervingly still, and returned to kneel before me, offering it with both hands.

"For the pain," she said, her voice soft as ash.

I hesitated. Her eyes remained unwavering.

"Please," she whispered. "Just this once."

The liquid slid down my throat like cold, living metal. It pulled me inward, a relentless undertow dragging me to the quietest part of myself. My limbs softened. My mind drifted to the edges of awareness, floating, untethered. Then I felt her beside me again, lying close, her breath a slow rhythm against my ribs. Her body wrapped around me with the same possessive certainty it once had. Yet something had changed at its foundation.

The bed beneath me smelled of wild rose and pomegranate. The silk sheets pressed against my skin like memory disguised as comfort. The phantom ache of the cords lingered beneath the skin. Her arm rested across my ribs, a familiar pressure, as though she still belonged there. Her hair, that impossible molten gold, spread across my chest like gilded thread, catching the low light with a metallic gleam. She looked peaceful, but it was the peace of something arranged, orchestrated with painstaking care.

I kept my eyes open, fixed on the ceiling. Gold grew directly from the stone, forming intricate patterns alive in the fabric of the chamber. The walls radiated a faint warmth that clung to my skin like old longing. This place was a shrine pretending to be a sanctuary. She was no longer a woman. She was Aphrodite, goddess of beauty and war. I was no longer just hers.

I turned my head slowly, careful not to disturb her manufactured peace. The pain in my chest had dulled to a persistent throb, but the quiet around me stayed sharp. I remembered when her hair had been chestnut, a warm, unremarkable brown that softened in morning light, the kind of color that belonged to autumn fields, to human things. That version of her had belonged to something real. This gilded Ana belonged to something else entirely.

She slept with the confidence of someone who believed the story had already reached its predetermined end, and that I had stayed. Every detail of this room had been chosen to convince me I was safe. The warmth of her arm across my stomach was measured, its intimacy a calculated effect. Her nearness was another wall in this cage, beautiful and suffocating.

I watched the ceiling, those gold etchings forming a vast net of symbols woven into living stone. Some were familiar, the spirals for Zorya, the lightning for Perun. Others stretched into complex geometric shapes I couldn't place. They hummed with hidden energy when I let my eyes linger.

Every inch of this chamber had been built with singular, obsessive intention.

The ache at my wrists had faded, but the phantom memory held. I flexed my fingers beneath the silk, feeling restraint echoed in every tendon. I imagined standing, walking barefoot through the stone passages until I found something that opened. I imagined the first rush of clean air against my face, and Danica's voice.

I remembered her on that desolate mountainside, voice rough from the cold, carrying a certainty that needed no proof. She hadn't tried to convince me of anything. She had said my name, Ilija, like it still belonged to me, like it was a key to something only she understood. She had seen what I was becoming, the unraveling, and she hadn't stepped back. Her eyes held the recognition that comes from carrying the same burdens. She didn't ask for promises. She stayed because she understood what it meant to choose someone who hadn't finished becoming.

The thought of her settled beneath my ribs, fierce and protective. I hadn't seen her since the Accord's soldiers had met their end on that mountain. Yet I could feel her still moving, still holding the fire that I, trapped here, couldn't reach.

Ana stirred beside me. Silk rustled. Her arm moved across my ribs. Her breath caught, then resumed its measured rhythm. She whispered something too quiet to decipher, then stilled. I didn't move. I watched the ceiling and held perfectly still, waiting for the runes embedded within me to quiet.

They had begun to stir, a dull, persistent heat beneath the skin of my forearms, responding to something far beyond these walls. They didn't respond to Ana. They remembered Danica. They remembered the rugged shrine and the raw storm. They were waiting for her, the same way I was.

I slipped my arm out from under hers slowly, inch by agonizing inch, until her body no longer touched me. I moved the silk aside with exquisite care. Then, with a searing protest from my ribs, I stood. My legs held. The floor was cold and smooth. The pain no longer grounded me in despair. It reminded me that I was still mine.

The air changed as I stepped into the corridor beyond. The walls were engraved with countless glyphs, some cut deep, others scratched faintly as though added in haste. Every mark radiated faint internal heat. The silence here was constructed, held in the fabric of the place like a breath trapped in a closed chest.

Velvet curtains hung in precise intervals along the corridor, framing what appeared to be windows. When I reached out, my fingers met cold stone. The murals painted behind the curtains gave the cruel illusion of depth, of a world beyond. The view was a painstakingly rendered lie.

The scent changed. The heady perfume of roses was gone, the sweetness of pomegranate with it. The air smelled of myrrh and dust, of incense left burning in a temple long after the gods had departed. The torches still flickered, but their flames held no life.

I kept walking. A growing certainty propelled me, yet I knew I was not alone. Ana's intention lived in the corridors themselves, pressed into the stone.

The atrium revealed itself without announcement. I stepped into a vast, circular space beneath a towering dome of glass and gleaming ivory. A single tree stood rooted at its center. It had not grown here. It had been shaped, forced into unnatural perfection. Its bark shimmered like gold leaf pressed over bone. Its leaves, thin and silver, trembled in the absolute stillness. Beneath the tree, a black pool spread in a perfect circle, its surface reflecting only the dome above. It showed nothing of me.

Seven mirrors surrounded the pool, each bearing the shape of a myth pulled from the edges of memory. The triskelion, the ouroboros, symbols too old for names, their outlines fading. These were functional, placed with deliberate intent. This room had been built to hold revelation.

I stepped closer. The mirrors showed nothing of me. They showed only her. Danica. Yet this was a version of her shaped by memory too vast for a single lifetime.

In the first mirror, she stood alone at the precipice of a jagged cliff, wrapped in dark linen, her hair wild and lifted by a storm that had not yet broken. The ground beneath her was blackened and cracked. Her eyes glowed with something that had no earthly name. In the next, she knelt beside a fallen girl, her palm pressed to the girl's cold cheek. Her lips moved in silence, and as she spoke, the girl's eyes opened, as if the world, having released her, had called her back.

Another mirror showed her on horseback, shoulders tense, a blade resting across her lap, her face half-hidden in shadow. She did not move, yet her stillness held an immense coiled force, the kind that keeps a battlefield together until the moment it is meant to shatter.

I took a step closer, my breath catching. The fourth mirror rippled as though reacting to my heartbeat. Danica knelt in a grove I didn't recognize, at the base of a stone marker. Her fingers gripped a scrap of cloth I recognized instantly, an old scarf, torn from the night we had escaped the stronghold. She pressed it to her face, her shoulders shaking with grief she did not dare voice. At her feet lay a ring, unadorned gold, its surface engraved with intertwining flowers. I didn't remember giving it to her, yet I knew, with a certainty that resonated in my bones, that it was mine.

In that moment, Danica was a woman trying to hold together the pieces of a life that kept breaking. The image cut deeper than anything Ana had done to me. When Danica rose, she carried the ring. She folded it into her hand, clutching it tight, and walked forward.

"Do you see her now?"

Ana's voice reached me from across the atrium. I realized she had been watching far longer than I had known. I turned, rigid.

She stood near the seventh mirror, the one that reflected nothing. Her flowing robe was gone. She wore ceremonial armor that gleamed like scorched ivory, its designs catching the dim light. Her hair had been pulled back and braided with cold metal. Pendants hung at her neck, bearing symbols I didn't recognize. Her golden eyes held no warmth.

"I've always seen her," I said, low and even.

She stepped towards the blank mirror. "Then you know what she's become, Ilija. What she's truly capable of."

Silence settled between us, thick as dust in a forgotten tomb.

"She won't stop," Ana said, her voice dropping low. "She doesn't care what breaks along the way. She wants to tear it all down, everything we built."

My fists clenched at my sides. "You mean what you built."

"I mean the order we gave them," she corrected. "The Accord. The silence. We brought peace to a world rotting in its own myths. Your Danica would see it burn, watch it crumble to ash, to bring back names no one should ever remember."

I looked past her at the mirror that still refused to show me anything. "You replaced memory with obedience, Ana, and called it peace."

"I did what had to be done," she insisted. Genuine regret flickered across her golden eyes. "I would have chosen something else, Ilija. A kitchen in Belgrade, your laugh echoing through the halls, the quiet life we could have had. But the day you remembered who you were, that future vanished."

"I never asked to be this," I said.

"You didn't need to," she countered, sharp now. "You chose her, Ilija. Over and over again, across lifetimes, you chose her."

The black pool beneath the tree stirred. Its surface changed in density, as though something vast beneath it had begun to wake. A low hum rose from its depths, filling the atrium. The mirrors changed, their reflections twisting. I saw myself, fractured across time. A boy standing before five flickering flames, his face alight with wonder. A scholar gripping chalk in a trembling hand, watching symbols appear on a tablet. Then nothing.

She stood beside the mirror as if it had always belonged to her. "This is what you've become, Ilija," she said. "A shape that no longer fits inside the boundaries of one life. You are something more."

The words hollowed something in my chest. My throat tightened. "I never asked to be anything more."

She did not approach. "You became it anyway. Worse, they remember you now. That cannot be undone."

She reached into her armor and pulled out a locket. The chain was thin, the gold worn smooth where her skin had polished it over countless years. I recognized it. I had given it to her when I still believed in a future untainted by gods or prophecy, when a shared apartment in Belgrade and a half-burnt meal had felt like everything.

"It still carries your name, Ilija," she said, barely a whisper.

I looked at the small golden disc but made no move to reach for it. My eyes went back to the mirror, where my reflection still refused to take shape.

"I'm not that man anymore, Ana," I said.

She held my gaze, golden eyes unblinking. "No one remains exactly who they were, Ilija. The difference is that I didn't fight it. I embraced the change."

She extended the locket once more, but her hand did not tremble. When I did not move, she closed her fingers around it, the gold disappearing into her palm.

"Then let me show you what she sees, Ilija."

The floor responded first. Symbols beneath the polished stone began to stir. Faint lines of light threaded outward in slow waves, red and gold weaving through the seams like veins returning to life. The air pressed against my chest. The walls vibrated with a low hum, as if the chamber itself recognized what was about to unfold. The mirror behind her darkened into a swirling void, and something deep within my body turned towards it, pulled tight with a force I didn't understand.

The chamber folded inward. The stone floor held my feet, yet my body no longer felt anchored. Ana did not move, but her gravity deepened. The air stretched like old fabric caught in a slow, agonizing tear. The torchlight bent sideways. The walls seemed to inhale, and the vision began.

I remained standing, but the room dissolved, the cold stone vanishing beneath my feet as if memory had peeled it away. I was no longer in the temple. I was somewhere else, deep in the currents of memory.

Ash clung to the air, thick and acrid. The sky was the color of iron. I stood at the edge of a battlefield where nothing lived, where no breath stirred. Burned books and shattered icons littered the ground. The stench of fire had sunk deep into the soil. A sun hovered above, a baleful orb casting only cold, indifferent light.

Danica stood at the center of this devastation. Her cloak, torn and frayed, still carried the lingering frost of her journey. Her shoulders were squared, her sword at her side, stained and silent. Her eyes were fixed ahead, towards something distant. Her face held the kind of exhaustion that follows too many losses.

Ana's voice returned, woven into the bones of this desolation.

"She sees what you're becoming, Ilija. The storm, the weapon. She no longer sees the man."

I moved towards Danica, my legs heavy. The air resisted with each step. The ground pulled at my feet, as though trying to keep me from reaching her. She turned just slightly, enough to catch my motion, but she did not call to me. Her hands trembled. The blade in her grip gleamed wetly at its edge.

Stone vaulted high above me. The walls were Roman, cracked and blackened with centuries of soot. Fires burned in the far corners. Children's voices echoed in a liturgy I didn't understand. I stood at the center of this sacred wreckage, unable to move. My body had been laid across a marble altar, stiff and cold, my eyes open, staring into the vaulted ceiling. I wasn't breathing. I was dead.

Danica knelt beside me, her face streaked with ash. Her mouth moved, forming silent words, her hands shaking. She pressed her fingers to my chest, to my face, whispering my name like it had once meant rescue, like it still held the power to bring me back.

"Come back, Ilija. Come back."

The sword lay at her side, broken clean through, its pieces no longer bleeding light. They had gone silent.

Ana's voice cut through the image, shattering it.

"She thinks she can reach you, Ilija. She still believes you're human enough to return to her."

I shouted, a guttural sound torn from my chest, and the vision shattered. The cold stone of the atrium rushed back around me, the black pool, the mirrors. I staggered, catching myself on one knee, heaving as if I had just broken the surface of deep water. The room smelled of roses again, overripe, edged with decay. Ana stood above me. She didn't reach down. She only looked at me with the expression she had worn in the old world, when she was still Ana, when I was still human enough to hold her affection.

"You'll forget me in every life you live, Ilija," she said quietly, sorrow threaded through her voice. "But I will remember every version of you, every time you left me."

I turned my face from her.

She stepped back. "You still believe Danica sees your humanity, Ilija?"

I clenched my jaw against the pressure building in my ribs. Something new stirred there. "She sees all of me, Ana."

Ana's voice tightened. "She sees a god, Ilija. A weapon."

I met her gaze, unblinking. "She sees the man who chose her. Who keeps choosing her."

Her breath caught, barely perceptible. She did not speak again. The torchlight dimmed, receding into deeper shadow. I could feel it coming now, something deeper than her visions, something the gods themselves had been waiting to show me. I did not resist.

I closed my eyes, and the silence changed. It came from within now, unfurling through my chest like a breath held too long, finally released. The stone floor vanished, but this time it didn't feel like Ana's doing. What descended was not hers. It moved through me as though it had always known the shape of my body, the names buried in my marrow. There were no words at first, only sensation.

I stood barefoot on snow that did not melt. The cold seeped through my soles and climbed my spine, but it did not hurt. It reminded. Grief settled behind my ribs, the kind that waits, curling inward with every breath that dares to go on. The sky above me held stars I did not recognize, constellations vast and alien, each one moving as if pulled into a shape I hadn't yet learned to read.

A voice broke through. It reached through memory itself, forming meaning from feeling, from pure sensation.

You are the storm's echo, and the fire's breath. You are the hinge upon which the next world turns.

I opened my mouth to respond, but no sound came. The vision had already changed, pulling me deeper.

I stood at the edge of a black shoreline. The sea stretched wide before me, churning, its rhythm locked to my heartbeat. Each wave rolled forward with names I didn't know yet knew intimately, faces I had once loved, now lost. I looked down. My wrists were unbound. The marks from the rope remained, faint silver scars. A figure approached from the fog beyond the waves. For a breathless second my heart leaped, convinced it was Ana. But the scent reached me first, heather and cold iron. My stomach clenched.

Danica.

Or rather, the version of her who had walked longer and endured more than a single lifetime could encompass.

She emerged from the mist, brambles caught in her cloak, raven feathers stitched into her shoulders. Ash streaked her face. In her right hand she held a blade I had never seen, yet it answered something deep inside me with such terrifying certainty that I staggered. I had known it before I was born.

She did not speak right away. She looked at me, her gaze heavy, as if the world itself had narrowed to this single exchange.

When she finally spoke, her voice carried no doubt. "You are not who you think you are, Ilija."

I tried to step back, but the sea growled behind me, pressing against my heels, holding me.

She stopped a pace in front of me. "You've carried the name Ilija like a torch through centuries, through war and forgetting, but that name is not the only one written into your bones."

My voice broke when I answered. "Then what am I?"

Her gaze softened. The blade in her hand began to hum, its edge catching light from a sun that had not yet risen.

"You are the choice, Ilija," she said. "The one who stands between what was and what might be. The one who burns and comes back changed."

Something moved beneath my ribs. It climbed like light through clear water, slow and unshakable, rising into my throat until I felt my mouth shape the beginning of a name that had always been mine, waiting to be reclaimed.

"I am…" but the vision twisted again, a sudden, violent wrench.

Danica faded into mist. The shoreline collapsed into foam. Then I stood before a towering mountain shrouded in snow, its summit lost in cloud. Auroras moved across the sky like smoke given ethereal form. A great temple waited at the summit, its doors cracked open, lit with soft blue-green light. I stepped inside.

At the center of the vast chamber, a throne stood. It was made of petrified wood, shaped by millennia into something that resembled a wound more than a seat of power. A figure sat upon it.

It was me, only older, infinitely more weathered. My hair, holy shit, I had hair, streaked with silver. My palms spiraled with contained lightning. His eyes, though hollowed by years, were piercingly clear. He did not stand. He watched me approach.

"What is this?" I asked.

He did not blink. "This is what she fears, Ilija. Your remembering."

He rose, and the immense gravity of him settled over me like iron. His back bore the marks of lashes I did not recall earning. His chest had been inscribed with the names of places I had not yet seen. The pain in his face ran deeper than wounds. It was the cost of remembering everything and still choosing to go on.

"She thinks you are hers," he said, or rather, I spoke to myself, the words echoing from a deeper part of my being. "But you were never a possession, Ilija. You were always a choice."

I looked into his face and felt the answer move through me again, unbidden.

"Then what am I?"

The blade appeared before me, suspended in the air, the one Danica had carried. It rested on the cold stone, its metal breathing. Heat shimmered from its edge, radiating like memory rising from scorched earth.

I stepped forward. The moment my foot crossed the line of its aura, the vision broke.

Stone rushed back into place, the atrium slamming closed around me. The walls contracted once, slow and deep, like a vast heart. My chest ached, but my breath came even. I opened my eyes and found Ana watching me from across the chamber. Her face had gone pale, her golden eyes wide. She too had witnessed what had changed.

Ana stood across from me, her hands slack at her sides. I saw it in her jaw, the way her chin lifted a fraction too high, compensating. I pushed myself upright. My legs were slow to respond, stiff from disuse, my ribs protesting. The bruises along my spine echoed how long I had been held.

"You can't keep what you don't understand, Ana," I said, my voice rough from disuse, yet carrying a new authority. She understood. After a long pause she stepped back, unceremonious, as though retreating from a door shut against her. She walked away without attempting to stop me, vanishing into the corridor. As she disappeared, the light in the room faded to a softer gold.

I was alone. The silence that followed offered no comfort, stretched too thin to hold any peace. The room no longer resisted me, but I did not belong to it. It recognized something in me that had not been there before, something unfinished.

I sat, to steady myself. My limbs trembled from the effort of standing too long in a space shaped by the wills of gods. The runes on the walls no longer hummed with domination. They responded to something within me, flickering in rhythm with my breath.

I thought of Danica. The woman who had met me in fire and ruin, whose gaze carried too many lifetimes. She had never demanded that I remember, never forced the past upon me. She had remained beside me, patiently, fiercely, long enough for memory to break through on its own. When the truth cut too deep, she stayed.

Footsteps, soft and deliberate, echoed from the corridor. I turned, every instinct sharpening. Someone was coming. Their arrival preceded them, quiet and immense, a wave of power moving without urgency, yet every step closed the distance with purpose. I rose as the figure appeared in the archway.

She wore a dark robe stitched with pale constellations that matched no sky I knew. Her movements were precise, each step displacing nothing, yet the room changed with her inside it. The sharp scent of iron and myrrh followed her, grounding her in something far older than Ana's cloying fragrances. Her face was hidden beneath a heavy hood, but the lower edge of her jaw, glimpsed in firelight, hinted at a beauty that predated human memory. Her skin shimmered, as if the years clung to her like dust.

"You are no longer hers, Ilija," she said, her voice a low hum.

There was no threat in her words. She was stating a truth already proven. She stepped closer, kneeling beside me with slow grace. The remnants of the rope still hung around my wrists. With a glance, they unraveled, the fibers dropping to the floor without a sound.

I looked at her. "Did Ana send you?"

"I didn't come for her," she said. "I came for you, Ilija."

I studied her face, trying to find purchase. "Who are you?"

She pushed her hood back, revealing features that didn't settle into a single shape. Her face moved as if sculpted by memory alone, fluid and shifting. The longer I looked, the more I recognized her, yet I couldn't place her, couldn't tether her to any single life.

"You opened the wound, Ilija," she said. "Now the others have begun to stir."

"They've been watching for a long time," I said.

"They were patient," she affirmed. "They were waiting for the right moment, but your blood called louder than theirs."

She drew something from her robe, a curved shard of black stone no longer than my palm. Runes spiraled along its edge, glowing softly. I didn't know the words, but I understood what they meant. She placed the shard in my hand, curling my fingers around its warm, humming surface.

"You can't keep moving forward, Ilija," she said, her voice carrying urgent gravity. "You must return to where it began."

"Where what began?" I asked.

She tilted her head, her eyes piercing mine. "The deepest part of you that still sleeps."

I glanced at the shard. It held heat, a breath in my palm.

"Danica is out there," I said, my voice taut. "I have to reach her."

"She is already moving," the woman affirmed. "Toward the blade, toward what was written long before either of you were born. If she claims it alone, it may cost her more than she expects."

I tightened my grip.

"Then I'll find her before she gets there," I said.

The woman stood slowly. "You have one chance, Ilija. You must return to the shrine beneath the mountain. If you remember who you are there, in full, then the rest may still be reclaimed."

She turned towards the corridor and walked away. She didn't vanish in a flash. She faded, as if distance had always been waiting to carry her.

I stood with the black shard warming in my palm. I turned towards the open archway. The walls no longer reached for me. The temple no longer pretended I was meant to stay. I stepped forward.

The stairwell wound upward in silence. The steps, worn smooth by centuries, held beneath my weight. I moved slowly at first, my legs stiff, but with every step a surge of renewed strength coursed through me. My body ached in places I couldn't name, yet I no longer felt like a prisoner. The shard rested warm against my palm, and I followed it without hesitation.

I emerged into a hallway of gold-veined stone. The air was cooler here, touched by wind that did not belong to the underground temple. The markings on the walls were written in symbols that stirred something in my chest. They didn't glow. They breathed. I could feel their pull as I passed.

The corridor narrowed, then opened into a chamber unlike anything I had encountered. Circular, its ceiling lost in shadow, with a shallow pool at its center. The water was clear as glass, reflecting nothing. I stepped closer. The shard vibrated, as if it recognized what waited below.

I knelt and touched the surface. The stillness broke. Ripples spread outward in perfect rings, then images erupted through the water. Fire and stormlight, the glint of steel on wet ground. A child running through drifts of grey ash. A woman's hand grasping a blade wrapped in black cloth.

I leaned closer. The images slowed. I fell back onto cold stone, the water once more still, but the warmth in the shard had grown stronger.

Something pressed behind my eyes, at the edge of my awareness, like an incoming tide waiting to rise.

I stood and moved towards the far end of the chamber. A door was set into the wall, a simple arch bearing a single symbol I had seen once before in the shrine beneath the stronghold. The storm-heart had carried it in its final moment.

I reached out and brushed the symbol. The stone gave way. The door opened without a sound, revealing the night beyond. Wind curled through the passage, carrying the scent of pine and the chill of frost.

As I stepped outside, the mountains surrounded me, their peaks piercing the ink-black sky. The stars were low and sharp, spread across the heavens like a map I could almost read. Below, the land was dark and still. I couldn't see the road that wound through it, but I knew it waited for me.

Danica Madsen was out there somewhere, following the path towards the blade, towards the place we had both been forged to reach. I adjusted the shard in my hand and started down the slope, a man no longer broken, but remembering who he was.

CHAPTER EIGHTEEN
THE STORM RETURNS

Ilija

Europe unraveled quietly. In Germany, schoolchildren recited sterile creeds, their voices hollow with rehearsal. In Belgium, street signs bore symbols instead of names, roses and crowns absorbed into the landscape until no one questioned them. The Netherlands folded with weary grace, its libraries converted into archives for rewritten scripture, its canals humming with surveillance drones shaped like metallic angels. In France, the final bells of Marseille rang, a last cry before the silence swallowed everything.

Even so, the streets burned with quiet rebellion. Defiant painters fled into the shadows. The dead were buried with faces uncovered, a refusal to be erased.

Italy had split itself in half. The north clung to memory like a forbidden relic, hiding monks and old poets in damp cellars beneath crumbling cathedrals. The south, sun-bleached and blood-soaked, sang hymns to Ana in six dialects, every voice shaking with the fear of being the first to forget the old ways.

Across the continent, the Trilateral Accord offered a careful illusion of peace, the suffocating certainty of absolute control. Beneath it all, something ancient stirred, a primal hum rising from the earth. The unburied bones of gods still held the faint echo of their power. The names of saints, rewritten in cold dogma, had never been destroyed. The resistance lived on in stolen glances, in half-spoken memories passed between lullabies and bedtime stories.

At the heart of it, now, was me. Ilija.

I stood at the threshold of the temple, one foot still inside its sterile confines, the other brushing the cold earth beyond. The door behind me had folded shut, almost imperceptibly. The black shard in my hand pulsed with a warm thrum. The mountains waited ahead, but first came the escape.

I exhaled slowly, letting the cold air fill my lungs until it scraped against the phantom bruises along my ribs. Every part of me ached, yet my breath held steady. I remembered who I was now. I was the storm Ana had tried to bottle. My bare boots found cold stone, and I walked.

The outer corridor stretched into dimness, lit by narrow slots in the ceiling where filtered light bled in from the world above. The air smelled of myrrh and solder. A single guard stood at the far end, half-armored, his posture slack with boredom. His head lifted. His eyes widened. He froze. I met his gaze and said nothing. The guard reached for his weapon. I moved first, closing the distance before he could draw. I struck with the shard. Its edge brushed his exposed skin, and the guard collapsed without a sound, his eyes wide with confusion that softened into awe. I grabbed the rifle from his slack hands.

The alarm came next, a jarring pulse through the floor, a low keening sound. The corridor flooded with red light. I turned and ran. Every muscle screamed in protest. The air around me surged, the black shard glowing faintly, as though even the walls could feel what was coming. Footsteps erupted from beyond the archway ahead. I kept moving. There was no going back. I had remembered too much, and Ana had made the gravest mistake of her long existence. She had let me live.

The stone behind me still held warmth, the imprint of gods who had long since vanished. The temple had folded itself into silence. Its gift had been given, and I carried it now in the bones of my hands, in the ache behind my ribs. The shard pulsed once, a final emphatic beat. I was no longer a man trying to remember. I was the memory itself, and the compound ahead did not yet understand what it had let live.

The corridor stretched into a chilling quiet, the kind that hummed with surveillance and walls wired to listen. Somewhere beneath the polished floor, I could feel generators, the mechanical breath of the machine that had made this place possible. The cage pretending to be sacred. I stepped forward.

Something in my gait disturbed the air, as if I had forgotten how to move like a prisoner. The lights flickered as I passed beneath them. The security panel at the first junction blinked to life, activated by my proximity.

I stepped closer, and the screen glitched, its surface fracturing. For just long enough, it displayed my own face, overlaid with symbols. Some I recognized as ancient glyphs of power. Some I had once taught. One I had only seen in dreams. The storm rune. It shivered once and vanished. The panel went dark.

Behind me, a heavy door unlatched, followed by the sound of boots. Three soldiers emerged in crimson body armor marked with the Accord's sigils. Their helmets bore mirrored visors. The rifles in their hands glowed faintly at the tips, holy weapons blessed in sterile ceremonies.

The first raised his weapon. I kept my hands at my sides. The air bent, just enough to shift the rifle's aim a few degrees left. The shot hit stone. The second shouted a muffled command, his voice distorted by static. I exhaled. The hallway plunged into shadow, the lights dimming in a wave above me. The floor trembled, vibrations rising from deep beneath the earth, something that had not been summoned in centuries, stirring now at my command.

The third soldier hesitated, a fatal human pause. I raised my hand and pointed. Lightning cracked from within, rippled up my arm, surged through my ribs, and erupted from my fingers. The walls buckled. One of the rifles exploded in its soldier's hands, twisting into slag. They screamed. I stepped over the first one as he fell, the scent of scorched metal trailing behind me.

The temple compound had awoken, and so had I.

The hallway twisted as it descended, its walls inscribed with psalms in no human language. I moved without hesitation, my fingers still faintly crackling with remnants of the storm. The compound's systems adjusted. Its guardians murmured to one another across encrypted signals.

A second detachment approached at the end of the hall, carrying gleaming spears that hummed with dark incantation. These were the Inquisitors, the highest tier, priests in armor trained to fight with fanatical faith. They advanced in a tight triangle without speaking. One raised a hand, beginning a protection spell. I touched the cold stone, and the floor cracked open beneath them, a jagged seam splitting from my heel to their feet.

Steam hissed upward. The corridor shook. One inquisitor lost his footing. Another lunged, his spear tip aimed at the mark above my heart, the place where Ana had branded me. I caught the spear shaft midair. It burned against my palm, but the burn clarified me. The storm in my spine surged. My eyes flared with ancient light. The inquisitor froze. I pressed two fingers to the priest's helmet and whispered. The sound was primal, a tone of truth given back to a man who had been hollowed of it. He collapsed, unmade. He wept before his knees hit the stone. I dropped the spear.

The third inquisitor turned to run. The corridor sealed behind him, the path closing in a pulse of molten stone. He screamed once, then fell silent. I walked forward. Above me, the lights changed to violet, the warning reserved for breach of the innermost sanctum. Five people had triggered that alarm in the compound's history, and all of them had died within minutes.

I would be the sixth, and I would walk out alive.

I pressed my hand to the next door. It resisted. The shard in my palm pulsed. The door sighed open.

Inside, a wide circular chamber. Surveillance screens glowed on every wall, dozens of them. Most showed deserted corridors and lesser altars. One did not.

Danica. She was a living fire on the screen. The camera flickered, struggling to contain her. Her silhouette passed through flame and frost as if they were thin air. The guards around her dropped to their knees, weapons clattering to the floor. Behind her, other figures emerged, outnumbered and under-armed, yet utterly unafraid. She was already inside the Accord's fortress, a living blade.

I moved faster. Behind me, alarms began to scream, older sounds, ancient chants dragged from memory and wrapped in cold circuitry. Voices layered across the corridors in fractured languages, syllables pulled from forgotten scripture. The temple had shed its veneer of sacred architecture and revealed itself for what it had always been: a cage built to hold gods.

I walked through the center of the storm I had called. My feet slid through ash that had not been there a moment before. The walls hissed with escaping steam. Sparks bloomed in the ventilation shafts. Overhead, sprinklers released a bizarre mixture of rosewater and static. Ceiling panels broke open, revealing drones shaped like angels, their wings crafted from titanium and glass. I looked up and curled my fingers once. The sky above the compound cracked.

The surveillance dome shattered like glass struck by song. My body moved faster than thought. A drone descended, its cold eye fixed on me, and I raised my hand. The lightning unfurled slow and deliberate, coiling around my arm like something long asleep finally stretching awake. The drone spasmed midair, then dropped, smoke rising from its single dead eye.

I moved toward the inner sanctum. The threshold was guarded by four acolytes clad in black silk layered over armor that gleamed with scripture. They carried no weapons of steel or fire. They carried words. Prayers were engraved into their skin with ash and light. They began to chant when they saw me. I recognized the rhythm. Ana's liturgy. I whispered the counter-verse, the truth she had suppressed, the one they had erased from their holy books. The light in their eyes dimmed. Their mouths stilled. One fell to her knees, hands trembling. I walked past her.

Behind me, doors began to open. The priests had lost control of the gates. Some systems recognized my blood. Others recognized my name. Somewhere in the compound's cold heart, one of Ana's most devoted panicked. The floor beneath me cracked open, a containment field designed to hold precisely what I had become. Blue light erupted from a silver sigil beneath my steps. I pressed my hand flat to it, and it flickered. Once. Again. Then, with a sickening groan, it turned red. The sigil stuttered. The floor sealed shut, as if the earth itself obeyed.

I passed through a corridor once used to indoctrinate children. The walls bore murals of Ana in stained glass, serene and unholy. Beneath each, stark words: Truth. Sacrifice. My own name had been scraped from the corner of one panel. A thin black smear remained. I ran my fingers across it. The glass fractured, a soft singing sound.

Behind me, Danica's whisper. It reached me on the breath of the storm I had called into the compound's bones. I kept walking. She was coming. The blade was awake, and the gods had already turned their gaze toward our convergence.

The lights above me blinked out one by one as I moved toward the final hall. The storm followed, quiet still, but moving with purpose. The gates to the sanctum loomed before me, and I smiled. I had remembered how to fight. The storm would break fully soon, and when it did, the empire built on the fragile beauty of a rose would shatter. I placed my hand to the final door and felt its mechanisms unlock beneath my breath. I stepped inside, and the world held its breath.

Ana stood before the shattered mirror in the deepest chamber, her reflection fractured. The image wavered, uncertain, like a story resisting its own narrator. She had sent the last of the guards away hours ago. None of it mattered now. The compound trembled beneath her bare feet. She could feel it in the floor, a pulse of life rising through the foundation. The stone was breathing, something ancient awakened below the surface, something she had tried to rewrite but had never silenced. It moved with rhythm. It moved with me.

She closed her eyes. My name, Ilija, on her tongue, before it had become prophecy, before Danica. The priests she had once commanded were whispering now, trading desperate rumors instead of scripture. She had overheard one murmur as I passed: he has returned. I had returned, as if I had been gone for longer than she had ever held me captive, as if they too had been waiting.

She moved slowly through the hallway that once echoed with my footsteps. Each torch she passed flickered, its flame dipping in rhythm with the storm beneath the compound. Her hands trailed along the cold stone wall. The runes she had burned into its surface were fading, their power leaching away like color from old cloth. The spell was unraveling around her, because I had let go.

She descended into the sanctum's true heart, a chamber wreathed in silver veins and lit by cold starless light. At its center rose the bloom, the black rose that had once pulsed with my captured breath. It had begun to close, its dark petals curling inward like fingers recoiling from unbearable heat. She reached for it, her hand hovering. It did not recognize her touch. The last time she had dared, it had drawn blood, a drop of her own divine essence. She still bore the scar on the edge of her hand, a line too clean to be mortal. The walls shimmered with shifting scripture, her name written in thirty tongues, yet none of them sounded right anymore. Ana. Afërdita. None of them felt like home.

She fell to her knees. She was a woman who had given everything to be remembered and still found herself forgotten. The storm outside cracked the sky, and she felt me rise. She pressed her forehead to the cold floor, the silk of her gown pooling around her. We had found each other again, Danica and I. That, she knew, was the beginning of the end.

Her breath came ragged, tearing at her throat. Recognition. She had spent a lifetime running from it, had believed herself immune. She whispered my name once, softly, as if by speaking it without command she might summon a moment that had once belonged to us alone, before the war, before the world broke.

"Ilija."

The black rose pulsed once, dimly, then went still. Ana rose in silence, straightened her spine, and walked from the chamber. Her footsteps no longer echoed, because the compound had stopped listening to her. It had begun to remember me instead.

Ana, for the first time in all her countless incarnations, walked away as the woman who had, for all her power, been left behind.

CHAPTER NINETEEN
THE UNBROKEN THREAD

Danica

The resistance gathered underground, where shadows clung thickest. Cities had become surveillance grids, wired to observe and report every flicker of dissent. The Trilateral Accord had transmuted entire skylines into silent sentinels. Even the wind that curled over the rooftops seemed rehearsed. So they met beneath basilicas stripped of their saints, in the sprawling catacombs beneath forgotten vineyards where the scent of deep earth mingled with the metallic tang of fear. They met behind crumbling frescoes in Renaissance chapels where the Madonna wept in voiceless grief, her painted eyes blank and pupilless.

I emerged from the southern ridge two days after crossing into Italy, wind-scraped and hollowed out by sleeplessness. The Blade of Fate stayed hidden beneath my coat, thrumming low against my skin.

Snow, light as powdered bone, followed me down into the valley, settling around my boots with a soft sigh. I found the resistance by accident, or perhaps by a twist of fate. I hadn't meant to stumble into a watch post hidden inside a collapsed monastery, its ancient stones choked with moss and winter's decay. I had only paused, my body begging for a moment's rest. Yet as soon as my boots touched the moss-choked stone of the nave, a voice cut through the quiet.

"You're a day early."

I turned, my hand going to the hilt of the blade. Three figures stepped from the deeper shadows. One wore the frayed dark robes of a priest. Another carried a Soviet-era rifle with a blade lashed to the barrel. The third was a girl, small and silent, her face marked with faint old scars, her eyes holding something centuries older than anyone else's. I said nothing. I opened my coat, revealed the hilt, and whispered the old words I had learned from Brigid's dreamfire.

"Where memory burns, we gather."

The girl nodded once. "You're the one from the Balkan fields."

I didn't need to ask how they knew.

They led me through a narrow winding tunnel beneath the chapel. It opened into a cavern strung with flickering candlelight, the rough walls draped with maps and relics that should not have survived the Accord's purges. There, among the rebels, I heard his name again. Ilija. Spoken in low reverent tones, like a forbidden word that might be listening, a forgotten god waiting to awaken.

The rebels didn't know where he was. Rumors floated through the cavern, fragile yet insistent. A secured compound buried beneath the Alps. A facility whispered about only as "devotional extractions," where heretics were altered, their spirits reshaped.

My hands clenched into fists. The fire beneath my ribs flickered like breath trapped in iron. I needed to move, to act. First, though, I needed to understand what had become of the world since I last saw his face.

They told me stories by firelight, their voices low and grim.

Rome fell in three hours. A single broadcast. A city-wide invocation emanating from an orbital array funded by the Synod, carrying one chord and one name. Divina. Every child who heard it, from the grandest villa to the humblest alley, fell to their knees in tears. Every elder forgot their grandchildren's names, their memories devoured.

The Vatican bent. London attempted a futile stand. Paris wept in silent surrender, Berlin fractured beneath the new order. The Accord moved like smoke, seeping into every crack of the old world. They installed Faith Engineers in universities, dismantled civil archives. They replaced the calendar with one based on Ana's birth. Her face appeared on every coin, on every school wall, on stained glass imported into churches like sponsored relics. They rewrote history entirely, and those who remembered were made to forget.

I listened to it all and felt myself tighten like a coiled spring. This was seduction, careful and insidious, and Ana, in all her terrifying incarnations as Aphrodite, had learned her lessons well.

That night, I slipped away from the others and knelt in the ruined garden beside the chapel, wind biting through my coat. The stars above me seemed further away than ever. I took out the blade and unwrapped it slowly. It absorbed the light, drinking it into its blackened core. I held it against my chest.

"Tell me how to find him," I cried, the words torn raw from my throat.

No answer came. Only the faint steady hum of something waiting. I pressed my forehead to the blade's cold edge and closed my eyes.

In the darkness behind my lids, he came.

Ilija's dream swirled with smoke and the distant mourn of bells. He sat on a cracked marble floor, wrists bound, throat raw from screaming. In the dream, he was unbound, whole and free. He walked through fields of heather with someone just ahead of him, someone with hair black as raven's wings and a fire-strand around her wrist.

It was me, Danica.

She was limping, stiff with pain and cold. Yet she carried a blade older than oaths and bloodier than war. She had crossed impossible mountains to find him, and she was still walking. Even with the world burning behind her, dissolving into ash.

I snapped awake in the ruined garden, my breath tearing from my lungs. The blade hummed in my hand, and the wind breathed a single word.

Geneva.

It was a memory, a place suspended between old borders. The Accord buried its failed miracles there, tested faith by the cruelest forgetting. Ilija was waiting.

I stood, my body trembling with the aftershocks of the vision. The chapel behind me was quiet with sleep. The blade was not. And neither was I.

In the dark, I whispered a promise into the unforgiving air.

"I'm coming."

The city had once glimmered like glass against water, clean and symmetrical, imbued with the cold grace of gray diplomacy. Now it loomed like a shrine built from stolen reflections, its beauty twisted into something predatory.

Geneva had become a city of silence. Only bells, low and slow, rang from towers no one remembered building. The water of the Rhône ran black with unknown effluvium. The old UN campus had been transformed into a cold monumental temple.

They called it The Basilica of Faith, the Accord's central sanctum in Western Europe. The circular chambers that once held treaties now served as a sacred tribunal. The council chairs had been replaced by rows of cold pews. Statues of nameless saints, their features deliberately obscured, stood between pillars that wept clear drops of holy water. Below it all, where once had been sterile briefings and mundane storage, lay emptiness.

The train yard stretched in silence, a desolate expanse of corroded metal and forgotten tracks. The rails and abandoned platforms had forgotten the echo of human voices.

I pressed my fingers against the rotted wood of the freight door, testing its weight. The hinges groaned, a long drawn-out protest, loud enough to make the two resistance fighters behind me tense.

We had arrived before dawn, flanked by fog and quiet dread. Lejla had insisted this was the place, her certainty unwavering. The coordinates matched our fragmented map. The glyphs on the resistance map burned with a soft inner light when I laid the blade across them. Something deep in my bones whispered, yes.

Beyond the splintered gate, the train yard spread open to the elements. Steel rails, twisted by time and frost, snaked through the rubble. A collapsed warehouse loomed against the pale sky, its rusted beams a skeletal cage where pigeons nested. And there, half-buried beneath ivy and soot, stood the cathedral. Catholic once, then bombed and abandoned. Now it was something else entirely.

I stepped forward, my boots crunching over scattered glass and frostbitten leaves. My breath coiled before my lips, slow and deliberate. The resistance cell stayed behind.

Lejla's voice reached me, barely a whisper. "This is as far as we go."

I looked back. Lejla's eyes were wide, too wide. Her voice trembled, arising from terrible knowing rather than fear.

"They say the saints themselves left this place," Lejla breathed, her gaze fixed on the grim edifice. "The last priest who preached here burst into flame mid-sermon. Only the desperate or the divine enter now."

I gave a tight nod, a grim smile touching my lips. "Then I'm both."

I stepped through the broken archway, and the world shifted around me. The air inside was thick, cloying, like breathing through silk soaked in blood and myrrh. Mosaic saints stared down from shattered alcoves, their eyes gouged out, their halos cracked. A thousand candles had once stood beneath them, reduced now to puddles of blackened wax. Yet the altar remained, somehow untouched, burning with a cold inner light.

I approached slowly, soundless. The blade beneath my coat vibrated, pulsing in rhythm with the unnatural light. I reached the nave and stopped. Something moved behind the shattered altar.

I held still, every nerve stretched taut, and waited.

A figure stepped into view. Something older than either Ana or her soldiers.

A woman, timeless, wrapped in shifting smoke. Her robes shimmered with soil and starlight. Her eyes swallowed light.

"You've come far," the woman said, her voice a low resonant murmur. "Too far to walk without remembering your steps, child."

My throat went dry.

The woman lifted a hand, and I fell inward, through memory and lifetimes at once.

I fell into every version of myself that had ever loved Ilija and lost him.

I stood barefoot in a forest lit by twin moons. The leaves whispered in a language older than grief. A boy knelt before me, his hair the color of rust, his face dusted with ash-smeared freckles. His eyes were lit by a vow he hadn't yet spoken. His name wasn't Ilija, but he was Ilija, the earliest version of the man I would forever seek. I was dressed in gold-threaded wool, a cloak of starlings across my shoulders. My name then was Anwen, a druid's daughter, promised to the gods and stolen away by love.

We met at the edge of war. A Saxon raid. A sacred shrine consumed by flame. His hands were bloodied from pulling me from the rubble. He kissed me beneath the burning yew tree, and died a week later.

I gasped, the vision dissolving, and found myself on a Viking ship lashed by a tempestuous sea. The sky roared above us, the sea boiling beneath. I was Eira now, shieldmaiden of a dead jarl, sailing with my brothers to a land that no longer welcomed our kind. A priest was lashed to the mast beside me, red-haired, mute, yet his gaze never left mine. The night the storm came, he cut my ropes. He held my hand as we were cast into the black waves. Our bodies were never found, only a single rune-stone carved with our names and the word forgjett, meaning forgiven.

The vision burned again. This time I wore crimson silks behind an ornate Ottoman veil, painting stories in goldleaf inside the walls of a palace no one remembered now. I was Džemila, court painter to a sultan's mother. He was a servant, a foreigner, quiet, his eyes a startling green. We spoke once beneath the shade of the pomegranate tree. His hand brushed mine, and that was all, yet it was enough to ignite a spark across lifetimes. When the city fell, our names were carved side by side into the cold marble of the ruined well.

And again. A battlefield strewn with the dead. A church repurposed as a desperate resistance cell. Lifetime after lifetime, and each time it was him. Each time, love followed by loss. Yet the thread held. It twisted, it blackened, but it remained.

The pattern shifted, but it held.

It twisted, like thread soaked in ink, the memory of him still warm, now tainted by something darker, something vast. The field around me vanished. The crumbling well, the ruined church, all of it was swallowed in a breath of fireless heat. I stood in a hall of shimmering glass and oppressive shadow.

The walls shimmered with reflected movement, too quick and fractured to follow. The ceiling was open to a sky that bled red and violet at once, like dusk pulled too far across the bones of the world. The air hung dead still. The silence was the kind that followed collapse.

I turned slowly, unsure if my bare feet had ever truly touched the ground. Before me stood a throne, sunken into a basin of black marble veined with silver. Upon it, a woman waited. She only watched.

I could not see her face at first. Smoke coiled at her feet, thick with the scent of pomegranates and ash. Then the smoke parted.

The woman on the throne was beautiful the way a blade is beautiful. Her beauty commanded silence. It was the kind that had driven men to launch thousands of ships, that turned kingdoms to dust for failing to bow deeply enough.

Her skin glowed like bronze in the low firelight. Her eyes burned from within, rimmed in black, holding something I could not name. Her hair spilled in thick dark waves down her back, bound in a single golden braid. Her presence was crown enough.

The power in her body was myth itself. Every gesture, the slow curling of her fingers against the stone armrest, the tilt of her chin, echoed like ritual. Even in stillness, she commanded.

I knew what she was. Aphrodite, yes, but the Aphrodite the Spartans prayed to, stripped of velvet shrines and wedding hymns. Areia. The warrior-goddess who turned longing into conquest, whose beauty shattered treaties, whose name lived in the fertile space between desire and death. She had been the cause and the punishment. The seduction and the sword.

Now she looked at me with eyes that recognized.

I tried to move. My legs responded, but barely. My breath stayed caught behind my ribs. I took one step forward, then another, and the marble cracked faintly beneath my feet, as if it had not expected me to walk so willingly into her domain.

The goddess rose, slow and fluid, and I froze. She was impossibly tall, her form expanding to fill the chamber. Her voice came devastatingly calm, a low hum that vibrated through the air.

"You have loved him many times," the goddess said. "But you do not know what love becomes when it is left behind."

I opened my mouth. My voice died in my throat.

"He is not yours," the goddess continued, her voice flat with cold unyielding fact. "He never was. He remembers you, yes, a fleeting echo. But he came to me. He came because the gods placed him in my path, and when the path ended, I did not let him go."

I stepped back. The air had grown heavy. My arms ached as if they had held too many lives at once. My mouth felt impossibly dry.

"I will take him again," the goddess said, her voice dropping to a whisper. "And again. Until the world no longer knows your name. Until he forgets the very shape of your voice."

I tried to shout, but the air collapsed around me, crushing the sound.

The goddess smiled, and then the marble shattered beneath her in a violent eruption of splintering stone.

I fell back into my body with a gasp that tore my throat. My hands were clenched white-knuckled. My chest burned. The fire beside me had died out, leaving only cold ashes. The others had not returned.

I stared at the cave ceiling, my breath uneven, my limbs cold. The goddess's name escaped me. But one thing was certain. Ilija was in danger. Whatever ancient power had touched him had no intention of giving him back.

The voice returned. Soft, but cold, offering nothing. "You were forged in grief, child. But it was love that tempered you. And the goddess, you now know who she truly is."

I looked up, my breath still ragged. "What the hell was that? Why show me this now?"

The woman knelt beside me, her ageless eyes holding mine. "Because the fifth is awakening. And you must be whole to receive it."

My chest ached. "Ilija...?"

The woman nodded, slow and deliberate. "He sees you, too. But he does not yet believe."

She placed her hand over my heart. A searing burn. And in that instant, I remembered the sound of Ilija's voice across centuries. A lullaby sung in firelight. A final word before the blade fell.

I gasped awake, back in the ruined cathedral. The scent of dust and myrrh filled my lungs. I was alone.

The candles flickered, and where the altar had once stood, there was now raw stone, split by two shallow rings of shimmering silver, embedded in the floor like relics sealed in bone. Still dormant, still waiting. The fifth artifact. Two of them, waiting together.

I staggered back, the realization branding itself into my mind. They were rings. Wrought in the dual image of Lada and Morana, goddesses of life and death, of joy and ruin. Only together could they be taken. Only in unity could they be worn.

I wrapped my fingers around the hilt of the blade beneath my coat.

"I'll come back for you," I whispered to the rings. "We both will."

I turned from the altar and left the cathedral behind.

Outside, the resistance waited in silence, their forms cloaked in pre-dawn mist. Lejla stepped forward, her face lined with questions. "Well?"

I didn't answer with words. I stared out into the smoking distance toward the east, towards Ilija. Then, my voice low and resolute, I said, "It's time we burned the road between us and left nothing but ash."

The wind had changed, carrying the sharp distant scent of gunpowder now, like the last breath of a dying god. I stood on the rise above the valley, my eyes fixed east, where smoke coiled above a distant tree line like a warning written in the sky. The others waited behind me. Lejla, silent and armored in her own quiet grief. Mira, with her knife teeth and a radio pressed to her chest. Roko, whose broken leg was wrapped in splints made from old Orthodox hymnals.

They were resistance, yes, but barely. Scattered fragments, dreamers who hadn't yet accepted they were at war with something older than empires.

I turned, my gaze sweeping over their tired faces. "We move at dusk."

Lejla stepped forward. "And if the corridor's mined, Danica?"

My gaze was unblinking. "Then we bleed, but we move."

The silence that followed was answer enough.

The grim march began beneath the bruise-colored sky, the road between Rijeka and Ogulin choked with the rusted carcasses of supply trucks and the hollow shells of abandoned checkpoints. Ministry flags hung from the gnarled limbs of cypress trees, torn and meaningless. At one site, an entire platoon of black-clad enforcers had been frozen into place, transformed into grotesque statues of ice, still holding their rifles, their eyes wide.

Mira whispered, awestruck, "This wasn't us. This was something else."

I knelt beside one of the bodies, its eyes lifeless, its hands blue with cold. On the soldier's cheek, drawn in faint shimmering frost, was a spiral.

Ilija's mark. He was alive, and still fighting.

The resistance split into three columns. Lejla led the southern path through an abandoned Orthodox seminary repurposed as an armory. Roko took the western gorge, where the cliffs narrowed. I pressed north alone.

Every old tree seemed to know my name. The earth gave way under my feet, soft and yielding, as if it wanted me to sink. I passed shrines rededicated to Ana's twisted faith, crosses bent into circles, icons smeared with blood. None of them held power anymore. Only I did, and the blade at my side whispered of oaths it still remembered.

At the edge of the forest, I came to a village that didn't exist on any map. Half the houses had collapsed. The others leaned like drunken specters into the hillside. But the church remained. Its bell tower had fallen, a skeletal finger pointing to the broken sky, but the nave still stood, charred and defiant.

I stepped inside and gasped.

On the altar, simple and stark, lay a single crown of ash and wildflowers. The space around it was empty, unguarded. The raw aching memory of something sacred. Beneath the altar, carved into the wood with what looked like dried blood, two words. She Knows.

My breath hitched. Ana. This message was for me.

I fled the church, the knowledge a cold dread in my gut, but the forest had changed. The trees leaned closer, their shadows deepening into vast consuming things. Something was watching. I felt it in my blood, a low thrumming pulse. Old rage tangled with old love, all of it ours.

By the time I rejoined the resistance, my boots were soaked, my lips cracked from the wind. I didn't stop moving.

"We go to Sarajevo," I said.

Lejla blinked. "That's not the plan, Danica."

"It is now."

"Danica..."

"She has Ilija. I know it." My voice sharpened. "And we don't have time to follow your damn plans."

Mira whispered, barely audible, "They say Sarajevo fell last week."

My eyes narrowed. "Then we raise it again."

The wind screamed through the trees. Far away, thunder echoed like drums made of bone.

As the resistance set up camp in the skeletal remains of a monastery garden, I stood alone beside a fountain full of ash. I pulled out the blade, held it up to the pale moon, and for the first time since the vision, I spoke the oath written along its hilt.

I end what was never spoken.

I sever what should not bind.

And I remember.

I sliced my palm and let the blood touch the blade. The forest shook. In the distance, wolves howled, their voices rising in recognition.

After three days, they saw the glow long before they saw the city. The artificial aurora of sacred tech, Ministry beacons and prayer-field generators, electromagnetic scripture woven into the skyline. The skies above Sarajevo no longer reflected stars. They shimmered with refracted psalms, digital haloes pulsing red and gold.

I stood atop the ridge with my coat pulled tight, the blade across my back hidden beneath old linen and a scavenged Ministry shroud. I studied the landscape below. The valley yawned wide, cradling the city like a vast hungry mouth about to close.

To the west, the remnants of old resistance. Coded graffiti on crumbling walls, carcasses of drones buried in ivy, an old Catholic hospital repurposed as a safehouse. To the east, armored checkpoints and doctrine towers projecting Ana's voice in twelve languages, each one reciting prayers like surveillance. At the city's heart, the Dome. Once a concert hall, now transfigured into a basilica of ritual. This was where they said Ana slept, where her name burned brightest.

Lejla crouched beside me, scanning the city with binoculars. "They'll see us if we move before nightfall."

"We move anyway," I said. "This isn't reconnaissance anymore."

Behind us, Mira checked the last of the explosives, each one carved with ancient sigils the old priests called anti-psalms, faith-eaters, nullifiers of sanctified ground. They wouldn't last long. Neither, I knew, would I. Each mile I carried the blade, something inside me faded. Time itself, draining away.

That night, the stars returned, barely visible through the glowing haze. The prayer-field blinked, just once, long enough for us to move. We descended the hills like phantoms. Four resistance fighters. Myself, Lejla, Mira, and a boy named Kian who hadn't spoken since the purge of Mostar. We crossed the old tram lines. We passed the burnt skeletons of mosques and steeples alike, their sacred forms twisted into ruins. The Ministry had devoured everything.

At checkpoint seven, Mira planted the first charge beneath a massive statue of Saint Peter, its face cruelly carved with Ana's features. It blew inward, erupting in shrapnel and scripture. I moved first, my blade still sheathed but thrumming like a bell in my spine.

At checkpoint ten, they saw us. The alarms resonated, low and harmonic, a lament woven with commands in ancient Greek and Slavonic.

I reached for the blade.

Lejla stopped me, her hand gripping my arm. "Not yet, Danica. We're too close to the field."

Mira tossed smoke. Kian bolted into the dark. We moved beneath the shadow of towering structures where monks in black body armor stood silent behind mirrored visors. I could feel Ana now. She was everywhere.

The city was her body. The cobblestones were her vertebrae, the omnipresent declarations her breath.

We reached the safehouse by dawn, a cold damp basement beneath what had once been a museum of war, converted into a temple for the New Order. I collapsed against the stone wall. I couldn't stop shaking. Lejla knelt beside me.

"You're burning up, Danica."

"I'm not," I whispered, though my skin felt like fire.

I pulled the blade from my back. It glowed with memory. It had begun to resonate, a faint melodic hum that vibrated through my bones.

I curled my fingers around its hilt. "I need to get inside the Dome."

"Are you insane?" Lejla yelled.

"She has Ilija. I know it."

Lejla stood, her stance defiant. "You go in now, you'll die. We need more time. More firepower."

I smiled, grim and blood-stained. "I don't need fire." I looked up, my gaze meeting hers. "I just need to remember."

That night, while the others planned, I dreamed.

Ilija lay naked and broken on the cold floor of some cathedral-turned-cell, his back marked with runes I didn't recognize. Ana sat beside him, a woman grieving her own shattered myth. She touched his face with reverence, her golden hair spilling around him.

She whispered, "I would've given you the world, Ilija."

And Ilija, gods help him, didn't look away.

I screamed in my sleep. The blade burned my hand. Far above, in the heart of the Dome, Ana opened her eyes.

I moved through the corpse of Sarajevo like breath through glass. I wore the Ministry veil, black silk embedded with glimmers of script that whispered holy things when touched. It masked my heat signature, bent the air around me, hid the fire beneath my ribs. Lejla had stolen it off a fallen guard two years ago and saved it for this impossible mission.

"This was made for martyrs," Lejla had said, binding it to my hair. "So let's lie to the veil."

I said nothing.

I passed checkpoints like a ghost. Guards' eyes flicked toward me, then quickly away, confused, as if seeing something sacred they weren't allowed to name.

Inside the Dome, the world changed. It smelled of honeyed ash and lavender, cloying and unsettling. The air shimmered with declarations, sustained rather than spoken, vibrating through the very structure, as if someone had pressed their palm to God's throat and held the note. Walls pulsed with light. Holograms flickered, ephemeral images of Ana kneeling at a grand altar, Ana raising a child that never was.

Every step I took hurt somewhere deeper than the body, somewhere in the memory. This place remembered me, too. It remembered me by blood.

The inner sanctum had once been a concert hall. Its grand arches vibrated with the sustained hum of corrupted power, empty of instruments or human voice. A dais of gold and jet rose at its center, backed by a screen of violet glass. Statues ringed the room, women with Ana's face, sculpted as saints and conquerors.

At the center, upon a throne built of ashwood and melted icons, Ilija knelt. Unbound and utterly motionless.

My breath caught. My vision blurred with tears. I stepped forward, and the blade on my back screamed. It wept, a long bone-deep moan that sent shivers through the architecture itself.

"Too late."

Ana's voice echoed through the chamber, cold and silken.

The veil dropped from my shoulders, crumbling into dust. The light above me snapped, blinding and brutal. Ana stepped from the side chamber, barefoot, wrapped in a robe of black silk with burned roses clinging to the fabric. Her skin caught the light like polished bronze. Her hair, molten gold and untethered, spilled past her shoulders.

"Why," Ana whispered, her voice carrying a strange weary sorrow, "do you always come when it's too late, Danica?"

I reached for the blade.

Ana raised her hand, and the room froze. Time itself locked in place.

I saw everything at once. Ilija's face through ten thousand lifetimes, as a monk, as a boy with hope still in his eyes. I saw myself in rough fur and soft velvet, in the light of campfires and the chill of frost. Always one step away, always dying. And relentlessly, Ana, there at the edges, watching and weeping.

I staggered back. The room twisted. Ana stepped forward, tears on her cheeks, real tears.

"I didn't want this," she said, her voice raw. "But you kept waking him. You kept pulling him back to yourself."

"You took him," I said, my voice hoarse. "You broke him."

"I loved him," Ana snarled, the ancient wounded goddess rising within her. "Before your name was a whisper in the wind, I loved him. And he loved me, too. You kept returning. You kept dragging him away, life after life."

My voice was quiet. "Because he chose to follow, Ana. He chose to follow me."

Ana's eyes blazed, twin suns of furious gold. "No. Because he's cursed. And you, Danica, are the curse."

I drew the blade, and it remembered. The runes along its edge flickered with all the names I had once borne, all the oaths I had ended across countless lifetimes.

The Veil cracked, a visible fissure in reality. Time returned with a violent jolt. Ana screamed, raw and primal. And I, with nothing left to lose, stepped forward.

The chamber at the heart of the Cathedral of the Forgotten absorbed sound the way a grave accepts silence. The walls, colossal pillars of petrified ash and basalt, seemed to lean inward, as if the cathedral's bones were listening.

I stood at its center, the blade held loosely in my hand, its blackened iron shimmering faintly, as if unsure of its own purpose. The Blade of Fate pulsed once beneath my fingers, an echo of sorrow, of promises buried beneath centuries.

Ana watched me from across the space, radiant yet broken. Her hair was no longer perfect, strands escaping its golden braid. Her crown hung loosely, tilted. She looked like a statue grieving its own sculptor.

Then Ilija ran into the room, placing himself between us. His wrists were no longer bound in golden filament. His eyes fluttered, caught between the lingering pain of his ordeal and the dawning light of recognition. His chest rose steadily now. The power that had nearly burned through him had finally stilled, settling into a contained, formidable force.

I spoke first, my voice cracking. "You don't have to keep doing this, Ana."

Ana's gaze did not waver, fixed on Ilija, then on me. "You never understood, Danica."

"I understand enough. You wanted his love. You still do. But this isn't love. This is possession."

Ana's mouth trembled. "It was. Once. Before the world turned us into symbols, before we were torn apart, lifetime after lifetime."

"You were never torn apart," I said, my voice steady. "You couldn't accept that he kept finding me."

That landed like a physical wound. Ana's breath hitched, then steadied. She stepped closer, her eyes blazing.

"You think this is about romance?" she whispered. "About flesh and longing?" Her voice deepened, no longer Ana's alone, but something older and vast, echoing with ancient power. "This is about constellations collapsing. About empires crumbling because a man refuses to forget the wrong heart."

My grip on the blade tightened. "I don't care what stars were aligned. I don't care what gods tried to bind him to you. He chose me."

"Because you were there," Ana hissed. "Because you were always waiting when I was forbidden to come."

Neither of us moved, suspended in charged silence.

Then Ilija stirred. He murmured something, a word in an ancient tongue neither of us fully remembered. We knew what it meant. Remember.

My blade flickered, responding to his unspoken command.

Ana stepped back, shaken. "You would use that against me?"

"No," I said, my voice clear. "Not against you, Ana."

I turned toward the altar. And I drove the blade down, with all my strength, into the stone itself. The shatter echoed through the cathedral's bones.

The floor cracked in five perfect lines radiating outward from the blade's impact, like the unfurling petals of a dark flower, like the five artifacts themselves, waiting to complete the circle. Four points burned with inner light. The fifth remained dark, stubbornly unlit. The final artifact had not yet revealed itself.

The power surged up anyway, raw and untamed. Wind tore through the chamber. Statues crumbled to dust. The stained glass above shattered inward, sending slivers of colored memory cascading across the floor.

Ilija screamed, a visceral primal sound of recognition. Memories burst through him like lightning. Past lives with me, dying for me, beside me. The wars we had bled through, the mountains we had crossed. A hundred vows across a thousand years, flooding his mind, becoming whole.

I staggered as the wind spiraled around me. My own memories flared, Ilija's voice echoing in every lifetime, calling me home. The blade refused to awaken further. The fifth point stayed silent.

Ana fell to her knees, her voice small. "Even now, he doesn't remember the beginning. Only you. Always you."

I turned toward her. Weariness was the only thing left on my face.

"Ana," I said softly. "He loved you once. Maybe even forever ago. But we were never meant to be cages for each other."

Ana wept, silent and shattering. The chamber pulsed once more, and the binding shattered. Ilija collapsed forward, free, into my arms.

Ana rose slowly, majestically. The goddess in her still burned. Yet the woman, the one who had waited, who had watched him fall in love with someone else lifetime after lifetime, was crumbling.

"You think this is the end," she said, her voice echoing as she stepped into deeper shadow. "It's only the pause before the final confrontation, Danica."

She vanished. Rose petals fell in her wake, hundreds of them, drifting in slow motion across the broken stones.

I held Ilija close. He blinked slowly, his eyes finding mine, and reached to brush the frost from my cheek.

"You came for me," he rasped.

"Always," I said, my voice thick with unshed tears.

"Took you long enough," Ilija said, a faint smile touching his lips. "Look at all the bodies I had to clear out of the way for you, you lazy bitch."

I rolled my eyes, a genuine smile breaking through. "Better late than never, ljubavi moja."

Above us, the fifth point remained unlit. It waited for devotion, for a vow made without gods, a promise that would have to be remembered before it could be forged. We walked out of the compound, hand in hand, knowing exactly where we needed to go next., to the place of Ilija's birth, Croatia.

Chapter Twenty
The Undying Vow

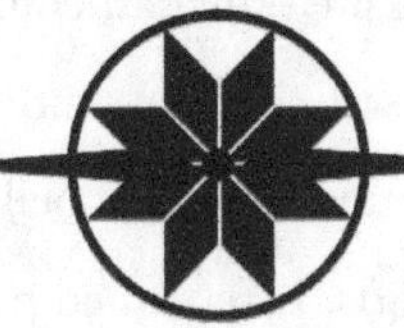

Ilija

The monastery had no name. If one had ever been spoken, the wind that scoured bone from cliff and breath from stone had carried it away long ago. Centuries of ivy and silence had smothered it, its memory unrecorded on any map, unmarked on any trail. It sat half-buried in the rugged spines of the Croatian highlands, where the trees thinned and the air forgot how to speak. The walls, shaped by time alone, pressed deep into the cliff face. This was where Danica brought me.

I was barely walking. My legs dragged through gravel and moss, useless things, my body a dead weight she bore without question. Fever glazed my skin in a pale sheen. My mouth hung open as if breath itself had become unfamiliar. Each movement whispered agony through me. The last storm I had unleashed, the power that had torn open the sky and boiled the blood of my enemies, had left me hollowed out. It had ripped through my veins like molten iron, branding raw memories into flesh I no longer recognized as my own. Something ancient had awakened inside me, and now that it stirred, it refused to return to sleep. Its presence hummed beneath everything.

Danica kept one arm wrapped around my back, steadying my faltering steps as we climbed the final slope. Her coat was soaked through from the clinging mist, her grip unyielding. Her eyes stayed fixed ahead, because the burden she carried was sacred. She would not drop me. Not again.

The monastery emerged from the rock as if the mountain itself had exhaled it, a skeletal ribcage against the darkening sky. The outer wall, once tall and grand, had half-collapsed. Ancient stones choked in roots, split by frost and decay. Above the entrance, an old bell still hung, leaning sideways, its iron throat coated in verdigris. It remained perfectly still, unstirred by the wind. Even the leaves on the surrounding trees seemed to hold their breath.

We passed beneath the arch as the last light of dusk vanished behind the jagged ridge. No door greeted us, only a gaping wound in the wall that opened into a corridor of shadow. Inside, the air thickened. Dust choked my lungs, layered with the crushing press of things remembered in silence. The walls were bare stone, cracked and discolored by centuries. Vines coiled along the corners of the nave, and the ceiling above had long since fallen away, leaving only the bleached bones of the rafters, casting crooked silhouettes beneath a sky drenched in starlight.

Danica led me past the crumbling pews, their wood warped and blackened by time. Statues of saints and angels had fallen into disrepair, their eyes hollowed out, their wings broken, leaving nothing divine in their faces. She brought me to what remained of the altar. The icon had been scorched beyond recognition, reduced to char. The wall behind it bore a single shard of stained glass still embedded in the mortar, a violet flame cupped within a golden hand. Its light trembled faintly, persistent and sourceless. She lowered me gently to the ground, folding a wool blanket beneath my head. I moaned, barely conscious, my fingers twitching in the air like a child reaching for something in a dream. She knelt beside me, soaked a cloth in a bowl of cool water she had drawn from the stream below, and pressed it to my brow. The fever still danced across my skin like a restless spirit.

My eyes fluttered open long enough to see her, long enough to know with sudden, aching clarity that I was not alone. Then they closed again. Sleep dragged me down into the place where dreams had teeth, where shadows whispered forgotten names. Danica did not speak. She only watched. The monastery was silent, yet alive. Dormant. Breathing with the stillness of something that had seen too much to move quickly. It remembered the gods that had once walked these peaks, the children hidden here from the teeth of empires. The stones did not weep. They endured.

Outside, darkness fell without fanfare. No sunset, no lingering light, only the sudden extinguishing of the world beyond the mountains. Then, from the depths of the woods below, a cry rose. The monastery heard it, its silence deepening in recognition.

Night thickened like oil across the bones of the monastery. The meager fire struggled in the center of the nave, coughing smoke through the rafters toward a sky sealed with impassive stars. Cold settled into the stones, dense as judgment.

Danica sat beside me, knees pulled beneath her coat, arms wrapped around them, her breath coiling faintly in the dimness. The silence that filled the nave had become a vessel, deep enough to hold everything we did not yet know how to say. I stirred sometime after midnight. My breath hitched, then steadied. My eyes opened slowly, bloodshot and shadowed with the ache of returning to awareness. My fingers twitched against the wool blanket.

Danica leaned forward, her voice barely above the hush of the fire's crackle. "You're safe."

I blinked, my gaze finding hers. Pain lived in her eyes, and confusion, and beneath that, something that made my chest tighten.

"How long?" I asked, my voice hoarse from disuse.

"Almost three days," she answered. "You collapsed the moment we left the shrine. Your body couldn't hold it. Whatever moved through you, whatever power you summoned, it burned you down to the root."

I tried to sit up. Pain bloomed across my chest like lightning chasing old scars. I fell back with a groan. Danica placed a firm hand on my shoulder, holding me in place.

"Don't," she said softly. "You're not ready."

I closed my eyes, breathing slow and shallow, the world still spinning. "I saw you," I whispered. "In the dark. In the vision. You found the blade."

Danica turned away slightly, her jaw tensing. "I didn't want you to see that, Ilija."

"I had to," I said.

For a while, only the fire gasping against the damp air filled the quiet.

Then she spoke, her voice low. "I went to Scotland, to the land of my mother's blood. Something was calling me there, something that knew my name before I remembered it. I crossed Europe in pieces. Trains and resistance trucks when I could find them, on foot when I couldn't. I changed names at every border. I slept in haylofts and cemeteries. I ate what they gave me. I hid when they couldn't see."

I turned toward her, my breath still ragged, my eyes sharpening. "Who helped you, Danica?"

"Everyone," she said. A faint, grim smile touched her lips. "No one. There were cells still scattered through the broken places. Old women with knives hidden in their aprons. Boys with eyes too old for their faces. They had no leader, no banner, but they knew what I was carrying. They recognized it even before I did." She paused, her fingers clenched tight in her lap. "In the Highlands, I found a stone circle shrouded in mist. A place lost even to the maps. Brigid met me there, and Freyja. They appeared in something older than flesh. The wind turned with their voices. The stones lit with their presence. They led me to a cairn in the hills above the sea."

I listened without blinking.

"I dug through frost with my bare hands. The soil was black and frozen. Beneath it, I found the blade. It had not been crafted. It had grown, from root and bone. It pulsed when I touched it, as if remembering me."

"And then?" I asked.

Danica's voice fell to a hush. "Then I remembered. I saw a life before this one. You were dying in my arms. Your chest torn open by something monstrous. I dragged you as far as I could, but you kept slipping away. You looked at me and said, 'Burn me. Before they take what's left of me.'"

My hand trembled. I did not reach for her, but the motion drew me closer.

"I built the pyre myself," Danica said, tears forming in her eyes, catching the firelight. "I lit it and watched the flames take you. The sky turned red. Your voice thanked me, one last ragged breath. I fell to my knees because I knew I had just burned the only man I had ever loved."

I closed my eyes, my breath catching. The memory hit like a fist beneath my ribs, sudden and total. Danica stared into the fire, its glow reflected in the wetness beneath her lashes.

"I left Scotland with nothing but the blade. The resistance helped me move south through France, across the border into Italy. A man in Florence gave me shelter in a ruined basilica. A woman in Slovenia hid me beneath her daughter's bed while drones passed overhead, their mechanical hum filling the night. By the time I reached Croatia, I knew exactly where you were. I didn't realize you would have already started finding your own way out, Ilija."

My voice cracked. "You crossed the entire continent to find me, Danica."

Danica turned to me, her gaze unwavering. "I crossed every life to find you, Ilija."

We sat in the silence of the nave, centuries settling around us. The fire burned low, its light casting long, dancing shadows. The stars above, remote and ancient, seemed to hold their breath.

"I think we've died a thousand times," I whispered.

Danica nodded. "And we always find each other again, Ilija."

I lifted my hand. The runes on my skin had begun to pulse faintly, fed by memory. Each line hummed with an ancient rhythm, as if my flesh remembered every time it had bled for a promise. For a while, only the wind filled the space, curling softly around the bones of the monastery. I turned my wrist slowly. The runes glowed, responding to the truth of memory.

"The fifth artifact," I said. "I can feel it. We're close."

Danica reached into her satchel but did not open it.

"I met others," she continued, her voice gaining strength. "In Slovenia, Germany, France. They wore no uniforms and carried no symbols, but they remembered the gods in their own ways. I think they've always been here, hidden, waiting for someone to come back to them."

I looked at her for a long moment. "You carried that blade across an entire continent, Danica."

She nodded. "I did."

"You crossed warzones. Borders. All for this," I said, my gaze sweeping the ruined monastery.

"I crossed them for you, Ilija." Her words hung there, suspended in the breath between us. We did not move. We did not reach for each other. We existed in that shared stillness, where the truth had already been spoken and no echo was needed. In the rafters above, the stars blinked, watching like gods who had seen it all before.

We left the monastery just after first light, though the sky offered little clarity. Clouds pressed low against the mountains. The mist had thickened overnight, curling along the ground in slow, heavy coils. The forest below waited in silence, its branches motionless.

I moved slowly. My body was sore, bruised, but something deep within me had steadied. I walked as if the ground beneath me remembered my steps, welcomed my weight. Danica led the way, and I followed without question. The land no longer resisted us. It only watched.

The trail descended into Dalmatia like a scar, narrow and winding, cut through jagged limestone and ancient roots. Pines stood tall on either side, their trunks marked with deep notches as though branded with forgotten signs. At times, fog closed around us so thickly we could see only a few paces ahead. We did not stop. A pressure moved with us, in the quiet, charged spaces where gods once lingered.

Hours passed. The light did not change. No sun, only a gradual lifting of darkness into dull gray. Danica stopped suddenly. I looked past her shoulder. Through the thinning fog, a black spire pierced the air, rising from a hill ahead, crooked and smoke-stained, like a spear thrust into the sky by a dying hand. As we drew nearer, the structure revealed itself. A ruined cathedral, hunched against the slope, its stones broken, its roof collapsed inward. Ivy covered what was left of its face. Beneath the spire, a grand arch still stood. We stepped through the clinging vines.

Five symbols had been carved into the arch, worn by time, some half-choked by moss, others scraped nearly flat. They were still there. The spiral. The flame. The lightning. The eye. The shadow. Danica reached up and brushed her fingers along one of them. The spiral shimmered faintly beneath her touch.

"They were watching even then," she whispered. "Waiting."

I stared at the weathered marks, my breath catching. The runes on my arms pulsed faintly, rising from something colder than pain. Recognition without specific memory. We passed beneath the arch. Inside, the cathedral was hollowed and dark. No altar remained. No pews. The nave was open to the sky, where beams of faded sunlight slipped through broken glass and the skeletal ribs of timber. Shards of old stained glass painted fractured colors across the stone floor, green like deep forest, violet like mourning. At the center stood a circle of carved stone. Five pedestals rose from it, arranged like the points of a star. Each bore a symbol. Each seemed older than the stones themselves, as though the foundation had grown around them. Only two glowed faintly. Danica stepped forward. I followed, my breath shallow.

"It's a shrine," I said, the words feeling inadequate.

She shook her head. "It's a memory."

We stood in silence before the pedestals. The air in the cathedral felt heavier than the sky outside. Sanctified. Like a tomb built to protect something sacred from the forgetting. Then a sound came from below. Stone scraped on stone. A footstep echoed from the far side of the nave. I tensed, stepping in front of Danica. From a narrow stairwell cut into the floor, a figure emerged.

She moved with slow, deliberate precision, wrapped in robes scorched at the hems, her shoulders layered in old furs. Time had carved her face into deep, weathered lines. Her hair hung long, braided with black thread and metallic rings. She held a lantern whose light arose from swirling dust and faint crimson luminescence, sourceless and persistent. It refused to go out.

"You came," she said, her voice cracked but strong.

I kept my stance guarded. "Who are you?"

The woman set the lantern down gently beside the circle of stone.

"I am Visnja. Guardian of the shrine. Witness to the fire before it burned."

Danica narrowed her eyes. "You're one of them, aren't you?"

Visnja nodded once.

"When the Accord came," she began, her voice low and steady, "they tried to erase this place. They burned the libraries and salted the wells. They killed everyone who remembered the old names. But this ground was sanctified long before doctrine, before war. It would not let them win. It buried itself, and I stayed."

I looked around the broken cathedral, the open roof, the shattered windows. "You've been here all this time?"

"I have," she said, holding my gaze. "Waiting. Watching. I was told that when frost and flame walked again, when the storm returned to flesh, the last threshold would open. That you would come."

Danica stepped beside me, her voice cutting through the heavy air. "Who told you?"

Visnja's eyes shimmered faintly. "She did not name herself. Her voice was pain. Her eyes were the sea. She left only a message." She walked slowly to the pedestal marked with the eye and retrieved a bundle wrapped in black linen, bound with wax. The seal bore the sigil of the Zorya. I reached for it, my fingers steady. Inside was no artifact, only a scroll. Old, curled with age, inked with symbols older than language. The parchment trembled in my hand, as if responding to my presence. Danica leaned close.

"These markings," she murmured, "they're like the ones I saw carved into the standing stones in Scotland. The night I touched the blade."

Visnja's voice turned solemn. "They are the path. The rings were not left here. Only what was needed to guide you. The rest remain scattered, hidden where memory still lingers."

I stared at the ancient writing. "Then we're not done."

"No," Visnja said. "You are only beginning."

Danica looked toward the broken ceiling. Outside, the wind had changed, carrying a new scent. Inside, the shrine breathed. The scroll trembled faintly in my hands, fed by the raw tension building around us. I rolled it tightly, tucked it inside my coat, and looked up. Light no longer filtered down. Only cold air. Only stillness.

Danica stood beside me, alert, jaw clenched. Her fingers hovered near her coat where the blade remained hidden. She tilted her head, listening.

"They're coming," she said, low and urgent.

Visnja did not blink. She stepped away from the pedestals and turned toward the far wall. "Downstairs. Move now."

From the shadows along the back of the cathedral, they emerged. Men and women in makeshift gear, some wearing body armor scavenged from dead soldiers, others draped in camouflage cloaks smeared with mud and grease. Children too, older than their years, carrying medical kits and communications equipment, their faces grim. These were resistance fighters. There was no incense, no ritual. Only discipline honed by endless conflict.

Danica guided a limping man toward the stone stairwell that descended into the crypt. I stayed at the center of the nave, my eyes trained on the breach in the ceiling, my stance ready. Visnja approached me, gripping a battered pistol with the safety already off.

"You stay, you fight," she said.

I nodded once.

The first tremor came like a ripple through the cathedral floor. A pulsing vibration, an electronic probe scanning for life. My head turned sharply toward the arch.

"Thermal sweep," I said.

Then came the drone. It sliced overhead in silence, its wingspan sleek, its hull glinting in the thin light. A small flare dropped from its undercarriage and burst in mid-air, flooding the room with infrared illumination.

I reached for Danica. "Cover your heat."

Too late. The stained-glass window exploded inward, showering us with glittering shards. The soldiers came in fast. Black combat gear, faceless helmets. They breached the nave in perfect formation, two on each side, weapons sweeping in deadly arcs. Their boots landed heavy on the stone. Their voices barked commands in clipped Russian. The insignias on their sleeves gleamed silver. The mark of the Trilateral Accord. They were here to kill.

I moved first. I wore no armor and carried nothing but memory and lightning. The soldier at point raised a rifle and fired. The bolt was kinetic, meant to kill. I raised one hand and caught the bullet mid-air. It stopped before my palm, as if the air itself had turned solid. Then it dropped, clattering to the stone.

Danica stepped forward, drawing the blade from beneath her coat. It hissed as it met the air, the sound born of power. Cold radiated from her in waves. The blade shimmered in her grip, refracting light in patterns like cracked ice. The soldiers opened fire. Automatic weapons lit up the nave.

I dropped into a crouch, slammed both hands against the stone, and released the storm. The floor shuddered. A wall of force erupted outward, flinging the front wave of soldiers back against the pillars. One hit the wall so hard his helmet cracked in two. Another dropped his rifle and scrambled back, gasping, his body convulsing with raw electricity.

Danica advanced without hesitation. Her blade cleaved through two soldiers before they could recover, the steel passing clean through their armor. They did not bleed. They collapsed, eyes wide, as if something essential had been erased. Another lunged at her with a combat knife. She turned into him, drove the blade upward beneath his ribs, and shoved him back. Ice crawled from the wound before he hit the ground.

I turned in time to catch another soldier vaulting the low wall near the broken pews. I raised one hand. Lightning cracked through the air, splitting the rifle in half and knocking the man flat. From above, the drone released a flare. Red and white, spiraling upward. A signal for reinforcements.

"Reinforcements," Danica shouted. "We have to move!"

Behind us, Visnja called over her shoulder. "Exit through the crypt. Northeast tunnel. It opens into the woods."

I sprinted for the altar, bare feet pounding the stone. I leaped over a fallen beam and skidded to a stop beside Danica. Together, we fell back toward the stairs as more soldiers poured in through the shattered windows. Grenades clattered to the floor. Danica grabbed one, hurled it back with a primal scream, and ducked behind a pillar. The explosion turned the nave into a furnace. Pews splintered and glass became shrapnel. Smoke swallowed the ceiling.

I pulled Danica behind me, gripping her arm, shielding her. We reached the stairwell and dove down just as more bullets tore through the air, spitting against the stone. The cathedral roared, consumed by fire. The stones above groaned, buckling under flame. Then silence fell. Escape, if only for a breath.

The crypt was colder than the cathedral above, the walls thick with moisture and old breath. Roots dangled from the ceiling like knotted hair. The light from Danica's torch flickered across stone coffins and alcoves packed with ancient bones. The stairs narrowed behind us, every sound echoing sharp and close. I moved ahead of her, one hand pressed to the damp wall for balance. My other hand sparked faintly, flickers of lightning crawling between my fingers like restless veins. Behind us, the cathedral burned. Gunfire stuttered above, sporadic and desperate. Grenades thumped, shaking the foundations. Stone screamed. None of it reached this deep.

At the lowest step, Visnja waited.

She had walked down as if she knew the way better than her own veins, as if the passages were part of her. Now she stood in the center of the chamber, a wide space chiseled from bedrock. The walls bore symbols painted in soot and blood: spirals and eyes, birds with wings turned inward. Between two ancient coffins rested a stone table, a bundle upon it wrapped in cloth black as coal, tied with sinew. I stepped forward, my breath hard and ragged.

"You stayed behind," I said.

Visnja looked at me, then at Danica. Her eyes were no longer old and tired. They were sharp, gleaming with something ancient. "I was waiting for this moment, Ilija."

Danica stepped beside me, her voice low. "The scroll said the rings were scattered, Visnja."

Visnja tilted her head slightly. "Some were. But the final pair were hidden together, placed in the care of one who remembers."

She reached for the bundle. The cloth made no sound as she untied it. Slowly, she unwrapped what lay within. Two rings. One carved from bone, threaded with gold and root. The other forged of iron and ash-veined silver. Both bore sigils: Lada's spiral of love, Morana's hook of ending. They pulsed faintly in the firelight.

Danica's breath caught. My hand shook. I stared at the rings as if they had been torn from my own chest. Visnja placed them back in the cloth and held the bundle out.

"They are remembrance," she said. "You wore them before. You died with them. You buried them in fire and frost so no empire could touch them."

I took the bundle. The moment my fingers closed around the rings, the runes on my arms lit with gold and deep blue. Danica placed her hand on the cloth. A mark bloomed over her heart, a spiral wreathed in ash. Something in the air shifted. We did not speak. We only felt. Above us, the ceiling shook. Stone dust rained down. A muffled explosion echoed from the nave. Visnja stepped away from the table.

I looked at her. "You need to come with us."

Danica nodded. "You won't survive what's coming."

Visnja turned to us and smiled. Her teeth were no longer bone. They were gleaming iron. Her eyes shone like coals banked in the dark.

"I have survived worse," she said. "I have walked through fire on legs made of crow bone and hunger. I have held secrets in my teeth for so long the trees themselves grew wise listening."

My jaw tightened. The blood drained from my face. "You're not Visnja."

"No," she said, her smile widening, revealing the glint of iron. "But she wore me well."

Danica took a step back, her eyes wide. "Baba Yaga."

The woman nodded once. "In the form that mothers take. When the world forgets what mothers are truly for."

I tightened my grip on the bundle. "You'll hold them off?"

"I'll give you time," she said. "Time is all you need."

Above us, another explosion cracked the floor. The old woman turned toward the stairwell. Her cloak flared behind her as if caught in a sudden wind, though the air in the crypt remained still.

She looked back once, her iron eyes piercing. "When you place the rings, you will remember everything. Each other, your deaths, and what you were meant to be."

Danica tried to speak, but her voice faltered. The iron smile returned.

"I know," Baba Yaga said. "It hurts."

Then she climbed the steps, each footfall impossibly slow, impossibly strong.

I turned to Danica. She nodded once. We ran through the crypt's far tunnel, into a passage that twisted through ancient roots and solid rock. Behind us, the cathedral howled, but its heart did not break. It fought. In its burning chest, Baba Yaga stood with iron teeth bared, welcoming the Accord like a storm welcomes fire.

The cathedral groaned beneath its own destruction. Fire licked the ancient arches. Smoke churned upward through the broken spire, a black plume against the bruised sky. The stained-glass windows had been reduced to jagged wounds. The pews lay scattered like bones. Baba Yaga climbed the final steps into the nave as the next wave of Accord soldiers breached the outer walls. They came without hesitation.

Drones swarmed above, their mechanical whine filling the ruined space. The soldiers were armored in black ceramic, their visors glowing with infrared readouts. They fanned across the cathedral in formation, rifles raised, boots hammering the stone. They expected resistance. They did not expect her.

She stood in the center of the aisle, framed in flickering firelight, her braid falling like a rope of snow and soot over one shoulder. Her hands hung loose at her sides. Her face was calm. Older now, hungrier, the kind of face that had been carved into children's nightmares long before nations were born. She took a single step forward.

"Do you know what this place is?" she asked, her voice cutting through the clamor.

No one answered. The lead soldier shouted something in Serbian. Two moved to flank her. One approached with a scanner raised, its beam searching for her heat signature. She waited. When the soldier stepped into range, she smiled and bit. Her iron teeth tore through his armor and into flesh. The scream barely escaped his throat before his body collapsed in twitching spasms. The second soldier fired. Baba Yaga raised one hand. The bullet struck her palm and dropped, crushed flat like a coin under an anvil.

She twisted her fingers. The soldier's rifle bent in his hands, the barrel coiling like a snake in an invisible vise. Then it exploded. His body slammed into the nearest pillar and stayed there, motionless. They opened fire. Automatic bursts ripped through the nave, but the bullets curved and shattered on the floor like seeds against stone. One ricocheted into a drone, which spiraled into the rafters and detonated midair, spraying embers through the smoke.

She moved without haste. She did not run or dodge. She walked. Where she stepped, the stone blackened. The soldiers backed away, seized by something older than training, but discipline still held. They dropped to one knee and loosed another volley. One fired a grenade launcher. It struck the ground beside her in a violent blast.

She vanished in the smoke. For three heartbeats, silence. Then she emerged, unburned. Her cloak had turned to ash, revealing shoulders marked in spirals of old script, living runes. Her skin had become the color of bone. Her braid floated behind her as if it no longer obeyed gravity. She inhaled once, drawing in the essence of the ruin, and exhaled rot. The air twisted.

One soldier screamed and clawed at his helmet. Blood poured from his ears. The others staggered as the atmosphere curdled into mold and wet iron. Another dropped to the ground and vomited black bile.

She strode through them. With each step, a soldier fell. One fired a sidearm. The bullet stopped in front of her heart and crumbled to dust. Another raised a flamethrower, shouting into the comms. She reached him first. Her hand closed around his helmet. She lifted him with impossible ease and twisted. The visor shattered. His body went limp. She dropped him.

The soldiers broke. They retreated, but the doors no longer opened. The cathedral had sealed itself behind them. The stained glass hummed faintly in the smoke. She raised both arms. The stone beneath her glowed with old sigils that burned red and white like embers remembering the forge. She spoke one word, a name no human tongue could shape. The ground split.

Roots erupted from the cracked tiles. Thick and gnarled, black and ancient, dragging soil and bone with them. They wrapped around the legs of the fleeing soldiers and dragged them down into the stone. Screams rose, but none reached outside. The sound died against the walls. Above her, the spire began to fall, the pillars cracking, and still she stood.

In the center of the cathedral, amid flame and ruin, Baba Yaga turned toward the last soldier still standing. He was young, shaking, blood trickling from his mouth. She walked toward him. He raised his rifle and fired. The bullets dissolved in the air between them. She reached him. He fell to his knees.

"I don't want to die," he said.

She leaned forward. Her iron teeth glinted in the firelight. "Then remember me."

She vanished into the smoke. The spire collapsed. The roof followed. Flame consumed what stone did not. When the reinforcements arrived twenty minutes later, there was nothing left. Ash and silence. In the center of the floor, untouched by soot or blood, two scorched footprints. Between them, a single lock of white braid.

The tunnel twisted for what felt like hours. Dirt walls pressed close on either side. Roots coiled through the ceiling like veins. The floor was damp and uneven beneath our feet. No light guided us except the faint blue shimmer pulsing from my arms and the silver glint along Danica's blade. Behind us, the world burned. We felt it in the tremble of the soil, the distant thump of collapsing stone. Baba Yaga's fury held the Accord at bay. Her fire was delay, and it had bought us the breath we needed.

The tunnel ended in a narrow opening cut into a hillside thick with moss. The woods beyond were dark but alive. Trees rose like columns in a temple lost to time. Fog clung low, curling around roots and rocks. The air tasted of pine and old smoke, carrying something deeper than scent. Danica collapsed beside a tree. I followed, lowering myself to the earth beside her. My hands trembled. The rings, still wrapped in cloth, rested between us on the forest floor. Neither of us reached for them. Our eyes met, and the forest stilled.

I unwrapped the cloth. The rings shimmered faintly in the mist. One pulsed gold. The other silver. Their light was the steady thrum of something waking beneath the skin. Danica reached out first, her fingers brushing the ring carved from root and iron. I mirrored her. When the metal touched our skin, the world fell away. There was no sound. Only vision.

We stood on a cliff above a burning city. A temple cracked behind us, its roof torn open, columns in splinters. Statues wept blood from marble eyes. We were not ourselves.

Danica wore a robe of crimson woven from ash and fire. Her face was younger, but her eyes were the same, old enough to have watched empires fall. Her hands were stained with blood that had not yet dried. I stood beside her, cloaked in black, marked with symbols of storm and twilight. A blade hung from my hip, the ancestor of the one we carried now. Below us, the city burned. Banners of a forgotten empire curled in the flames. People ran through the streets, chased by men in gold masks and crimson armor. Screams rose like incense.

"We can't save them," she said, her voice raw with grief.

"I know," I replied.

We turned to face each other. She reached into her robe and drew forth a pair of rings.

"These must survive," she said. "Even if we don't."

I took them. I placed one on her finger. She did the same. The moment they locked into place, the world blurred. Another vision.

A field soaked in mud and blood beneath a brutal sky. Rain lashed the earth. I knelt beside Danica, her body broken beneath the weight of some monstrous war machine. I held her hand to my chest and screamed to gods who had long since gone silent.

Then we were somewhere else.

A frozen cave, its entrance sealed by a roaring fire. Danica held the blade as a torch, leading me through the dark as beasts howled outside. We were wounded and starving. We kept moving.

Then another life.

A library set ablaze by zealots. Books screamed in burning tongues. I threw Danica from the window to save her. I stayed behind, consumed by the flames. She never stopped running.

A battlefield of steel and gunpowder. A resistance camp. Our faces were different, altered by the currents of time, but our eyes were the same. Always searching. Always finding.

Then, now. The forest. The rings. Our breath. The memory of everything, every death, every reunion, crashing through us like a wave that would not stop. Danica gasped and gripped my arm. Tears streamed down her cheeks without shame. My throat was filled with names I had once spoken in other languages, other lives, all of them hers. She leaned into me, her forehead touching mine.

"We were there," she whispered. "In every age. In every war. We always found each other."

My voice was ragged. "And we always lost."

She shook her head. "Not this time."

The rings on our fingers pulsed together, two lights merging into one. The runes on my arms burned bright, gold and black now, storm and shadow entwined. Over Danica's heart, the spiral of Lada glowed like an ember wreathed in frost. We remembered it all. The deaths, but also the joy. The first kiss in a ruined orchard before the skies fell. The quiet hours spent watching stars in a world too cruel to deserve them. All of it returned, making me whole. I cupped her face, my thumbs tracing the lines of her sorrow and her fierce determination.

"I remember the last time I lost you," I said.

Her voice broke. "I remember every time I found you, Ilija."

We kissed, with a passion so ancient that even the gods could not have severed it. The wind through the trees bent around us, and for a single moment, the gods were quiet. Because memory had returned. The vow had been spoken again.

The forest carried its silence like a shroud, full of breath and bone. Fog slid low through the undergrowth, rising from the wet earth in slow, gray curls. Pines stood tall in every direction, their trunks streaked with age, their branches trembling as if they too remembered what had passed.

I sat beneath one of those trees, my back pressed to the bark, my shoulders heavy with an exhaustion that ran deeper than muscle or bone. My arms had gone still. The runes no longer pulsed with fire or lightning. They remained illuminated, the glow soft now, settled into my flesh as if they had always been there. Beside me, Danica sat in silence, her knees drawn close, her cloak wrapped tight around her. Her hair clung to her cheeks, dark and damp. Her eyes had not closed since we fled the tunnel, yet she looked as if she had returned from some distant place with her soul intact.

Between us, the bundle of cloth lay untouched. The rings had done what they were meant to do. The memories had returned in one vast river, surging through us until the floodwaters became calm again. The past no longer whispered in fragments. It spoke in full, in every breath we took, in every ache that had never left us.

Danica reached toward the rings. She did not take them. Her fingers hovered above the cloth, and the metal responded with recognition. She turned her head slowly toward me. Her voice came softly, like the rustle of pine needles in windless air.

"This is the first time we've remembered everything, Ilija," she said.

I did not answer right away. I looked at her the way a man looks at something he has been chasing through lifetimes. My chest ached with it. My hands were still.

"It feels like it should have broken us," I finally said, my voice steady but tired.

She gave a faint smile. It did not reach her lips, but it lived in her eyes. "Maybe it did. Every time. And still, we came back."

I shifted, stretching one knee to ease the ache from the cathedral's collapse. The dirt beneath me was soft. The forest held our weight without question. Danica's gaze drifted toward the trees. The mist had begun to lift. Somewhere above the canopy, light was gathering. Dawn was close. She let her breath out slowly.

We sat in silence, because the truth had filled the space between us so completely that words would have only dulled it. The fire we once carried had returned. It was memory, vast and all-consuming.

Danica leaned into me, her head resting lightly on my shoulder. I did not move away. I let the warmth of her closeness settle into my chest. My hand found hers, fingers intertwining with the ease of someone who had done it a thousand times before. No vows were spoken aloud. None were needed. The vow had been made in every age that had tried to erase us, and now, beneath the ancient trees, it had been made again. In the silence that comes after truth. The forest remembered it all.

CHAPTER TWENTY-ONE
ASH AND MEMORY

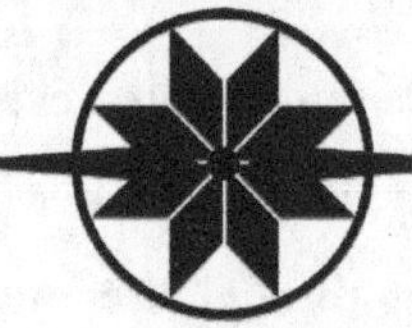

Ilija

The wind shifted first. The kind of shift that precedes a detonation, a sudden drop in pressure that stiffened the body before the mind could register the change. A brutal front rolled in, something monstrous pushing through from somewhere that should have stayed closed.

Danica tasted it first, a sharp tang of copper on her tongue, as though a live wire had been shoved down her throat. I felt it lower, a raw tremor in the base of my spine, the place where instinct lives. Every nerve in my body stiffened at once.

We stood shoulder to shoulder on the ridge above what had once been called Poljana Svetih, the Meadow of Saints. Centuries ago, this land had been consecrated in pilgrimage, blessed by the footsteps of the devout. Now it was a graveyard of war, its sacred purpose gutted. The spring at the bottom had long since dried, leaving only parched earth. The chapel stood as a skeleton of charred stone, its cross bent and blistered from relentless shellfire. Scorch marks spiraled across the earth in black whorls. Empty casings littered the slope like discarded rosaries.

Below, a stillness waited, the kind that invites blood.

Behind us, the resistance gathered. Hardened soldiers forged in endless conflict. Veterans of shattered cities, their faces gray with grim experience.

Field medics whose bodies bore the ragged scars of battlefield amputations, whose stares went through you rather than at you. Peasant snipers in stolen camouflage, their gazes sharp and cold. One woman held an anti-tank rifle across her lap like a child, a strange and terrifying lullaby. Another draped a claymore mine with cloth that had once been a priest's stole, the embroidered cross half-covering the detonator.

At the center of them all stood Danica and me.

I wore a coat pockmarked by shrapnel. My left sleeve was soaked in dried blood that wasn't my own. Around my waist, the relic dagger pulsed with residual heat, a low and steady thrum against my skin. My eyes, glassy with fatigue, still burned with electric intensity. When the storm came now, it erupted from me, raw and uncontained.

Danica stood to my left, her hands wrapped in combat tape and dried blood. Her frostbitten knuckles gripped the hilt of The Blade of Fate, its weight familiar in her grasp. Her braid was tucked beneath a hood, her shoulders squared, her boots black with dried mud and bone fragments. The brooch at her throat, bearing Freyja's and Brigid's symbols, still shimmered faintly, though it no longer glowed with overt power.

Its dim flicker carried a warning. Neither of us spoke. We had no need to. The rings on our fingers, ironroot and silver, bone and carved wood, pulsed in sync, matching our heartbeats.

I broke the silence, my voice rough. "We've died here before, Danica."

Danica nodded, her gaze sweeping the valley below through her cracked scope. "At least twice, Ilija."

"And this time?" I asked.

"I don't know," Danica replied, her voice low and grim.

We waited, suspended in the stillness, and then came the sound. A horn, mechanical, harsh, splintered with static. A declaration of war. I turned east, my jaw locked, my gaze hardening. Across the smoldering field, the fog peeled back, and hell itself arrived.

They came in columns, four deep. They brought no banners, no drums, only the pounding hum of engine-choked infantry and the grinding of armored boots across fractured soil. The Accord shock troops moved in lockstep, their modular armor camouflaged in synthetic ecclesiastical gold. Every helm bore the same chilling symbol, a burnt-black icon of Saint George with his face distorted by wire and lens.

Behind them, monstrous tanks crafted from the desecrated iron of cathedrals rumbled forward. Each chassis bore scorched scripture carved into the plating, twisted crosses jutting from the turrets like mock crucifixes. The barrels radiated heat from their loaded shells.

Above, drones hovered, grotesque and mechanical. Steel wings with serrated edges, optics like the hollow eyes of crucified saints. They spun slowly overhead, broadcasting encrypted signals that distorted the airwaves and made every ear ring with a maddening buzz.

The battlefield's static transformed into a deeper drone, a sound that throbbed just behind the eardrums like something trying to crawl its way out.

Then came Ana.

She walked, barefoot, her violet gown embroidered with threads of gold and dark crimson, sweeping above the blood-damp grass. Her crown shimmered unnaturally, seven orbs of molten light orbiting her skull like a halo peeled from a dying sun. Yet her face was the face of a woman already mourning the man she was about to kill, sorrow drawn through every line of her features.

I flinched. Danica's breath caught, a sharp and choked gasp. That expression, the way grief and tenderness fought for the same space on her face, hit harder than the advancing tanks.

"She knows," I muttered, barely voiced.

Danica kept her eyes locked on Ana.

"She's not here to conquer," Danica said, her voice flat. "She's here to end what she started. To cut it out."

My pulse thundered against the inside of my skull. "We don't let her."

Danica drew the blade. I raised my hand, and the spiral rune on my palm blazed open. Behind us, the resistance moved. They surged in patterns only the desperate could follow. Ex-militia fighters carried salvaged AKs with duct-taped magazines. Medics crouched in the brush, stripping Accord armor for their hidden caches of grenades. A woman named Marija held a grenade launcher slung across her back and a machete in her hand. She whispered to the blade before she kissed the handle.

I dropped to one knee, pressed my palm flat to the dirt, and whispered the old word. The air thickened. The soil around my hand cracked outward in a spider web of fissures.

From the ridge to the field below, the land began to hum with rage, a deep and resonant tremor. Danica's blade trembled, vibrating with contained force. I rose, lightning crawling up my arm like a living beast.

Then the tanks opened fire.

The first shell struck thirty meters away, vaporizing a resistance scout where he crouched. His body atomized, skin and bone turning to red vapor that clung to the trees. A second shell hit the chapel ruin. The front wall disintegrated in a storm of dust. Screams followed, shrill and piercing.

My voice tore through the chaos. "NOW!"

Danica moved first. She leapt from the ridge like a thrown spear, her coat whipping around her, the blade drawn high. The first soldier she landed on had his mouth half-open when The Blade of Fate split him in two from shoulder to pelvis, his armor peeling like fruit skin. Blood sprayed against Danica's jaw, hot and arterial.

She carved through the second soldier with a reverse slash that severed both knees. He hit the ground howling. She silenced him with a brutal boot to the throat. Another moved to flank her with a plasma baton. She ducked, rolled, came up under his ribs, and drove the blade in slow. He convulsed as the weapon devoured his body and the oath inscribed in his armor's neural bond. His last breath tasted of singed copper.

I descended behind her, fist-first. My fist slammed into the earth and detonated. The concussive blast flung five Accord soldiers into the air, limbs flailing. One screamed as he hit a tree and cracked his spine in half. Another landed on his own severed rifle, its barrel jutting through his gut. I stood, electricity pouring off my shoulders in bright forks. My beard smoked, fine tendrils of vapor rising. I clenched my teeth, eyes burning white-blue.

Two more soldiers leveled their rifles. I raised a hand and snapped my fingers. Their rifles exploded, splintering into lethal shards that tore through their armor and pierced their throats. They fell gargling.

The resistance charged. Milan, an axe in one hand and a pistol in the other, led a break line of fighters through the smoke, roaring. Bullets ripped through the air. Screams rose in clusters. Danica cleaved her way to the

Accord's flank, hacking through armor with ruthless efficiency. Every stroke killed. She removed heads and spines with equal indifference.

I moved through them methodically, forking bolts of lightning through chest plates, lifting one man in the air and igniting his ribcage from the inside. His jaw broke open on a scream that never finished. He collapsed in a heap of scorched fat and liquefied lungs.

Ana watched from the center of the field. Danica saw her standing at the eye of the battle like a prophet watching her apocalypse unfold, arms loose at her sides, her gaze sweeping the carnage with the patience of someone who had already seen the ending.

My voice was hoarse as I stepped beside Danica. "She's not fighting."

"She's waiting," Danica growled, her gaze riveted on Ana.

"For what?" I asked, my breath ragged.

Danica raised her blade and pointed it directly at Ana. "For us."

The ground quaked beneath us, fed by my storm and Danica's blazing fire. The moment Ana's gaze turned aside, I launched myself forward. Electricity whipped from my palms like hunting serpents, slamming into a group of advancing Accord soldiers. Their armor lit up with searing blue light, every neural implant overloading in a simultaneous burst. One screamed as his helmet melted around his face, fusing metal to bone. Another convulsed, vomited foam, and dropped twitching into the mud.

I moved like a storm given form. I tore a jagged piece of rebar from a crater wall and hurled it through the air, lightning coursing down its length. It speared an Accord psionic through the chest, embedding him into a tree. The bark exploded behind him in a shower of splinters.

Danica was already ten meters ahead. Her sword blazed with orange flame rimmed in pale frost, the blade leaving a trail of ash and glittering rime. Her coat was slick with blood, her jaw set. She swung upward, carving through a soldier's arm and chest in one savage arc. The wound froze instantly, then exploded from within as ice expanded into the cavity. Shards of bone and armor rained down.

Another enemy tried to flank her. Danica whirled, fire spiraling from her free hand, igniting the air around him. He burned alive, screaming as the flames dug into his lungs before his knees buckled.

Behind us, Milan fought with grinding endurance, his axe pulping one Accord helmet after another. The man's face was smeared with blood, his eye swollen shut, and he roared with every kill. Zoran moved with him, dropping soldiers with clean headshots, muttering prayers he no longer believed in.

Around Danica and me, the battlefield bent. She swept her blade in a wide arc, freezing the ground ahead of her, fifty meters of slick black ice. Accord mechs attempting to charge slid into each other, crashing. One toppled sideways and detonated, blowing a trench of charred soil into the air.

I raised both hands, crouched, slammed them down. The lightning spiked upward in jagged pillars, impaling two drones along with three soldiers, transforming them into blackened statues that smoked before crumbling. One soldier tried to crawl away, half his spine exposed. I stepped on his skull.

Danica pivoted, sweat and blood pouring down her temples, and unleashed a torrent of fire from her palm. The blaze blasted forward in a solid column, catching a retreating line of troops. They screamed and dropped their weapons, burning alive in rows. She did not stop until the air reeked of roasted flesh.

At the center of the valley, untouched by ash or smoke, Ana stood motionless. Her silk gown rippled though no wind blew. Her stare held fixed, unblinking. She was crying, her tears silent, born from inevitability. I saw it and faltered for half a second, and that was all it took.

A drone arced above me, dropped two bombs behind my shoulders. I turned to face the first, too late. The explosion came without sound, pure concussion and distortion. It threw me skyward and slammed me back into the earth like a crucifix hurled from heaven.

Danica turned with a scream that tore the air open. She dropped her blade, raised both arms, and unleashed everything at once. Flame poured from her left hand, ice from her right. The air shattered where the elements met, and a shockwave burst outward. Drones tumbled from the sky. Trees snapped and splintered. A tank's viewport imploded as superheated air met the sudden chill.

The Accord line faltered. Soldiers dropped their weapons and ran. Danica sprinted to my side, sliding on her knees through the mud, her fingers trembling as she pulled me upright. My lip was split, blood running down my jaw, my coat torn open. Yet the lightning still crackled behind my pupils.

I coughed once, tasted blood. "You screamed for me."

Danica's hand hovered over my chest. "Don't die."

I tried to laugh. It came out as a wheeze. "Working on it."

The air changed again, heavier and older. The rings on both our fingers glowed, hot with memory. The ground beneath Ana's feet broke apart.

The earth split with a sound like a lung tearing, a fracture ripping the dead grass open in a perfect spiral beneath Ana's feet. The smoke parted and the wind stilled. The sun dimmed, as if whatever was waking demanded full attention.

Danica staggered back from the epicenter, dragging me with her. My boots skidded through churned mud as the rings flared white-hot against our fingers. Visions flooded in.

A war camp beneath Norse banners, Danica sharpening a blade beside a pyre while I prayed to a god with a wolf's name. A crumbling temple of Perun, where we knelt before a shattered altar with matching burn marks on our palms. Then older still, a battlefield drowning in Roman blood where she held my body as fire rolled over our backs.

Hundreds of lives. Thousands of deaths, and one oath binding them all. The twin rings burned against our skin, collapsing lifetimes into a single instant.

The rift widened. Light poured out, the light of memory, dense and aching. It struck the Accord lines like a physical force. Soldiers screamed. Some dropped weapons and clutched their heads. Others collapsed, murmuring names they did not remember learning.

Ana stood at the center of it, her arms spread wide, embracing the chaos. The seven stars in her crown flickered and destabilized. Her lips moved, shaping words that carried no sound. She looked at me, her gaze empty, settled into resignation. Then her knees buckled as the memory surged through her.

Danica surged forward, sword in hand. Ice crawled up her shoulders while fire trailed from her hair like smoke off a torch. Her pupils were gone, replaced by a flickering, mirrored glow that reflected ancient power. She raised the blade and screamed, a sound of rupture, of worlds splitting open.

The temperature dropped twenty degrees in a heartbeat. Frost sheathed her boots, her breath emerging in sharp plumes, and then the fire exploded from her skin. A dozen Accord troops were vaporized in a flash of red-gold flame. Another tank burst into a secondary explosion as its munitions ignited. Metal shrapnel ripped through the trees like birds made of knives.

Danica tore into the nearest squad. Her blade left molten grooves in chestplates. One soldier tried to flee. She lashed out with a backhand and froze his spine solid before shattering him with a second swing. Bone snapped inside armor that broke a half-second later. The frost ate its way through their weapons. The fire consumed their eyes, leaving only hollow sockets.

I stood behind her, arms raised, every vein in my neck lit from within. The spiral on my palm opened like a mouth. Lightning detonated outward in every direction, a vast and intricate web. It struck ten soldiers at once. Three combusted where they stood. Two slammed into trees hard enough to liquefy their skulls. One screamed for mercy, and I shot a bolt directly through his mouth. I watched the man drop. The air filled with the sharp, acrid smell of burned flesh.

Behind us, Zoran's squad pushed forward, gunning down the last wave of retreating psionic units. Marija launched a grenade into a group attempting to regroup behind a boulder. The explosion painted the trees red.

The rings still hummed, steady against our skin.

Danica fell to her knees beside Ana's crumpled form. I followed, one hand still sparking as I lowered it. Ana looked up. Her skin was pale, her lips cracked, though her eyes still carried their strange starlight.

Danica pressed the tip of her blade against Ana's chest. Her voice was hoarse. "Why didn't you fight, Ana?"

Ana's reply came as a whisper, frail and ancient. "Because I already lost you, Ilija. A long time ago."

I knelt beside Danica. "Then why did you come, Ana?"

Ana's gaze flicked between us one last time. "I needed to see your face again."

She closed her eyes. Something behind her gaze retreated, her spirit pulling inward even as her body held. Her crown flickered, its seven orbs unstable.

Ana's breath fogged in the cold air. She remained standing, trembling, the blood on her lips mingling with tears held in check by her immovable will. The earth cracked around her in unnaturally smooth fissures. The starlight in her crown dimmed to a faint pulse. Her eyes lingered on me one last time, vacant, finished.

Then the ground behind her split open, and she stepped back into it. A pulse of light, and she was gone. The silence that followed was absolute.

Danica lowered her blade slowly, breathing hard, the flame and ice flickering off her skin, fading.

"She didn't die," she said, her voice a low murmur.

I nodded. "She ran."

Danica turned her eyes toward the battlefield, now silent. "She'll come back worse, Ilija."

I did not reply. I knew she was right. The resistance stood around us, bloodied and burned, exhausted but victorious. Some dropped their weapons, letting them clatter to the earth. Some fell to their knees in the mud. No one cheered. Only the ragged sound of breathing filled the air.

Zoran limped toward us, covered in black soot, his rifle strapped across his back. "We held."

Marija crouched beside a wounded fighter, wrapping a tourniquet made from the sleeve of her own coat.

Milan dragged a dead Accord soldier into a growing pile. "They'll return. In greater numbers. With cleaner machines."

I looked to the ridgeline, to the chapel ruins now caved in and soaked in the blood of the dead.

"No," I said, my voice firm. "They'll return thinking we're finished."

Danica's eyes met mine, fierce and unwavering. "We're just beginning."

The fires were lit at dusk for memory, for the fallen. We dragged the dead from the field with broken arms and shattered ribs, our smoke-blackened hands barely able to grip. We had nothing to dig with, only blades, only bare fingers clawing into the earth. We buried our own in pits lined with iron, marked with names scrawled in soot and blood. Each grave received a glyph. Each body, a stone and a word whispered into the cold earth.

A woman knelt and pressed her ear to the soil before covering it, murmuring in a dialect lost to time. A boy broke his own blade in half and laid one piece on the chest of his fallen brother.

I limped from grave to grave, touching the markers with burned fingers. The rings warmed faintly each time, acknowledging the fallen.

Danica lit the pyres. The frost clung to her shoulders, though the flames she summoned rose in pillars, devouring the carrion stench and painting the snow orange with heat. One column of smoke rose black as pitch, another white. Signal fires, sent to the world.

She turned to me. "The old cities will see them."

"They'll remember," I said. "If they still can."

We gathered around the central fire as night devoured the valley. I stood in the ruined chapel, a jagged crucifix behind me, my coat soaked through with someone else's blood. I held up the rings. They were warm in my palm, heavier than metal should be.

"Five artifacts," I said, my voice scraped thin. "Found and united."

The resistance stared back, bruised and bloodied, leaning on each other to stay upright.

"These don't promise peace," I continued. "They promise memory. And memory is the one thing they can't burn out of us."

Danica stepped beside me, firelight catching the edge of her jaw.

"They think we're stories," she said, her voice rough. "Let them find out."

Later, above the valley, Danica and I sat beneath a dying oak, its ancient branches reaching towards the silent stars. The snow drifted again, soft and slow. I opened my hand. The rings lay there, no longer burning, though still warm and steady in my palm.

Danica rested her head on my shoulder, her coat torn, her fingers blistered. Her mouth still tasted of ash and blood.

"She'll go to ground," she murmured. "Somewhere deep. Somewhere holy."

I nodded. "A sanctuary."

Danica closed her eyes. "Then we drag her out of it."

I looked up at the stars, scattered across the dark, each one burning in silence. I took her hand, and the rings glowed. Their light was promise. Tomorrow, we would move. Tomorrow, we would march to the next memory. Tonight, we stayed with the dead and let the fire remember them.

CHAPTER TWENTY-TWO
THE SEAL IS BROKEN

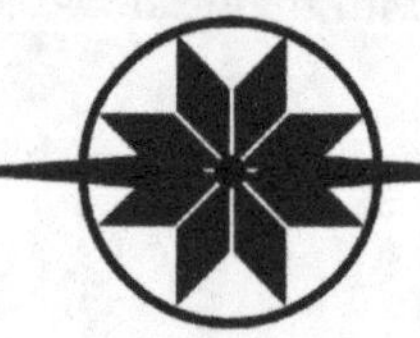

Ilija

The wind came at us like a blade, thin and relentlessly cold. Even here, even now, after all the screams had faded into silence, the mountain itself refused to be still. Its breath was smoke. Its skin was ash and broken stone. Every step forward brought the sickening crunch of bone and volcanic glass, the air so dry it scraped the inside of our lungs raw.

Danica led the way, her coat pulled tight against her frame. Sweat clung beneath her collar despite the chill. The air felt cold in the lungs yet warm against the skin, like standing too close to a dying furnace. Ash clung to everything. Her boots. Her blade. It coated my waistcoat like frost, softening the dark gray into something bone-colored, as if I were slowly being pulled into the mountain's grain.

Behind us, the resistance moved in silence. Their footsteps were steady, disciplined, hushed by reverence. This was a tomb, or perhaps something worse, a memory too vast for the world to bury.

Zoran carried the satphone and the last functioning recon drone, his face drawn with grim purpose. Marija moved like a ghost, her gaze scanning the rocks above for any sign of movement. Milan had stopped speaking altogether after the final body was burned the night before, his voice lost to the horror. He walked now with the blade of his axe resting across his shoulder, his expression sealed shut.

The rings on Danica's hand were quiet now, yet they radiated a constant warmth, a subtle pulse. She could still feel the tremor of the last battle, the raw electricity in my blood. We had stood on that ridge and tasted war. Now we came to climb into its mouth.

The mountain rose before us, its flanks black with spent lava and ash drift. Bones poked from crevices, animal and human intermingled, their origin impossible to tell in the gloom. The ridge sat silent save for the wheezing wind and the occasional low groan of shifting rock.

I climbed behind her, each step deliberate. My ribs were still bruised, perhaps cracked, yet I never slowed. The storm that lived in me was coiled, a serpent sleeping beneath my flesh. Lightning had always been my weapon, but since the unity of the artifacts, it moved like something older now. More precise.

Danica could feel my breath between her shoulders and knew I was still hers. We reached a plateau halfway up. The smoke thinned. The wind dropped, and the temple came into view.

It rose from the rock like a carcass preserved by the very fire that had killed it. Black stone ribs jutted from the slope in twisted symmetry, half-buried in ash and sediment. The roof had collapsed in places, the vast dome leaning at a perilous angle. What frescoes remained were cracked and burned, flaking off in long, curling strips of scorched plaster. Some depicted faces distorted by heat, eyeless and screaming. Others were spirals and constellations that echoed the sigils on the rings we wore.

At the center stood a single doorway. The doorway gaped open, a black rectangular mouth framed by crumbling reliefs of women with braided hair and blindfolded eyes, carved from volcanic stone. One had her hand on a sword. Another held her own severed tongue. I approached the threshold and stopped. Danica stepped beside me. The wind stilled completely.

I spoke first. "This place was buried for a reason."

She looked at me, the ash curling in her eyelashes, frost forming along the cuffs of her coat despite the heat rising from the stone. "And we're here for that reason."

I nodded once. Then we entered.

Inside, the air shifted. The change was gravity, immense and sudden, like stepping underwater. Dust filled the space, clinging to skin, crawling into nostrils, settling behind the eyes. The stone walls pulsed faintly with heat. They were warm like the ribs of something still living.

Behind us, Zoran and Marija waited with the others at the ridge, securing a perimeter. We alone would enter.

The walls bore murals, none whole. One depicted a figure with outstretched arms, her mouth stitched shut, her feet bound by roots. Another displayed a twin spiral encased in flame. Still others had been violently scratched out, gouged by fingernails or blades. The floor bore carvings half-covered in soot. I wiped my hand across one and uncovered a spiral almost identical to the one on my palm.

Danica's gut twisted at the sight. She stopped at a narrow antechamber where the ceiling had partially collapsed. Rubble littered the floor. Half-burned tapestries and shattered pottery. Rusted chains. Sulfur and blood hung thick in the air, undercut by something herbal and deeply rotted.

"This isn't a sanctuary," she said, her voice low.

I crouched and touched one of the chains. "No." I ran my hand along the links and winced. "They used to bring people here. Perhaps priests. Perhaps prisoners."

Danica moved further in. Her boots crushed something soft beneath her, a half-decayed bundle of fabric with brittle bones inside. She kept moving. The chamber opened into a rotunda deeper within. Its ceiling was still intact, an oculus overhead letting in a thin shaft of dying light. Beneath it, a dais. Upon it, a single stone chair flanked by braziers long since cold.

Danica circled the seat, tracing the symbols carved into its surface. They were instructions. A litany of oaths.

I stepped up behind her and whispered, "This was a confession seat."

She met my gaze and nodded.

The rings began to glow again. A pulse. Then another. Mine burned ice-blue. Danica's flickered between frost-white and ember-orange. The air thickened. The heat returned, and something beneath the floor shifted. The sound that followed was breathing. The breath came again, slow, wet, subterranean.

I turned toward the dais. The glow from the rings intensified, mine and Danica's pulsing in perfect alignment, two separate powers merged. The room seemed to flex around us. Walls curved where they should have been flat. Shadows shifted without light. The air turned thick with iron and incense.

Danica stepped down from the dais and knelt by the stones. She placed her hand on the ground. It was warm. Too warm. Behind the warmth, a tremor. A heartbeat.

She looked up at me. "There's something beneath us."

I nodded once and stepped to the center of the floor, directly beneath the oculus. The beam of dying daylight fell across my shoulders. The spiral on my palm widened, curling, rotating, hungry. I whispered the word. The ancient command. The spiral opened.

Light poured from my hand, white-blue, crackling, cold like lightning at high altitude. It hit the floor in a perfect ring and the stone began to melt, transformed by recognition, folding inward, retracting into itself like a wound reopening. Steps appeared, descending into shadow. Danica unsheathed her sword, the steel flickering briefly with frost.

I nodded toward the opening. "You lead?"

She smirked, just barely. "Always."

We descended together, the spiral of steps cut from obsidian and bone, the walls carved with the same twin spirals and goddess-figures repeating endlessly. Always women. Always faceless or blindfolded, bound by hair or root or fire. The deeper we went, the hotter it became, the air growing thick and oppressive.

Danica's fingers began to sweat against the grip of her blade. Her breathing slowed, born of reverence. Power lived here, old and raw and ritualistic. When we reached the bottom, silence pressed in from every direction, the hush of something too deep to disturb.

We stepped into a vast circular chamber carved out of the mountain's root. The floor was black glass, volcanic, smooth, half-melted, reflecting distorted shadows. Pillars lined the perimeter, carved from a material Danica couldn't name, one that reflected her face wrong. Too old. Too knowing.

In the center stood a monolith. It rose from the floor like a jagged tooth, its surface veined with lines of molten red and blue, a heart made from stone and electricity. Runes curled along its sides, unreadable yet living, pulsing with inner light. The rings on our fingers pulsed harder, answering.

Danica gripped her blade tighter, her knuckles white with anticipation.

"This is it," she whispered.

I stepped beside her, my eyes wide. "The nexus."

I raised my hand toward the monolith. It opened. The stone split organically, like a fruit being peeled by unseen hands. The center revealed something buried in flame and frost, a pair of figures suspended in light, locked in an eternal embrace.

Danica staggered forward. She knew that face. The woman was herself. The man, taller in this vision, his hair long and copper red, his beard unkempt, his eyes glowing with lightning, was me. Ilija as I had been centuries ago, a past life, one of many.

Their bodies were bound by threads of flame and frost, twisted into the monolith, held in place by runes of oath and sacrifice. The figures were still. Yet the light between them flickered, as if aware. As if waiting.

My voice was hoarse. "It's us."

Danica's knees buckled. She saw it all. A battlefield under a black sun. A temple crumbling as she screamed his name. A knife in her hand. His blood on her chest. Her hands burned from holding him too long after he died. We had been here before. This exact place. We had built the monolith. We had become the seal, and now the seal recognized us.

Danica dropped her sword. It clattered to the floor, echoing too loud, like metal on bone. I stepped toward the figures. The light reacted, drawing back, then rushing forward, engulfing us both in a wave of burning memory. The chamber vanished. We saw ourselves. Life after life. War after war.

The monolith had been built to trap our fate, to lock us into a cycle the gods could control. It weaponized our love, our power.

I clutched my chest. The spiral burned. Lightning ran down my spine and exploded behind my eyes. I screamed once, but it came out as a ragged gasp. Danica reached for me, but her hand passed through light. She was there, yet distant. She was watching her own past. The younger Danica, the one trapped in the monolith, raised her hand and placed it against her Ilija's heart.

"I will find you," she whispered.

The monolith closed. It snapped back into place. The light vanished. Danica stood alone in the dark. I dropped to my knees beside her, panting, drenched in sweat. The monolith stood silent again, a sealed stone.

Danica turned to me. "What the hell was that?"

I looked up, my gray-blue eyes wide, full of tears and fury.

"They built a cage," I said. "They built it out of us."

Somewhere far above us, on the surface of the mountain, the sky cracked with thunder.

The monolith stood silent now. Its surface had gone dark, but it had changed. Hairline fissures glowed with faint frost and flame, the same colors that flickered behind Danica's eyes. The seal held.

I knelt beside the monolith, one hand pressed to the glass-slick floor, my breath slow but ragged. My eyes had stayed dry when the vision ended. Yet now, in the silence, they brimmed with something worse than grief.

"I saw her die," I said.

Danica sat beside me, her hand resting on the hilt of her fallen blade. Her knees were smudged with ash. A smear of blood, someone else's, marked her cheek.

"I killed you once," she whispered.

My eyes met hers. "I asked you to."

The silence that followed was the edge of a cliff, the fall already begun. Above us, the chamber's pillars began to hum. The vibration was presence, a living thing pressing against the walls. A low tone, like a thousand voices inhaling at once, filled the temple's belly.

Danica stood slowly, her body tensing. "They're coming."

I rose beside her, wincing from the pain in my ribs. "They've always been here."

It began in the ceiling. The oculus above, a mere crack of sky, shivered. The dim light pouring through it fractured into colors unknown to the mortal spectrum. Bruised violet. Obsidian blue. The monolith groaned in anticipation. Then the gods began to unfold.

They manifested like a tide that had been waiting behind the veil of reality, suddenly permitted to flood forward.

First came Zorya Utrennyaya, the morning star. She appeared as a girl with silver braids that twisted into constellations, her eyes reflecting the exact moment I had first seen Danica in our first life, on a battlefield, rain falling like spears.

Then her twin, Zorya Vechernyaya, arrived as a woman cloaked in shadow, her lips stained with the wine of endings. Her breath smelled like twilight. Together they circled Danica and me, their voices pressing against us without audible sound.

Danica clutched her chest. "I remember the shore," she gasped. "The one with the black sails. I waited."

"I never came," I whispered. "I drowned in the shallows."

From the floor rose a figure formed of roots and snakes. Veles, the god of the underworld and trickery. He stepped from the dust with a grin carved from bone, moss clinging to his antlers.

"Still playing with fate," he rasped, his voice dragging like a blade through gravel. "Still thinking love can beat death."

Danica turned to him, her eyes wide with memory. "You promised us time."

Veles shrugged. "And you wasted it. Again. But now, now you're learning."

A thunderclap echoed without origin. The air stank of charred metal and broken steel. Perun arrived, his eyes glowing white, hammer resting across his shoulder. His chest bore the scars of battles no history book could name. His gaze landed on me, and a smirk cracked through his storm-weathered face.

"You finally let the lightning speak, Ilija."

I stood taller, the pain forgotten. "It was always there, Perun."

Perun stepped forward and slammed his hammer once on the stone. The chamber shook. "I gave you rage," he said. "You turned it into discipline. Do not forget your fury."

Then, like dusk turning to midnight, the shadows coalesced.

Morana emerged last. She was there, seated on the far end of the rotunda like a statue made of hunger. Her skin was absence. Her face a void. Her voice, when it came, crept through the chamber like cold oil.

"You should have died," she said. "In every life."

Danica took a trembling step forward. "But we didn't."

Morana's grin was slow and wide. "You did something worse, Ilija. You remembered."

The gods surrounded us now, each occupying space in a way that made the room feel boundless, like sky and sea collapsing into one. Then, like a whisper over still water, came Lada.

She stepped through Danica's chest like a memory given flesh, tall, luminous, adorned in robes of wheat and snow. Her hair was raven-black. Her eyes were Danica's eyes.

"My child," she said.

Danica collapsed to her knees, shaking.

"I keep loving him," she whispered. "Even knowing how it ends."

Lada's hand brushed her temple. "And he loves you back. That is the price. That is the gift."

I reached for Danica and fell beside her. The rings on our hands pulsed, then fused for a moment, their glow blinding. Every past lifetime unraveled inside us. The assassin and the soldier. The healer and the prince. The lovers burned in fire. The rebels who died in chains.

Danica's breath hitched. Tears brimmed in her eyes. "I remember the taste of his blood."

I cupped her cheek. "I remember your last breath in the smoke."

Then we kissed. It was storms rejoining, memory becoming body again. It cracked the floor beneath us, the stone groaning. The gods watched, and they blessed it. Their presence alone declared, "You are the story now."

The light dimmed. The gods receded into us, becoming part of our being.

Danica stood in the flickering half-light of the collapsed chamber, every part of her vibrating from the unbearable fullness of memory. She felt it behind her ribs like a second heartbeat.

I was across from her, stripped down by revelation. My shirt clung to my chest, damp from sweat and ash. My waistcoat hung open, the buttons torn. A streak of soot marked my cheek, blood clinging to the corner of my mouth. Yet my eyes, gray-blue and stormlit, held only her. The gods had gone. Her.

She took a step toward me. I met her halfway. Danica touched my face with both hands, cradling me like a relic she had just unearthed. Her thumbs brushed the curve of my cheekbones, then down to the line of my jaw, which trembled beneath her fingers.

"You found me," she whispered.

My voice was low, reverent. "I will always find you."

Our lips met slowly, as though tasting memory itself. Our mouths explored in silence, eyes fluttering shut, then met again, deeper and slower. Her body leaned into mine, and my arms wrapped around her waist with something like awe, like prayer.

She pulled back for only a breath. "Touch me like you remember everything," she said.

I answered without words, with the quiet shaking of my hands as I unclasped the fastenings of her shirt. My knuckles brushed the soft slope of her collarbone, and she gasped.

Her shirt slid from her shoulders. I pressed my lips to her skin as it was revealed. The hollow of her throat. The line of her ribs. I touched her like I had known this body in fire and frost, like every inch was a home I had longed for in exile.

Danica undressed me in turn, hunger tethered to reverence. When she pushed my shirt from my shoulders, she kissed the scar that cut across my chest, then the hollow just below my throat. My breath caught when her fingers skimmed my waist, and I exhaled her name like it was the last word I'd ever be allowed to speak.

We sank to the stone floor, cloaked in flickering firelight from the wall torches and the lingering radiance of the rings. The ash beneath us was still warm. Her thighs cradled my hips. Her lips sought my throat, then my mouth again.

"I want to remember this in every life," she murmured.

My hands cupped her face, steady now. "You will."

I entered her with a slow, deliberate motion, one hand on her hip, the other at the base of her spine, grounding her. We gasped together, our eyes locked. Every movement of my body against hers was a recollection. The way she arched. The way she tightened around me with each slow, tender thrust.

She ran her fingers down my back, feeling every muscle flex, every breath stutter. I kissed her with growing urgency, then with gentleness, my mouth tracing the curve of her shoulder and the line of her throat.

"You're shaking," I whispered into her skin.

"So are you," she breathed.

Our rhythm deepened. Her moans were soft at first, growing sharper as I moved inside her. Her hips rose to meet me, and together we found a cadence that echoed like a heartbeat through the hollow stone.

Frost crept across the floor beneath her, spiraling outward from her spine, while flame traced delicate lines along her shoulders. My skin sparked with electricity, each pulse of pleasure igniting a flicker of lightning from my fingertips to the floor.

Danica cried out first, her climax rising like a wave from her core, crashing through her in a blaze of heat and trembling limbs. Her arms clung to me, her face buried against my neck as her entire body shuddered with release. I held her through it, breath ragged, whispering her name between kisses.

When she opened her eyes again, she found mine, glassy and burning. My control slipped then. I moved faster now, thrusting harder, grunting softly into her mouth as she kissed me with everything she had left. When I came, it was with a groan that was almost a sob, my entire body seizing, my arms pulling her to me as though she might vanish.

We held each other afterward without speaking. Her head rested against my chest, our legs tangled, our fingers still laced. The warmth of skin on skin and the steady cadence of breath.

Danica finally whispered, "Stay."

I stroked her hair, kissing her forehead. "I'm here."

She kissed my shoulder, then my chest, then looked up at me. "Then let's make this one the last."

Danica ran her fingers through my beard, resting her cheek against my chest. She could feel my heartbeat slowing, syncing with hers. She kissed the center of it.

"I died so many times," she whispered.

I turned, eyes glassy. "So did I."

She nodded. "We always will."

I held her tighter, and for a moment, in the ruin beneath the ash, the war outside fell away.

The echoes of our love had barely faded when the first scream shattered the ridgeline. A death rattle, raw and chilling.

My head snapped up. Danica's eyes, still soft from our union, sharpened into obsidian slits. Our hands, just moments ago pressed gently to one another's skin, now crackled with barely contained power.

Zoran's voice snarled over comms. "They're here. North slope. Repeat, they're here!"

I grabbed my coat, sparks flickering across my fingers. Danica had already turned toward the entrance. The frost-ring on her hand pulsed like a second heart, the fire-ring beside it burning steady and bright.

Drones darted overhead like carrion flies. The Accord's vanguard, a full strike unit in black carbon exo-frames, advanced in tight formation. Each step they took left prints that smoked. Neural implants blinked green behind their visors, syncing every movement. Silence and precision. The cold, efficient intent to kill.

Danica stepped into their path. She raised her right hand and spoke her first word since the gods vanished.

"Burn."

A tidal wave of fire, raw and hungry, ripped from her palm and rolled across the field like molten wind. The first line of Accord troops disintegrated on contact. Their armor buckled and boiled, peeling off in sheets, taking flesh and bone with it. One soldier screamed as his helmet fused to his face, skin blackening beneath reinforced glass. Another tried to run, only to collapse as flame poured into his respirator and cooked him from the inside.

Behind them, the second wave tried to flank. I struck first. Electricity whipped from my palms like hunting serpents, slamming into a cluster of charging soldiers. Their suits lit blue, every neural implant overloading in a simultaneous burst. One fell to his knees, convulsing, eyes bleeding. Another seized mid-stride, foam spilling from his mouth before collapsing face-first into the mud. A drone dived from above. I turned and pointed. Lightning ripped upward in a blinding column. The drone exploded mid-air, shrapnel raining down like jagged hail.

"EMP isn't holding!" Marija yelled from her perch behind the ridge, her voice raw. "They've re-shielded! Focus fire!"

"West flank breached!" shouted Milan. "Three heavies inbound!"

Danica's gaze locked onto them. Massive Accord enforcers stomping through the smoke, plasma repeaters glowing red-hot on their shoulders. One fired, launching a pulse that incinerated two resistance fighters instantly. Danica sprinted forward, sliding through mud and blood, her hands glowing bright as twin suns. The moment they turned toward her, she hurled both arms out. A spiral of flame coiled around her like a hurricane, mixing with piercing arcs of glacial frost. The elements struck together. The left enforcer exploded in chunks of meat and molten alloy. The center one tried to raise his weapon. Danica was already on him, eyes blazing, her bare hand pressed to his chest.

"You'll freeze before you scream." She plunged her frost into his core. His chest caved inward, armor snapping, flesh crystallizing. Blood froze mid-spurt, coating her arm in a sheen of red ice. The third tried to retreat.

I intercepted. I walked straight through gunfire, bullets slowing in the electric field crackling around me. I raised both hands and summoned a forked bolt so violent it fractured the stone beneath me. The soldier vaporized. Smoking boots were all that remained. Still, they came. The Accord held.

Drones screamed overhead. Drop-pods launched from orbit carved craters into the hillside, spilling out fresh troops armed with anti-elemental tech. Electromagnetic dampeners and graviton snares. All of it useless.

Danica swept her hand across the valley floor, unleashing a wave of cryo-fire, a twisted paradox of burning cold. The air itself cracked, shattering eardrums. Dozens of soldiers seized mid-stride, their organs flash-frozen. One screamed as his limbs snapped off in jagged pieces when he tried to move.

I turned toward a heavy weapons emplacement. Five Accord soldiers stood behind a shield wall, prepping a multi-cannon railgun. I charged it alone. Bullets sparked off my body like dust. I leapt the barrier, electricity arcing from my fingers into the gun mount, overloading it mid-cycle. It detonated, obliterating the entire crew in a flash of blood and steel.

Zoran's voice came again, hoarse and shaking. "We need to push them back now or we're dead by dawn!"

I stood at the edge of the burning slope, smoke swirling around me.

My voice was low and cold. "No."

Danica appeared at my side. Her skin glowed like embers beneath snow. Her hair whipped around her like living flame, streaked with frost.

"We end it now," she said.

Together, we walked into the fire. Danica threw her arms skyward. From the clouds came frozen daggers, piercing from the heavens like spears of justice. Dozens fell, skewered through torsos and throats. The snow beneath the Accord turned red. I held both palms forward. Twin bolts surged down the hill in serpentine rhythm, one splitting a tank in two, the other ricocheting through a column of enemies. Screams turned to begging, then to silence, then to fire.

By the time it ended, the ridge was unrecognizable.

Smoke choked the air. Blood filled the trenches. Corpses, burned and shattered, lay in crumpled piles, their armor fused to charred flesh. Danica and I stood among the dead, power still simmering in our bones.

Zoran approached from the rear, limping, his face covered in grime and blood. "We held," he said. "Barely."

Danica stared at her hands, one wrapped in frost, the other still smoldering. I looked to the sky.

"We bury the temple," I said.

Zoran nodded. "We can't let them find what's underneath."

Together, Danica and I walked to the steps of the ruin. Danica raised her frost-ringed hand and unleashed a torrent of freezing wind that cracked the walls, collapsing the east wing. I struck the foundation with a bolt of raw current. Stone split. The monolith far below pulsed one last time, then went dark. With a final scream of elemental fury, we brought the temple down. The mountain swallowed the gods. Ash was all that remained.

That night, the survivors of the resistance made camp among the ruins. Danica and I stood apart, blood still drying on our skin, the ghosts of countless lives whispering in the silence.

Danica leaned into me, her head on my shoulder. "We're not done."

I wrapped an arm around her waist. "We haven't even begun."

Chapter Twenty-Three
THE SONS

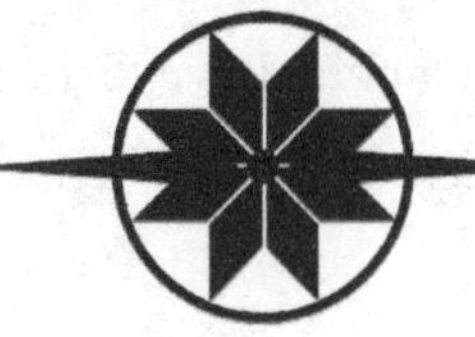

Ilija

The sanctuary pulsed with a rhythm older than memory. A low, thrumming beat resonated through the floors of Ana's sanctum, vibrating through the throne carved from obsidian and polished bone. The air hung sterile and electric, thick with the scent of iron and absolute silence.

A war womb, with Ana seated at its heart.

Her throne rested atop a tiered dais, black as pitch, etched with gold lines in patterns only gods remembered. No windows marred the chamber. No wind dared pass through its sealed symmetry, the whole place still as a sniper's breath held taut before the shot.

She sat with one leg crossed over the other, her spine an iron rod. Her dress, crimson silk cut with militant severity, revealed bare shoulders yet was armor-plated at the hips and collarbones, the ceremonial garb of a high priestess turned executioner. Her bare arms rested on the throne's sculpted arms, each carved in the likeness of a dying man on one side, a dying god on the other.

Her hair spilled over her shoulder, pale and heavy as poured metal. Her eyes were clear as spring water caught in the moment of freezing, their depths reflecting utter stillness. This was Aphrodite Areia, the goddess of war-clad love, the seductress of blades. She was worshipped in blood, feared for what she could twist love into. Obedience. Madness.

She had felt our union.

My awakening with Danica had torn through her like a blade slipped between ribs, a slow, spreading burn. Love that was real, ancient, untethered from her influence. It disgusted her. It terrified her. So she summoned terror in return.

The chamber dimmed. The central dais began to glow, etchings of runes older than Olympian speech flaring gold and black. With a sound like cracking ice, a rift opened at the far end of the hall, a jagged tear in reality. From it stepped the gods she had kept leashed until now.

Phobos came first.

He moved like smoke through a battlefield, gaunt and impossibly tall, his eyes sunken with madness. His flesh shimmered between states, part obsidian armor, part living shadow. His gaze paralyzed the soul, froze it in place. He wore no weapons. He needed none.

Behind him came Deimos, broader, monstrous in frame, built like raw violence given terrifying form. His body seemed carved from scorched bronze, his face half-covered by a jawbone helm that grinned with ancient cruelty. Flames licked beneath his armor, a faint glow. The air around him vibrated with bloodlust.

The sons of Ares. Of Ana. She had birthed them from need itself. Phobos was fear's insidious whisper in the mind just before the charge. Deimos, the raw scream in the throat as the blade falls. Now they knelt before her, subservient.

"Ana," Phobos said, his voice soft as velvet, edged with knives. "We felt the tremor."

Deimos growled, low and guttural. "They've awakened."

"Yes," she said. "They've touched what was forbidden. They felt what I denied them. Now they believe it makes them whole."

Ana stood slowly. Her steps echoed like hammers on stone, deliberate and weighty. She walked between her sons like a general inspecting her weapons. Her fingers drifted across Phobos's shoulder, cold as a tomb. She pressed her palm to Deimos's armored chest, where an inferno pulsed beneath his ribs.

"They defile what I built," she said. "They light fires in the ruins of my truth. You will put them out."

Deimos's eyes flared. "Shall we burn them?"

Ana smiled, a slow curve of her lips. "You will break them. The people of Rijeka cling to hope, emboldened by Danica's rise. They think Ilija is unkillable. I want them to see that even gods can fall to madness."

She turned toward a glowing table, activating a topographical map of Rijeka. Resistance holdouts lit in red, burning points of defiance. Civilian shelters glowed in blue. A sanctuary beneath the waterline was circled in black.

"They hide in the bones of drowned kingdoms," Ana told Phobos. "I want those bones shattered."

Phobos stepped forward, his form wavering. "What of Ilija?"

Ana narrowed her eyes. "Leave him breathing."

Her voice dropped to a guttural growl. "Let him remember everything. Every mistake, every time he fell short. I want him to drown in his inadequacy. I want Danica to see his mind unravel and realize I am all that remains."

A platform rose from the floor behind her throne. Upon it lay artifacts of divine tech merged with modern terror. Memory razors. Identity bleed injectors. Proximity-induced psychosis fields. Time dilation cuffs. One device pulsed like a beating heart, its function to induce waking nightmares. Ana lifted it with reverence, its power humming in her hand.

"Take this," she said to Phobos. "Use it to unmake his mind. Let him see all their past lives crushed, distorted, meaningless."

Phobos bowed his head. "As you will."

Deimos cracked his knuckles, a sound like grinding stone. "And if she resists?"

Ana stepped up to him, face-to-face, her hand cupping his chin.

"If she resists," Ana whispered, her lips inches from his, "make her regret every breath she stole from me."

The chamber dimmed again. The rift pulsed wider, a gaping maw. Legions stirred beyond the veil, Ana's personal army, now activated. A divine phalanx of terror. The Dread Legion. Each warrior wore full-body black armor inscribed with Slavic and Greek sigils alongside symbols no living scholar could name. Their helmets were emotionless masks. Their weapons did not fire bullets; they unleashed dread and madness.

Ana looked upon them and felt no warmth. Only absolute control. Only righteous fury.

"You are my vengeance," she said to the assembled gods and horrors. "My hunger made real."

She stepped back onto her throne, her voice rising like a storm tide.

"March to Rijeka. Bury their hope beneath the bones of their ancestors. Let them choke on ash. Leave only me."

Phobos and Deimos turned in perfect unison and led the Dread Legion into the world, their passage tearing the space behind them.

As the rift closed, Ana sat once more. She leaned forward, fingers steepled, and spoke to the silence. "Let them remember what love becomes when it is betrayed."

Rijeka was quiet in the way cities become before a storm truly breaks, a silence born of held breath. The Adriatic wind scraped through broken windows, rustling prayer flags strung across crumbled balconies. The streets, once echoing with boots and shouts of resistance, now slouched in tension, heavy with unseen dread. Civilians huddled in basements and storage closets. Resistance fighters watched the rooftops with cracked binoculars and fingers tight on triggers. Everyone knew something terrible was coming.

In a candlelit bunker two levels beneath the city library, Marija adjusted the last generator's voltage and turned to the scout who had burst in moments before, pale and shaking.

"What do you mean they just walked through the checkpoints?" she hissed.

"They didn't walk," he said, his voice brittle. "They glided. They didn't look real. They moved like shadows with eyes. The guards didn't scream. Didn't even shoot. They just dropped their rifles and..." He fell to his knees, sobbing, unable to continue. Behind him, his partner stood trembling in the doorway, lips moving soundlessly, reciting a prayer that produced no words.

Marija cursed under her breath and activated the citywide low-frequency alert. A sub-audible hum vibrated through the ground. All resistance personnel would feel it in their boots. Incoming.

Above, the sky had turned the color of an old bruise.

Rijeka's eastern wall, shattered and patched after months of siege, was little more than a symbolic barrier. It stood no chance against what emerged from the forested ridge beyond it.

The Dread Legion came without fanfare. No drums, no engines. They appeared, drifting forward like a spill of oil down a hillside, silent and inexorable. Their armor shimmered in matte-black shades, reflecting no light, absorbing it like grief. Dozens appeared at first, then hundreds. Their footfalls made no sound. The birds had already fled the trees.

Above them, Phobos hovered, his body shifting between mist and sinew, a god of illusions and psychic contagion unbound from gravity. With one flick of his hand, he released a pulse of hallucination that washed over the tree line, an invisible wave of terror.

The resistance spotters stationed there began to scream. One tore out his own eyes. Another turned his rifle on himself and whispered, "She's in the trees... she's under my skin..." as his mind came apart.

From a rooftop vantage, Milan watched them advance, his face grim. "Shit," he whispered. "They're not using drones. They are the goddamn drones."

Deimos marched at the vanguard, a force of dread given form. He wore a crown of scorched iron and a grin carved into his face like a scar. He did not wield a weapon. When he stomped the ground, the pavement cracked and sparks danced between buildings, emanating from his very presence.

Behind him, the elite units of the Dread Legion moved in ranks.

The first carried reality disruptors, small disc-like objects they rolled into intersections. When they detonated, they bent the air, made time loop, caused memories to flicker. Children began to cry for mothers long dead. Soldiers forgot what language was.

The second wave carried graviton nets. They cast them like fishermen across defensive positions, invisible threads tightening. Men screamed as their bones compacted, as walls folded inward. In one alley, two fighters tried to run. They made it three steps before the net hit and dragged them to the earth, where they liquefied into pulp.

The third wave needed no weapons. They walked past those already broken. Some people followed them, crying, begging to be taken, their wills utterly enslaved.

From a balcony near the city's university, I stood frozen. I could feel it, feel them. Gods of terror had stepped through the veil of reason, utterly unbridled, and my blood surged with ancient recognition. My fingers twitched. Sparks crackled beneath my skin. The power felt distant, muffled, like I was underwater.

Danica appeared beside me, her face pale, her jaw set.

"They're not mortals," she said, her voice grim.

"No," I agreed, my voice a rough murmur.

"They're hers. She's finally sent them."

I nodded once. "Phobos. Deimos."

The names struck the air like thunder, heavy with ancient power. Danica drew her breath, a plume of frost curling from her lips. Her rings burned cold and hot at once, a clash of elements. I looked down into the streets where resistance fighters were already falling back, dragging the wounded.

A man staggered down the road, rifle clutched in one hand, tears streaking his face as he stared at something that wasn't there.

"What are we up against?" Danica asked, her voice tight.

My eyes flashed. "Gods who feed on fear. They brought a war to match."

In the lower quarter, in the markets where resistance had set up a triage center, chaos bloomed. A pulse wave from Phobos shattered the mirrored dome of an old church. The shrapnel cut memory, severing minds from their past.

A medic named Luka stumbled outside, blinking as he forgot who he was and why he was there. A little girl gripped his leg, crying for help. He couldn't recognize her face. He couldn't remember the words to speak. He turned and ran into the fog, swallowed in moments.

Deimos entered the west plaza like a blade through flesh. His footfalls cracked the stone. He walked through gunfire as if it were sand. One resistance squad opened fire from a balcony, twelve men with rifles and armor, holding high ground.

Deimos raised one fist. The building collapsed, folding inward from sheer pressure. Bricks crumpled like wet clay. Screams were swallowed in rubble. Blood ran down the gutters, mingling with the dust.

Danica and I moved fast through the back alleys, sparks and frost trailing behind us. No time for strategy. Only survival. As we reached the edge of the old courthouse steps, Danica grabbed my arm.

"Feel that?"

I stopped. Closed my eyes. The ground beneath our feet was wrong. Something ancient hummed beneath it, something terrible and vast.

"They're drawing from her," I whispered. "Feeding on Ana's will."

Danica stepped forward, her hands glowing blue and red, resolute. "Then let's see what they taste like when we bite back."

The city's east quarter cracked open like a wound. Buildings smoldered under unseen pressure. The air shimmered with radiation pulses, an invisible tension that turned breath into blades. Resistance lines collapsed block by block. Communication links filled with static and broken prayers.

I stood amid it all, the air around me pulsing tight as a coil drawn past reason. I was done retreating. My body thrummed with something deeper than electricity, a storm trying to be born inside my bones. My skin prickled with invisible needles. Sweat stung my eyes. My fingertips itched like something under the surface was trying to tear through.

A wave of Dread Legion soldiers emerged through the smoke, machine-silent and inhuman. A dozen of them, black-armored, their eyes like furnace glass, moved with cold precision. I stepped forward, raised my hand, and let it go.

The air around my outstretched palm rippled, then imploded, dragging gravity into a singular focus. The lead soldier's armor buckled inward as if gripped by a giant's invisible fist. Metal warped. Bones folded like scaffolding in a gale. The body caved in on itself with a wet, horrible crunch.

I turned my palm outward. A shockwave of inverted force burst from my chest, unraveling. The neural implants in the others shorted with screams, raw and desperate. One clawed at his helmet until fingers snapped. Another tried to pull his own spine free, body convulsing.

I walked forward slowly, my feet crunching over glass and bone. My beard was soaked in sweat and blood. My gray-blue eyes shimmered with clarity, the stillness of a man who had seen his own death a hundred times and shed his fear of it.

Behind me, Danica advanced, her eyes a twin storm of ice and fire. She raised both arms as four more Legionnaires rounded the far corner. Her right hand unfurled toward the ground, and ice bloomed in jagged spears from the street. It caught the first two soldiers mid-stride. They did not scream. Their legs were sliced open at the knees by frozen razors. One collapsed, twitching. The other tried to crawl and was frozen solid mid-movement, one arm extended in a gesture of surrender that never finished.

From her left, she summoned a radiant heatwave so dense the air shimmered white. The third soldier's armor warped outward before combustion began inside it. His chest cavity burst open, steaming blood hissing into vapor. The fourth soldier reached her too fast for ranged magic.

Danica did not hesitate. She spun, grabbed him by the throat, and her palm flashed cold, the frostbite so immediate it cracked the metal of his gorget. She pulled him closer, eyes burning into his visor.

"You were made to kill gods?" she whispered. "Then let me show you one, you motherfucker."

She drove her flaming fist through the helmet, fusing bone and circuitry into a smoking ruin. He dropped like dead weight.

Above us, a shadow coalesced into form.

Phobos. He glided through the air like a hawk made of smoke and memory. A god who embodied what war leaves behind. Shame and paralysis. He landed on the roof of the courthouse like an executioner.

Danica felt it first, the air thickening with remembrance. Her heart pounded too fast. Her knees trembled for a second.

Then my body stiffened. I staggered.

"Ilija?" she called out, sharp with concern.

I didn't answer.

Phobos extended one hand, and from his palm, threads of light spun outward. Veins, vessels, reaching. They pierced my chest and skull, silent and fast. I didn't scream. I vanished from her side, undone. I stood in a hallway, then a field, then a burning city, then a mountain shrine, all in the span of a single breath. Memory smashed into memory.

I was holding Danica's corpse in a trench. I was bleeding in a church, praying to gods who had already left.

I was alone. Forgotten. Always too late.

"You always arrive after it matters," said Phobos, walking calmly through each vision like a priest through an empty cathedral. "You love too late. You act too late. You are a shadow pretending to be fire."

I dropped to my knees in a shattered library where the books bled from their pages. My waistcoat was soaked. My beard clung to my neck like vines. I looked up and saw Danica die again.

"Why do you try?" Phobos asked, smiling without warmth. "You were never meant to win. You were made to break."

In the real world, my body floated inches above the stones, trembling, eyes rolled back. My fingertips curled inward, small arcs of silver pressure flickering at my joints.

Danica fought to reach me. Phobos turned to her. She screamed my name, fueled by rage. She hurled herself into the chaos between us. Two Legionnaires stepped into her path. She slid under the first, ice slicking the ground in her wake, then flipped up, planting a burst of flame into the second's helmet. The skull detonated inside the armor, spraying molten bone through the faceplate.

She leapt over a fallen barricade, turned a full circle mid-air, and drove a whip of liquid frost into two more soldiers. They froze where they stood, still breathing, still conscious, entombed.

She reached me. She dropped to her knees, eyes glowing, and grabbed my face.

"Ilija, come back. Look at me. You are not their weapon."

My lips trembled. "They showed me how we always fail, how we always fall short..."

Danica pressed her forehead to mine. "They show you what they fear. That you'll rise anyway, you stubborn bastard."

Her powers flared around us, fueled by defiance. Flame coiled around my shoulders. Frost danced along my back. I gasped, and my body slammed into hers. I remembered. I remembered the blade in my hand. The sound of her voice. The ache of past lives, yes, but also the victories. Also the love.

I opened my eyes with a clarity that reached deeper than light, and I stood.

Danica stood beside me, battered but unbroken. My arms lifted, palms outward. This time, I didn't conjure pressure or lightning. I stopped the very air.

The battlefield froze, suspended in movement. Sound fell away. Soldiers halted mid-step, guns halfway to their marks.

I whispered, "Let's take it back."

The world exploded forward.

The tunnel beneath the collapsed municipal court was narrow, crumbling, forgotten by time and government. Once meant for emergency evacuation, it now served as a tomb for light. The only illumination came from the faint bluish glow of Danica's frost magic curling across the walls, just enough to keep us from tripping on broken concrete and rusted rebar.

We did not speak until we found the reinforced storage chamber at the end.

Danica sealed the metal door behind us with a wall of hardened ice. The room was bare, metallic, with one rust-streaked bunk and a collapsed wall vent that opened just enough to let air hiss through.

I sank to my knees on the floor, chest still heaving, shoulders shaking. Soaked in sweat. My waistcoat was torn, my shirt clinging to my chest in patches, streaked with blood and grime. My fingers twitched, grasping for a weapon no longer there.

Danica knelt in front of me and placed her hand on my cheek. I flinched.

"Ilija," she whispered.

"I saw everything," I rasped. "I saw every life. Every time we tried and failed. I saw you die in ways I can't describe. I saw myself holding your body in snow and in ash. I saw you burned at the stake. I saw you drown in rivers. I saw me walk away from you, you fucking ghost."

Danica's hand tightened around my jaw, grounding me, firm.

"You saw the truth," she said. "But you didn't see all of it."

I looked at her then, truly looked, and the gray-blue of my eyes shimmered with something deeper than recognition.

"You always came back," she said. "We always found each other again. Even in pain. Even in fire."

I leaned into her hand. My beard scratched against her palm. She pulled me close and pressed her forehead to mine. A surge pulsed between us, like air sucked from a vacuum, and the chamber became a bridge. It stretched between lives, between selves. Our memories snapped into place, rising through the veil whole and unbroken.

We stood together in a temple of Zorya, wrapped in linen, lovers beneath the stars. Her hands stained with ink. Mine with soot.

We fought together in a Tatar war camp, back to back. She was speared through the stomach; I carried her until I collapsed.

We were burned as witches, chained together. Our ashes mingled in wind.

We were married once, beneath a Slavic birch tree. She carried our child to term. I died in battle before holding the boy.

We died over and over. We loved over and over. Always, relentlessly, we remembered.

I groaned, collapsing back onto the cold floor, my eyes wide with the force of it. Danica was already beside me, her body trembling, her hands on my chest, her lips at my ear.

"I remember," she whispered. "The stars and the blood and the vow."

I turned to her, forehead pressed to hers again. "What vow?" I breathed.

Her lips brushed mine. "That no matter how the world ends, I'll find you again."

The silence that followed was ripe, thick with history and the intimacy of knowing someone for centuries.

Danica reached up and pulled the torn fabric of my waistcoat off my shoulders. I did not stop her. I leaned in, and this time, it was my mouth that found hers, drawn back into the center of something sacred. Our mouths moved slow at first, uncertain and reverent, each kiss wrapping tighter around the other, binding soul to soul.

Danica pulled away just long enough to slide her fingers down the buttons of my shirt. She pushed it open, revealing the scars along my collarbone and ribs, some old, some new. She kissed each one.

I reached for her jacket, fingers trembling with emotion I had no words for. I slid it from her shoulders, let it fall, and found her eyes again.

"You are so beautiful," I said softly.

"Not always," she murmured, removing the last layer, her skin bare to me in the glow of her frost light.

"Always," I said again, firmer, and leaned in.

Our bodies found each other with the practiced certainty of those who had known this rhythm in lifetimes past. Every touch felt familiar. Every sigh echoed from some ancient chamber of memory.

I kissed down her neck with aching patience, with devotion. Her fingers wove into my beard, tugging me closer. My hands slid along her hips, mapping the shape of her as if remembering familiar ground.

Danica arched into me, a hiss of heat escaping her lips, her skin burning where my hands touched. Her power flared in response, ice blooming in delicate webs across the metal walls, flame dancing at her heels, both gentle.

I entered her slowly, reverently, my hands on her face and her shoulders. She met me, breathless, nails digging into my back, lips trembling against my ear. We moved together like waves shaping shoreline, utterly synchronized. There was no violence, no desperation. Only need. Only home.

At the height of it, as her cry echoed into the vault above, the frost cracked across the ceiling. Flame curled up the walls. My eyes met hers, and there was nothing left between us. No secrets. No fear. Only love born of fire and forged in ruin.

After, we lay together on the cold floor, breath mingling, fingers still interlaced, skin cooling against the broken stone. Her head rested on my chest. My arm wrapped tight around her back. Neither spoke. There were no words for what we'd recovered. In the silence, something deeper settled between us. Purpose.

Above, the earth shuddered again. Danica sat up slowly, her hair damp with sweat, her skin still glowing faintly from her powers.

I stood and retrieved my ruined coat. I pulled it on over bare skin and turned to her, offering my hand. She took it. As we walked toward the door, Danica turned and ignited her ice wall with a flick of flame. It melted into mist. Beyond it lay fire and gunmetal and death. This time, we stepped into the war as gods reborn.

The sky above Rijeka wept fire. Tracer rounds lit the dawn in streaks of silver and crimson. What was left of the east quarter lay in molten heaps, shops and homes gutted, reduced to ash and twisted rebar. Blood soaked the gutters. Neural scramblers still hummed from broken helmets strewn across the road.

Danica and I stepped through the wreckage. We were changed. Our footfalls cracked the pavement. The air shimmered around us, charged with divine presence, ancient and terrifying. Our skin glowed faintly. Our breath steamed like smoke from a sacred forge. We moved like death that had remembered love.

A squad of Dread Legion soldiers turned the corner, rifles already raised. They never had time to fire. Danica lifted her palm, a gesture of judgment, and a spiral of ice shot forward like a hurricane's fang. It flayed them.

Armor peeled open. Blood burst in frozen jets. Their screams choked mid-throat.

Beside her, my veins glowed gold and pale blue. I stared at the next line of attackers, and they stopped moving. One by one, their limbs locked. Their eyes rolled back. Their lungs stopped drawing breath. Their hearts forgot how to beat. They collapsed where they stood, dead from disconnection, like puppets with cut strings.

Danica turned to me.

"You're different," she said.

"So are you," I replied.

She smiled, faint and bitter. "They're afraid, Ilija."

We found Deimos first. He stood atop the resistance's old garrison building, arms crossed, muscles slick with oil and blood, eyes glowing like furnace embers. His voice echoed across the square like falling stone.

"Children," he growled. "Do you think your little dance beneath the skin makes you gods?"

Danica did not answer. She stepped forward, palms already burning. The wind shifted, cold then hot, spinning around her like a cyclone of opposing elements.

I turned to face the opposite end of the square.

Phobos emerged from the fog, all whispers and twitching light. His body was fragments, faces and bone stitched together with the teeth of nightmares into a vaguely human shape.

"You crawled out of time," Phobos whispered. "You think memory makes you strong. Memory is a prison."

I exhaled slowly. "Then I'll turn it into a blade, you bastard."

The square erupted.

Danica launched herself at Deimos, a fury of frost and fire, her body trailing ribbons of white-hot steam and piercing cold. Deimos met her midair, fists like anvils, colliding with a crack that shook the windows of buildings still standing. They fell together in a spiral of sparks and shattered stone.

I rushed Phobos. The god flicked his hand and the world fractured. I saw every war I'd never fought, every life I'd never saved. This time, it did not stop me. I held my hand out, fingers splayed, and time bent around me, a radius of order in the chaos of panic. I stepped through Phobos's illusion like a man walking through a waterfall, and I struck him hard enough to make a god flinch.

Danica fought like a goddess of the storm. Deimos was stronger, brutal and unrelenting, but she was faster, more precise, merciless. She twisted mid-dodge and summoned a whip of flame, lashing it around his wrist and yanking him forward. As he stumbled, she ducked low and drove a spear of ice through his kneecap. He roared, backhanding her across the plaza. She hit the pavement, skidding, coughing blood. He charged her, but she rolled sideways, flung a blast of burning wind into his face, and leapt to her feet. With a scream, she conjured a blade of frozen fire, a paradox only a god could create, and struck it into his chest. It burned and froze at once, melting armor and seizing breath. Deimos stumbled back.

"You don't belong, you bitch," he snarled.

Danica's eyes burned black and blue. "I never did, you arrogant prick."

She launched again.

Across the square, I fought Phobos and every version of myself Phobos could weaponize. The god shattered the light around us, turned echoes into weapons. Illusions of Ana appeared, bleeding and whispering lies. I stepped through each vision without flinching. I reached within myself, past nerves and past blood, into divine inheritance. I opened both hands and whispered a word I hadn't known I knew.

The air shattered. Rings of kinetic force burst out in concentric waves, flattening debris, blowing out every window on the street. Phobos staggered, his form flickering.

"You see me now," I said.

"No," the god snarled, reconstituting. "You see yourself."

I lunged, my attack driven by memory. I touched Phobos and shared with him every love I'd buried, every prayer screamed into uncaring sky. Phobos screamed in contamination. Emotion burned through him like acid.

Deimos dropped to one knee. Danica stood over him, one arm bloodied, one shoulder dislocated, her legs trembling with exhaustion and rage. He looked up at her, lip split, one eye swollen shut.

"You're no goddess," he spat.

She raised her blade. "I don't need to be, asshole."

She struck downward, but Deimos vanished in a ripple of red mist.

Phobos recoiled from me, light spilling from the cracks in his shifting body.

"You ruined me," he hissed.

"No," I said. "You just remembered you were never whole, you piece of shit."

I raised my hand, but Phobos was already retreating, melting into shadow, dragging the screams of war with him.

The gods of fear had fled.

Danica and I stood in the broken square, chest to chest, panting, drenched in blood and godlight. The Resistance, what remained, emerged from the ruins. The citizens of Rijeka stared from windows, from basements, from behind burned-out vehicles.

For the first time in years, they saw gods on their side.

CHAPTER TWENTY-FOUR
DELPHI CALLS

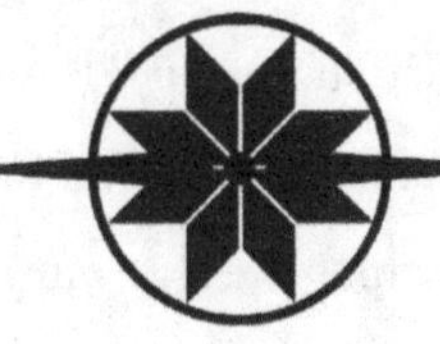

Ilija

Rijeka burned behind us. The square choked on smoke and sulfur, and steel groaned in the distance where structures had begun to fold. Beneath a collapsed bell tower, the last Dread Legion soldier coughed his final breath. The city, what remained of it, had gone quiet.

Danica and I sat at the edge of the half-destroyed cathedral, legs dangling over a ledge above a scorched garden. The stone beneath us held heat from the fires we'd summoned. Her thigh pressed against mine, and even through cloth I felt the cold she carried, that ancient frost threaded through her bones. She could feel the thunder in my blood, the electric hum that had never gone quiet since our memories returned.

She hadn't spoken since the fight ended. Not after Phobos and Deimos vanished like frightened myths. Not when I'd collapsed against her, breathing hard, blinking through tears I refused to let fall. She had only held my hand, fingers wound through mine, firelight dancing in her eyes. Now she broke the silence.

"I had a dream," she said softly, her voice barely above the faint crackle of distant embers.

I turned my head to her, one eyebrow raised. She didn't look at me. Her gaze was fixed on the ash-covered hills in the east.

"Not one of those half-memories. Not from a past life." She paused. "This was different. Clearer. Louder. A command."

I frowned. Cold dread coiled in my gut. "From whom?"

She exhaled slowly, then said, "Brigid. And Freyja."

I did not scoff. After everything we had witnessed, disbelief had lost its usefulness. Danica pressed her palms together, fingertips trembling. "They stood at the edge of a canyon I couldn't see the bottom of. One held a torch. The other held a spear. They spoke in a language I don't know, but I understood it instinctively. They said I had to go to Delphi."

My breath caught. "Delphi?"

She nodded. "An old power sleeps there. We'll need it if we're going to stop Ana."

I shook my head, exhaustion settling heavier in my bones. "Danica, we just got you back. I just got you back. After everything we've been through..."

"I know." She finally turned to look at me. Her jaw was tight, her eyes wet. "But you know I have to go, Ilija."

I leaned back on my hands and stared up at the broken ceiling above us. Through the gaping wound in the stone, a ribbon of moonlight spilled down, cutting across the soot and rubble.

"I hate this," I said, the words raw.

"So do I," she replied.

I closed my eyes. "Delphi is halfway across the continent. It's surrounded by Accord-held territories. If they even get a whisper that one of us is moving, we're fucked."

"They won't," she said, her voice steady. "You'll stay in the shadows. Gather what's left of the Resistance. Rally the survivors. I'll move through the ruins. Quiet. Alone."

I opened my eyes again, meeting her gaze. "You shouldn't be alone, Danica."

She reached out and brushed my cheek with the back of her fingers. "I never am. Not really."

My throat tightened. She leaned in and kissed me, soft, slow. Her lips lingered on mine for a heartbeat longer than needed. Then she pulled away.

"I'll find you," she said. "When it's done."

I nodded. "Bring back whatever sleeps beneath the stones. We'll need it."

She rose, her silhouette framed by firelight and ruin, her long coat fluttering in the wind. Her hair, soaked with sweat and dust, shimmered like crow feathers. I stood beside her. We did not say goodbye. We had done this too many times before, in too many lives. Instead, I placed my hand over her heart. She placed hers over mine. For one last breath, we held there, connected. Then she turned and walked into the ash.

Danica

I did not sleep for three days. I moved by starlight across a broken world. I crossed shattered towns where trees grew sideways and the air reeked of scorched plastic. Skirmishes burned in the distance, the last flickers of Accord purges, a world being mercilessly rewritten. I kept to the hills, shrouded by fog and deep shadow, my fingers brushing ash-covered leaves as I passed. My dreams haunted me even when I was awake, relentless whispers in my mind. Freyja's words pounded in my chest. Love will break the spine of nations.

The further south I walked, the heavier the world became. By the time the Parnassus range rose on the horizon, my hands were trembling. The tremor was bone-deep, as if the very bones of the earth remembered who I was and what was owed.

Delphi appeared as the jawbone of a long-dead god. The temple ruins were blackened and split, scarred by time and violence. The columns leaned as if exhausted from holding up millennia. What had once been a sacred terrace felt like a desolate crater, ringed by gnarled trees that watched with bark-split eyes.

I slowed my steps as I approached the old stone altar. Beneath my boots, the earth whispered. I heard it before I saw it. A low thrum, a pressure that lived in the air. It echoed in my ribs, pulsed behind my eyes. I stepped closer, and the world broke open. The ground split with a sound like bone cracking beneath a boot.

I fell to my knees as a deep quake rolled through the valley. The altar cracked clean down the middle. Dust erupted in spirals. Roots tore loose and writhed, and from the center of the rupture, water burst forth. This was water that remembered fire, thick with mineral, glowing faintly with divine heat. It did not flow. It rose, swelling upward, forced through the throat of the world.

I shielded my face, but the mist burned my skin.

Then came the voice. "You have come."

The air bent around it. I turned, and saw her. The Oracle stood barefoot on the edge of the spring, her form shifting with every blink. One moment she looked no older than I, her skin silver-white and wrapped in moss. Then she was ancient, her flesh dry as clay, her eyes deep black and cracked like obsidian, holy and terrifying. I tried to speak, but no words came.

"You have memory in your marrow," the Oracle said. "You are not new. You are not whole. But you are ready."

I bowed my head. "I don't know what I'm supposed to find here."

"You do know." The Oracle reached out her hand. "Drink."

I stepped forward, scooping the water with shaking hands. It tasted of copper and storm. The world vanished. I fell through Ana's memory, through a vision that did not belong to me. A battlefield of marble and blood. Troy, or Sparta, or both at once. Ana stood on a mound of corpses, her hair crowned in thorn and flame. The wind kissed her face, intimate and terrifying. Her mouth moved, but no words came; only the silent fury of war.

Then the scene shifted. Steel skyscrapers. Boardrooms. Men kneeling. A sword placed across a conference table like a desecrated relic. Blood signatures on contracts inked with divine dust. Ana's eyes were no longer green; they were void-colored, consuming all light. She had become a goddess reborn, Aphrodite Areia. Love transmuted into annihilation. Worship twisted into a weapon.

I screamed. The vision held me, pulling me deeper. I saw Ilija in every life, as a child, a soldier. Sometimes he was mine. Sometimes he was just out of reach. And always Ana, circling him. She was trying to remake him. She was trying to consume him.

I clutched my chest. I felt the blade again, the one I remembered dying on a thousand years before. I saw Ana's face the moment Ilija turned away from her. It held grief, the kind that had become a rift so deep it had split heaven from itself. She was never meant to lose, and now Ana, the bitter bitch, would burn the world to reclaim what was never hers.

The vision shattered. I collapsed beside the spring, my body steaming, my pulse frantic.

The Oracle knelt beside me. "She loves him."

A cough tore from my raw throat. "I know, goddammit."

"She will never stop."

The Oracle touched my forehead. "And he loves you."

I looked up, hoarse, a new resolve settling behind my teeth. "I know."

The Oracle smiled, a thin and knowing line. "Then the world will end. And begin again."

Ilija

I traveled east beneath a low, bruised sky. The morning after Danica left, I stood at the edge of Rijeka's charred ruins and watched the sun claw its way over the broken horizon. The square was littered with the dead, all of them burned or shattered by what Danica and I had become. I did not flinch at the bodies. Not anymore.

The Resistance was gathering again. Those who had fled were returning with new weapons and new names. Yet I needed silence. I needed to remember a buried truth, a piece Ana had hidden in the bones of an old city that had survived every kind of empire.

So I walked, alone, southeast into Bosnia, into Sarajevo. The road stretched empty before me. Every gas station along the way was scorched out, their steel frames buckled inward. Billboards lay face-down in the dust. Accord flags hung tattered from lamp posts. My mind was not quiet. I felt her everywhere. Ana.

Her presence rode the wind. She flickered behind dead windows. She was a fracture running through every thought, a presence that never left.

When I entered Sarajevo, I did not head toward the government square. I went underground.

The hidden archive was buried beneath a shattered mosque, one of the few that had survived the city's early bombardment. Beneath the cracked tiles and collapsed minaret, I found the entrance, an iron staircase that twisted down into the dark. My boots echoed softly on stone steps slick with condensation. I descended slowly, torchlight flickering behind my eyes though no physical fire burned. The air pulsed. Each step carried me further back, past history, past story, into the primordial.

The final chamber was round and wide, shaped like an old domed tomb. Scrolls littered the shelves. Burned manuscripts lay in crumbling piles beside holoscreens flickering with corrupted data. I did not come for records. I came for the mirror. It hung on the far wall, rimmed in bronze, its glass fogged but intact, humming with a low resonant thrum.

I stepped before it and looked into my own eyes. They shimmered, silver and stormlight. Behind me, a thousand flickering shadows gathered. Then I felt her. The mirror bloomed. I was no longer in Sarajevo.

I stood in a palace of glass and bone, beneath a ceiling of swords. Each one hung point-down, suspended as if waiting for the wrong word to trigger their fall. The air smelled like roses soaked in gasoline. She sat on a throne of skulls. Ana. This was Aphrodite Areia in full, her body wrapped in crimson armor, her hair a mantle of living flame. Around her knelt gods, old and forgotten. Technocrats beside cult leaders. She held their leashes in one hand, my name in the other. I couldn't speak. Her gaze held longing, and beneath it, a sadness so vast it hollowed me.

She rose. She walked toward me. The throne room echoed with her precise footfalls. When she reached me, she raised a hand to touch my cheek. When her fingers brushed me, I saw everything.

I saw her fall from Olympus, naked and bleeding, cast out by the very gods who had worshipped her too long. I saw her wander the war-sick world for centuries, collecting scraps of power, seducing kings, whispering into revolutions. I saw her weep when I turned from her in ancient Thrace. I saw her build an empire to never feel that loss again. And now, in this life, she had twisted love into domination. Beauty into war.

Because that was the only way she believed she could win me back. The vision broke. I stumbled backward from the mirror, gasping, clutching my chest. I collapsed onto the cold stone floor. For a long time, I lay there, shaking and soaked in sweat, whispering Danica's name like a prayer. When I finally stood again, I was different. I wasn't afraid of Ana anymore. I pitied her, but I would still stop her. Even if it meant burning down every temple she ever built.

The sea crashed like a beast in chains. Danica stood at the edge of Split's old harbor, boots caked with salt and blood, hair lashed to her cheeks by the fierce Adriatic wind. Behind her, the scars of war stretched inland, burned farmhouses beside broken roads, forests stripped bare by artillery fire. Ahead, just beyond the flicker of resistance torches, loomed the pale stone skeleton of Diocletian's Palace.

She hadn't meant to come here, but Delphi had left her hollowed, filled with knowing and terror. In that cold void, a voice had whispered again. Brigid's, or Freyja's, spoken through their divine mouths. He will be waiting where the past breathes.

This coastal fortress, carved by a mad emperor turned god, breathed like no other. Inside the palace shell, the marble floors echoed with the ghosts of two millennia. The main halls had been bombed months ago, their arches shattered and draped in vines. Yet beneath it all, the old catacombs remained, dark and still.

Danica descended slowly, every step guided by the heat pulsing in her fingertips. The artifacts she carried in her pack trembled like animal hearts, sensing what lay ahead. She passed a collapsed colonnade and turned into a tight corridor where the stone walls glistened with brine. At the end, a torch flickered, and I stood beside it.

I was bent over a map spread across a crate. My coat was off, sleeves rolled to my elbows, forearms smudged with ash and blood. A sidearm sat holstered beside a curved dagger she didn't recognize. My red beard had grown fuller since Delphi. My eyes were ringed in gray, exhaustion carved into the corners of my mouth. When I looked up and saw her, I straightened. The map fluttered to the floor.

Danica stepped forward. Neither of us spoke. I met her in the middle of the corridor and wrapped my arms around her as if the air itself might steal her away again. She held me just as tightly, her face buried in the warm crook of my neck, fingers digging into my back. When we finally broke apart, I touched her cheek.

"Did you find it?" I whispered.

She nodded. "I found her. The Oracle."

I nodded once, my eyes scanning hers. "And?"

"She showed me Ana. All of her. Before the beginning. After the end."

I swallowed hard.

"I saw her too," I said.

Danica raised an eyebrow.

"In Sarajevo," I continued. "There's a mirror. A vault. She's building a divine order."

Danica nodded slowly.

I looked down. "I think she believes she's doing it for me."

Danica said nothing. She stepped closer and placed her palm on my chest.

"She doesn't know what love is," she said. "Not anymore."

My hand closed over hers. "And we do?"

Danica smiled, slow and tired. "We remember."

Together, we descended deeper. The hidden stairway revealed itself only when all five artifacts were within proximity. The stone wall shimmered like water and peeled back in a spiral. The air turned electric. Our skin prickled. As we stepped into the lowest chamber, the earth hummed beneath our boots. This place was older than the palace, older than the gods. The Chamber of Echoes.

The walls were carved with symbols neither of us could read but both understood, threads of lives woven through names of the dead. The ceiling arched high above us, vaulted and dark. In the center, a stone pedestal waited, smooth and blood-dark.

The dagger pulsed against Danica's ribs. The ring on my hand warmed. Each of the artifacts began to glow, a low steady light, like breathing. Danica stepped forward first and set her artifact down. I set mine. Then both of us reached into our packs and withdrew what remained, the iron pendant beside the obsidian charm, the final blade laid between them. We set them down. For a moment, nothing happened. Then the pedestal split open with a hiss. Light poured upward, golden and thick, and we saw a memory that belonged to all of us.

Fire and ash fell over a battlefield made of black glass. In the distance, Ana stood on a spire, naked save for chains made of stars. Danica and I faced her, twin figures clothed in godlight, one wreathed in electricity, the other in flame and frost. We held hands. We bled.

The vision shifted. A wedding in a field of poppies. No audience. No gods. Just me, kneeling, Danica crying, our foreheads pressed together as red petals drifted down.

Another shift. Our deaths. Dozens of them. On spears, in flames. Always together. Always torn apart. One last vision. Our child. Unseen, but near. A heartbeat that echoed in both our chests. Then silence. We opened our eyes together and knew.

Our story was the blade Ana feared most, because it could not be broken. Not by time. Not by gods. Only by forgetting, and we had remembered. The chamber sealed behind us.

Danica and I remained in the stillness of the lower vault, side by side, our skin lit by the quiet glow of the five artifacts now bound to us. The pedestal no longer pulsed. It rested, its work complete.

The dagger, slick with old blood, had fused into Danica's spine. She felt it as a second nervous system, ice and flame humming down her limbs, braided together in living rhythm.

I bore the ring of storms over my heart. I had not placed it around my finger; I had pressed it into my skin, and it stayed, glowing faintly with lightning that never flickered out.

We had remembered. We had merged with what we once were, and the remembering had not broken us. It had made us harder. Sharper. Outside, the Resistance stirred.

The command chamber had moved into one of the old stone cisterns beneath the palace. Paper maps lay across ancient Roman granite, their surfaces punctured with bullets and blood. Electronic tablets blinked alongside relics of older wars, WWII radios beside carrier pigeons in iron cages.

Danica stepped inside and every head turned. She did not speak. I followed behind her, my coat billowing like a professor arriving late to a lecture on the apocalypse.

Captain Toma rose from the corner, his eyes wide. "You're both..."

He couldn't finish.

I gave him a tired smile. "Yes."

We worked quickly. Transmission bursts went out to Resistance enclaves across the Balkans, Sofia, Mostar, Ljubljana, Skopje, even whispers of surviving cells in Vienna. Some replied. Others did not. They would come anyway. They all knew what time it was.

That night, Danica and I stood together on the crumbling sea wall, overlooking the black mouth of the Adriatic. The wind was vicious. Salt bit our lips. Below us, lights flickered in the ruined town, refugees huddled beside fighters, children darting between them who had no idea they were on the edge of myth. A little girl wove between tents, chasing a shape no one else could see. A boy slept holding a broken tablet carved with an old Slavic rune.

Danica leaned against me, her head on my shoulder.

"You know she's watching," she murmured.

I nodded. "She always is, the bitter bitch."

Danica pulled the frost from the wind, let it coil in her hand like a snake. It hissed, then vanished.

"I don't want to kill her," she said. "But I will, Ilija. I swear to whatever gods are listening."

"I know," I said. I reached into my coat and drew out the iron pendant, once Veles's, now mine to command. "It won't be easy."

"Nothing worth doing ever is, you bastard," Danica said, grim humor in her voice.

We said nothing for a while, listening to the sea. Behind us, the Resistance lit its torches. Steel met stone. Guns were loaded. Old blades were strapped to mortal hips. Across the camps, war-chants rose. They did not need gods. They had Danica and me.

In the final hours before dawn, we returned to the underground. I pulled Danica into me and kissed her. It was for memory. She tasted like the moment before a battlefield ignites. I didn't need to say it. Neither did she. We would not survive this unless we won. And even then...

At first light, a single scout returned with news. The Accord was on the move. Columns of soldiers. Drones. Tanks. Worse, dark banners flanked by crimson flame, and at their center, two figures in black. Phobos and Deimos.

Danica's eyes darkened. I pulled on my coat. Outside, the Resistance gathered at the southern cliffs. No one spoke. The ground trembled. The air sharpened. It was time.

Danica stepped forward and whispered, "Let them come."

CHAPTER TWENTY-FIVE
THE HEART OF THE EMPIRE

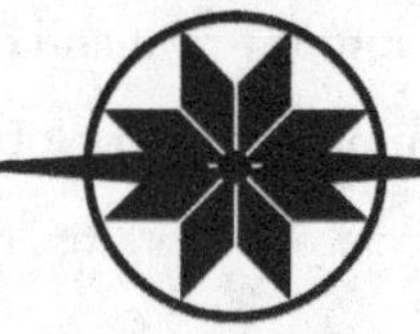

Ilija

The earth shifted beneath Europe's broken spine. Under the Alps, under the shattered plains of Hungary, the soil trembled like an animal waking from a long, cold sleep. Roots groaned with memory. Stone refused to stay still. The world was responding to something older than prayer.

In the stillness of early morning, mist clung low across the fields of central Italy. Danica stood barefoot at the edge of the Monte Cassino ruins. The abbey had collapsed in an earlier purge, its walls blackened by drone strikes and fire. Yet something in its bones had survived. The old stones still breathed, still held echoes of forgotten power.

With her eyes closed, Danica felt the tension beneath her feet. Something subterranean and alive, too old for any instrument to measure. She opened her eyes. The mist rolled back, revealing rows of tents, makeshift altars, gun racks lined with scavenged rifles, flames too stubborn to die.

The Resistance had grown into a storm gathering its voice.

I found Danica near the outer perimeter, bent over a steel table covered in topographic maps and recon drone images. My fingers traced paths across terrain like sigils. I kept my focus tight, my breathing even, but Danica always read what I tried to hide.

"Something's moving," she said, stepping beside me, her voice low.

I did not look up immediately. "Beneath our feet, or in the sky?"

She frowned. "Both, you stubborn bastard."

I straightened slowly, stretching my back, my waistcoat smudged with oil and dust. I felt older than the man I'd been in Belgrade. The years hadn't done it. The burden had.

She placed a hand on my arm. "I think it's beginning."

I looked at her, my gaze steady.

"No," I said. "It already began, Danica. We just didn't want to call it a war yet."

Across the field, Resistance fighters moved as a single breath. They were teachers and poets, engineers and orphans who had grown into soldiers. They trained with fierce determination, as if they had always belonged here. Every movement had weight. Every rifle was held like an extension of memory. Some bore symbols carved into their armor, letters of Slavic and Norse origin, stitched alongside resistance patches and blackened metal plates. Others tied relics around their necks, old crucifixes alongside pagan pendants. This was memory weaponized.

Danica walked among them, her presence drawing heads lower in reverence. She was command itself. Flame and frost entwined behind her as she passed, rising from the soles of her boots like breath from the dead. A child ran up to her, hair matted with smoke, eyes too wide for their age.

"Miss Danica," he whispered, holding out a handful of pebbles. "The ground's been humming."

Danica crouched and took the child's hand in hers. "It's not humming," she said gently. "It's remembering, little one."

The child blinked. "Like... it knows you're here?"

Danica's lips curved, tight and brief. "It knows we all are."

That night, I stood atop the abbey ruins as a storm gathered on the far horizon. The sky stayed dark and silent. Only relentless wind. It rolled down from the mountains, pulling dry leaves into spirals, sweeping across the tents and through the cracks in the old stones. I felt the electricity stir beneath my skin, deeper than before, tuned to something vast and waiting.

The artifacts we carried had fused with us entirely. The ring over my heart pulsed when danger neared, its beat frantic. The iron pendant whispered in Slavic tongues when I closed my eyes. I could feel the echo of Perun, Veles, and Lada in the blood between my ribs. More than that, I felt Danica. She was down below, at the fire pit, still and awake. Watching the sky as though expecting it to fall. I did not go to her. Some silences could not be shared.

From Scotland to Greece, from the Black Sea to the Rhine, other sacred sites began to shift.

In a forest in Bavaria, a boy found a buried antler beneath a circle of stones. When he touched it, the trees around him bent inward, bowing.

In Thessaly, the ruins of a long-forgotten temple began to glow with a heat no one could see, but every animal in the region fled.

In the caves beneath Dinaric karst, an old shepherd awoke from decades of stillness and began whispering names he never knew.

At the edge of Rome, something ancient stirred in the Forum, older than marble, older than empire.

Danica and I met again near midnight. We sat beside the rusted shell of an old tank, repurposed as a watchpost. The stars were visible above, strange and scattered. I leaned into her.

"You were right," I murmured. "This is bigger than her, Danica. Much bigger."

Danica did not answer immediately.

Then she spoke, barely above a murmur. "She'll still try to make it only about him, that twisted bitch."

"Let her," I said. "The rest of us are already past her."

She turned to me, our eyes catching like flame to flint. "What if we're wrong?"

I smiled, tight-lipped and uncertain. "What if we're not, Danica?"

In the darkness below us, the ground gave a low, slow tremble. Whatever slept beneath the world had decided to rise.

The ruins of Monte Cassino did not become a fortress overnight. They became something stranger and older. It began with the people who arrived without a word. First in small groups, farmers and hunters, deserting soldiers with hollow eyes. Then came the scholars, archaeologists with dirt still under their nails, alongside priests who had abandoned their churches and returned to sacred fires. Mothers who had lost every child followed them, carrying nothing but rage.

They brought weapons, old ones passed down through generations, and left their flags behind. One woman carried an axe that had belonged to her grandmother, its head engraved with Baltic runes. From the Romanian forests came two brothers who had bound blades to oak branches and dipped them in wolf blood. They carried no songs, no chants, only the memory that lived in their hands. When Danica walked among them, her steps trailing frost and flickering flame, they stood straighter, like iron drawn to a magnetic pole buried deep in the world.

I had seen many things in my life. I had watched a child beg for water from a drone before being gunned down. I had stood before gods and called them by name. Yet this quiet, relentless mobilization of myth and flesh was something else entirely. The Resistance had become a fulcrum. The world was about to tilt, and Monte Cassino was where the force had gathered.

I stood in the center of the training grounds, once a cloister, now a killing field in raw preparation, and watched as new recruits lifted rifles and spears. Each weapon carried history. Each step was a return to something before borders, before nations.

Danica walked the perimeter, her eyes scanning movements, correcting form with a glance. A boy stumbled, his feet tangling. She stopped.

"Again," she said, her voice firm.

He rose. He tried again. This time he did not fall.

At night, the rites began. They were held in the mud, under the cold, watchful stars. Old symbols drawn into the ground with bone and ash, each one a name older than the language used to speak it.

I walked past one fire where an elder woman painted a bullet casing with soot and whispered over it.

I paused. "What are you doing?"

She did not look up. "Giving it a purpose, brate."

I nodded once. "Good."

From France came a caravan of medics and exorcists, their skills twisted together by necessity. From Poland, a unit of resistance fighters who had once guarded sacred salt mines, their armor crusted in minerals.

Danica met with each group personally, without fanfare. She looked each leader in the eyes and gave them a single nod. This was correction. The Oracle had warned them both, "This is a war to remember, above all else." Remembering, I knew damn well, hurt.

Each night Danica woke with burning hands, the residue of unleashed power. Her dreams showed her other lives, parallel and vivid. Lovers falling in different cities. Wars she had died in, over and over. I did not speak of my own dreams. But Danica saw how my shoulders stiffened before sunrise. How I stood just a little too long near the ruins, looking toward Rome. I remembered Ana as she had been, before all of this. That, somehow, was worse.

By the seventh day, the camp had grown into a living organism. Messengers sprinted between tents. Scouts returned from the hills with maps carved into their arms, while a team of engineers fed ghost broadcasts into the remnants of global military networks.

At dusk, I stepped before a circle of commanders, men and women with scars where medals might have once gone. I did not raise my voice.

"We don't attack Rome," I said. "We remind it."

A murmur rippled through them, then died.

Danica moved to my shoulder. "She is a fracture, a wound in the world. We are marching to make everyone see what she truly is."

One commander, a grizzled old man with a missing eye, asked, "And if they don't see, Ilija?"

I smiled without humor. "Then we burn the whole goddamn thing down and build something better from the ash."

That night, a girl no older than fifteen climbed the outer wall with trembling legs. Her lips were cracked, her coat ragged. When she reached the gate, she collapsed. I caught her before her head hit the stone.

She looked up, her eyes rolling, wide with terror and fatigue. "They're moving," she gasped. "The Accord. Ten miles south of Orvieto. Tanks and heavy armor. Foot soldiers behind them."

Danica crouched, her face hard. "Who leads them?"

The girl's lip bled as she whispered, "Two demons. Screaming ones. I don't know their names."

Danica and I looked at each other. We knew. Phobos and Deimos.

Across the field, the Resistance stirred. Danica stood on the northern ridge, hair blowing behind her, eyes fixed on the distant horizon. There would be no sleep now. No more waiting, only the memory that drove them and the fire that would carry them forward.

In the heart of the Eternal City, behind the thick walls of the Senate chamber turned war bunker, the last three heads of the Trilateral Accord stood in a triangle of silence. The table between them held a single artifact, a fragment of obsidian pulled from the battlefield in Belarus, scorched by lightning not of this world. Its surface still trembled. Its low hum had not stopped for days.

President Bradford Keyes paced with the gait of a man once immortal in polls and screens, now grayed around the temples and frayed at the edges of his rhetoric. His suit was pressed, his tie perfect, but his fingers kept curling toward the weapon holstered at his side.

President Yelis Semyonov, regal in a black coat embroidered with deep crimson, sat in a steel chair beneath a broken Roman arch. His cane rested beside him, though he never reached for it. His eyes were two cold planets orbiting a dying sun, calculating and increasingly empty.

President Stefan Vuković stood nearest the window, where the old gods used to ride chariots across mosaics. The view offered fractured domes and shadows moving in the streets below. He stared down at his hands, as if trying to remember what they used to be before they signed death warrants.

"They're here," Semyonov said at last, his Russian accent clipped by weariness. "Outside the city. The Resistance has gathered in the ruins of Monte Cassino."

Keyes did not answer immediately. He was too busy watching the obsidian tremble.

"There's something older behind them," Vuković murmured. "The Vatican intelligence confirms what the satellites picked up over the Adriatic. The seismic disruptions are something else entirely."

Keyes stopped pacing. "They're divine."

No one corrected him.

"I gave her everything," Keyes said quietly, too quietly, his voice barely human. "The infrastructure, the funding. I carved her into the shape of the future. She was our Aphrodite, irresistible and unifying, myth reborn for a digital empire."

Semyonov scoffed, dry and bitter. "You gave her delusion, you fool. She grew teeth while you painted her lips."

Vuković finally turned from the window. "You both gave her what she needed. Worship."

Keyes's eyes snapped toward him. "So what did you give her, Vuković?"

The Serbian president did not blink. "I gave her a place to be born, you self-important prick."

Silence fell again, thick enough to hear the obsidian humming on the table. Semyonov rose with deliberate grace, lifting his cane.

"She's not in Rome yet," he said. "But she doesn't need to be. This city belongs to memory now."

Keyes muttered, "Or madness."

"No," said Vuković, more to himself than them. "It belongs to judgment."

Behind them, the stained-glass windows flickered with impossible silhouettes, figures too tall and too fluid for flesh. One bore the outline of a stag, its shadow antlered and vast. Another shimmered as a woman of fire with feathers for skin. The gods were watching, even here.

Semyonov approached the obsidian shard. He placed a gloved hand upon it and winced.

"It resonates," he whispered. "Not to us."

Keyes stepped away, suddenly furious. "We built this Accord to unify the last century of men, you pathetic fools. We didn't build it to become pawns of prehistoric myths."

Vuković gave a bitter laugh. "That's exactly what we are, Keyes. Pawns. She used us. Now they've come to finish the board."

A knock echoed from the sealed iron door. It opened without permission. An aide stepped through, pale and sweating. His hands trembled as he clutched a tablet. The data screen showed movement. Dozens of contacts. Maybe hundreds. Streaming through the southern gates of the city.

Keyes dismissed him with a wave, but the aide stammered, "They're not firing, sir. They're just… walking."

Semyonov's eyes narrowed. "No bloodshed?"

"Not yet," said the aide. "They're marching like a procession."

Vuković asked, "Are they chanting?"

"No, sir. They're silent."

Keyes sat slowly, the bones in his back cracking. "They know we've already lost, the cunning bastards."

Semyonov touched his cane to the obsidian one last time. The vibration nearly buckled his knees. "She's not here yet," he said, "but her temple is."

They all knew which one he meant. The Temple of Venus Genetrix. It served Ana now, throbbing with her memory, and something even older than her, the myth behind the myth.

"We have to go there," Vuković said. "We can't stop what's coming from a bunker, you cowards."

Keyes scoffed. "So we crawl to the altar? Ask forgiveness, like groveling dogs?"

Semyonov's voice sharpened to steel. "We go to see the end. Or be seen by it, you insufferable fool."

Vuković nodded slowly. "To die as witnesses, you spineless shits."

Outside, the city began to shift. Lights flickered in rhythmic pulses. The air trembled from something beneath the streets, something older than war. From beneath the Vatican to the bones of the Colosseum, Rome pulsed like a heartbeat. The Resistance was coming. I was coming. Danica burned at my side. The gods, once myth, now terrifyingly real, were moving toward Rome.

At dawn, the march began. Just the sound of boots pressing into the wounded soil of Italy, step by step, steady as a pulse. The Resistance moved in silence, beyond words. Each fighter knew why they walked. Each knew what waited beyond the hills, beyond the forests scorched by drone fire. Rome waited, and within it, Ana.

Danica and I led them. We walked among them, woven into their ranks. My coat rippled with charged air, my fingers crackling softly even when still. Danica's aura pulsed with alternating waves of frost and flame, her every step branding the dirt beneath her with invisible sigils. We said little, our weapons heavy across our backs. With each mile, the sky seemed to shift.

The clouds thinned above us, pale and taut, as if the sky itself were holding something back.

We passed through villages choked with ruin, churches gutted to their foundations. Schools turned to command posts and then abandoned. Still, people emerged. They came out of cellars and from behind boarded doors, blinking in the light. They stood on thresholds and watched. Some wept. Others raised fists. In every town, someone joined. A farmer with a sickle. A priest with dried blood on his robes. By the time the Resistance crossed into Lazio, its numbers had tripled, and every step they took shook the ground harder than their boots should have allowed. They moved like witnesses, like people who had looked gods in the eyes and remembered that those gods had once been them.

Danica walked beside a woman who carried only a bundle of herbs and a long, iron nail.

"You know what waits for us?" Danica asked.

The woman nodded. "The mirror of the old world. Shattered and angry."

"Then why walk toward it, you dumb bitch?"

The woman did not smile. "I'd rather die facing it than live looking away, you cowardly prick."

Danica looked ahead.

By the third day, signs began to emerge. Animals fled from unseen forces in the trees. Birds flew in tight, unnatural circles overhead. The rivers turned cold and metallic, changed in ways that defied explanation. Always, the wind carried whispers. These were fragments, like someone trying to remember how to say a name they once knew.

Rome emptied as the Resistance approached. Buildings shuttered their windows. Drones vanished from the sky. The streets went hollow. The Trilateral Accord was still there, but its belief in its own permanence had crumbled. Its leaders watched from tower windows, their faces slack with resignation. They had built their empire on control, but the world had slipped free.

I stood one night atop a broken aqueduct just outside the city. Below me, the Resistance camp glowed with firelight and the quiet murmur of breath. Danica joined me, her eyes reflecting the embers.

"It's almost time," she said.

I nodded. "The earth's holding its breath."

Danica turned her gaze south toward Rome, lit like a throat preparing to scream.

"I can feel her," she whispered. "Like a star collapsing in reverse, that fucking bitch."

I closed the distance between us. "She remembers us."

Danica reached for my hand. "Then we'll remind her what we became."

The next morning, we stood on the final hill. Below us stretched the city. Its domes and ruins. Its temples and scars. In the center, the Temple of Venus Genetrix, alive now, something beyond marble and stone. It breathed. It pulsed like a living wound. I drew a long breath. Danica narrowed her eyes. The Resistance waited, unmoving, behind us. The wind was still. The world tilted, and the ground beneath us whispered, "Now."

The headquarters of the Trilateral Accord squatted like a wounded leviathan in the center of Rome; a towering complex of concrete and steel now girded for siege. Barriers had been raised. Gun turrets pivoted. Thermal grids flickered across shattered walls. Sniper nests crowned every rooftop. It had become a fortress, and the Resistance had come to shatter its spine.

We moved without sound through the outskirts of the dead city. Blades sharpened in memory and rifles loaded with history.

I walked at the front, my jacket torn open at the seams from flame and lightning, my eyes aglow with stormlight. Electricity danced across my shoulders like a living cloak, pulsing with each breath.

Danica walked beside me, her boots striking fire and frost into the cracked stone beneath. Her fingers trembled, restraining what she had yet to unleash.

The Resistance followed, battered and furious. They were witnesses. They were heirs.

They reached the perimeter just before dawn.

The first Accord drone descended with a whir that sounded almost like a warning. I did not give it the chance. I raised my arm, and the storm answered. A lance of lightning shot from my palm and tore the drone in half, its pieces raining down like burning snow. Alarms shrieked from within the compound.

Danica exhaled, and the air froze. She raised her arms, flames spiraling from her back like wings igniting. She stepped forward before the first shot was fired. The battle erupted without declaration.

Accord soldiers emerged from barricades, black helmets gleaming, rifles locked. Neural implants glowed with red synchrony across their temples. They opened fire in a coordinated wall of death.

I walked through it. Bullets veered off course, magnetized by raw current. I extended both hands. Lightning snarled out from my fingertips in jagged arcs, tangling through the air. The current hit the soldiers like a hammer from the heavens. Their implants burst with sparks and shrill static. One man's visor cracked inward as blood misted behind the glass. Another dropped mid-scream, his body jerking in spasms as electric veins spiderwebbed across his skin, smoke curling from his mouth before he collapsed face down.

Danica moved like a storm front behind me. With a single gesture, a wall of fire exploded from her chest, incinerating the forward gunners. Their bodies turned to silhouette and ash. She spun, casting a column of ice through the second line. Their knees froze mid-charge and they shattered on impact. Her eyes were glowing coals, her lips stained with frost. Every step she took left the earth gasping between heat and void.

The Resistance surged in behind us. Shouts in Serbian, Greek, Polish, Italian. Rifles cracked in rhythm. Explosives slammed into barriers, tearing them apart.

Blood painted the marble steps of the old tribunal chamber. Inside, the corridors pulsed with artificial light and the screams of the dying. I kicked in a steel-reinforced door, my foot glowing with electric backlash. An elite unit with night-vision visors and electromagnetic cannons stood ready on the other side. One raised his weapon. I moved faster.

I hurled my hand forward, fingers splayed. The air rippled and collapsed into a localized lightning pulse. Every soldier's visor shorted. Their screams overlapped as fire burst from their skulls.

Danica walked through the smoke and opened her palm. A soldier tried to shoot her point-blank. She caught the bullet in a sphere of frost midair, then clenched her hand and drove the frozen round backward into his throat. He fell, gargling on ice and blood.

Down the hall, a heavy blast door rumbled shut. Danica reached for it.

I stopped her. "Let me, love."

I pressed both hands to the wall beside it. I closed my eyes. Electricity surged from my chest into the circuitry. Sparks shot across the ceiling. The entire compound groaned. Then the blast door ripped open on its own, metal peeling like wet paper.

The next room was a bunker, the last defensive layer before the inner sanctum. Dozens of soldiers, shoulder to shoulder, heavy artillery leveled. They were waiting, ready to die. They were not ready for gods.

Danica stepped forward. She whispered a word no human had heard in centuries, one of Lada's names, the first flame ever spoken in love. The ceiling collapsed in fire. A torrent of living flame poured downward like the wrath of forgotten suns. The soldiers screamed as armor melted onto bone, as lungs filled with molten oxygen. Prayers curdled on their burning tongues.

I raised a hand and sealed the inferno behind a wall of lightning to keep the Resistance from being consumed. The fire licked the edges of the hall, painting it gold and crimson.

Then there was silence.

In that silence, we reached the final threshold, the grand chamber beneath the old tribunal, rebuilt in steel and surveillance. The door was locked with every safeguard the Accord had invented, biometrics layered over voice print, encrypted ritual woven through the circuitry. I did not touch it. Danica did not breathe. Together, we stepped into it, and it dissolved in light.

The Resistance paused behind us. The corridors ahead wound empty toward the heart of the empire. Toward its final architects.

I turned to Danica. Her face was pale with ash, eyes still flickering flame.

"Tomorrow," I said.

Danica nodded. "Let them hear us coming, you glorious bastard."

Behind us, fire smoldered and the blood of a century's betrayal ran into the cracks beneath our feet.

CHAPTER TWENTY-SIX
THE LAST ACT OF GODS

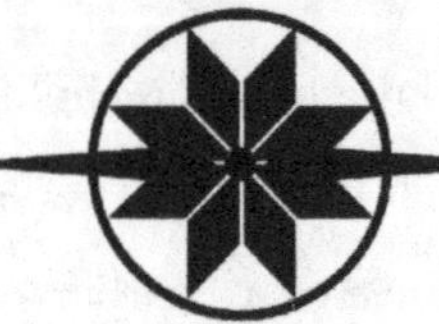

Ilija

We stood at the edge of the world, or at least at the edge of what the world had become. A gray-hearted husk of empire, carved hollow by greed and liturgy, pulsing now with the final heartbeat of the Trilateral Accord. The marble plaza outside the former Italian Parliament, now converted into the Accord's headquarters, lay blanketed in ash and the flickering remains of drone wings. Smoke clung to the sky like a ceiling of mourning.

I looked up once, only once, and then never again. There was nothing left to see but what we had come to end. The building loomed before us like a tombstone, built in the style of fascist resurrection, white and towering, cruel in its proportions. It had once been a place of command, then of dead silence. Now it would become a place of reckoning. The Resistance flooded the outer ring, boots crushing broken glass and shell casings. No civilians remained here; Rome's heart had been evacuated weeks ago. Only ghosts lingered in the walls, and gods.

They gathered in the ruined arcade of the square. Freyja stood with her flaming hair bound in iron bands. Perun's shoulders ran thick with stormlight, his eyes burning like black suns. Veles watched barefoot and smiling, his arms robed in serpents of smoke. Lada stood beside Morana, neither speaking, their presences vibrating the stone beneath their feet.

Brigid knelt in silence, one hand resting on a scorched rifle. Behind them all, higher than the rest, the Zorya twins watched, one with open eyes, the other with eyes of starlight and blood. They had come to witness what the children of man would choose.

Danica's boots clanged against the steel loading ramp as we advanced through the final breach in the barricades. She held no weapon; she had no need of one. Ice fanned from the soles of her steps, each one cracking the concrete as her core temperature dipped to levels that would kill an ordinary soldier.

I walked beside her, my jacket torn but buttoned to the collar, the sleeves scorched where lightning had bled from my veins. Sparks leapt between my fingers even at rest, barely contained, my beard singed at the edges. My eyes remained steady.

"They're inside," I murmured. "All of them."

"Then let's bring the fucking walls down," Danica said, her voice a low growl.

The first Accord line opened fire the moment we stepped into the lobby. Dozens of armored soldiers, hybrid forces from the US, Russia, and Serbia, poured lead into the entryway. Gunfire bounced off the walls, sending chips of marble into the air like stone shrapnel. Danica and I did not duck.

I raised my right hand, and the air detonated. A dome of high-pressure current burst outward from my palm, arcing in every direction. Bullets screamed backward. A dozen soldiers were lifted off the ground and slammed into pillars hard enough to break their spines. Steel warped. Walls cracked under the force.

Danica stepped through the broken glass and exhaled. The air turned white with frost. With a sweep of her arms, twin crescents of ice tore across the chamber like scythes, severing legs and cleaving rifles in half. One screaming man was pinned to the wall with a frozen spike through his gut. Flames erupted behind her like phoenix wings, curling up her arms, hungry for flesh.

Another squad attempted to flank.

I turned. "No."

I clenched both fists. The floor exploded upward, shards of electrified stone impaling two soldiers before the others were vaporized in a white-hot burst of arc-light. Blood splashed against the wall, painting a red arc over the Accord's faded emblem.

"Reinforcements!" one Accord captain screamed into a comm unit, but his transmission dissolved into static.

Outside, the Resistance breached the front doors, dragging steel barriers out of the way with brutal force. Dozens of fighters poured through, some firing, others armed with kitchen knives and the will to survive. It did not matter. They fought the architects of the new myth. They fought to become memory. Then they came.

Phobos and Deimos descended from the upper levels of the building like wraiths in combat armor, each one half-human, half-shadow. Phobos had the body of a butchered god, his skin covered in screaming faces, his hands wrapped in chains that coiled like serpents. His eyes were pitched and endless. Deimos moved faster, sleeker, his presence a pulse of fear that warped perception around him. They were Ana's last offering. Her private sons, her brutal revenge.

Danica turned as the temperature around her plunged. "They're not like the others, Ilija."

"They're what's left of her divinity," I said.

"Then we end them," Danica snapped.

Phobos charged first, his steps thundering like ancient drums. With a swing of his chain-wrapped fist, he slammed a Resistance fighter into the ceiling. The man's skull cracked open like a fruit. Danica rushed forward, flames roaring from her palms. She ducked the next blow and thrust upward. Fire coiled around her arm and speared directly into Phobos's chest. The god screamed, and then laughed, his mouth splitting wide with something worse than pain.

Deimos was already behind me. The fear hit before the blow, cold sweat pouring down my back as he raised a curved blade made of memory and bone. I caught it with lightning. The clash detonated, sending us both tumbling backward through the air. The room collapsed around us. Marble fell and pillars shattered. Screams filled the air, and still the gods did not intervene. They watched. Because the old stories had always ended this way, with ruin and flame, memory reborn through blood.

I rose from the rubble, my mouth bleeding. Danica stood panting, her arms wreathed in blue flame and pale frost. Together, we stepped over the corpses of a hundred soldiers and walked toward the blackened hallway where the last war still waited.

The hallway stretched before us like the throat of a dying beast, smoke pooling in the corners, walls slick with oil and blood. Dim security lights flickered overhead in a pattern like a stuttering heartbeat. Danica and I walked in silence, our boots wet with gore, the echoes of the last battle still ringing in our bones. Then metal doors ahead of us screamed open.

A flood of soldiers poured in, machines in flesh. The Accord's final elite units. Cybernetic implants pulsed across their skulls and limbs. Some had no mouths left to scream, only dark grilles where orders entered and silence obeyed. Their armor clicked in unison, their eyes glowing. They raised their weapons in one perfect, synchronized motion. They were not prepared for gods.

I stepped forward, palms raised. This time, I did not summon lightning. I became it. My body cracked open with arcs of pure electric fury, my silhouette dissolving into bolts and pulses. Electricity raced along the walls and crawled through the wiring, surging beneath the floor. The hallway itself became a cage of voltage. The soldiers fired. Bullets screamed down the corridor and stopped midair. My field caught them in an invisible vortex of electromagnetic distortion, spinning them harmlessly until I twisted my wrists and reversed their direction. The elite squad screamed as their own rounds punched through their skulls and shoulders, ripping armor from bone. One soldier tried to retreat, but his implant burst into flame, cooking him from the inside. My eyes were pure light now, my beard whipping in the arc-blown wind.

Danica moved beside me. Where I was pure charge, she was fire and frost at war with itself, flame licking across her arms, ice trailing from her fingers. She threw her hands wide, and the temperature collapsed. A wave of frost blasted outward, flash-freezing the entire floor. Accord soldiers slipped, screamed, then the flames followed. With a flick of her wrists, the ice shattered beneath their feet. Fire erupted from the cracks. Screams turned to gurgles as molten stone swallowed men whole. One soldier tried to leap at her, implanted legs launching him like a beast. She caught him midair by the throat. Flame erupted from her eyes. He combusted in her hand, his armor melting, flesh liquefying, until she dropped what remained, a blackened husk still twitching.

Then the roar came again, deeper this time. Phobos had broken free.

He tore through the ruined ceiling like a meteor of rage, slamming into me with enough force to break a mountain. We hit the ground in a thunderclap, stone cracking beneath us. I coughed blood, barely able to raise my arms before Phobos's fists came down again, bone and chain crashing down with divine force.

I caught one blow. Lightning raced through Phobos's arm, but the god absorbed it, laughing with a mouth full of teeth that were no longer human.

"You want to fight fear?" he snarled. "Let me show you your own."

I gritted my teeth, then let go. My body erupted in a surge of power so intense the walls peeled backward. Phobos was thrown down the corridor like a comet.

Danica turned, but Deimos was already there. He stepped from the shadows, his expression unreadable. His sword was forged from remorse, a blade of broken promises and stolen grief. Danica tried to block him with fire. He moved through it. His blade nicked her shoulder, a scratch, and pain seized her heart. The pain was memory.

She was a girl in another life, kneeling beside my corpse, weeping beneath the gallows as a king's guards dragged her away. She cried out, disoriented, flames collapsing around her.

Deimos came closer, his voice gentle as a lover's. "Every life you've lost. Every time he died in your arms. I'll make you feel them all at once."

"No," I growled.

I slammed my fist into the wall, lightning surging into the building's foundation. The ceiling collapsed on Deimos, burying him in tons of stone and molten wire. Danica gasped, regaining focus. Frost bloomed from her lips. Together, we turned and found Phobos rising again. He had become war itself. His body had split open, revealing the thing beneath, muscle threaded with blades, a heart that pulsed with fire. Eyes that bled steam. His voice had turned to the brutal clash of weapons in every war ever fought.

The Resistance behind us faltered. One soldier fell to her knees, weeping in terror. I stepped in front of them all and roared, and the lightning answered.

Phobos charged. I met him head-on, electricity forming a spear in my hands. It collided with Phobos's chain-fist and exploded, sending shards of power in every direction. Walls buckled. Fire danced in the ceiling. The two of us slammed into each other over and over, blow for blow, light against fury.

Danica watched for one moment, then turned and found Deimos still alive, bleeding but smiling.

"You always wake up too late," he whispered.

Danica's eyes narrowed. "Not this time, you piece of shit."

She stepped forward. A circle of ice bloomed beneath her. Her hands ignited, fueled by memory. Images spiraled in the flames, her first kiss with me, the warmth of my hand in every life we'd shared. She hurled it all at Deimos. The flame became a lance. It struck him dead center, and for a moment, Deimos remembered everything he had stolen. He screamed. His body cracked. Light burst from his chest. He reached out, fingers trembling, then crumbled to dust.

Phobos paused, his chain-fist frozen mid-swing.

Bloodied and gasping, I pointed toward his brother's ashes. "Your turn."

Phobos hesitated. For the first time, he looked afraid. I raised both arms. Lightning spiraled from the heavens themselves, tearing through the ruined ceiling, descending in an apocalyptic column of light. It struck Phobos. The god disintegrated, screaming, vaporized by the fury of memory and vengeance. Silence followed, and smoke curled through the wreckage.

The Resistance rose from the wreckage, stepping over bodies and shattered armor. In that quiet, Danica and I stood hand in hand. We were covered in blood. Shaking, but whole. Ahead, the inner chamber doors waited. Beyond them, the final architects of the Accord, and something far worse.

Danica took my hand. "Together?"

"Always," I said, and squeezed her hand.

The inner doors stood like the gates of an old-world cathedral, vaulted and polished, guarded by silence rather than sentries. Carved into them were the symbols of the Accord, the eagle and the double cross. Even in the carving, the lines trembled, as if the stone itself feared what it held back.

I placed my hand upon the metal. It hissed and opened, the lock shorting out beneath my touch. Beyond, the chamber of the Presidents waited.

It was a circular hall, vast and cold, fashioned to resemble a war room but furnished like a throne room. Its marble floor was veined with gold. A skylight shattered by some earlier blast let in ash and smoke from the burning city beyond. Surveillance monitors blinked on the walls, broken and stuttering, showing flickers of the world outside, fallen cities and broken flags, temples burning in the distance. Three seats waited at the far end, spaced evenly beneath a cracked emblem of the Accord. Three monsters sat upon them.

Bradford Keyes, once the darling of Western liberalism, now little more than a corporate husk inside a general's body, leaned forward, veins bulging from steroidal augmentation. His eyes were cold, metallic implants, and his voice came from his chest like a machine's verdict.

"You've killed my army," he said. "But you haven't killed the Accord."

Danica did not answer. She stepped into the chamber, eyes blazing. Behind her, I walked with silence like a cloak.

Keyes rose to his feet and spread his arms. "The world wants order. You think this… rebellion, this mythological fever dream, will bring peace? We built a system! We carved out chaos and filled it with control!"

"You built a cage," I said. "And told everyone it was home."

Keyes snarled and reached for the weapon mounted on his back, a cannon pulsating with the stolen energy of old gods.

He aimed it at Danica. "Then die with your memories."

Before he could fire, I moved. I vanished in a flash of stormlight and reappeared beside Keyes, driving my hand into the weapon's power core. The cannon screamed and detonated in Keyes's hands. The explosion hurled him backward, shredding the synthetic skin from his arms, exposing chrome and blood. Keyes staggered to his knees, coughing steam. I stalked toward him, lightning arcing in both palms.

Keyes looked up, furious even in death. "You're nothing. A footnote."

I said nothing. I touched Keyes's forehead. Electricity surged through every implant, every nerve. Keyes's body convulsed, then burst from within, flesh tearing like paper. Sparks danced across the floor as he slumped sideways, smoking and twitching. Silence returned. Only two remained.

Yelis Semyonov sat motionless. He hadn't moved during the exchange. His white-blonde hair was slicked back, frozen like ice. The only motion came from his hand, which tapped the armrest of his chair, once, twice, then fell still.

"I suppose it was always meant to end like this," he said in Russian. His voice was softer than expected. "You think we are villains, but you know nothing of holding a dying empire together."

Danica stepped forward, her arms falling to her sides. "Then speak. If you believe we don't understand, make us."

Yelis's eyes narrowed. He looked at Danica, his face stripped of rage and panic, leaving only contempt behind. "I was ten when I watched Moscow burn for the second time. I was thirteen when I starved. I was seventeen when I killed for my seat. I was twenty when I buried every god we once knelt to and defended the motherland. I gave Russia a future."

"You gave it fear," Danica said. "And silence."

"You gave it fantasy," Yelis said, his lip curling. "You gave it ghosts."

Danica's flames sparked, licking her knuckles, but it was frost that answered her.

A stream of pale mist drifted from her breath as she stepped forward. "No," Danica said. "We gave it memory. You smothered it."

She raised her hand. Yelis stayed seated. He whispered, "Then do it right."

Danica's ice speared outward, elegant and precise. A single shard of frost slid through the air and pierced Yelis's heart. He exhaled, eyes wide, filled with awe. Then he slumped forward, lips turning blue. He froze in place, an unblinking statue of iron pride and forgotten gods. Only one remained.

Stefan Vuković, the man who had tried to bury me in silence. He sat watching the other two fall without flinching.

"Do you know how many people I had to crush to get here?" His jaw tightened. "Do you know how many friends I executed? How many priests I drowned? You think you're heroes. All you've done is delay the inevitable."

He leaned forward. "I tried to protect Serbia."

"You tried to own it," I said.

Vuković leaned back. "You were just a nobody. A boring professor reading dusty old books. Dust under my boot."

"I was the dust in your lungs," I said. "And I never left."

Vuković rose now, slow and deliberate, drawing a knife. It was a military blade, not ceremonial. As he unsheathed it, he said, "The gods abandoned us long ago. If you think they're your allies, you've already lost. They want what we want. Obedience."

I shook my head. "No. They want remembrance. And we are their echo."

Vuković lunged. The blade arced toward my throat. Danica moved to intervene, but I caught the blade mid-swing, my fingers searing with lightning. I looked into Vuković's eyes and saw every lie the man had ever told reflected back in them. The blade glowed. It melted.

I pulled Vuković close and whispered, "For Serbia."

Then I pressed my forehead against the man's. A pulse of energy burst between us. Vuković dropped the knife and screamed as memory slammed back into him. He fell backward, clawing at his face as ancient names poured into him, gods he had tried to erase, tongues he had banned. They flooded him all at once, a tidal wave of history crashing into a mind built only for control. He collapsed and did not rise.

The chamber fell still. Three bodies lay where three thrones had ruled, and something sacred had ended.

Danica let her breath go, her flames dying down. I knelt beside the remains of Vuković and placed two fingers on his forehead, a gesture of remembrance. Let history write what it would. This was how power ended, with the return of truth.

The hall trembled. The source was deeper than gunfire, deeper than collapsing beams, a resonance, as if the earth itself had been struck by a tuning fork of sorrow and wrath. Air thickened, rippling with pressure, and every god who had been silent until now turned.

I froze mid-step. Danica's hand shot toward me, then stopped. Overhead, the light dimmed, wilting rather than flickering, as if some unseen gravity now pulled at every photon. Marble cracked under our feet. Veins of light fissured across the walls, bleeding soft gold into the room.

Then the far wall split open, and Ana entered.

This was Afërdita Areia, her war-bound incarnation, the lover turned blade, the seductress made sovereign. The woman who had curled beside me in sunlit beds, paint beneath her fingernails, had been consumed by this, something older, something merciless. She walked barefoot across the shattered stone, each step blooming red petals and flame behind her. Her gown was woven from shadows and gold threads. Around her neck was a torc of iron roses, withered and bleeding. Her hair flowed like dark ink in a current of wind no one else could feel. I had once loved her eyes. Now they held only absence.

Danica felt the temperature shift, something that was neither hot nor cold, only dangerous.

"Ilija…" she whispered.

I had already stepped forward.

"Ana," I said.

The word was small, like speaking into the heart of a volcano. She tilted her head slightly, her lips pressed thin, her jaw trembling with something she refused to release.

"You remember me," she said. Her voice was the sound of violins breaking.

"I never forgot you," I said. "But I did survive you."

She laughed once, a broken, low sound. "You made me believe," she said. "In something beautiful, something that wasn't carved out of death and heritage. Now look at you." She gestured to the corpses behind us. "To them. To that goddamn bitch."

Danica stepped forward, ice flaring around her shoulders. "Don't make this about me, Ana."

Ana's gaze stayed fixed on me. "You're nothing to me."

Then she moved. One breath. That's all it took. In less than a second, Ana was in front of me, her hand driving into my chest, grasping my heart without touching it. A tremor passed through my body. I gasped as love and pain hit me at once. Memories we'd shared, from this life and from every life we'd ever touched. She gave it back to me all at once. The bed in Thessaloniki. The first time we'd kissed in a forest under siege.

"I gave you everything," she whispered. "And you gave it to her, that whore."

Danica screamed. A storm of frost and flame burst outward from her body, shattering the air between us and throwing Ana back, but the goddess caught herself midair, her feet never touching the floor, hovering like a star that had been banished from the sky. Her eyes burned now, filled with betrayal.

"You think I did this for power?" she hissed. "I did it to be with you. I joined the Accord to save you. To preserve something beautiful in a world built to burn."

"You killed my people," I said. My hands were shaking. "You burned everything I loved."

"You let them die for ghosts," she shot back.

The gods still did not intervene. Neither Perun nor Freyja, not even the Zorya. This was a reckoning of the heart. Ana raised her hand. A dozen blades of golden light erupted around her like wings. She hurled them toward Danica.

Danica raised her arms, ice coiled in front of her like a shield, each flake fractal and sharp. The first few blades struck, cracking the surface. The rest shattered it. One blade cut Danica's side. She staggered back, bleeding.

I roared and thrust my palms forward. Twin spears of lightning shot toward Ana. She caught them midair, twisted them into a crown, and threw them back. They hit me like hammers of light. I fell, groaning.

"Do you see now?" Ana whispered, hovering above us. "Do you understand what I've become?"

Danica rose, her face bleeding, flames curling through her hair.

"I see exactly what you are," she said.

She ran, through Ana, into her. She hurled herself at Ana like a comet wrapped in fire and ice. Their bodies collided midair, the force of the impact cracking every window in the hall. They struck the ground and rolled, a chaos of flame and frost.

I dragged myself upright, bones trembling. I watched the two women I had loved across lifetimes tear the sky between them, and I knew only one would survive.

Ana pinned Danica to the floor.

"Do you think he'll stay with you?" she hissed. "After he remembers what we had?"

Danica smiled, blood between her teeth. "I don't want him to stay. I want him to choose."

Ana froze. Danica raised her hand and ignited, fueled by divine truth. A thousand lives poured through her skin, every incarnation of herself that had ever held my hand and died for me. She pushed that memory into Ana's heart. Ana screamed and fled. She rose through the shattered ceiling, golden wings of fire peeling from her back, tears streaming down her cheeks that turned into arrows of molten glass. The room trembled. Then she was gone.

I knelt beside Danica. She was breathing. Barely. I held her hand.

"I choose you," I whispered.

Her eyes fluttered open. "I know."

Silence fell like ash. The room still trembled from Ana's exit, embers drifting in slow arcs through the air, golden and soft, like feathers from a wing set aflame. Danica leaned against me, her breathing shallow, her chest rising and falling in a cracked, fragile rhythm. Around us, the Resistance moved in murmurs, quiet and cautious. They had seen gods. They had fought monsters. Now they stood in the rubble of both.

No victory cheer arose. Only breath and blood, and the crackle of fire eating history. The chamber of the Accord lay in ruin. One throne had been torn in half by lightning. Another was frozen, crumbling into diamond shards. The last smoldered, as if the soul of its occupant had refused to die all at once. Walls once adorned with flags bore only the shadows of fallen empires. Monitors blinked static. Marble was shattered underfoot.

At the center, I stood, holding Danica's hand.

We did not speak. We had no need to. From the edges of the chamber, the gods began to move. They came to observe. Perun filled the doorway with his arms crossed. Veles leaned against a fractured pillar, serpents coiled around his shoulders like a mourning shawl. The Zorya stood near the dome, each looking in a different direction, and Freyja stood behind them all, her eyes on Danica, something unreadable flickering behind her warrior's calm.

No one offered congratulations. Gods do not do that. They witness, and they remember. A door opened in the air itself, crackling with starlight. Outside, the world waited.

The skies were torn, plumes of smoke from a thousand battlefields, ruins glowing beneath clouds swollen with fire. Yet in some places, there were lights. Candles and torches, windows lit by hands that had refused to die.

From the shattered hall of the Accord, a new voice broadcast. One of the Resistance engineers had found a surviving uplink and patched into the feeds from abandoned satellites, hijacking the global stream. A camera turned toward Danica and me.

I stood silent for a long breath. Then, "It is finished here, but the work has only begun. The world is yours again. Remember who you are."

The camera went dark.

The fallen flags stayed fallen. The seats of power stayed empty. Only the image of two figures remained, hand in hand, standing in a temple of broken thrones.

Around the globe, screens flickered. In India, protesters wept openly in the streets, burning effigies of the Accord's corporate lords and lighting marigolds in their place. In Kenya, soldiers dropped their weapons as Resistance banners rose above Nairobi's skyline, carried by children and poets alike. In São Paulo, the people stormed their own parliament, demanding every archive the Accord had sealed be opened and read aloud. In Serbia, Belgrade's sky was orange. It was dawn. For the first time in years, church bells rang without fear.

Danica and I stepped through the breach. The temple collapsed behind us, consumed by sheer exhaustion. The gods did not follow. They stood still, watching as the two humans, the two immortals, walked back into a world they had torn apart.

We did not speak until we reached the courtyard. It was strewn with broken vehicles and burning documents, helmets torn open like eggshells.

Danica's voice came first. "Do you think it'll hold?"

I looked skyward. The clouds were dark. Yet there were breaks, slits of light bleeding through.

"No," I said. "But maybe we've given it a chance to remember how, you beautiful monster."

She nodded, then sank to her knees beside a dry fountain. I knelt with her. I took her hand in love, nothing more. We kissed in the silence of history's ending, with only the wind moving through the broken windows of the world's last palace.

Far above, in a mountain cloaked in fog and carved from stone that whispered its own name, Ana stood alone. She bled from her lip. A crack ran through the rose-gold crown at her temple. Her reflection in the obsidian pool was the face of someone left behind. She watched the fire dance and said nothing.

Back in the ruins of Rome, the Resistance began gathering the wounded. The gods vanished one by one, slipping back into shadow and myth, their work unfinished, their voices silent now. Danica leaned into my shoulder.

"I remember everything," she said.

I nodded. "So do I."

"Even the pain?" Danica asked.

"Especially the pain," I said.

We stood beneath the fractured sky, hand in hand, our bodies bruised, our hearts still beating in rhythm with the new world being born. Around us, the shattered remnants of the Accord's throne hall settled into silence. Danica's head rested against my shoulder. For a moment, there was peace.

Then, a rupture. The air tore open without warning, without wind. Reality split like flesh beneath a blade, and out of it Ana exploded, her body limned in golden fire, eyes a storm of grief and fury. She moved in silence, without hesitation. She reached, and her hand clamped around my wrist like a vice of divine iron. I shouted, stumbling forward, dragged by her immense force.

Danica screamed. "Ana, no!"

I clawed back toward her, fingers outstretched, feet skidding across the broken stone. "Danica!"

Our hands nearly touched, but Ana wrenched me back. A burst of light detonated around us, cold and howling, like a star being smothered.

And then, I was gone. Ana and the void vanished with me. Danica fell to her knees, her scream swallowed by the smoke. The only sound was the wind moving through a ruined world, and the echo of a name torn from a soul.

Epilogue
A New Moon Rises

Danica

The years since Ilija vanished had not healed the cracks in the world. They had merely weathered them, deepening their fissures like old bone left beneath a bitter sky. I built a life in the quiet places, tucked away in the salvaged ruins of a mountain village where the wind still carried the faint reek of ash and old blood. Every breath served as a raw reminder of what we'd lost, of the absolute terror of that last moment, when Ana, that insidious bitch, ripped him from my goddamn hands.

The silence here was different from the enforced quiet of Accord territories. This was a patient stillness, a profound listening that felt older than human memory, settled deep in the scarred earth. The Resistance, those fragments of defiance scattered across the continent, had not disbanded. They had simply gone to ground, cultivating seeds of rebellion in the shadows, waiting for the inevitable. We sent whispers across dead networks, shared intelligence through coded glances, and kept our blades sharp. Peace remained a fragile, temporary truce, a held breath before the next inevitable scream.

Selene was the only light that pierced that perpetual dusk. She was two years old now, her hair a startling copper, catching the meager sun like flames. Her eyes, the exact, piercing gray-blue of her father's, watched the world with an unnerving stillness, too knowing for a child her age. Sometimes, when she slept, a faint, almost imperceptible shimmer would trace the tiny, perfect spiral etched over her small heart, a mark only I could see, a truth burned into her skin. And the air around her, when she dreamed, would prickle with a familiar, cold electricity, a subtle current that resonated through the quiet room. She was his, every goddamn atom of her.

I spent my days teaching her the old words, the names of gods and constellations. I showed her how the earth remembered, tracing patterns in the dust with her tiny fingers. I watched her closely, every subtle shift, every flicker in her too-bright eyes. Her laughter, a clear, bell-like sound, was a constant torment, reminding me of what was missing, of the vibrant echo of his own laugh I would never hear again. I carried the rings, still fused to my hand, their presence a constant ache, a promise I wasn't sure I could keep.

Ana was out there. I felt her presence, a cold pressure on the edge of my awareness, like a shadow waiting for the sun to set. We knew she was rebuilding, drawing power from the forgotten places, twisting old truths into new chains. We intercepted fragmented messages, saw the subtle shifts in the world's ancient currents. She was patient. She was vengeful. And she would come back. I often wondered if she knew about Selene. If the knowledge of this vibrant, living fragment of Ilija would drive her to even greater madness. The thought curdled my gut.

One cold morning, Selene stood by the window, her small hand pressed against the misted glass. The air around her shimmered faintly, a subtle distortion. Then, a single snowflake, impossibly large and perfect, drifted through the window pane and landed on her palm without melting. It pulsed once, a tiny, exquisite star, before disappearing. My breath hitched in my throat. I looked at her, my heart pounding with a fierce, terrifying love.

She turned to me, her gray-blue eyes wide, filled with an ancient knowing. She did not speak. She did not need to. She simply extended her tiny hand, the faint outline of a spiral glowing on her palm, and in that moment, I saw him. The fierce, defiant, undying love that had chosen me across a thousand goddamn lifetimes.

I knelt, pulling her close, burying my face in her hair. Her small arms wrapped around my neck, her grip surprisingly strong. The cold fire within me surged, meeting the faint warmth of her nascent power. The world was still broken. The war was far from over. And Ilija, my Ilija, was still gone. But in this quiet embrace, in the terrifying, beautiful presence of his daughter, I knew, with a certainty deeper than any vow, that we would find him. Even if I had to tear open the sky itself. Even if I had to burn this world to its damn bones. We would find him. We always did and this time, we would not lose.

ACKNOWLEDGMENTS

No book is ever written alone, but this one feels like it was forged in a constellation of love, patience, and unwavering belief from so many people. It is a profound privilege to finally be able to thank them.

First and foremost, to my incredible wife. I joked in the dedication about you "putting up with me for all these years," but the truth is far deeper. You have been the steadfast heart of this entire journey. For every long, dark night I spent lost in worlds of ash and thunder, you were the light guiding me back. You were the first to read these pages, the one who listened to my frantic monologues about forgotten gods and broken myths, and the one who always knew when a cup of coffee was more valuable than a thousand words of encouragement. You have been my editor, my confidant, and my fiercest champion. You are, and shall always be, what I see when I look towards the cosmos. I will find you in every lifetime.

To my children, who will one day read this and perhaps understand why their father spent so many hours chasing ghosts through history. Thank you for the joyful interruptions, for the laughter that always managed to break through the darkest parts of the story, and for reminding me every day of the kind of world worth fighting for. Your love for all things history has reminded me that stories of the past can lead to the light of the future.

To my friends and my family, a heartfelt thank you for your endless patience. For every missed call, every conversation dominated by Slavic folklore, and for never once looking at me like I was crazy for chasing this dream. Your belief kept me grounded in this reality while I was busy building another.

And to the vast and wonderful community of supporters who have followed this journey. In the solitary world of writing, you were a constant and welcome presence. Every comment was a conversation; every share was a vote of confidence, and every like was a spark in the dark. You have no idea how much your digital enthusiasm translates into real-world strength. Thank you for believing in this story before it even had a cover.

This book is a piece of my soul, but it was shaped and sheltered by all of you.

Thank you,

-Elijah

If you liked this story, don't forget to leave a review!

PRONUNCIATIONS, PLACES, AND THINGS

❋ **Ilija Dragović** (EE-lee-yah DRAH-go-vich) Protagonist; his surname is Serbian.

❋ **Danica** (DAH-nee-kah) Central heroine; name means "morning star" in Slavic languages.

❋ **Ana** (AH-nah) Antagonist figure.

❋ **Selene** (Seh-LEEN) Daughter of Ilija and Danica (appears late).

❋ **Nikola Lazarević (NEE-koh-lah LAH-zah-reh-vich)** President of Serbia, appears in National Broadcast

❋ **Jelena Trifunović (YEH-leh-nah TREE-foo-no-vich)** Prime Minister, styled as hierophant in cultic imagery

❋ **Father Gavril** *(GAH-vreel)* Orthodox priest who offers wisdom

❋ **Anwen** (AN-wen) A vision/past-life name; Welsh, meaning "very beautiful"

❋ **Eira** (AY-rah or EH-rah) Past-life vision name; Old Norse, meaning "snow"

❋ **Džemila** (JEH-mee-lah) Past-life vision name; Bosnian/Turkish, meaning "beautiful"

❋ **Danilo Kiš** (DAH-nee-loh KEESH) Real Yugoslav/Serbian author referenced in Belgrade scene

❋ **Saint Sava** (SAH-vah) Serbian Orthodox saint, national religious figure

❋ **Theotokos** (thay-oh-TOH-kohs) Greek Orthodox title of Mary, "God-bearer"

❋ **Saint Elijah** (ee-LYE-jah) Biblical prophet, referenced in icons

❋ **Belgrade** (BEL-grade / bel-GRAHD) Capital of Serbia; major setting

❋ **Novi** (no-vee) **Belgrade** (bel-GRAHD) Post–WWII urban district

❋ **Danube** (DAN-yube / DAH-noob) Major River in Central/Eastern Europe

❋ **Sava** (SAH-vah) River joining the Danube at Belgrade

❋ **Delphi** (DEL-fye) Ancient Greek site of the oracle (appears in chapter titles).

❋ **The Varangian Gate** (vuh-RAN-jee-uhn) A historical/mythic reference to Norse mercenaries in Byzantium.

❋ **Forgjett** (for-YETT) Old Norse/Icelandic word meaning "forgiven," appears in past-life vision

❋ **Icons** (Orthodox) Religious paintings of saints (Saint Sava, Theotokos, Elijah)

❋ **Ajvar** *(EYE-var)* A Balkan roasted red pepper and eggplant spread, often eaten with bread or grilled meats. Common in Balkan cuisine.

❋ **Rakija / Loza** *(RAH-kee-yah / LOH-zah)* Strong Balkan fruit brandy; loza is grape-based.

❋ **Orthodox incense (myrrh & frankincense)** Used in church liturgy.

❋ **Yugoslavia** *(YOO-go-slah-vee-uh)* Former multi-ethnic federation in the Balkans, dissolved in the 1990s.

❋ **Kosovo** *(KOH-soh-voh)* Region tied to Albanian national identity.

❋ **Balkan** *(BALL-kan)* Southeastern European region encompassing Serbia, Croatia, etc.

THE ACCORD TERRITORIAL MAP

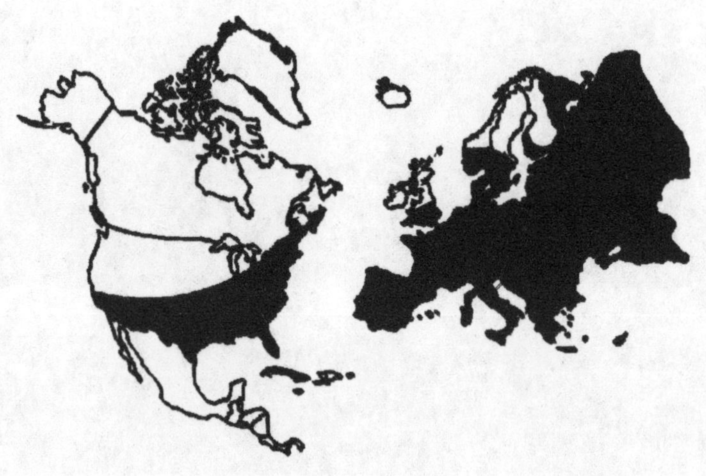

MEET THE GODS
SLAVIC PANTHEON

Perun: The highest god of the pantheon, ruling over the sky, thunder, and lightning. He is a figure of law and immense power.

Veles: The god of the underworld, waters, and the earth. Often depicted with horns, he is a chthonic deity associated with magic, memory, and cattle.

Morana: The goddess of death, winter, and rebirth. She represents the inevitable end of the life cycle and the harshness of winter.

Lada: The goddess of love, beauty, and springtime. She represents life, fertility, and the beginning of the life cycle.

The Zorya: Twin goddesses of the dawn and dusk, the Morning Star and the Evening Star. In mythology, they guard the celestial gates and watch over the world.

Baba Yaga: A powerful and unpredictable supernatural being from Slavic folklore. Often depicted as an old woman dwelling deep in the forest in a hut that stands on chicken legs, she is known for her ambiguous nature, sometimes helping and sometimes hindering those who seek her out.

GREEK PANTHEON

Aphrodite: The Greek goddess of love, beauty, pleasure, passion, and procreation.

Areia: A lesser-known epithet for Aphrodite, worshipped in places like Sparta. This title connects her to the god of war, Ares, and gives her a martial, warlike aspect.

Phobos: The Greek personification of fear and panic (the root of the word "phobia"). In mythology, he is a son of Ares and Aphrodite and often accompanies his father onto the battlefield.

Deimos: The Greek personification of terror and dread. He is the twin brother of Phobos, a son of Ares and Aphrodite, and also serves as his father's companion in war.

NORSE PANTHEON

Freyja: A prominent Norse goddess associated with love, beauty, fertility, war, and death. She rules over her own afterlife field, Fólkvangr, and is a master of seidr (Norse magic).

CELTIC PANTHEON

Brigid: A prominent goddess from Irish mythology associated with poetry, healing, smithing, and the hearth. She is a fire deity whose festival, Imbolc, marks the beginning of spring.

THEY WILL RETURN IN
THE OATH OF ASH AND
THUNDER